DEEP AS THE MARROW

Also by F. Paul Wilson

HEALER (1976)*
WHEELS WITHIN WHEELS (1978)*
AN ENEMY OF THE STATE (1980)*
BLACK WIND (1988)
SOFT & OTHERS (1989)
DYDEETOWN WORLD (1989)
THE TERY (1990)
SIBS (1991)
THE SELECT (1993)
IMPLANT (1995)

The *Adversary* Cycle:
THE KEEP (1981)
THE TOMB (1984)
THE TOUCH (1986)
REBORN (1990)
REPRISAL (1991)
NIGHTWORLD (1992)

Editor:
FREAK SHOW (1992)
DIAGNOSIS: TERMINAL (1996)

*[combined in THE LaNAGUE CHRONICLES (1992)]

DEEP AS THE MARROW

F. PAUL WILSON

A TOM DOHERTY ASSOCIATES BOOK

NEW YORK

DEEP AS THE MARROW

Copyright © 1997 by F. Paul Wilson

This book is printed on acid-free paper.

A Forge Book
Published by Tom Doherty Associates, Inc.
175 Fifth Avenue
New York, NY 10010

Forge® is a registered trademark of Tom Doherty Associates, Inc.

Design by Brian Mulligan

Library of Congress Cataloging-in-Publication Data

Wilson, F. Paul (Francis Paul)
    Deep as the marrow / F. Paul Wilson.
        p.   cm.
    "A Tom Doherty Associates book."
    ISBN 0-312-86264-4
    I. Title.
PS3573.I45695D44   1997
813'.54—dc20   96-30502
                                          CIP

First Edition: April 1997

Printed in the United States of America

0   9   8   7   6   5   4   3   2   1

To Meggan and Coates
upon the start of their life together

Acknowledgments

Special thanks to Robert Surgent for sharing his treasury of Stupid Car Tricks.

Also, thanks to Mary, Meggan, Coates, Parvez Dara, Harriet McDougal, Steven Spruill, Al Zuckerman, and the National Drug Policy Foundation.

Fear by day and night, fear as deep as the marrow.

—James Baldwin,
The Fire Next Time

DEEP AS THE MARROW

WEDNESDAY

"... and then you know what Jimmy did?"

John VanDuyne struggled to concentrate on his six-year-old daughter's story about the baddest boy in her kindergarten class. It wasn't easy. His gaze kept shifting back to the angry face on the screen of the little TV on the kitchen side counter.

"No, Katie," he said. "What did he do?"

Katie slurped up a big spoonful of her Lucky Charms and chewed as quickly as she could.

Morning was the brightest part of the kitchen's day, but even now, with the spring sun cascading through the windows, it was still fairly dim. A 1970s kitchen, with dark-oak cabinets and furniture, a Congoleum floor, and harvest-gold appliances and countertops. If he ever decided to buy the place, he'd want to brighten it up. But each year he put off the decision and renewed his lease.

He watched Katie swallow convulsively. She was really into this story. Excitement shone from her bright blue eyes.

My eyes, he thought. The round face, clear skin, and long, dark, glossy hair are her mother's; and she's going to be petite like Marnie. But those are VanDuyne eyes.

She said, "Well, he took his pencil and he ..."

John heard the words "racist" and "genocide" and couldn't help glancing at the TV again. A very angry black congressman, his jowls trembling with rage, was letting the President of the United States have it with both barrels.

John knew him—or at least knew of him: Floyd Jessup.

D–NY flashed through his mind and he had to smile at the reflex . . . a natural response after you've been in Washington awhile.

No surprise about Jessup's reaction. The President had made his official announcement last night, and here was the congressman, not twelve hours later, venting his considerable spleen on *Good Morning America.* His staff hadn't wasted a second.

" *. . . and to think that we supported this man, we helped put Thomas Winston into the White House! And what does he do? He drives a knife into the back of the already-oppressed African-American community!* "

John ripped his attention back to Katie and found that he'd missed what bad boy Jimmy Clifton had done. He tried to cover.

"Oh, wow. Did he get in trouble?"

"Yep!" Katie said with a quick nod and a satisfied smile that revealed a gap on top. She'd lost her first tooth just last week. Her upper right-front incisor now belonged to the Tooth Fairy. "Had to go down the hall and see Sister Louise."

"Is that bad?"

Katie stared at him as if he had two heads. "She's the *principal,* Daddy."

"Oh, right. Sister Louise. Of course."

Despite the fact that he'd been raised a Baptist, John had opted to enroll Katie in a Catholic school—Holy Family Elementary in Bethesda. It had a great reputation as one of the best primary schools inside the Beltway. Even had a waiting list.

John was delighted Katie was getting along so well in school. She'd suffered some separation anxiety at first—perfectly understandable, considering what she'd been through—but now she looked forward to catching the school bus and riding off with her friends every morning. Made it worth all the strings he'd had to pull to get her in.

Pulling strings . . . the name of the game around here. When he'd been a practicing internist in Atlanta he hadn't known a thing about strings. But he'd learned fast: a couple of years as a Health and Human Services deputy secretary and he could pull with the best of them.

He glanced at his watch. "Oops. You're going to miss the bus."

She grinned. "And then I'll be Latie Katie."

"Yes, you will. Did you take your pill?"

She searched the tablecloth around her cereal bowl for it. "No, I—"

"I have it."

John looked up as his mother approached them from the far side of the kitchen, holding up an amber vial.

"Thanks, Nana," Katie said, sticking out her hand.

Nana—she was still Helga to her peers, and she'd once been "Ma" to John, but she became "Nana" to the family once Katie began speaking. Not a day passed that John didn't thank heaven that his mother had come to Washington to stay with them. He and Katie couldn't have got along without her.

She shook a pink, red-speckled tablet into her granddaughter's upheld palm.

John watched his mother and realized how much she'd aged within the past few years. Seventy-five and looking every minute of it. Two or three years ago her hair had been just as white, but she'd looked sixty-five. Living proof that stress makes you old.

But her slide seemed to have slowed and halted since she'd begun yoga classes last fall. He'd noticed a new spring in her step over the past few months.

Tall and trim—John's father had been tall, as well—and just beginning to develop a dowager's hump, she still took impeccable care of herself, keeping her thinning white hair softly permed; she was never without a touch of pink lipstick, even this early in the day. Her natural high coloring accentuated the blue of her eyes.

She didn't have a full closet but she bought good quality clothing and then wore it to death. No housecoats, no polyester, and God forbid she ever appeared in an outfit that didn't match. This morning she wore lightweight wool beige slacks and a blue-and-beige turtleneck.

Katie popped the pill into her mouth and washed it down with a gulp of orange juice. The tablets were chewable but she'd never liked the flavor, so she'd learned to swallow them whole. She was an old pro at it by now.

One of those tablets, twice a day, every day, for . . . how long? John wished he knew. He *did* know what would happen if she missed a dose or two.

His throat tightened and he had to reach out and touch her, smooth some fly away strands of her shiny, dark hair. So fine . . . baby fine. Nana combed out the knots every morning and braided it into a pair of pigtails. Katie tended to prefer a single, looser French braid like the bigger girls', but Nana didn't think that was neat enough. Nana liked things neat.

Katie looked at him. "What's the matter, Daddy?"

"Nothing. Why?"

"You look funny."

He crossed his eyes. "Is this better?"

"No!" She laughed. "Now you look goofy!"

"And he will look even goofier," Nana said, ever the voice of reason, "if you miss your bus and he has to drive you to school."

John checked his watch and got to his feet. "Can't do that. Got an appointment with Tom this morning."

"About this mess he has created?" she said, nodding toward the television.

"No. His regular checkup."

Her lips were tight as she shook her head. "Well, Tommy has really done it this time."

He nodded. "That he has, Mom. That he has."

John buttoned Katie's navy-blue uniform blazer over her plaid jumper. Here was another thing he liked about Holy Family Elementary: the uniform. No daily contretemps over what to wear, what the other kids were wearing, and why-can't-I-wear-that-too tantrums. All the girls wore one-piece blue-and-gray plaid jumpers over a white blouse with a neat little Peter Pan collar, blue knee socks, and saddle shoes; all the boys wore blazers of the same plaid with blue slacks. And that was that.

But no rules on hats, so Katie was allowed to wear her favorite: a red beret. After she adjusted it over her hair, they began the predeparture ritual:

"Got your lunch box?" he said.

She held it up. "Check!"

"Morning snack?"

"Check!"

"Afternoon snack?"

"Check!"

"Got your pencil case?"

She held that up. "Check!"

"Got your emergency quarter?"

She felt in her blazer pocket. "Check!"

"Then I guess you're ready to go. Say good-bye to Nana."

He watched his mother and his daughter exchange a quick hug and a kiss; then he took Katie's little hand in his and led her out the door.

A crisp April morning—spring was here but winter wasn't letting go. One of those days it felt good to be alive.

And for John, this was the best time of day, the time he felt closest to Katie. He wanted that closeness, needed it, and knew she needed it too—desperately. He'd worked hard to let her know she was loved and cherished and that no one was ever going to hurt her again.

When they reached the corner, they stopped and waited for the bus.

"Do you think Jimmy Clifton's going to get in trouble again today?" he said.

She shrugged. "Maybe. I hope they don't kick him out."

"Ooh," he teased, nudging her with his hip. "That sounds like somebody I know likes Jimmy Clifton."

"I do not!" she said. "I just think he's funny."

Methinks the lady doth protest too much, he thought, but he didn't push Katie any further. She seemed genuinely worried that the boy would be kicked out.

John doubted that that would happen to Jimmy, being Senator Clifton's son—but you never knew. Those nuns weren't easily impressed. And they had about fifty other kids on a list waiting to take his spot.

"If he's really funny," John told her, "maybe Sister Louise will keep him around just for laughs."

"He's not *that* funny," Katie said.

As John laughed, the yellow Holy Family Elementary bus rounded the far corner and made its way down the street.

He squatted next to her, pulled her close, and gave her a big hug. "Daddy loves Katie."

She threw her free arm around his neck. "Katie loves Daddy."

He held her tight against him, cherishing the moment. In a few years she'd become self-conscious and find such public displays of affection too embarrassing for words. But for now, she was delighted to be hugged by her daddy.

He released her as the bus pulled to a halt at the curb. He let her run to the open door by herself. A few seconds later she was waving and smiling from one of the windows. When the yellow bus and the red beret were out of sight, he headed back to the house.

Not a bad house, he thought as he approached it. A twenty-year-old brick federal in a neighborhood of colonials and other federals on small, wooded lots. A neighborhood that screamed *Washington, D.C.* Nana— Ma—tolerated it. Said the layout was out of date, with no flow for company.

But when did he ever have company?

If he bought it he'd have to do some heavy renovation. *If* he bought it. When he'd come to Washington he hadn't known whether he was going to like it around here. Still wasn't sure.

When his old boyhood friend Tom Winston became President of the United States, he'd asked John to come along. Said he wanted some Georgia boys around him in Washington, that John was already treating his high blood pressure and he wanted him to keep on doing so. But John guessed the real reason was that Tom had known how he was hurting, how his life had fallen apart, and had offered him a breather.

John had come to Washington looking for more than a change of routine and a change of scenery—he'd been hoping for a whole new life.

He didn't know if he'd found that. But he had found a peace of sorts, and that was a start. A good start.

2   MacLaglen was fully into Snake mode now.
Last night he'd been sitting in front of the tube—or rather the eight-by-twenty-foot wall screen of his projection TV—watching President Winston commit political *sepukku*, when the call came. He'd been expecting it.

One word: "Go."

The word had begun the transformation. He'd called Paulie and told him the snatch was on and going down tomorrow. He'd gone online, spent some time lurking the hacker boards, then went to bed. When he'd hit the pillow he was still mostly Michael MacLaglen.

But upon opening his eyes this morning, he was all Snake. The adrenaline had begun to flow—just a mild buzz now, but he knew it would build throughout the day to a rush that would last the duration of the snatch. And this one could go a couple of weeks—easy.

He licked his lips. He hoped so.

Snake had been following the yellow bus for about a mile in his new Jeep Grand Cherokee. He tapped on the steering wheel and acted impatient, looking like any one of the other dozen or so agitated commuters trapped behind the school bus.

But inside he was cool, very pleased that the laws kept him behind it, forced him to stop whenever it picked up a kid, forbade him to scoot around it when its red lights were flashing. Nothing easier than following a school bus.

He watched with satisfaction as it picked up the blue-blazered package and carried it off to school. Right on schedule, just like every other school day.

As he passed the package's father, he stole a look. Dr. John Van-Duyne. Tall dude—six two, Snake guessed; fortyish with longish brown hair graying at the temples. Looked a little like that Charlie Rose guy on the tube except for the intense blue eyes. Casual, conservative dresser, leaning toward slacks and button-downs and sweaters. Like me, Snake thought. Moved well, walking with a long, easy stride. Maybe a basketball player in high school; a shooting guard, he bet. Trim, good shoulders, probably watched what he ate. Snake knew he worked out regularly, knew he had a fairly set routine for every day of the week.

The doc looked fit on the outside, but Snake had him figured for a mushy core. Still living with his mother. A mama's boy. A wimp. Good. He'd fold up like wet cardboard and do exactly as he was told.

Which was how it should be. Snake wouldn't put up with any heroics or ad-libbing from this guy. Because this was already one weird piece of business, what with the cash payoff coming from a third party instead of the package's family. The family—the doc—would have to buy back his little package another way.

Get ready, doc, he thought as he left VanDuyne behind and continued in the wake of the school bus. Your routine's in for a big change. Real soon.

3 Back in the house, John found his mother standing before the kitchen TV, watching a replay of key moments from last night's Presidential address.

" . . . *can break the backs of these criminal empires. We can pull the economic rug out from under them by denying them the tens of billions of dollars—not tens of millions, tens of billions of dollars—they rake in annually from their illegal activities. And we don't need to mobilize our military, we don't need to mount an armed assault on them. All we need to do is change a few laws . . ."*

She glanced up at him. "Has that Tommy Winston gone crazy? Was he sipping at the schnapps before he went on TV last night?"

John could tell by the rhythm of her speech that she was upset. His Dutch-American father, raised all his life in the south, had married a girl from the old country. When she was upset her voice jumped half an octave and a Dutch accent began to creep into her otherwise perfect English.

"No, Mom. He was sober."

"Then I am thinking he has gone mad. It is the only explanation."

John shrugged. "You won't have to go far in this town to find someone to agree with you. His staff has been trying to talk him out of it, but you know Tom when he gets his mind set."

"You knew? Why didn't you tell your mother?"

"It was a secret. I got wind of it last time I was at the White House but I never thought he'd go through with it. Besides, they made me promise not to tell anyone."

"Even your mother?"

"Even my mother."

She had the remote in her hand and started hitting the button, stopping on each channel just long enough to catch the topic, then moving on.

"Look at this. On every channel it is the same. That is all they are talking about. In Holland this would not create such a fuss. But here . . ."

She walked to the other side of the island and freshened her cup of coffee. She held up the pot for John but he shook his head.

"Tom expected this," he told her. "He's figuring—hoping—the initial ruckus will die down and people will stop emoting and begin thinking."

"Let me tell you what *I* am thinking, John VanDuyne," she said—and using his first and last name meant she was *really* annoyed. "I am thinking it is a good thing you are only renting this house. Because your old friend Tommy Winston is going to be chased back to Georgia very soon, along with everyone he brought with him."

"I am thinking you could be right," John said.

4 The inbound traffic along Massachusetts Avenue seemed heavier than usual, giving John extra time to check out what the wonderful world of talk radio had to say about Tom's address to the nation last night. He hit SCAN and let his tuner skip up the dial. Almost immediately he heard Tom's voice.

"*. . . so we've been attacking the problem with the full force of all the federal government's law enforcement agencies and all the local police departments for a quarter of a century now, and where has it gotten us? We've spent three-quarters of a trillion dollars, jailed hundreds of thousands of people, but have we solved the problem? No. It's worse. Are the streets any safer now after all these hundreds of billions of dollars? No. They are not. So what's the solution? More of the same . . . ?*"

He moved on, stopping whenever he heard an angry voice. Which was often.

Everyone was shocked, but not everyone was enraged. Howard Stern seemed to think it was a great idea, long overdue; Imus didn't seem to know what to think.

But the call-in shows presented a chorus of condemnation from everywhere on the political spectrum: right, left, and center.

"Tommy, Tommy," he said softly. "What have you done?"

As he crawled downtown, John's mind tuned out the radio. His thoughts drifted back to his boyhood and all the years he had spent with the kid from the neighboring farm. From grammar school in Freemantle through Georgia State, Tommy and he had been inseparable.

The things they did . . . God, they were lucky to have survived.

Both were reckless, assuming like most kids that they were immortal and serious harm happened to other kids—ones who weren't quite as smart and agile as they—but Tommy had always had more of the dare-devil in him. Always Tommy who thought up the most outrageous stunts.

John remembered the time he discovered he could drive his car down the wall of the sand pit outside town. The pit's walls looked steep and sheer, but one night when he was seeing how close he could get to the edge with his old wreck of a Chevy—a junker that was ready for the scrap heap—he got too close and the car began sliding down the incline. To his relief, the walls were soft and slowed his progress. He made it to the bottom in one piece and was able to drive out the other side. He picked up Tom and damn near scared the crap out of him by driving up to and over the edge.

Which gave Tom a wonderful idea.

The next night they got Eddie Hennessy, one tough s.o.b., in the back seat and went cruising through the woods, supposedly looking for parkers to spook. While they were driving, Tom bemoaned the fact that Bonnie Littlefield had left him for another, and how miserable he was, and how he didn't see much point in going on living. He timed his despair so that it reached its deepest point as they approached the sand pit. With a shout of "Shit! I can't go on without her!" he wrenched the wheel to the right and went over the edge of the pit.

Well, Eddie Hennessy went into a bug-eyed panic in the back of the car. He lunged forward, reached over the front seat, and wrapped his arms around Tom's face and neck, shouting that he didn't want to die and screaming, "Mama! Mama!"

John was laughing so hard he nearly wet himself, not realizing that Tom couldn't see a damn thing with Eddie's arms wrapped around his face. He lost control of the car; it slewed sideways and toppled over. Rolled three times before it came to a stop at the bottom of the pit.

No seat belts on any of them, but somehow they came out with only a few scratches.

John shook his head. Yeah . . . lucky to be alive.

They drifted apart after college: Tom to Duke Law, John to Tufts School of Medicine. He'd finished his residency and was just starting as an internist when he got a call from Tom: "I'm thinking of running for Congress. Want to help?"

Starting then, John had played a part in every one of Tom's campaigns. The disintegration of John's marriage coincided with the beginning of the Winston presidency. When Tom offered him a post in the Health and Human Services Agency, John jumped at the chance.

So here he was, inching through the traffic around DuPont Circle. It finally loosened up on Connecticut Avenue, but instead of heading for HHS, John continued downtown. He was due at the White House.

5

"You don't have to be here, Mac," Paulie said as the barber fastened the plastic drape around his neck. "I mean, I know how to get a haircut on my own."

Snake stiffened at Paulie calling him "Mac"—he should know better than to use any sort of name when there was a third party in the room. He forced himself to relax. Mac was such a common term. Could mean anything. Probably what Ronald McDonald's friends called him. He didn't like it, but he guessed it was okay . . . just so long as Paulie didn't call him Snake. But how could he? Only packages' families and friends ever heard that name. To Paulie he was simply Mac. Not Mike, not MacLaglen . . . just plain Mac.

Snake leaned his chair back against the wall of the private cubicle and stared at Paulie DiCastro—a stocky guy of average height, thirtyish with long red hair and beard, blue eyes, and fair skin. The least Italian-looking Italian he'd ever met. Snake had booked him with one of these upscale men's hair stylists on Connecticut Avenue because he wanted a quality job. Who the hell knew where Paulie would have ended up if the choice had been left to him?

Snake had hired him for jobs through the years. For all his whining, Paulie was a stand-up guy. He followed instructions, and that was the number-one priority. Even when things had got a little dicey with the last package, Paulie had hung in there. Poppy had been a little freaked, but it all worked out. Usually Paulie and Poppy just baby-sat the packages until the buyer came through with the ransom, but this time Paulie was going to do the actual snatch.

Thus the beard. Snake had told him two months ago to stop dying his hair and start letting his face grow. It looked pretty shaggy now, but the guy with the scissors would trim it up nice and neat.

And tonight, after the package was safely tucked away, Paulie would shave it off. Anybody looking for a guy with a beard wouldn't give him a second look.

Next step after the haircut was to get him into normal-looking clothes. Paulie and that girl of his both had this thing for black. Look at Paulie now: black T-shirt, black leather pants, black fingerless gloves, black boots, long black coat—Paulie even dyed his hair jet black most of the time. And Poppy . . . she had these straight, severe bangs and shoulder-length pink-burgundy hair that looked like it had been cut with a laser; she dressed in slinky, low-cut black dresses with spider-web lace down the arms and fishnet stockings. Even had black lipstick and finger-nails. Looked like a vampire hooker. A couple of tattoos high up on her arms that Snake had never got a close look at and loads of earrings. Christ, she must have had ten in her left ear alone last time he saw her. And if that wasn't enough, she had a nostril ring and an eyebrow ring. Who knew where else she had a ring. Between the two of them the only thing that wasn't black was their skin and Poppy's hair—which probably *was* genuinely black when it wasn't dyed that weird color.

Snake didn't get it. He wouldn't be caught dead in Paulie's get-up. Like carrying a flashing neon sign that said *Look at me!* Hell with that.

"I'm footing the bill, Paulie. Just watching over my investment."

"Yeah, but I feel like a little kid. I mean, what next? A booster seat?"

Snake permitted himself a smile. Paulie was never completely happy unless he had something to whine about.

"I'm just making sure that—What's your name again?" Snake said to the barber—oops, sorry: hair stylist.

"Raynoldo," said the stylist. He had a delicate build and a delicate mustache and dark hair slicked back tight against his scalp.

"Yeah. Raynoldo. I just want to make sure Raynoldo here does it right. And that means off with the ponytail."

"Aw, Christ!" Paulie said. "Do we really have to do that? I mean, isn't that like goin' kinda far?"

Snake ignored the question. The ponytail wasn't up for discussion.

"And I want to make sure the beard looks good too," he said. "*Neat* is the word. Hear that, Raynoldo? Neat."

"Yes sir," Raynoldo said. He gave Snake a quick, delicate smile. "Neat it will be."

Probably thinks me and Paulie've got a thing going, Snake thought.

"The beard I don't care about," Paulie said, still whining. "I mean, I only grew it for the gig. But the tail, man. Plenty of chauffeurs got ponytails. I can—"

Sudden fury overcame Snake. *The goddamn jerk! He said chauffeur!*

He catapulted out of his seat and pulled the scissors from Raynoldo's fingers. He grabbed Paulie's ponytail, yanked it taut, and snipped it off about two inches from his head.

"You talk too much, Paulie," he said through his teeth, handing the scissors back to Raynoldo and tossing Paulie's hair into his lap. "End of discussion."

Paulie glared at him but said nothing.

Good, Snake thought. Just so long as we know who's boss here.

He felt the rage cool as quickly as it had flared, the way it always did. One second he was ready to kill; another second and it was as if nothing had happened.

He didn't like the outbursts, but sometimes they served multiple purposes. Like now: He wouldn't have to listen to any complaints from Paulie about the change of clothes waiting for him. He was going to be dressed right for the pickup this morning. Chauffeur's livery all the way.

He glanced at his watch. Time was a-wasting.

"All right," he said to Raynoldo. "Let's get going. Make him nice and respectable looking, and make it quick. We're on a schedule here."

6 "*. . . so let's remove the outlaw glamour from drugs. Let's make drugs dull, and let's portray people who use them as dumb. One of the definitions of stupidity is the inability to learn from experience. Nothing we've tried has worked. It's long past time for a change of tactics. . . .*"

John twisted the knob and cut off Tom's voice as he hit another major snag near Pennsylvania Avenue. Cars were backed up on 17th Street. When he reached Lafayette Square he saw why.

Hundreds of people were gathered on the grass, setting up tables and tents wherever they found an open patch, one even holding an impromptu prayer meeting on a nearby corner. Across the park, on the far side of the section of Pennsylvania Avenue in front of the White House that had been blocked off and turned into a pedestrian mall in 1995, he could see chanting, sign-carrying protesters marching in front of the wrought-iron fence.

The circus had arrived.

John edged his car toward the cadre of armed, grim-looking members of the Secret Service uniformed division manning the visitors gate. Twice the number he usually encountered. One started to wave him off, but then let him approach when John held his ID and pass out the window.

John knew most of the gate guards by now. This guy must have been one of the reinforcements.

As his ID and pass were being scrutinized, John said, "They didn't waste any time, did they. Must all be early risers."

The guard grunted. "The first group showed up around ten o'clock last night."

He checked the appointment book in the gatehouse, then hurried back to the car and handed John his ID.

"Really sorry for the delay, Dr. VanDuyne," he said. "You should have told me right off who you were."

Yeah, being the President's personal physician did have a certain cachet.

"No problem," John said. "I understand perfectly."

The huge gate closed behind his car, and an iron beam rose out of the pavement as a further bar to entry. John had heard it could stop a two-ton truck doing forty miles an hour.

He parked in the visitor's area, removed his black bag from his trunk, clipped his ID badge to the breast pocket of his sport coat, and walked around to his left.

The White House—or "Crown" as the Secret Service called it.

He couldn't see them, but he was sure the White House SWAT team was positioned on the roof. He was more aware than ever of the infrared sensors, electric eyes, audio monitors, pressure sensors, and video cameras monitoring his every step, feeding everything to W-16, the Secret Service command post under the Oval Office.

He tried to forget all that, tried to appreciate the setting. The South Lawn was greening up, the trees were starting to bud, and the Washington Monument loomed over the scene like a monolithic guardian. The cherry trees were in bloom along the Potomac—he made a mental note to take Katie and Nana for a ride along the basin this weekend. Washington was a wonderful place to be in the spring.

Although this spring might be different. . . .

John quickened his pace. Good thing he'd had this appointment set up in advance. He was concerned about Tom's blood pressure. Hairy enough to be the first line of medical defense for the leader of the free world, but when he was also your oldest friend . . .

At the ground-level doorway between the two stairways that framed the South Portico, another uniformed agent checked his ID. This was unusual. Most times he simply breezed in.

He entered the State Floor and bore left through the diplomatic reception area into the warren of executive offices in the west wing. In the hall he spotted a familiar and unhappy face.

"Hey, Bob," John said. "I'm looking for the boss."

Robert Decker, Supervisory Special Agent, Secret Service, was a veteran of that exclusive club, the presidential detail. Today he looked harried and hassled. His gray suit was uncharacteristically rumpled, as if he'd been wearing it all night. John noted his tired eyes. Maybe he had.

Decker jerked a thumb over his shoulder. "Down in the exec offices. Anything wrong, Doc?"

John shrugged. "Just doing his monthly blood pressure."

"Do me a favor and give him a checkup from the neck up while you're at it, will you?"

"All this getting you worried?"

"We're already getting category-three death threats. I've canceled all tours and that's earning me a ton of flack. Talk to him, will you?"

"I don't see what I can do. He can't exactly take it back."

"Sure he can. He can go back on the tube tonight and say that he never said those things. It was his evil twin."

John waited for Decker to smile . . . and waited. . . .

"You're kidding, aren't you?"

"Look at this face," Decker said grimly. "Is this the face of someone who's kidding?"

"That bad, huh?"

"Worse," Decker said, then walked off.

John continued down the hall. He stopped by the small, dungeonlike clinic that shared this ground-floor corner with the White House physician's office to offer a courtesy hello to Jeff Stein, the young doc who manned the clinic. Jeff could have taken Tom's blood pressure every *day* if need be, but the President preferred his old buddy.

And John didn't mind. It was a way of keeping in touch with Tom, of piercing the wall of "splendid isolation" that was inexorably rising around him.

A blond nurse whose name John forgot sat at a desk, doing a crossword puzzle.

"Where's Dr. Stein?"

She moved a folder over the puzzle, hiding it. John imagined things could get pretty slow in a little clinic like this.

"He went for some coffee, Dr. VanDuyne. Can I help you?"

"No. Just letting him know I'm here. Maybe I'll catch him later."

He continued on toward the door with the presidential seal and pushed through.

The executive offices, normally a calm, well-ordered complex, were jumping with frenzied activity: aides and secretaries hustling back and forth, shouting across the rooms and between the offices, phones ringing off the hook.

Not at all a party atmosphere. Grim expressions on everyone. And the grimmest was on the face of the small, compact curly-haired, middle-aged woman approaching John right now: Stephanie Harris, White House Press Secretary.

"You're here to sign the commitment papers, right?" she said.

She'd be upbeat and four-square behind her boss when she faced the cameras later, but not now.

"Nope. Just the usual blood pressure check."

She stuck out her arm. "You want blood pressure? Check mine. It's got to be a record."

"Think you can top Bob Decker's?"

"Definitely! He thinks this is a security nightmare? It's nothing compared to the PR catastrophe! The phones have *not* stopped, not for an instant. Do you know how many calls we get on an average day? Forty-eight thousand. We've had that many already since midnight, most angry as hell. The damn fax machines have run out of paper so many times we've stopped refilling them. Beat Decker's? I can *double* it!"

John laughed but wondered if Tom's pressure would beat Stephanie's. "Where is he?"

She turned and pointed. John had to smile at his old friend, an island of calm in a sea of turmoil: President Thomas Winston, code-named "Razor" to the Secret Service, looking as sharp as ever—tall, and serene in his dark blue suit, talking to a pretty young woman. Every strand of his dark, just-the-right-amount-of-gray-at-the-temples hair in place, the tanned, chiseled features composed into a relaxed, confident expression. John was willing to bet Tom's pressure was all right. This was a man who caused more hypertension than he suffered himself.

Tom glanced up and spotted John. He smiled, pointed at him to indicate that he should stay where he was, spoke a few final words to the young woman—an aide no doubt—then started toward John.

"Welcome to the funhouse," Tom said, shaking hands.

"I warned you."

"That you did, good buddy. You and a lot of other people." He turned and nodded to the young woman he'd just left. "See that angel-faced young thing over there? That's Heather Brent. She's going to be our designated mass-media spokesperson on the decriminalization issue."

"She looks about twelve." John was exaggerating, but she did look awfully young.

"She's twenty-eight and the happily married mother of two. She's also a world-class debater who firmly believes in decriminalization. She can verbally slice and dice you without losing one iota of that fresh-faced charm. She's going to be a *potent* weapon in this war." He glanced around. "Let's go upstairs so you can check me out in peace and quiet. It's a little crazy down here."

7 Poppy cracked up when she saw Paulie.

She'd been working out to her *Buns of Steel* video when he walked through the door. One look at his short, blow-dried hair and she started laughing so hard she collapsed on the floor. She could barely breathe.

"I don't look *that* bad," he said, grinning sheepishly. "Do I?"

Poppy managed to stifle her laughter. Gasping, she stared up at him. He'd been looking weird anyway, letting his hair go back to its natural red, but now, with it trimmed all around the ears and off the collar, and his beard clipped down to a quarter inch and neatly edged along his cheeks and throat, she like barely recognized him.

"You look so totally . . . *straight*. Like you should be running a bookstore or something."

She got up off the floor and gave him a hug. As her arms went around him she touched the back of his collar where his ponytail had been. She started laughing again.

"Ooh, look! Your neck! I never seen your neck before!"

He pushed her away—gently, but she could tell he was beginning to get pissed. He went to the cracked mirror over the sagging sofa and examined himself.

"Christ, you're right. I could be a fucking bookworm!"

"But one who's into leather."

"Yeah, well, not for long. I better get changed."

Poppy brushed off the crud her black bodysuit had picked up from the rug. This place Mac had rented for the job was a dump. The only good thing was they wouldn't like be here that long.

She sobered as she realized what the haircut meant: The snatch was a go, and Paulie was definitely doing the deed.

A fleeting spasm gripped her stomach then let go. The whole thing had seemed like such a lark the first time she'd helped Paulie baby-sit one of Mac's "packages" three years ago. They'd hung out, listened to music, eaten fast-food take-out, and taken turns keeping an eye on the handcuffed, blindfolded guy in the next room. When the ransom got paid, they drove him to a deserted spot in the woods off one of the freeways and let him go.

Easy. No pain, no strain, and lots of gain when Mac paid Paulie his share.

But good as it was, the money never like lasted that long. When they had it, they spent it—mostly on high living.

And she did mean *high*. Poppy had been like heavy into speed back then—oh, she'd do a little toot now and again, and grass for sure, but speed was her favorite.

And so whenever Mac called and said he had another baby-sitting job—like maybe a couple, three times a year—they always said yes.

She was amazed how none of their "packages" was ever reported missing. Paulie said Mac had told him you wouldn't believe how many people got snatched every year. Kidnapping was a growth industry and Mac a major player.

But growth industry or not, the last job had like turned her off to the whole thing.

She followed Paulie into the smaller bedroom and watched him begin to change his rags.

"Did Mac give you any idea who you're gonna be snatching?"

"Nope."

"I wish you weren't doing it."

He removed his earrings, then stripped down to the black jockeys she'd bought him for Christmas. Paulie was about half a dozen years older than Poppy, but he still looked good for a guy pushing thirty. So maybe his nose was on the large side, and his face a little pockmarked, but she liked his curly hair, even if it was thinning on top. His deep blue eyes had like grabbed her first time she saw him. Still grabbed her. He didn't work out but had a naturally muscular body. Cool tattoos too. She especially loved the Grim Reaper on his right upper arm. She'd be turned on now if she wasn't so damn worried.

He looked up at her. "Why not? He's paying me extra, and we could use the money."

"Yeah, I know, but . . ."

"But what?"

"But I don't want you to, like, get hurt."

He smiled. "Don't worry. No rough stuff. The package thinks it's going for a limo ride. I drive up, I open the door, the package gets in, I close the door, I drive away. Simps."

"'Package,'" she said. "Why does he always call them 'packages?'"

Paulie took the white shirt off its hanger and slipped into it. "That's the way he is. You want me to explain Mac to you? He's a genius. How'm I supposed to explain a genius?"

Poppy stepped over and helped him with the buttons.

"I don't know. I just wish he wasn't like so mean."

"He's not mean. He's a totally straight shooter. Has he ever stiffed us? Ever even tried? No."

"Yeah, but last time—"

"All right," Paulie said, slipping into the gray pants. "I admit, things got a little rough. But that had nothing to do with us. That was all tho fault of the package's family. Buyer, I mean." Another of Snake's words.

Poppy shuddered. "A *little* rough? That was more than a *little* rough. That guy—"

"Look, I didn't like it either, but it worked out, didn't it? I mean, he's back home, right? And he ain't all that much worse for wear."

"Easy for *you* to say. I told you I didn't ever want to do this again."

Paulie stepped forward and put his hands on her shoulders.

"Look, Poppy. Didn't we make a deal? Didn't I promise this is the last one? Well, I mean it. This is going to be a huge score; that's why Mac's paying us so much. He's a good guy that way. If he makes out big, *we* make out big."

The thought of being set up with a big cash stash was *so* appealing. Just the two of them, traveling around . . . no strings . . . no Mac. . . .

"Okay, fine," she said. "I want the money too. But there ain't enough of it in the world to make me go through something like that last job again."

"This will be different, I promise you. We don't have to worry about the package's family not paying up because the money's coming from somewhere else."

Poppy stared at him. "I don't get it."

"Well, neither do I, completely. Mac didn't give me no details, just that someone else is paying him. All we got to do is baby-sit the package for like a week or so and then walk away. That's it. No persuaders, no worrying about somebody holding back on the money—it's totally guaranteed."

At the mention of "persuaders" and what they'd had to do last time, Poppy shuddered again.

"I still don't like it."

"Hey, Poppy—two hundred large in cash for a week's work. We can go away and never come back."

She threw her arms around him and held him tight.

"Oh, I hope so. And then I never want to see Mac again. He scares me."

"Hey, you're wrinkling my shirt."

Poppy let him go and helped him with his dark gray clip-on tie. That done, he shrugged into his jacket. Then he put on this dumb cap and—

"I hardly recognize you," she said.

He grinned. "You ain't seen nothin' yet. Watch."

He turned away from her and reached into a brown paper bag on the dresser. After rattling around in it and then fiddling with his face, he whirled and faced her again with a flourish.

"Ta-da!"

The transformation was so totally awesome, Poppy took a step back. His normally rectangular face looked round, his nose was wider and flatter, and his eyes hid behind super-dark sunglasses. The only skin showing was between the bottom part of the shades and the upper edge of his beard.

"Jesus, Paulie! How the hell—?"

He pulled a soft white cylinder from the inside of his cheek and held it up.

"A few cotton plugs"—he pointed to his nose—"some nostril dilators, some shades, and I bet I could fool my own mother."

He stepped around the corner and studied himself in the bathroom mirror, obviously very pleased.

"How cool is this? I mean, can you just see me going up to my mother and saying, 'Mrs. DiCastro, you seen Paulie around lately?' Would that be cool or what?"

Poppy stepped up behind him and slipped her arms around his waist. Seeing Paulie transformed like this made her feel a lot better about this snatch. Still . . .

"You be careful, Paulie. You pick up this package, whoever he is, and get back here safe and sound."

He nodded, still staring at himself in the mirror. "And then I shave off this goddamn beard and get my hair back to black and—"

"And I'll have my old Paulie back again."

He turned and kissed her. "Right."

She rubbed her pelvis against his. She was beginning to feel hot and didn't want to let him go.

"Mmmm, I love a man in uniform. How about you and me, like—?"

"Whoa, no." He pulled away and slipped past her, returning to the bedroom. "That's all I need: Show up late and miss the snatch. You know what Mac would do? I don't even want to think about it."

Neither did Poppy.

She followed him through the bedroom and noticed a pair of black leather gloves on the bed—fingered gloves.

"Hey, Paulie, these yours?"

He turned and looked. "Oh, yeah. My driving gloves. Almost forgot."

"No fingerprints, huh?"

He shook his head and held up his fists. "No tattoos."

"Oh, right."

She'd got so used to the letters on his fingers between the first and second knuckles that she didn't see them anymore. But someone else would notice them sure: *l-o-v-e* on his left hand, *h-a-t-e* on his right.

He slipped them on and flexed the fingers.

"How do I look?"

"Like you're ready to drive the President."

"Who knows?" He grinned. "I might be."

"Not funny, Paulie."

"Yeah, that'd be a little much to handle, even for Mac." He stared at her. "You all set?"

"I think so."

"Let's check the room one more time."

She followed him into the darkness of the master bedroom and wrinkled her nose at the smell. The last renters must have kept a dog in here. A sharp, acid odor permeated the room.

Paulie flipped on the light and checked out the two windows. He'd hung room-darkener shades in both, then nailed plywood over them. He tapped his toe against the box sitting on the floor by the bed.

"All our supplies are up to date, right?"

"Yep."

"You sure?"

"What do you think I am, an Appleton?"

His smile had an edge to it. "No. I still don't know what an Appleton is. You keep using that word and—"

"Sorry." She should like keep her mouth shut about Appletons. "Just a family expression."

"Yeah, well, I just want to make sure we got everything we need. Is that okay?"

"Sure." She knew the checklist by heart: "Three sets of cuffs, fifty feet of rope, duct tape, two flashlights plus extra batteries, three blindfolds, a first-aid kit, a gag, our masks, and a good supply of yellow jackets."

The last were the downers she used to use to bring her off the quartz when she wanted to sleep. They kept them in case the package got antsy and noisy.

"Cool. We're set, then."

Paulie returned to the front room where he took off his cap and pulled on his long black-leather coat, completely hiding his chauffeur's livery.

Poppy straightened his lapels. "Nervous?"

"Nah."

"Come on," she said with a smile. "Truth: You got to be like just a *little* bit nervous."

"Okay. Maybe just a little bit. I mean, like I know Mac's got this whole thing planned down to the last detail, but still . . . things can go wrong. Shit happens."

That it did. Oh, did Poppy know how shit happened.

And suddenly a worm of dread was squirming through her gut. She didn't want anything to happen to Paulie. He was a good guy. They had good times and good sex, and he never hurt her, which was more than she could say about some of the creeps she'd hooked up with since . . . since she'd been on her own.

But it was more than that. Paulie took good care of her. She needed that, because whenever she tried to go it alone she like always seemed to mess up.

She could see staying with Paulie forever. Because as far as she knew, he didn't want kids. And that was just fine with her.

"Everything will be all right," she told him.

"Yeah. I know that. I'm just a little edgy is all. I could use a couple of hits of Mary. You know . . . to relax me."

"That's all you need. You know how Mac feels. He finds out you been tokin', he'll like kill you."

"You got that right." He straightened his shoulders inside the leather coat; then he clasped her head between his gloved hands and kissed her hard on the lips.

"See you later."

Before she could grab him for a last hug, he had picked up his cap and was heading for the side door to the garage.

"Be careful."

Poppy watched as he backed the old white panel truck out of the garage and coasted down the street.

"Please let everything go smooth," she whispered.

Almost like a prayer. She used to pray, but you couldn't pray about something like this, could you? Maybe she could pray that this time nobody got hurt. Yeah. Somebody might answer that one.

With the truck out of sight, she turned away from the window.

Now the hardest part: waiting.

She stretched. She felt so *tense*. Used to be she'd pop a pill to loosen up. Now she had another way.

She went back to the thirteen-inch portable TV-VCR combo they'd brought along and restarted the *Buns of Steel* tape. Best way she knew to kill time. She turned down the sound, jacked up the latest Jawbox on the portable CD player, and got down to it.

She was determined to get in shape again. She'd been a real hardbody back in high school but she'd let herself go to hell. Drugs and fast food—bad news.

She still ate too much garbage, and she'd get around to changing that. But first the drugs. She wanted off the drugs.

She'd been so totally rattled by the last snatch that as soon as it was over she dove head first into the coke . . . and did way too much. She'd never been strung out like that before. Scared the hell out of her.

That was when she'd decided: no more coke. No more downers, either. Oh, she'd take a hit on a nail now and then, and maybe keep a few thrusters handy—just for diet help—but for the most part she was going to get back into her body and start treating it right. And once this was over she'd like *keep* treating it right.

Once this was over . . .

The job had just started and already she had this bad feeling.

She concentrated on the routine on the screen, adding two-pound steel dumbbells to work her upper body. She felt her heart start to pump, the sweat begin to sheen her skin. Soon she'd be working into a high—not a pill high but another kind. And it was almost as good.

Almost.

8 "One-fifty over ninety," John said, not happy with the numbers but relieved they weren't through the roof.

Usually he took Tom's blood pressure in the ground-floor clinic, but today he was upstairs in the Monroe Room. He'd been to the top floor of the White House on numerous occasions, but this was the first time he'd ever done a medical exam here.

"What do you call that?" Tom said. He had his suit coat off and his left shirtsleeve rolled up.

"Borderline. And considering the circumstances—"

"Not bad."

John unclipped the cuff from Tom's arm. "Watch that sodium. I don't much like you staying at ninety on the diastolic; it gets above that and I'm going to hit you with some pills."

"That mean no more pork rinds?"

"Damn right! They're loaded with fat *and* sodium. Pure poison for a guy like you."

Tom fell silent as John rolled up the BP cuff and stowed it in his bag. When he looked up, Tom was standing at the window. His sharp profile was why the Secret Service had come up with "Razor" as his presidential code name. As he stared out at the protesters beyond the front fence, he looked very much alone.

"Surprised by the response?" John said.

Tom turned and shrugged. He'd left his leader-of-the-free-world face downstairs. "George Reedy says the White House robs people of their political instincts. We begin to think we can do anything." His smile was tight, his eyes bleak. "Maybe he's right. Look at them. They want to crucify me."

"You expected less?"

"I thought I was pretty persuasive last night. A whole hour of network prime time . . . I thought I'd convince *somebody*."

"You probably did. But they're not out there marching, and they probably can't get through on the phone or fax. Maybe e-mail."

He barked a laugh. "E-mail! The queue is endless!"

"You'll probably find a lot of support on the Internet. Lots of free-thinkers out there."

He stared at John, holding his gaze. "How about you, good buddy? I change your mind?"

Clearly the answer was important to him, and John longed to tell him what he wanted to hear.

Tom had announced last night that he was going to the International Drug Summit in the Hague next week to advocate a cease fire in the war on drugs. John was already familiar with most of the arguments, but he'd hoped some rhetorical magic would make him a believer.

He shrugged. "Intellectually I can see it. But emotionally . . ." He shook his head as he tapped his chest. "Something in here won't go along with the idea of an America where I can drop by the local drugstore for some toothpaste, some dental floss, and a fix of heroin."

Tom smiled tightly. *"Et tu, Brute?"*

"What can I say? You've got a fight on your hands. The fight of your life." *And you're going to go down in flames, old buddy.*

"I need your support, Johnny."

"No, you don't. I'm just one guy. You need the support of those four-fifty odd guys on the Hill."

"No, Johnny," he said softly. He put his hand over his heart. "I need your support here. I need to know the one guy I could always count on is still watching my back. Somehow it'll be easier to win knowing you're with me." He jutted his jaw defiantly at the protesters. "But with you or without you, I *am* going to win."

John knew that look. He remembered the time when they were seventeen and had been tipping a few brews behind Ebersol's gas station outside Freemantle. A couple of the guys started making fun of the beat-up old Kharman Ghia Tom drove, wondering if it could top fifty. Tom couldn't defend the car's speed, so he said something like, "Yeah, but I can drive all the way home without ever using the brake."

Well, nobody believed that, so they challenged him to prove it. A crazy idea, an insane dare—he'd have to drive through the center of Freemantle to reach his house on the far side of town. Four traffic lights stood between him and home, and they were *not* sequenced. Freemantle's lights changed whenever they damn well pleased.

John never expected Tom to take them up on it, but he drained his beer and said, "Sure. Follow me and watch. You see my brake lights once, you guys can have the car."

Truth was, nobody wanted that pint-size rust bucket, but after checking to make sure the brake lights worked, everybody piled into their cars to follow. Everyone except John. He got in beside Tom. No discussion. It was understood, expected.

Off they went. John still got shaky when he remembered that ride. The first light was green, and that had been fine. But the next three turned red as Tom approached. He never slowed. Playing the manual gear shift like a Stradivarius, he passed stopped cars ahead of him on the left or swung onto the shoulder and shot by. But never once did he hit the brake pedal. Ran three red lights, and each time he flashed through an intersection his face wore the same expression it did now, with that same jutting jaw.

And he seemed to be demanding that same kind of loyalty now. But John couldn't quite bring himself to slip into the passenger seat on this trip.

"Why, Tom?" John said. "It's not only bad policy, it's bad politics. Even your own party—"

"Will eventually come around." He ground a fist into his palm. "The ones that really irk me are the budget cutters. They wail about federal spending? Well, I'm giving them something real to cut: sixty billion a year. Every year. For what? Drugs are more available on the street now than they've ever been. Sixty *billion*, Johnny. The truth is, I want that money. I've got better places to spend it."

"But the social cost . . ."

"How can the social cost be higher than what we're paying now? You mentioned buying heroin at the corner drugstore. You can do that now, John—on the corner *outside* the drugstore. Legalization is not going to change availability—drugs are everywhere *now!* And you talk about social cost? What about every sociopath in the world fighting for a piece of the profits?"

"My point exactly," John said. "Why become the enemy?"

"Aw, Johnny," he said. "Don't look at it that way. There's so damn much money in drugs that the cartels have been able to corrupt entire police forces, *buy* entire town governments . . . towns with airports. It's mind-boggling and stomach turning. And the worst of it is, they can make those kinds of profits for one reason and one reason alone: We've declared their commodity illegal. If we legalized it, we could even start *taxing* the profits on the legal sale of those same drugs. I see a net gain of seventy or eighty billion dollars."

"All of it dirty money," John said.

"No dirtier than taxes we take from tobacco and alcohol. It's money we can put toward educating people to stay away from drugs, and rehabbing those who are already hooked."

"Come on, Tom. Do you really want to collect taxes on crack? I mean, don't we have enough crackheads and crack babies already?"

"Crack wouldn't even exist if cocaine were legal. It's just like the hundred-ninety-proof industrial-grade alcohol of the Roaring Twenties. People bought it to spike their drinks. It had a *huge* market—which disappeared overnight when Scotch, beer, and wine became legal again. The same will happen to crack when you can buy cocaine powder, cocaine drinks—where do you think the "Coca" in Coca-Cola came from?—even cocaine chewing gum."

"Cocaine chewing gum—Christ!"

"So I'll give in on crack. But what I—"

The phone rang. Tom picked it up, listened for a few seconds, said, "Thanks," then hung up. He started for the door, motioning John after him. "In here."

He followed Tom into the presidential living quarters where a giant rear projection TV was already on. John had been here two or three times for drinks and dinner. Tom grabbed the remote and switched to *Today*. An elderly, balding man with thick, horn-rimmed glasses was speaking to the camera. The screen tag read MILTON FRIEDMAN.

"Friedman?" John said. "The economist? Wasn't he—?"

The screen answered his question by adding FORMER ADVISOR TO PRESIDENT REAGAN.

Bryant Gumbel asked him what sort of America he envisioned after the decriminalization of drugs, and the professor said he saw an America with half the number of prisons, half the number of prisoners, ten thousand fewer homicides a year, inner cities in which there was a chance for poor people to live without being afraid for their lives. . . .

Professor Friedman fielded several more questions, each answer stressing the propriety—for economic as well as philosophical reasons—of legalizing drugs.

As the station cut to a commercial, Tom hit the mute and turned to him.

"*That's* why I'm going to win. My staff has been talking to the mass media for weeks. The networks, the major magazines, and newspaper chains are ready to support me on this."

"They sure didn't sound that way as I was driving down here."

"Oh? You'll notice that they all carried my address in toto. They'll start off with subtle support. Like Milton Friedman there. He's opposed antidrug laws from the git-go. When he was with Reagan, he pushed for it. But the millions who saw him just now don't know that. They heard him say drugs should be legalized and they saw 'Former Advisor to President Reagan.'" He mimicked a viewer: "'*Reagan?* Really? Hmmm . . .' Believe me, none of that was accidental. You'll see a lot of Friedman in the coming months. William F. Buckley will be out there too. And—"

"Buckley?" John couldn't believe it. "You and William F. Buckley on the same side?"

"He's favored decriminalization for years, and hasn't been shy about saying so. We'll have senior judges from all over the country who are refusing to hear drug cases because they think the laws are unfair. . . ."

"If you think that's going to make any difference . . ."

"Every night, every day, every random act of violence, every drive-by shooting, every overdose, every single crime that can be blamed on the *huge, unconscionable* profits from *illegal* drugs—and believe me, those points will be punched home—will be dragged before the viewing public. So will all the statistics that certify the War on Drugs as unwinnable. The facts are on my side, John."

"But the *people* aren't."

"They will be. They'll see that there'll always be a sizable segment of humanity that wants drugs and will find ways to get them. We have millions of them in this country—twelve million occasional marijuana users alone. They're here and they're not going away. Passing laws won't change them. And we sure as hell can't lock up all of them."

"I can't see the average American citizen surrendering to the druggies."

"Changing tactics is not surrender. Look, we have millions of Americans who want to dose themselves with various chemicals. Mostly they're only hurting themselves, and if they happen to hurt somebody else while under the influence, we already have laws on the books for people who do damage while intoxicated. Let's deal with them as people with a hang-up, not criminals."

Tom radiated sincerity and conviction. He was a mesmerizing speaker and a master of mass media. And he truly believed.

"You know," John said slowly, "you just might bring this off."

"I *am* going to bring this off. I may not get complete legalization, but I *know* I can get marijuana decriminalized. That's a foot in the door. And once that door is open, it's just a matter of time."

John was beginning to believe him.

And then the phone was ringing again. Tom answered, listened, then turned to John.

"I need to get back down to the offices. Heather's getting ready to leave for the talk-show circuit and I have to speak to her. Want to hang around?"

John shook his head. "I've got to head over to my own office. I'm sure HHS will be neck deep in this before the day is out. But I want to come back and check your pressure again before you head for the drug summit."

"Good idea. But you still haven't answered me: Are you with me on this?"

"Publicly, I'll stand with you, of course. But privately . . . I'm not there yet, Tom."

"You will be," Tom said with that crooked smile. "I know I can count on you."

John didn't argue. He was nowhere near as sure as Tom.

9 Snake hovered over his keyboard, staring at the monitor as he wove through the now familiar memory banks of the C&P Telephone mainframes. He'd been inside every day this week, smoothing the way to the switching programs, finding the path of least resistance, the one that left the fewest traces. And that was rarely the most direct path.

He'd spent the last two weeks probing the system until it felt like home. Like old times, reminding him of his high school days as a phreaker when he'd pull all-nighters with his Apple II+, hacking into phone companies, banks, and universities all over the country, free in cyberspace, hunting the electronic grail of system mastery, suffused with the sheer joy of the doing. He'd never stolen, never destroyed data. Never even left taunting electronic graffiti like some of his jerkier brother hackers. He wasn't looking for attention; he was looking to see how far he could go, how many barriers he could overcome, how *deep* he could get. The idea was to conquer the hacked system, defeat all its security, open all its doors, declare victory, and move on.

Snake felt an echo of that old thrill even now. He smiled. Mikey MacLaglen had been such an idealist. Such a nerdy purist. Such an asshole. So awed with the novelty and grandeur and immensity of cyberspace that he'd missed out on endless opportunities to exploit his power.

Truth was, he hadn't even realized he *had* power.

Just as well. If he had he wouldn't have been able to resist exploiting it, probably would have been caught, and would even now be on the FBI's hacker list.

No thanks.

He could have been nabbed in college too. He'd been heading for an engineering degree at MIT when he started hacking cable boxes for his classmates who wanted free HBO and Showtime. Somehow a video pirate named Mitchell Fuller—hacker handle: "Brushman"—caught a blip about Mike MacLaglen's skills and offered him a job hacking video boards for satellite dishes. The six figures he offered was four times the entry-level salary his engineering degree would net him after graduation—*if* he could even find a job—and all tax free.

Things were great until Fuller ripped off Mac's elegant and excruciatingly difficult hack of the latest VideoCipher board. When Mac complained, Fuller laughed in his face and said, "Whatta you gonna do—sue me?"

Something snapped in Mac then. He'd always had a bad temper but that was the first time he completely lost it. A red haze seemed to envelop him and suddenly he had a tire iron in his hand and was beating Fuller over the head. Before he could stop himself, Fuller was unconscious. Shocked, Mac stared down at the battered, bleeding s.o.b. and wondered what to do. He still wanted to kill him, but he was thinking now . . . and he had a better idea.

He dumped him in the trunk of his car, then called Fuller's wife. He told her she wouldn't see her dear Mitchell alive again unless she delivered $100,000 in cash. Now. When Fuller came to, Mac let him talk to his wife, to tell her how to get the cash together. The way Fuller looked at him when Mac made him get back into the trunk, the fear in his eyes, wondering if he'd ever see daylight again . . . it somehow opened a door within Mac, and stirred something on the other side.

Fuller's wife delivered the money within hours. She never called the cops or the FBI. Couldn't. They'd want to know how her husband earned his money. It all went down so smooth and fast, Mac wished he'd asked for more. But a deal was a deal and, after all, he was netting a hundred large for less than a day's work. He let Fuller go. And he got out of the video-hacking business. He'd found a better line of work.

Snake was born.

Simply amazing how many people were out there making tons of money illegally, or in legit cash businesses but not declaring it.

They became Snake's prey. They weren't fighters. The sight of a pistol, a hint of casual brutality with a promise of more to come—letting them know they were no longer a person; they were a commodity, a *package*—usually bought instant cooperation. Snake liked calling their buyers—their families or business cronies—threatening all sorts of injury if they didn't pay up quickly and quietly. Even if they hated the guy, they were stuck.

Snake remembered one time when a package's partner told him to go ahead and kill the fucker . . . and do it slow. Snake hadn't been prepared for that, but he'd come up with the solution. He told the partner he would indeed kill the guy slowly, and during the process extract the full details of their gun-running operation . . . which he'd record and send to the ATF.

Snake had the ransom within hours.

Yeah, like Fuller's wife, the last thing any of these clowns wanted was the attention of a federal agency.

Trouble was, Snake couldn't do it alone. He needed someone to baby-sit the packages. Paulie DiCastro had fit the bill. Not the brightest bulb in the box, but no dummy either. And his rep was dependable: A guy who showed up when he was told to, did what he was supposed to—mostly he made deliveries—then went home and kept his mouth shut.

Snake had used Paulie for his first couple of jobs, and things went swimmingly. But on the third job, Paulie had brought his new girlfriend along. Poppy. Paulie swore she was all right, and that this would be better. This way they could take shifts watching the package. One would be on duty while the other slept. Snake hadn't liked the idea—this Poppy was a wild card—but it'd been too late to call off the snatch.

He had held his breath through that whole gig, but things turned out okay.

This job, though, was a little different. Snake usually made the snatch himself. He could say he was better at it, more experienced, that he was the only one he could trust not to screw things up, but truth was, he liked doing the snatch. He liked to see that look in the package's eyes when he realized what was happening to him.

Snake had never known anything else that even approached the rush he got when it dawned on the package that he'd become property—*stolen* property. That his life was no longer his own. Someone had taken control of his world.

Someone who called himself Snake.

Even now Snake could feel the first faint stirrings in his groin.

But this would be different. This would be a kid, and kids weren't in control, anyway. So he'd found it easier to let go of the actual physical snatch.

Besides, he had a lot more riding on this one. Other people involved. Heavy people. Snake preferred to operate on his own, but the heavies had come to him and made an offer he couldn't refuse. Literally. Offered him a fortune for this job, but even if they hadn't, you didn't say no to these guys.

He'd been startled that they were even aware of his little enterprise, and rattled by *how much* they knew. They told him they liked the idea that he was experienced in the art of the snatch and so they were hiring him. That was it. Not: *Do you want to do one for us?* More like: *Here's what we want you to do.*

Snake was trusting Paulie not to screw up. He knew this would be the last job with Paulie. Poppy would see to that. Snake had the distinct impression the only reason Paulie was in on this one was because the payoff was so big. Poppy'd got all spooked when the last snatch got a little rough. Last time he'd seen her she'd looked like a rat on an electric grid, waiting for the next shock.

Too bad. Paulie was a reliable dude. Hard to replace. But that's what you get when you let yourself get attached.

He stretched, picked up the snub-nosed .38 special he kept by the keyboard—a Colt Cobra . . . something about that name—and swiveled in his chair, sighting at the toys that filled his current domain. Three computers—two Pentium 166s and a Mac 7100/80 Power Station—each with a hex-speed CD-ROM drive, all of them up and running twenty-four hours a day, connected to an HP 1200-C printer and a flat-bed color scanner; three cellular phones, all hacked to the same account; a projection TV with Surroundsound, a laser-disk player, two VCRs, a CD player with a 100-disk switcher, all hitched to a pair of Bose 701s and a monster fourteen-inch subwoofer.

Yeah, his living room looked like an electronics store, but hell, this was where he *lived*—at least for now. He loved his gadgets, especially his recently hacked USSB satellite system, but he couldn't think of anything here he couldn't walk away from. He had bank accounts all over the world, and he could always buy more toys. He moved once a year anyway. Presently he was renting this neat little Cape Cod on a cozy, tree-lined street in Alexandria. He waved to his neighbors when they waved first. He was perfectly happy not knowing any of their names. Why bother? He'd be moving again when this gig was over.

No attachments. They colored your thinking. Tied you down. Women were the worst. Like leeches, always wanting to latch on. Who needed the hassle? He could download all the women he needed from the net.

He returned to the keyboard and tapped in his final patch on the switching program. Now, as far as the C&P Telephone computers were concerned, his phone line and Dr. John VanDuyne's line were the same.

He dialed the number of Holy Family Elementary School in Bethesda. He'd been given loads of intelligence on the place. A lot of politicos and well-connected people sent their kids there, and the principal, Sister Louise Joseph, had a rep as a pretty sharp cookie. Who knew? She might have a caller-ID rig on her phone. Snake wasn't taking any chances.

He told whoever answered the phone that he was Dr. John VanDuyne and he needed to speak to the principal on an urgent matter about his daughter. Half a minute later a cool, clear voice came on the line.

"Yes, Dr. VanDuyne. This is Sister Louise. How may I help you?"

Snake closed his eyes and tried to be someone else.

"Good morning, Sister. It's about my daughter, Katie."

"Is something wrong?"

"Well, yes. Her mother was in a serious car accident in Atlanta."

"Oh, dear, I'm so sorry."

"Thank you. I just got a call from the trauma unit and she's in critical condition. I'm going to have to pull Katie out for a few days and take her down there. I don't know how much school she'll miss. . . ."

"Easter vacation begins next week, so you don't have to worry too much about school."

Easter? Was Easter soon? Snake hadn't even thought about that. But he couldn't let the sister know. "I know. And that's good, I guess," he said. "This may be the last time Katie will see . . ."

He let his voice trail off into silence.

"I'm so terribly sorry," Sister Louise said. "If there's any way we can be of assistance."

"Thank you. I have to run over to my office now; then I'm heading home immediately to pack our things. I've sent a driver to pick up Katie and bring her home."

"A car? What service will you be using?"

A thrill of alarm shot through him. He hadn't planned on telling her in advance. She might decide to look it up.

"Oh, I haven't called one yet. I have a few I use now and then. Whichever one can get a car over there the soonest, I suppose."

Silence on the other end of the line. Obviously she didn't like the idea of not knowing precisely who to expect.

Snake looked at the phony ID he'd made up. Reliance Limo existed but he had no idea what their company IDs looked like. Neither would Sister Louise . . . he hoped. He'd give her the name if he had to, but he'd hold back as long as he could.

This was kind of fun.

Finally she said, "Well . . . just make sure the driver has proper identification. We make a point of being very careful about any break from routine with our little charges."

"Which is one of the reasons I enrolled Katie at Holy Family. But please don't say anything about the accident. Just tell her it's a surprise trip back to Georgia."

"Which is very much the truth."

"Unfortunately, yes. I'll explain everything to her when she gets home."

"Very well. Have your driver present himself at my office when he arrives and I'll have Katie brought here. I'll explain to her that you called before he arrives."

"Thank you very much, sister."

He terminated the call and leaned back, his heart racing, his nerve ends twitching. He felt so great, he laughed aloud.

"God, I love my work!"

10 Paulie parked the panel truck on the bottom level of the under ground parking garage like he'd been told, and looked around. Not too many cars down here, and no people.

He turned on the radio again. The old van had only AM. He spun the dial, hoping in vain for some music. *Any* music. Yeah, like he had a chance. Only old farts, news junkies, and born-agains listened to AM.

He stopped at a random number somewhere between 800 and 900 and heard a replay of part of the President's drug talk from last night.

He grinned. Some shocker, that one. Legalize drugs. Who'da thunk? The commentators all saying it wasn't such a big surprise to anyone paying attention—the Pres and his boys supposedly sending up signal flares over the past six months—but Paulie had never been much into politics.

Legal drugs? Weird to think of dropping by the liquor store and pick up a six of Rolling Rock longnecks, and, oh, yeah, while I'm at it, how about a couple of B-40s and a pack of Wowie Maui filter kings? Or buying a box of Little Debbie hash brownies from Abdul at the local 7-Eleven.

Didn't seem right. The whole street ritual was half the fun . . . finding your source, negotiating the price, passing the green, slipping the buy into your pocket, and drifting away, feeling cool 'cause you scored clean once again.

Getting it legal seemed so damn . . . ordinary. Like being a citizen.

Irritably he wrenched the radio power knob to OFF. What was the goddamn world coming to, anyway?

Had to calm down. He felt like an overwound spring, ready to go *sproing!* and bounce all over the inside of the truck. He wanted to get this over with.

Easy enough to baby-sit a package: Snake drops him off, you spend a few days to a week cooped up in a rented house keeping him blindfolded and tied to a bed; a couple times a day you feed him and take him to the bathroom. And when the money's paid, you let him go and leave the house behind. Simps.

But this . . . actually doing the snatch. This was a whole other deal. He had a sudden vision of half a dozen Metro squad cars, lights flashing, sirens screaming as they screeched to a halt all around him, doors flying open and a swarm of steely-eyed SWAT dudes, all armed to the teeth, pointing their Glocks and shotguns in his face.

Paulie shuddered. He didn't like guns. He didn't even own a .22.

I'm a lover, not a fighter, as he liked to say.

And he wanted to reach thirty.

What was that old expression? Do it by the time you're thirty. Well, he was just about thirty and he'd just about done it all.

Grew up mostly alone—his mother working two jobs to keep food on the table while his lard-assed dad shacked up rent free with some bimbo on the other side of town and didn't contribute a goddamned penny because he was "disabled." Yeah, right. An ambulance chaser and a coked-up quack had got him declared totally and permanently disabled after a car accident. But not disabled enough to keep him from lifting weights in his girlfriend's garage. The only thing total and permanent about his father was that he was an asshole.

But before Paulie left home for good, he'd made an honest man of his dad. Waited for him in the parking lot outside his favorite bar. Got him with a Louisville Slugger as he was unlocking his car. Never knew what hit him. Took his wallet to make it look like a mugging and left him with a ton of broken bones.

Now you're totally and permanently disabled, you son of a bitch.

He got something out of his system with that. Pretty much the first and last totally violent thing he'd done in his life.

But he'd done just about everything else. Steal, cheat, swindle, lie, threaten, do second-story work; he'd be a mule, a numbers runner, a courier, or a wheelman. You need something done, you call Paulie DiCastro. He'll take care of it.

But not anymore. Not after this gig. With the money Mac was paying, he wouldn't need to work for a *looong* time.

And besides, Poppy had had it with this life. She'd changed after the last baby-sit. She'd started exercising and eating vegetables and that sort of stuff. And to tell the truth, she was looking damn good.

Not that she hadn't turned heads before. He still remembered the first time he saw her. He was sitting at the bar at The Incarnate Club on Avenue A in Manhattan when she walked in. She'd poured herself into this slinky tight black latex outfit that showed off every curve of her not-too-thin-but-no-way-fat figure. Tall—had to be pushing five-ten— with nice hips, long sweet legs, and a real nice set up top. He was made helpless, completely ga-ga by the way her purple China-doll hair swung back and forth when she walked, the way her black-lined blue eyes stared out from under those heavy bangs that looked like they'd been sliced with a scalpel. The eyebrow ring, the nostril stud, and some cool tattoos: a red heart on each upper arm, with GLORY inside the one on the right and 89 in the one on the left. He bought her a drink, found out she'd come in to hear the goth-industrial battle of the bands the club was featuring all week—same as Paulie. One thing led to another and soon they were back in his place.

And if he thought she'd looked good *in* that outfit, out of it—*mama!*

He was starting to get a woody just thinking about her.

Yeah, Poppy was cool—in more ways than one. She had places in her she never let him see, even when she was stoned. Some major pain tucked away inside, things she never talked about. Something to do with those tattoos, maybe? She always managed to worm out of explaining them. Whatever—somehow she got to him. What he'd expected to be just one more in a long line of live-ins turned out something more. A lot more.

Beaucoup weird, but Paulie had arrived at a place where he couldn't imagine living without her.

A tap on the side window made him jump: Mac, staring at him, leaning close to the glass. He rolled it down.

"Jesus, Mac! You scared the shit outta me."

He said, "Back out and follow me." Then he walked away.

"Well, hello to you too, Mac," Paulie muttered as he started the van.

Talk about weird dudes. Mac was about as strange as they came. He looked like a college professor or something. A good six feet, big shoulders—maybe like a professor who worked out. Always dressed in Dockers and penny loafers and crew-neck sweaters or tweed jackets—one jacket even had suede patches on the elbows, for Christ sake. Brown hair, short all around, none on his face, no jewelry, not even an earring. The ultimate straight. Until you took a look in his eyes.

Paulie knew hit men, stone killers, with warmer eyes than Mac's.

Mac. The name was something that had always bothered him, mainly because it was the only handle he had for this guy. Mac who? Mac the Knife? Maybe. He did carry a big one. Also carried a .45 automatic—always. Mac the Gun?

Mac the mystery. He never saw Mac between gigs. Paulie'd get a call, show up where he was told—could be Kansas City, Phoenix, West Palm, anywhere—baby-sit the package, collect his money, and that was it. Mac dropped off the face of the earth until the next time.

Not that it mattered much. Paulie wasn't exactly looking to hang with the guy. Probably a security thing so that Paulie couldn't finger him. Not that he'd ever consider it. He had his rep as a stand-up guy to consider. And besides, Mac had always been straight up with Paulie—never shorted him or kept him hanging. He paid on time, to the dime.

You had to respect that.

Also had to respect how smoothly Mac's gigs ran. Like well-oiled machines. Everything went down by the numbers. . . .

Except the last one.

And if Poppy was calling the shots now, that would have been Paulie's last one too. They'd had a fight about doing this gig, with Poppy shouting and throwing things, and almost walking out. That was when Paulie realized how important she was to his life.

So they cut a deal: One last gig and then they were out of it. They'd take the money and run, find an island somewhere, and just sleep, sunbathe, eat, drink, and screw.

Yes.

He cruised the truck over to where Mac was backing a shiny new Lincoln Town Car out of a slot. He motioned Paulie to pull into the space.

Paulie parked the truck, then got out and ran a gloved hand over the Lincoln's gleaming black finish.

"Flash ride. Where'd you get it?"

"Get in. We'll talk inside."

The windows slid up as Paulie slipped into the passenger seat. All sound from the outside world faded to zero when he closed the door. Like being sealed in a coffin.

"It's rented," Mac said in a low voice, looking straight ahead through the windshield as he pulled an envelope from the inside pocket of his brown herringbone jacket. Paulie checked him out: No patches on the elbow this time. "The Maryland omnibus plates are borrowed."

Paulie tried not to look too interested in the envelope, but he was hoping he'd find some dead presidents inside. He was just about tapped out. He had to hold himself back from snatching it when Mac handed it over.

"Here are some papers you'll need," Mac said. "Just in case."

Paulie lifted the flap, looking for green paper. The first thing he found was a supply of business cards. He held one up.

"'Reliance Limousine Service.' Is that who I am?"

"For the next hour or so, yes. You'll find a Reliance Limo ID and Maryland driver's license with matching names. Plus directions to your pickup neatly typed on Reliance Limo stationery."

Paulie emptied the envelope. No green, but boy, Mac was thorough. The bogus license and ID were beauties.

"Where'd you get these?"

"I made them."

"No kidding?"

"All it takes is a color scanner, some DTP software, and a little time."

"Amazing. I—" And then a couple of words on the itinerary caught his eye and he straightened in the seat. "Hey, Mac. Does this say Holy Family Elementary School? *Elementary* School?"

Mac was still looking straight ahead. "You got it."

"You mean I'm snatching a *kid*?"

"You are."

"Oh, shit! Oh, fuck! Not a kid!"

And now Mac turned to him, letting those stone-flat dirt-brown eyes bore into him.

"You got something against kids, Paulie?" he said in a voice smooth as satin . . . and just as cold.

"No. I got nothing against kids. That's why I don't want to snatch one."

"You don't look at it as a kid. You look at it as a package. Just another package."

"Yeah, but a *young* package. People get upset about an old geezer getting snatched, but, man, they go off the fucking *wall* about a kid."

"It's not like we're going to molest her or anything."

"*Her?* Oh, shit! A little girl? Just great. Poppy don't like kids."

"She'd better like this one."

"She's gonna go ballistic."

"Poppy will do what she's told."

Paulie wished there'd been more heat behind those words. But Mac said them with the same soft flat tones he'd use ordering a cup of coffee . . . black, two lumps.

Truth was, Poppy *would* do what she was told . . . up to a point. . . .

"You're the one who brought her in," Mac said. "I went along. Poppy's had a free ride so far. Now it's time for her to earn her keep. She can be a nanny for a week or so." He smiled . . . a cold flash of teeth. "We've called it baby-sitting all along. Now it really is."

"Yeah," Paulie said, slumping back in the seat. He didn't like this . . . didn't like it at all. "How old is this 'baby?'"

"Six. Don't let her age spook you. This is going to be a walk. I've called the school. They're expecting you. You drive up, belt her into the back seat like a good, safety-conscious driver, then you cruise away and bring her back here. What could be simpler?"

"How about you doing it? That would be a whole lot simpler."

"I would, but I've got to cover this end."

When Paulie said nothing, Mac reached out and poked his upper arm with a finger. Paulie stiffened. He didn't feature being poked. But when he looked at Mac he saw what he hadn't thought possible: The guy's eyes were even flatter and colder than before.

"You're not backing out on me, are you, Paulie?"

"Nah," Paulie said through a sigh. "I ain't backing out."

He had to admit it: He was afraid to back out now.

"Good. Because a deal is a deal."

"Yeah. A deal is a deal."

But how the hell was he going to explain this to Poppy?

11 Snake strolled into the lobby of the Marriott in Bethesda and went straight to the bank of pay phones. He'd already scouted most of the larger hotels inside the Beltway—this Marriott was *just* inside the Beltway—and knew which ones had the kind o phone he needed.

Of course he could have called from his house or his car or a playground using the mobile PCMCIA modem card on his laptop, but that would have involved a cellular call, and cell calls were about as secure as a loudspeaker.

He found an AT&T Dataphone 2000 and slipped into the seat before it. Airports and hotel lobbies were the best places to find these phones. They provided their own keyboards or a port for jacking into laptops and notebooks. Snake had brought his own. After charging the call to Charles Porter, a credit account he'd set up just for this gig, he jacked the phone clip on the wire running from the back of his Thinkpad 701C into the port, then popped open his computer and let the butterfly keyboard expand.

As he waited for the rig to run through its boot-up routine, he glanced around the lobby. Only a few people about and none of them paying the least bit of attention.

He logged onto the IDT account he'd recently set up for a nonexistent someone named Eric Garter, accessed the e-mail service, and uploaded the text he'd written earlier and stored in memory.

Thirty-seconds later, with his message zapping through the Internet, he logged off. He unplugged the Thinkpad from the Dataphone, snapped the top shut, and headed for the front doors and the parking lot.

So easy, so anonymous, so completely untraceable.

So *safe*.

Too safe, maybe. Too easy.

Almost a letdown.

12 Paulie eased the Lincoln to a stop before the front entrance of the Holy Family Elementary School. Didn't look much like a school. More like a big old house, two sprawling stories of dark stone and cement with ivy crawling all over it.

He reached for the keys but hesitated.

He didn't want to do this.

It just wasn't right.

Okay, it's one thing to snatch a guy. He's an adult. Another man. He should be watching his ass but he got careless, so now he's snatched and somebody's got to buy him back. That's life, dude: You pay for your mistakes.

But a kid . . . shit. Kids can't protect themselves. They don't know the rules. They're sitting ducks. And putting the screws to some guy through his kid . . . that was low. Worse than low—it was unmanly.

Paulie slammed a gloved fist against the steering wheel. God*damn*, Mac!

He was tempted to shift the car back into drive and burn rubber out of here. Pick up Poppy from that rented dump in Falls Church and roar off to parts unknown.

But Mac would be pissed out of his mind. He'd come looking, and sooner or later he'd catch up to them. And that would be ugly. Only one of them would walk away from that scene, and Paulie doubted it would be him.

And besides, he'd made a deal.

He hadn't known a kid would be part of the deal, but . . . a deal was a deal.

Is that how it really is? he wondered. Or am I just yellow?

How low will you go, Paulie? he asked himself. When do you say enough is enough?

He should've listened to Poppy and stayed clear of this one.

Growling with disgust, he grabbed the keys and got out of the car. He adjusted his dumb chauffeur's cap and headed up the front steps.

A middle-aged woman at the desk inside the door phoned, spoke a few words, then led him back to the principal's office.

The lighting wasn't the greatest but he kept his shades on. The less these people saw of his face, the better.

The principal's office . . . jeez, did that bring back memories.

Sister Louise was an older nun, all in black from head to toe. The only skin showing was on her hands and face—and that was encased in something that looked like a cut-out Whitman Sampler box. Looked about as comfortable as a vise. She stared out at him from that box through thick rimless glasses that magnified her watery blue eyes. Her jutting lower jaw made her mouth look weird when she smiled.

Which she did when she greeted him.

"Good day, Mr. . . . ?"

"Anderson," he said, glad he remembered to look at the ID Mac had given him. "James Anderson."

"And you're here to pick up . . . ?"

What is this? Twenty questions? She knows damn well who I'm here for.

"The VanDuyne child. Katie VanDuyne."

"Oh, yes. Dr. VanDuyne called and told me you'd be coming." She stuck her head out the door. "Camille, would you fetch Katie VanDuyne from K-B and bring her here?" Then she turned back to Paulie and held out her hand. "Your identification, please, Mr. Anderson."

He fumbled in his pocket. Suspicious old broad, wasn't she. Mac might be a mean, sneaky, rat bastard, but he'd covered all the bases. Paulie pulled out his Reliance Limo ID and hoped she wouldn't notice how his hand shook when he handed it over. But he held back on the driver's license. No need to appear *too* cooperative.

Sister Louise's brow furrowed as she studied the ID.

"This isn't a photo ID."

"No, ma'am."

She looked up and studied him just as closely with those old blue eyes. She was still smiling but Paulie began getting a bad feeling about this nun. She had this sweet-little-old-lady air about her but she was a sharp old bat, and suspicious as all hell.

"Do you have an ophthalmologic condition?"

"Beg pardon?"

"An eye condition, Mr. Anderson. Is there something wrong with your eyes?"

"No, ma'am."

"Then why are you wearing your sunglasses indoors?"

Paulie felt himself begin to sweat. He didn't like the way this conversation was going, and he liked the way Sister Louise was looking at him even less.

"Habit, I guess."

"You may take them off."

Paulie struggled with the best way to go. Refuse and push her from overly cautious to downright suspicious, or cooperate and graduate.

He took off the glasses.

"There now," said Sister Louise as her searching eyes bored into his. "Isn't it easier to see?"

"Yes, ma'am," he said, trying not to look away.

"And please remove that hat. We don't wear hats indoors. It sets a bad example for the children."

"Yes, ma'am," he said, making sure he opened his jaw so he wouldn't be speaking through clenched teeth.

He felt naked.

And then someone he assumed was Camille delivered a dark-haired little girl in a plaid uniform to the office.

"Hello, Katie," Sister Louise said. "This is Mr. Anderson. Remember how I told you earlier that your father was taking you on a trip back to Georgia? Mr. Anderson is going to take you home now."

The kid looked up at him with her baby blues and smiled. Jeez, she was little. And cute.

"You're gonna take me to my Daddy?"

"That's right, miss," he said, turning on the charm—for Sister Louise's sake as well as the kid's. "I'm taking you home, then taking you and your dad to the airport. And then you're off to Georgia for a vacation."

She said, "Oh," and that was it. Didn't seem too overjoyed.

He held out his hand. "Ready to go?"

Pulling on a red beret, she said, "Sure," and turned to Sister Louise. "Bye, Sister."

"Just one moment," said the nun, staring at him like she wished she had X-ray vision. "Tell me, Katie. Have you ever seen Mr. Anderson before?"

The kid shook her head. "No."

Sister Louise's fingers drummed the desk. "Before I let you go, I think I'd first like to make one call."

Oh, Christ! Who was she calling?

"We're on a tight schedule, ma'am," he said.

"This will only take a second," Sister Louise said, reading a number off her desk top as she punched it into the phone.

Paulie's heart kicked into overdrive. His mouth, already dry from the cotton plugs, suddenly felt like a stretch of desert highway. This was bad. *Very* bad. He widened his stance to keep from wobbling as he began planning his getaway. Did he grab the kid and take her with him? Or did he simply make a fifty-yard dash for the car and head for the hills?

He took a slow, deep breath and waited, hoping to hell Mac had this covered.

13

Snake sat before his home desktop Pentium. He was still hacked into the C&P mainframe, still sitting on VanDuyne's line, monitoring his calls. Two so far, both for his mother—one from a bridge partner, and one from the doc himself. Since both had originated in the District, Snake had let them through. The call he was watching for would originate in Maryland.

This little exercise in caution was probably overkill, but it would be a damn shame if he let the whole gig go to hell because he couldn't hang out an extra half hour or so and keep an eye on—

There!

Snake bolted upright. A call from the 301 area. He checked the number and it matched Holy Family Elementary's. Had Paulie fucked up?

He hit ENTER on his keyboard, sending in a preprogrammed command that would shift the call to his phone. He waited with his hand poised over the phone on his desk.

And waited.

When it didn't ring, he glanced at his monitor screen. Had Holy Family hung up? No! The call was passing through to VanDuyne's.

Shit!

Frantically Snake pounded on the keyboard, entering another command to send the call his way. Two rings already at the VanDuyne house. If the mother picked up . . .

He jumped as the phone next to him suddenly began to ring. He leaned back, caught his breath, then picked up in the middle of the second ring. He cleared his throat and modulated his voice to a soft, even tone.

"Hello?"

"Dr. VanDuyne, this is Sister Louise from Holy Family."

"Yes, Sister. Didn't the driver arrive? I told him—"

"Yes, he's here, doctor. I just wanted to double-check with you before I released your daughter to a stranger."

Snake closed his eyes and thanked the stars he'd stayed hacked in to C&P.

"I appreciate your caution, Sister. The driver should be Jim Anderson of Reliance Limo."

"That is correct. Very well. I'll let Katie go with him then. Sorry to bother you."

"Absolutely no bother at all, Sister. You can't be too careful these days."

He hung up and slumped in his chair, staring at the monitor and relishing the furious pounding of his heart.

No, sirree . . . no way you can be too careful.

14 Paulie was so dazed with wonder, trying to figure out how Mac had worked that bit of magic, that he almost forgot to strap the kid into the backseat. He quickly pulled open the back door and buckled her in.

Good thing too. That Sister Louise was standing on the front steps, watching his every move.

His fingers shook a little and his knees still felt a bit wobbly. He'd thought it was all over back there in her office, but Mac had had it covered. No doubt about it: The guy was a genius.

"What's this box?" the kid asked.

"Oh, that?" he said. "That's candy."

"For me?"

"For all our special customers. Help yourself."

"My Nana doesn't like me to eat candy before lunch."

"This is a special day. Your daddy told me to make sure I told you to eat all you want. Go ahead. Don't be shy. Plenty more where that came from."

He got behind the wheel and hit the ignition.

"Wave to your principal," he said as they rolled toward the street.

Paulie made sure he waved too.

Good-bye, you old bat. You're one sharp cookie, but I'm hooked up with a dude who's even sharper.

Which reminded him . . . He pulled out a cellular phone and pushed two buttons to dial a preprogrammed number. A few seconds later he heard Mac say, "What?"

He wanted to ask him how he'd managed that phone thing but decided to stick to the script.

"Loaded up and on my way."

"Right," and Mac broke the connection.

"Who are you calling?" said that little voice from the back seat.

"That was the, uh, dispatcher. Just letting him know I'm heading for your house. How's that candy?"

"Deee-licious!"

"Excellent. Keep eating."

"Okay. What's this blanket for?"

"That's for in case you get cold or sleepy."

"Oh. My daddy's a doctor, you know."

"Is he, now."

"Yeah. But he doesn't see sick people anymore."

"Really?" Paulie had been wondering what this was about. Maybe he could get a clue from the kid. "What's he do?"

"He works with other doctors. But they're not sick."

"Where does he work?"

"In a big, big building."

So much for prying information out of this one. Paulie glanced in the rearview mirror. The kid had the box of chocolates on her lap and was digging in.

Keep eating, he thought.

"You want some candy, mister? They're real good."

"No thanks. I'm on a diet."

He glanced back again. Cute little thing. Happy with the chocolates and so trusting. Complete faith in him . . . because he said her daddy had sent him.

Jesus, he felt like a rat.

15 Before leaving the White House, John VanDuyne stopped by the press office and found Terri Londergan in her cubicle. Her desk was littered with yellow sheets, all scribbled up this way and that. She had a phone receiver crammed between her shoulder and her ear and was taking furious notes on a fresh yellow sheet.

She looked up and smiled at him, rolling her dark, dark eyes as she pointed to the phone.

"Yes, he will," she said into the receiver. "Yes, I'm sure he will. . . ."

John watched her as she did her deputy press secretary thing, fielding questions from some far away newspaper or magazine editor. He loved the way her blunt-cut raven hair fell across her face when she tilted her head and how she'd toss her head to flip it out of the way. Her sharp nose and strong jaw were softened by her full-lipped smile. Oh, that smile. It had drawn John the length of the executive offices when he'd spotted her talking to Stephanie Harris last year. And he'd stood there like a dummy until Stephanie had introduced him.

A few minutes of conversation with Terri and he'd been completely taken by her. After that he'd made a point of running into her on his regular White House visits, but it wasn't until a few months ago that he'd mustered the nerve to ask her out. They'd been dating ever since.

Terri was in her mid-thirties—about ten years younger than John— but had the poise and self-assurance of someone older. She and Katie had met and spent a few evenings together—in the neutral territory of restaurants—and seemed to get along fine. Katie was always asking when they were going to see Terri again. John was ready to admit to the possibility that he might find someone else, that there might be life and even love after Marnie.

". . . of course," she was saying. "He'll answer all those questions at the press conference. That's right. Right. Have a nice day. Goodbye."

She hung up and then cradled her head facedown in her arms on her desk. She spoke into the chaos of papers under her nose.

"No more calls! *Please*, no more calls!"

John placed his black bag on her desk, moved behind her, and began massaging her tight shoulder muscles, working a thumb along each trapezius.

She groaned and the sound excited him.

"Ooooh, that feels good. You do know what a girl needs."

"Rough morning?"

"The roughest. Ever. Times ten. I—there . . . oh, yes . . . right there. I was in a hundred percent agreement when I listened to him last night."

"You were?"

That surprised him. He knew she didn't use any drugs, and with her strict Irish Catholic upbringing he'd assumed she would oppose legalizing them.

But then, she'd already proved herself to be remarkably liberated regarding sex, so why not the same attitude toward drugs?

"Yeah, I were. But now I'm not so sure."

"Why the change?"

"The phones! The calls from Europe were already backed up when I walked in at six this morning. They've been going wild ever since. Anyone with a newsletter, a local radio show, a fanzine, an online chat nook, everybody in the western *world* wants more information." She lifted her head. "And oh God the West Coast is just waking up. I'm going crazy!"

He laughed. "Now *there's* a good reason to change your principles."

"I have my principles," she said, turning and smiling up at him. "But you learn quickly in this town that you've got to be practical too."

"In other words, if this is going to cause you extra work, drugs should stay criminalized."

"You got it, Doc," she said, still smiling. She pulled on his tie and drew his face down to hers. "C'mere," she murmured. "Gimme a kiss."

And kiss her he did. On the lips. He loved the feel of those lips on his. He started thinking about—

The electronic warble of her phone jumbled his thoughts. She picked up without breaking the kiss and held the receiver to her ear. John heard an indecipherable staccato buzz.

Terri pulled away from him. "Go ahead," she said into the receiver. "Oh, great! Yeah, put him through."

She turned back to John. "I've got to take this."

"Sure," he said. "We still on for tonight?"

Her expression became pained. "Oh, I don't think so. The boss has called a meeting and God knows how long it's going to run. I could be here till ten or eleven. Maybe later."

"I understand."

She smiled. "You're an angel. Let's make it same time, same place tomorrow."

"You've got a deal."

She smiled and turned back to the phone. "Hello? Yes, this is she." She blew John a silent kiss as he waved and left her.

He allowed himself a rueful smile as he headed for the outside. If he hadn't been in favor of this decriminalization stuff before . . . he was *really* against it now.

16 By the time Paulie returned the Lincoln to the bottom-level of the garage, the kid was sound asleep, thanks to the Valium-laced candy. Great idea. Maybe he'd keep the leftovers for himself.

He wound around the entire lower level, checking it out, looking for people leaving or retrieving their cars. He found none. All quiet.

He pulled to a stop behind the panel truck, lining up his passenger-side rear door with its back end. Then he got out, opened the panel truck's rear doors, leaned through the Lincoln's rear passenger door, and wrapped the kid in the blanket.

Now the hairy part. Now something could go wrong.

He straightened up and scanned the level again. No one in sight. He set his jaw and bent to it: quick—one, two, three—he transferred a limp, kid size, blanket-wrapped bundle from the car to the truck. He closed and locked the truck's rear doors.

He was breathing hard and not from the exertion. Done. The worst was over. All he had to do now was leave the Lincoln in the panel truck's spot. Mac would come by later and take care of the car.

He could relax. Just drive back to Falls Church and transfer the kid to the house and—

Oh, shit! Poppy! He'd forgot about her. She was going to go bug-fuck nuts when he showed up with this kid.

The worst part over? Not even close.

17 It took John a while to extricate himself from the area around the White House. When he finally reached HHS, he had to wade through a seemingly endless gauntlet of friends, colleagues, and vaguely remembered bureaucrats stretching from the lobby, into the elevator, and down the halls, each with an opinion about last night's announcement.

Finally he reached the relative sanctuary of his office. Phyllis, his secretary, handed him a cup of coffee and said, "Where do you want me to begin?"

She was fiftyish, thin, with very black skin. She wore her hair in a short, frizzy natural style that framed her narrow face. Despite regular lectures from John, Phyllis still smoked—on the coldest day of the year she'd be out in the courtyard on her break sucking on a butt. She rarely smiled and usually looked as if she'd just bitten into a lemon. This morning she looked as if she'd found a particularly sour one.

"How about with anything that hasn't to do with decriminalization? Like OPC, maybe?"

The main thrust of his post here at HHS was a program called Operation Primary Care. Its purpose was to stimulate medical schools to emphasize primary care in their curricula and encourage medical students to enter family practice and general internal medicine training programs. So far it was being well received.

"Well . . ." she said slowly, shuffling through the blue message slips in her hand, "a couple of schools that have been on the fence about having you speak to their students have called, looking to firm up a date."

"Now there's some good news."

"But they want to know if you'll also address the issue of drug decriminalization."

"Yikes." He rubbed his jaw. Like it or not, he too was caught in the spotlight. "All right," he said. "Sort them out and set up the dates."

"And about drug decriminalization?"

"Be as vague as you can. Just set the dates."

He'd duck those. He was no expert on drugs or drug laws. He had no business talking about the issue. What he did want to talk about was the crying need for primary-care physicians, and to do that he'd shoehorn himself into these medical schools anyway he could.

John dropped into his desk chair and found his monitor on and waiting for him. Good old Phyllis—the soul of efficiency. The e-mail envelope was blinking in the lower right corner of the screen.

That was the one thing Phyllis couldn't check for him. He punched in his password and found thirteen letters waiting.

Let me see if I can guess what they're all about.

He ran quickly through the queue: no surprises. They all had one thing on their minds. . . .

Except the last. This wasn't internal. It came off the Internet. . . .

```
Item 4321334   10:31
From: DAEMON@ANON.NONET.UK     Internet Gateway
To: J.VANDUYNE01      John VanDuyne
Sub: Katie
From daemon@anon.nonet.uk
Received from: anon.nonet.uk by relay1 with SMTP
(1.37.109.11/15.6) id AA080380591; 16:13:11 GMT
Return-Path: <daemon@anon.nonet.uk>
Received: by anon.nonet.uk (5.67/1.35)
id AA 26085; 10:31:16 +0200
From: daemon@anon.nonet.uk
Message-Id: <9502271831.AA26085@anon.nonet.uk>
To: vanduyne01@hhs.com
```

Subject: katie
We have Katie. She is being well cared for. We do not want money. We merely wish you to perform a service. If you perform that service, Katie will be returned unharmed.

!!!BUT!!!

You will be unable to perform this service if anyone knows that you are under duress. Therefore, no one must know that Katie is missing.

!!!NO ONE!!!

Is this clear??? We sincerely hope so. If you inform any local or federal authorities of your plight, you will no longer be of value to us. And, subsequently, neither will your daughter. And we will dispose of her like any other useless object.

ARE WE MAKING OURSELVES CLEAR?

Please do not doubt our determination or resolve. Your daughter's life depends on it. Don't do anything stupid. We'll know.
You will be contacted again soon.
Snake
=END=

John sat staring at the screen. If this was someone's idea of a joke, it was *not* funny. Who the hell—?

He checked the return address and noted the UK suffix. It had been sent from England. Who did he know in England with a sick sense of humor?

And then he realized that the message had come through one of those anonymous remailers he'd read about. E-mail routed through the remailer server was stripped of its origin data and forwarded anonymously.

A chill washed through his arteries. He grabbed his phone and hit the speed dial for Katie's school. When the receptionist answered, John said he wanted to check on his daughter.

"Oh, she was picked up a while ago," she told him.

His office tilted. He had to clutch at his desk to keep from toppling backward. He tried to speak but could not find a sound that even approximated the horror that filled him. Every vowel and consonant had deserted him.

"Dr. VanDuyne?" the receptionist said. "Is anything wrong?" When he still couldn't answer, she said, "I'll get Sister Louise."

On hold, he sat and trembled, gasping for breath. His heart seemed to have quadrupled in size and threatened to burst from his chest.

One thought raced through the circuits of his brain in an endless loop: *Not my Katie! Please, God. Not my Katie!*

His darting eyes found his monitor and locked on the e-mail message still on his screen . . . one particular paragraph seemed to expand in size:

> You will be unable to perform this service if anyone knows that you are under duress. Therefore, no one must know that Katie is missing.
>
> !!!NO ONE!!!

Sister Louise came on the line. Concern was etched in her voice.

"Dr. VanDuyne? Is something the matter? Isn't Katie home yet? It's been more than half an hour since your driver left with her."

John swallowed quickly, trying to find a little moisture. He had to be very careful, but he had to say *something.*

"My driver . . ."

"Yes. That Anderson fellow from Reliance Limousine. I called you about him just before he left. That was you I spoke to wasn't it? Great heavens, don't tell me—"

He wanted to scream at her: *How could you let her go?*

"No-no!" he said quickly. "Everything's fine. My . . . my allergies are just kicking up."

"Thank the Lord. For a moment there . . . but she should be home by now, shouldn't she? If you want I can call the police and ask them—"

Oh, Christ don't do that!

He forced a laugh that must have sounded ghastly. "Well, what do you know . . . here she is now . . . just pulling in the driveway. Must have got stuck in traffic. Thank you, Sister. Sorry to bother you."

"No trouble. I'm just glad she's safe. And have a safe trip to Atlanta."

"Yes . . . thank you."

John fumbled the receiver back into its cradle and leaned on his desk. Atlanta . . . *Atlanta?*

He stared at his monitor screen. Despite the e-mail, despite what

Sister Louise had said, he still couldn't believe it. This whole thing had an unreal feel about it. He had to be dreaming. That had to be it. Soon he'd wake up and—

He jumped as his phone rang. He snatched it up.

"What?"

"Secretary Grahmann is on twenty-two. He wants—"

"Tell him I'll call him back."

"Yes, but—"

"I'll call him *back*, Phyllis." He wanted to scream at her. How could she disturb him *now?* "And hold all my calls. I'm not speaking to anyone right now."

"Are you all right?"

"*No* calls!"

"Yes, sir."

John lurched from his chair and staggered around his desk. He had a strange, floating sensation. His office seemed to have shrunk. The walls pressed in on him.

Katie. Oh, God, Katie. Where was she? What were they doing to her? What did they want with her?

What did they want from *him?*

He rushed back to the screen and reread the message.

. . . We do not want money. We merely wish you to perform a service. If you perform that service, Katie will be returned un-harmed.

A service. What kind of service? What did that *mean?* He didn't have any special skills. What could they want?

But he couldn't think about that. All he could think of was Katie, alone, surrounded by strangers, terrified. . . .

Christ, if he lost her . . .

He stopped at his window, looking up at the overcast sky.

Hasn't she already been through enough, God?

He needed help. He had to call the FBI. They were headquartered right down on Pennsylvania Avenue. Hell, he could call Tom and Tom would call the director and the whole goddamn agency would be combing the country for this Snake creep.

But then another section of the message burned into his retinas.

. . . If you inform any local or federal authorities of your plight, you will no longer be of value to us. And subsequently, neither will your daughter. And we will dispose of her like any other useless object.

But he couldn't handle this alone. What did he know about dealing with kidnapers? Maybe with Tom's help he could keep the FBI's involvement ultrasecret.

Don't do anything stupid. We'll know . . .

And that was the really chilling part. *We'll know.* Obviously this Snake already knew plenty about Katie's schedule, and about his own. He knew John's e-mail address and—what had Sister Louise said? *"I called you about him just before he left."* That meant this Snake had been able to intercept a call to him from Holy Family. Was his line tapped? Did they know *everything?* What about . . . ?

A sudden thought struck him like a sledge hammer: Katie's Tegretol! She needed it twice a day. If she didn't get it—

"Oh, Christ!" he said, and dropped back into his chair.

He hit the function key for reply mail and banged in a message. He wanted to spew every obscenity he knew at this scum, but he held back. If he angered Snake, who would suffer the brunt of that anger?

Be calm, he told himself. Be cool. Think this out. Don't let the bastard know he's made a basket case out of you. Stroke the slimy son of bitch.

Snake—
Your message received and understood. I have told no one. I will follow all your directions to the letter. You are in control. Please do not hurt Katie. But please listen.
THERE IS SOMETHING YOU MUST KNOW!
Katie has a seizure disorder. A form of epilepsy. She needs medicine twice a day, every day. If not, she will start convulsing. She'll have one convulsion after another until she's . . .

His fingers paused over the keys, balking at the next words. He forced them to type on.

> *. . . brain dead.*
> *You must believe that what I am saying is true. I am not playing games with you. You have my daughter. She is the most important thing in my life. I have no idea how I can be of use to you or anyone else, but I will do exactly as you say, do anything you want, but you must get her some of this medicine. I can arrange to send you some, leave some somewhere, or call any pharmacy you choose and have a supply waiting there. You must believe that THIS IS NOT A TRICK!!! THIS IS A VERY SERIOUS MEDICAL PROBLEM!!!*

John sat back and searched his panic-scrambled memory for what he knew about the psychology of kidnapers. He remembered reading that many of them tended to depersonalize their victims. He tried to add something that would make Katie a person to this madman.

> *Katie's had it tough so far in her six short years. I know that sounds hard to believe. How tough could a doctor's daughter have it, right? Believe me, fate has not been kind to Katie. Her epilepsy is only part of the story. Please don't make it any tougher on her. Please don't hurt her. Please. I'll do anything you want, just don't hurt her.*

He heard a noise . . . like a sob . . . and realized it was his own voice. He was crying.

Quickly he wiped his eyes, added his name to the bottom, then hit the function key that would send the message—queue it into the Internet, route it back to the remailer that would forward it to Snake . . . whoever he was.

To the U.K. and back? How long would that take? Ten minutes? An hour? Two? He had no idea. He didn't know that much about the Internet. It was all so big, so anarchic.

One thing he did know: He couldn't stay here. He'd go crazy waiting around for his e-mail icon to start blinking. He—

That reminded him. He had to keep this secret. What if Phyllis knew his password and decided to help him out by checking his e-mail? She'd find out about Katie. He returned to his desk and changed his e-mail password from KATIE to . . . what?

He couldn't think. He looked at the message still on the screen and could think of only one word, one that would be almost impossible to forget.

He typed in SNAKE.

Then he grabbed his coat and fled, averting his face as he passed Phyllis.

"Dr. VanDuyne," she said. "Are you leaving?"

"Yes," he said without turning.

"Is something wrong?"

"I'll be on the beeper."

He hurried along the hall, avoiding eye contact with everyone. When he saw a cluster of people waiting for the elevator he ducked into the stairwell and galloped down.

Minutes later he was driving through downtown D.C., heading for home . . . but not directly. He had to cook up a cover story for his mother. Not only because of what the message had said—

. . . no one must know that Katie is missing. !!!NO ONE!!!

—but also because he didn't know how she'd react. He had a vision of her clutching her chest and keeling over.

But John wished he could tell *someone*. Just one person, so he could share the burden, *talk* about it.

Never in his life, not even during the darkest hours when Katie had been hospitalized in PICU three years ago and it wasn't yet clear she was going to live, had he felt so alone.

Why Katie? Because of me? What have I got that anybody wants? What kind of "service" requires someone holding my daughter captive?

He heard horns blaring behind him and looked up. The light was green. He hit the gas but after a hundred yards realized he couldn't go any farther.

He pulled onto the shoulder, leaned his head against the steering wheel, and began to sob uncontrollably.

What if Katie was already dead?

18

Paulie had left the garage door open, so now he just guided the panel truck into the narrow space, turned off the engine, got out, and pulled the door down.

Dark. Safe. Quiet.

But not for long. Not after Poppy saw the kid.

He could get tough, of course—tell her to shut up and live with it. But when Poppy wasn't happy, somehow neither was he. He'd never been like that with anyone else. He didn't get it.

But no sense in putting if off. Sooner or later he was going to have to face the music. Might as well be sooner.

He opened the rear doors, lifted the blanket-wrapped package in his arms, and headed through the door into the house. Another one of Mac's touches: always a house with an attached garage.

"Oh, honeeeee!" he called, being careful not to use her name, but trying to keep things light. "Here I am, home from a tough day at the office."

He found her standing in the middle of the living room waiting for him. She was grinning, as he'd hoped she'd be.

"Hey, honey, yourself," she said. "Did everything go . . . ?" Her grin faded as her eyes took in the bundle he was carrying. "What the hell is that?"

"It's the package."

Her face got a funny look as she backed away a couple of steps, like he'd just told her he had AIDS or something.

"Oh, no. Oh, God, no. Not a kid. Don't tell me that's a kid!"

"Yeah. It's a kid. Six years old."

"Oh, shit, Paulie. *Shit!*"

"Hey, keep your voice down. And don't use my name. She's out cold now, but she could wake up any minute."

"Take her back! Tell your good buddy you don't want to have anything to do with snatching a kid."

This was stupid. He wasn't going to stand here jawing with Poppy and holding the kid. She was starting to get heavy. He stepped into the "guest room" and gently placed her on the bed. The longer she stayed out, the better.

"She's already snatched," he said. "I can't undo that. So we're stuck with her, like it or not."

Poppy was standing at the guest room door, her gaze flicking from Paulie to the blanket-wrapped lump on the bed and back to Paulie. Her shocked expression was gone, replaced by red-faced anger.

"I can't believe you never told me!"

"I didn't know. How could I tell you if I didn't know myself? He hit me with it this morning when I went to pick up the limo."

"I don't want any part of this."

"I don't like it any more than you do, but we're stuck with it."

"What do you mean 'we'? I didn't sign on to baby-sit no kid. I'm outta here."

She turned and headed toward the other bedroom.

This was awful. Paulie hurried after her and grabbed her arm. He wanted to shout but kept his voice down to a harsh whisper.

"You can't walk out on this, Poppy."

"Watch me."

"We made a deal!"

Her eyes flashed. "The deal didn't include no kid! This could turn out like that Limbaugh thing."

"Lindbergh."

"Whatever. I don't want nothin' to do with it! Now let me go!"

He released her arm and she continued toward the other bedroom. He couldn't make her stay or he'd wind up baby-sitting her *and* the package. He'd have to try something else, like maybe guilt. From years with Poppy he knew that guilt tended to work on her pretty good.

"Fine. Leave me hanging. Walk out and leave me with a kid I don't know nothin' about. Bad enough if it was a little boy, but this is a little *girl*. How'm I supposed to take care of a little girl?"

She stopped at the door and turned, eyes blazing. "Damn you, Paulie!"

"Hey, quit saying my name."

"I oughta shout it from the goddamn roof!"

"You oughta *help* me, Pop—honey. We both got sucker punched on this one. I thought we were a team. It ain't right to jump ship as soon as the going gets rough."

She wandered around the room muttering, "Damn, damn, damn!"

under her breath, over and over. That was good in a way . . . at least she wasn't in the bedroom packing up her stuff.

"I don't see why you're mad at me," he said. "I didn't know a thing about this."

She wheeled on him. "I knew we shouldn't have trusted him! I *knew* it. I didn't want to take this job in the first place, but would you listen? Nooo! You said . . ."

Paulie let her rattle on. She was blowing off steam. In a few minutes maybe she'd run out.

Took more than a few minutes, but finally she quieted and stood there in the middle of the living room, glaring at him.

"All right," she said. "I'll help you out. But so help me God, this is the last time we have anything to do with you-know-who. Is that totally clear?"

"As a bell," he said, reaching for her to seal it with a kiss.

She danced away. "I gotta see to the kid. And I like totally hate kids, you know. I ever tell you that?"

"Like a zillion times."

"Well, that ain't changed."

"But you never said why."

"I just do, is all. If I liked kids I'd've had some by now. But I don't. I'll never have kids. Ever. You understand that?"

"Sure." Christ, she was acting crazy. "No kids. No problem. That's all fine with me." He tried to lighten things up. "This one's only on rental anyway. We get to return her in a few days or so."

Another glare, this one even meaner than the first—like she was trying to bore holes in his skull or something.

"We'd better," she said. "Because I don't know no more about taking care of kids than you do. What do I do with her?"

"What else? Make sure she can't walk or talk when she wakes up . . . just like all the other packages."

"Great, Paulie," she said with a venomous glare. "Tie up a little girl. Just *great!*"

He watched her stalk off into the big bedroom. He was about to offer to help but thought better of it. She looked like a cranky wildcat with PMS, ready to scratch his eyes out if he got too close to her. Better to back off and let her do it her way . . . alone.

19

Poppy approached the blanket-wrapped lump on the bed gingerly, as if it might rear up and bite her. She didn't want it to wake up.

A kid. Of all things, a damn kid.

Well, wasn't that where the word came from anyway? *Kid*napping?

What were they going to do with a whiny, crybaby kid?

Cautiously, she pulled the blanket aside to take a look.

Skinny little thing. Wearing a uniform. Probably a private school. Rich kid. But that dumb red beret—where'd she get that?

Poppy knelt so she could get a look at the face.

Round, kind of cute, with chocolate smeared on her lips. Nice hair . . . long, dark, braided.

Poppy wondered what color her eyes were, but wasn't about to pry up a lid to see.

As she knelt there, staring at the child, a strange thought came to her.

How old would Glory be now? Probably about the same age.

Would Glory have looked like this little thing? She'd had dark hair and . . .

Poppy leaned forward and pushed up one of the kid's eyelids—just far enough and long enough to see the color—then let it drop.

Blue eyes . . .

Just like Glory's . . .

Poppy shook herself. This was doing her like no good at all. She hadn't thought of Glory—hadn't allowed herself to think of her—in years. Glory was gone. Long gone. And there was no coming back from there.

She busied herself with trying to find a way to bind, gag, and blindfold a six-year old. All their supplies were geared for adult sizes.

20

"Damn!"

Snake slammed the heel of his palm against the Dataphone—in the Mayflower Hotel this time—nearly dislodging it from the wall.

He glanced around. One passerby through the lobby stopped to stare at him for a second, then passed on. Probably thought he was talking to his stockbroker.

He shackled his rage. After all, he went online through these hotel phones to *avoid* detection. The last thing he wanted to do here was make a scene. But damn, he *really* wanted to punch his gloved fist through the Dataphone's blue screen.

He reread the VanDuyne E-mail on his Thinkpad screen one more time, just to be sure he wasn't seeing things, then saved the message to his hard drive.

The kid's a goddamn epileptic! All that primo inside information on VanDuyne and his brat but not one rotten mention of epilepsy, or medicine.

A defective package—the worst!

Served him right for getting involved with someone he didn't know. In the first place, he never would have touched an upright citizen; in the second, never an upright citizen's kid; and third, he'd never pick up a sick package—anything could go wrong.

So what did he have on his hands now? An upright citizen's sick kid.

He wanted to scream. He wanted to—

He disconnected and walked away from the phone bank before he did something stupid. When he was cooler, he came back to another phone and punched in Salinas's private number.

"Il Giardinello."

Snake had expected to hear Salinas's butt boy, Allen Gold. But this voice was thickly accented.

"It's me," he said, snarling. "Tell your boss the package has been picked up but it's defective. Tell him I want to talk to him *now*."

"Defective? What do—?"

"I'll tell *him*. I'm only going to explain it once."

"Hold on."

Snake waited what seemed like a long time before the guy came back on the line. "He is not here right now, but he is on his way in. He says to give me your number and wait there. He will call you back as soon as he arrives."

Snake read off the number on the phone and hung up; then he sat back and waited. He calmed himself. No snarling during his next conversation. He didn't like Carlos Salinas, didn't trust him, and wouldn't be working with him if he thought he had a choice, but you didn't snarl at a guy who had his fingers in most of the drug trade east of the Mississippi.

21 It stank in here. Carlos Salinas could barely breathe in the thick, wet, sulfurous air. And the glare from the overhead bank of 600-watt sodium lamps spiked his eyes through his sunglasses.

And yet, Carlos Salinas was impressed. Deeply impressed.

He'd come to this tiny apartment in Southeast D.C. to inspect a business opportunity. Instead he'd found . . . a miracle.

"Behold my own dwarf hybrid," said their host, a thin, bearded, middle-aged ex-hippie who wore a cowboy hat and referred to himself only as "Jeff." Carlos knew he was really Henry Walters, age 45, who lived off Dupont Circle and had been an independent drug dealer—strictly hallucinogens—for most of his adult life. "I call it Lizard King Indica Hybrid. Look at those buds, will you? I cloned out these babies barely six weeks ago and you could start your harvest right now."

Carlos stared at the "sea of green"—Jeff's term—and marveled. The entire front room had been taken over by eighteen-inch plants with serrated leaves and hairy tops—"calyxes," Jeff called them—waving back and forth in the gentle breeze from a trio of oscillating fans. They clustered in children's plastic swimming pools that in turn sat on metal platforms. Shades, duct tape, and heavy drapes sealed the windows. Rubber tubing snaked from plant to plant, supplying water and fertilizer; heaters warmed their roots from below while the sodium lamps above bathed them in artificial sunlight twelve hours a day. A large metal tank kept the air rich in carbon dioxide for maximal growth.

"And the beauty part of the operation," Jeff said, "is it's all computerized. The whole room is rigged with sensors that monitor light, temperature, humidity, CO_2, and water levels. The computer's modem allows me to keep tabs on every one of my seas of green from a phone booth, and a smart interface lets me make adjustments over the wire. I've rigged the place with motion detectors so I know if someone's broken in.

And last, all my computers are infected with Deicide, a virus that wipes out the hard drive should the wrong dude try to access it."

"You appear to have thought of everything," Carlos said.

Inside his suit he was bathed in sweat. A man of his weight should not frequent jungles, even indoors. Yet despite his discomfort, he was almost mesmerized by the gentle swaying of the leaves and calyxes. They seemed almost . . . happy. Where had plants ever been treated so well?

A wave of nostalgia engulfed him for an instant. His first brush with the drug trade had involved marijuana. Many moonless nights on the beach west of Cartagena, transferring bale after bale of Colombian Red from trucks to trawlers bound for the Gulf Coast of the United States. The "square groupers," as they were known, were the most profitable "catch" for those crews in the early seventies when America's domestic marijuana was so poor.

Smuggling . . . it was in his blood. After all, he was a *paisa*. His ancestors had left the Basque regions of Spain in the 1600s and settled in the Andes, in Antioquia Province around what would later become the city of Medellín. When Spain fixed the price of gold in Colombia, his forebears smuggled it out to Jamaica where they got the higher market price. Down the centuries it became an Antioquian tradition: Sneak out coffee, emeralds, and quinine; smuggle electronics, appliances, and perfumes back in past the rapacious import duties.

True to another *paisa* tradition, his father had kicked him out at age sixteen, telling him: If you succeed, send money; if you fail, don't come back.

He had succeeded.

"Yeah, the technology's great," Jeff was saying, drawing Carlos back to the present, "but it's the plants that are truly awesome—four pounds of top-grade sensemilla per hundred. This ain't no Maui Zowie, you know what I mean? The stuff I started smoking in the sixties was maybe one percent THC. Lizard King is connoisseur stuff, man—tests out to *fourteen* percent. An absolutely bodacious high. Brings down a minimum of five hundred bucks an ounce."

"How many plants in this room?" Carlos said.

"Two hundred."

Carlos glanced at Allen Gold, his lean and lupine chief bean counter. "Allen?"

Gold stood near the door, his arms folded across the front of his Armani suit, the sodium lights reflecting off his blond hair and the wire rims of his glasses.

"That's sixty-four thousand per crop," he said without hesitation. "At roughly eight crops a year, figure half a mill per room per year."

Carlos looked at Jeff. "That is a good living. Why do you need me?"

"I want to expand," Jeff said. "Look. Grass is a thirty-something-billion-dollar industry. I can't produce it fast enough to keep my customers happy. I'm ready to move up to warehouses." He extended his arms over his tiny jungle as if blessing it. "Imagine it, man. A twenty-thousand-square-foot sea of green. Cosmic!"

"You are not afraid of President Winston legalizing your crop?"

"Never happen. This is a growth industry, and I need a banker—somebody with connections . . . you know, for security and such. You're that guy."

Gold's cell phone beeped before Carlos could reply. He saw a troubled look steal over the young MBA's features as he muttered monosyllables into the receiver.

"Everything is all right?" he said as Gold turned toward him.

"It's Llosa," he said. "He just got a call from your new contractor saying something about the package being defective. He insists on speaking to you right away."

Defective? Carlos felt a sudden tightness in his chest. Had something gone wrong? Had the child been hurt? He prayed not.

"Have Llosa tell the contractor to give a number and wait. I'll call him from my office." As Gold passed on the instructions, Carlos turned toward the door. "We must go," he said.

"That's it?" Jeff said. "I took a risk bringing you here, you know."

"We will be contacting you."

"I'd like an answer soon," Jeff said. "After all, I ain't getting any younger."

"You must be patient," Carlos said, giving the man's shoulder a gentle squeeze. "Otherwise you could be worried about getting older, eh?"

Jeff blanched behind his beard. "Hey, I didn't mean any—"

"You will be contacted," Carlos said, smiling grimly as he walked out into the cooler, fresher air of the dirty hallway. He didn't like to be rushed.

"Any details from our friend that you didn't mention?" he said to Gold when they were seated in his Lexus and his driver was gliding them back to Georgetown.

Gold shook his head. "No. Pretty damn enigmatic." His voice took on a whiny tone. "Just like the rest of this kidnapping thing. If you'd let me in on the big picture, maybe I could help."

As much as Carlos trusted Gold, this "big picture" was best left under wraps.

"All in good time, Allen," he said. "But tell me: What did you think of that little demonstration back there?"

Carlos did not really want to talk about marijuana—he was more concerned about the "defect" in the package MacLaglen had picked up—but he did not want to listen to Allen's whining about not being trusted.

"A warehouse-sized setup like that could be *very* profitable. But I hope you're not considering investing—"

"Not me," Carlos said. "But I can connect him with some money people—"

"And take a cut." Gold smiled. "That's my man. For a moment there I was afraid you were thinking about getting back into handling product."

"No." Carlos shook his head slowly. "I've handled more than enough in my day."

How many years had he been in the trade? Certainly half his life—and he was looking down the barrel at fifty.

His first brush with cocaine had come when he joined up with fellow *paisa* Pablo Escobar, who was transshipping kilos of the white powder from Chile to the U.S. in spare tires. Cocaine was a small business back then, a cottage industry run out of Chile. But everything changed when Pinochet took over in 1973. The cocaine refiners fled to Colombia and into the arms of Pablo Escobar and Jorge Ochoa . . . just about the time cocaine use exploded in the U.S.

Colombia, Medellín, the world—especially Carlos's world—would never be the same.

Carlos had done his share of mule work in "Los Pablos," but along the way he became the group's peacemaker. He discovered a knack for bringing warring factions together, striking a deal, and letting each feel that the other party had given up more.

And so when Jorge Ochoa—"El Gordo"—called a summit meeting of all the major players in the cocaine trade, it was only natural for Pablo Escobar to send Carlos Salinas to represent his interests.

April 18, 1981, the day he landed on Ochoa's private mile-long airstrip at his estate on the Caribbean coast near Barranquilla. Jorge Ochoa— "the Fat Man"—personally came down to the air strip to greet them and bring them up to the main house. Hacienda Veracruz, as Ochoa called his estate, was the size of a small province, with its own zoo, a private bull-ring, and a stable of prized *caballos de paso*—walking horses.

The traders arrived as suspicious competing factions, feudal lords, vi-ciously protective of their individual fiefdoms; they left with an agree-ment to pool their resources and their product in a combined effort to keep the lines of supply wide open into their biggest market: the United States.

Later the Americans would say that this meeting marked the birth of the Medcllín cartel. True, he guessed, but none of them ever referred to themselves as a cartel. They were *la compañía*.

"Call him," Carlos told Llosa as he entered the sumptuous back office of his restaurant. Llosa dialed, then handed him the receiver of the Louis XVI-style telephone.

When Carlos recognized MacLaglen's voice, he did not let him speak. He said, "Hold now while we check the line."

He signaled to Llosa to run a scan. Llosa was good at this.

Carlos Salinas shifted his two-hundred-eighty pounds in the over-sized chair as he waited. His back was killing him.

Even though only a handful of people knew his private numbers, Carlos hadn't accepted an incoming call in years. Who knew where they were originating? His research had assured him that MacLaglen was just as careful as he, but even public phones could no longer be trusted. America was turning into a fascist state. Almost as bad as his homeland.

So he always called back, using his secure line—and *never* to a cellular phone. Even his own line was suspect; he constantly had it checked and rechecked.

He wondered which of MacLaglen's favorite phones he was calling from. He knew most of the man's habits, his favorite hotel lobbies and street phones, his accomplices, Paul DiCastro and Poppy Mulliner. He probably knew more about Michael MacLaglen than anyone else in the world.

Carlos could have used some of his fellow *paisas* for this job. After all, kidnapping was an art in Colombia. But he'd decided an American would be better. He did not want any Colombians involved should anything go wrong.

Carlos had become aware of MacLaglen when he kidnapped a gun runner Carlos had dealt with. He watched MacLaglen then, saw how he handled his next snatch—a videotape bootlegger. Very smooth. He had talent. Here was their man.

Llosa looked up from the lights and dials on his scanner box and nodded. Carlos pressed the recorder button before speaking.

"So, Miguel. You have picked up the package, I am told. I am delighted that the first phase is completed."

Clean scan or not, Carlos believed in revealing as little as possible over the telephone.

"Yeah. That went fine. But the contents are defective."

"So my associate informed me. How so?"

"You ever hear of epilepsy?"

"Epilepsy?" Carlos smoothed his mustache and glanced at Gold. *Epilepsy?* He'd seen people convulse after too much cocaine. Was that what this child would be doing? "You are saying that epilepsy is involved here?"

Gold stood near the window. He spread his hands and shrugged, offering his that's-news-to-me expression.

"Damn right it is," MacLaglen said. "Why didn't anyone know about this?"

Good question, Carlos thought. He'd received excellent in-depth intelligence on the President and his doctor friend, all of it free. That something this important could have been overlooked annoyed him. Well, as the saying went, you get what you pay for.

"Or did somebody know about it," MacLaglen was saying, and Carlos could hear the anger rising in his voice, "and neglect to tell me?"

"Calm yourself, Miguel. No one neglected to tell you anything. It was somehow missed. It is not, after all, something that one parades around. Certainly for a man of your talents this is not an insurmountable difficulty."

"Don't give me that. This is a major glitch. It shows incompetence right at the source. What *else* don't we know, señor?"

"I have the utmost confidence in you, Miguel. I am certain everything will be fine."

"This means more contact with the package's point of origin. It broadens the interface. The more contact, the more chance of something going wrong."

Carlos was growing impatient with MacLaglen. Time to put him in his place.

"I have three words for you, Miguel: Deal with it."

Cold silence on the other end of the line. Carlos let it continue for a few seconds. He'd used the stick; now for the carrot.

"By the way," he said cordially, "you are due the second installment. You may pick it up today, at which time I will inform you of phase two."

"I'll be over around five."

The line went dead.

"Manajate!" Carlos muttered as he hung up and swiveled toward Allen Gold. "Our friend is angry."

"I'd say he's got a damn good right to be," Gold said. "It's inexcusable. We should have been told." He shrugged. "Could be worse, though. She could be a diabetic. Then MacLaglen would have to learn how to give insulin injections."

Gold was right: It could be worse and it *was* inexcusable. Bad intelligence could ruin everything. Carlos wished he could mete out suitable punishment to the man responsible, but that was not possible—not to someone so high in the United States government.

"MacLaglen is arriving later to pick up his second installment. Have the cash ready."

"Sure thing," Gold said, making a note in his ever-present scratch pad. "How many more installments?"

"One."

Gold whistled. "He'll need a wheelbarrow to cart that one out in cash."

"He won't see a penny of it until this is all over."

"Come on, Carlos. What's this kidnapping all about? What's our goal here?"

"All in good time, Allen."

He wondered if he'd ever tell him that the goal was to see President Thomas Winston either dead or out of office.

Carlos sighed and leaned back in his chair. He pressed a button to start the automated low-back massage. Heat and gentle, padded pistons began to ease his perpetual backache. Ah, good.

He wished he didn't have to shoulder this entire burden himself, but it was far too sensitive to entrust to anyone else, even Allen.

I should have refused, he thought. I should have kept my mouth shut when I heard about Thomas Winston's legalization plans.

But how could he have kept silent? What threatened the drug trade threatened him.

And threatened *la compañía* even more.

If only he weren't *El Mediador.*

He'd earned that title after the 1981 summit at Hacienda Veracruz. Carlos had impressed Jorge Ochoa at that meeting—enough so that El Gordo called on him whenever *la compañía* needed someone to quell the all-too-frequent flare-ups between rival subgroups.

He became *El Mediador*—the top negotiator for *la compañía*. He dealt with the low-down and high-up. He arranged with *cara de Piña* Noriega to set up cocaine labs in the jungles of southern Panama. Later he was paying the Sandanistas for the use of their airfields to refuel *la compañía's* cocaine-loaded planes. All along he took his fee in product, which he sold off through his own network in Miami. Life was good.

But then the so-called War of the Cartels broke out in 1988, and nothing could stop the bloodshed. Carlos tried to get the message into their thick heads that there were enough billions to go around, but no one was listening. His old friend Pablo Escobar went crazy, declaring war on the rival Cali cartel, and on the Colombian government itself. Blood quite literally flowed in the streets of Medellín.

Carlos Salinas watched the carnage with growing dismay. He had a new wife then, the beautiful Maria, and he wished to keep her out of the line of fire. But what else did he know?

He decided to trade on his reputation as *El Mediador* by going into an ancillary service.

But he needed guidance. When he learned of a young man named Allen Gold, fresh out of the Wharton MBA program, who'd been arrested in a cocaine sting operation, Carlos got him off and hired him. Through various fronts set up by Gold, Carlos began investing heavily in the stocks of small independent banks up and down the East Coast.

When he gained controlling interests, he began maneuvering his own people on to the boards of directors.

The best move he'd ever made. Even while the war raged, the white powder flowed unabated—as did the profits. And all that tainted money needed sanitizing. Who better to trust than *El Mediador*, Carlos Salinas?

And even after the Cali *compañía* eclipsed Medellín, the negotiating skills of Carlos Salinas remained in demand. In 1992, Miguel Rodriguez Orejuela, a Cali leader, retained his services to help NAFTA get through Congress. Carlos moved to the Washington area and made sure money from the Cali *compañía* got into the right pockets. Of course, he took his cut, and pocketed a bonus when the bill was signed into law.

Free trade . . . it was wonderful. No more need for offshore air strips and risky flights across the border. Now the Mexicans were moving truckloads of Colombian product into Texas every day.

And along the way Carlos Salinas discovered that Washington was much more convenient than Miami as a center of operations for his banking business, especially after all the high-placed friends he'd made here during the NAFTA legislative battles.

Life got better. The landscape of the cocaine trade was changing yearly, but so what? The cocaine princes came and went—Pablo Escobar was dead, and most of the leaders of the Cali *compañía* were in jail—but Carlos Salinas remained. Did the jailings and killings affect the trade? Not by an ounce. The only result was the consolidation of the power of the Colombian *compañías* into fewer hands—mostly into Emilio Rojas's—but no matter. As long as drugs remained illegal, the profits would need laundering.

And Carlos was here to help . . . for a cut.

But there would be no cut for this service. Instead he'd been offered a simple flat fee for stopping President Winston's plan: one billion dollars.

And if he succeeded, he'd be more than mind-numbingly rich.

He'd be a legend.

If he succeeded.

No, don't think *if*—think *when.*

Because if he *didn't* succeed . . .

Better not to think about that. Better to think about how this opportunity to become a legend had dropped into his lap exactly ten weeks ago when he received the first of a series of anonymous calls. The caller used a voice distorter, but Carlos eventually learned who he was. And was shocked. This was a man no amount of money could have bought, yet he was *giving* him information about the president's plan.

At first Carlos did not believe him. Legalize drugs? *All* drugs? Impossible . . . *unthinkable!* Never happen. Had to be a trick, part of some weird scheme to entrap him.

He passed the story—along with his misgivings—to Emilio Rojas, the current head of the Cali *compañía*.

Rojas scoffed at first, but he began making inquiries, tapping *la compañía*'s many sources, even in the White House itself.

And Rojas learned it was true. Not just marijuana and the occasional mushroom—*all* drugs. Cocaine included.

How they'd all laughed back then, thinking what did it matter what this loco president wanted, the American people would never accept it. But then as more information flowed in from Carlos's big shot source, *la compañía* began serious research. What they learned scared the living *mierda* out of them.

Emilio Rojas himself made a trip to the United States to meet with Carlos. Emilio came *here*.

Carlos remembered sitting in this very room, just the two of them, and listening with a sick feeling in his gut as Rojas told him how, with a plan promising lower crime rates and lower taxes, backed by support from the media, the pharmaceutical industry, and the tobacco states, this Thomas Winston just might do it. Not total decriminalization, perhaps, but a beginning that would eventually finish most antidrug laws.

And where America went, the rest of the world would surely follow.

Rojas admitted that for a while he and *la compañía* had been panicked. But when they calmed themselves, they set about making plans. They examined every possibility. No cost was too great. How could it be? With billions of dollars coming in every month, they would spend any amount necessary.

Although Rojas had tried to appear calm and confident, Carlos could sense his fear, his rage. This was not some little brawl for a bigger piece of the market—this was a war for their very lives.

This upstart gringo, this Thomas Winston, could wipe out their global empire with the stroke of a pen.

Carlos agreed that he had to be stopped. But how?

A bullet was the first thought, but that was discarded immediately. Assassination would make a martyr out of Winston—the last thing they wanted. They could hear the speeches: A heroic president has been shot down by the evil drug lords. We must carry his brave plan forward and put an end to these criminals so powerful and arrogant that they will kill our president to preserve their profits! Do not let the drug lords get their way! Honor the slain president's commitment! Legalize drugs now!

No . . . a martyred President Winston would be an even more formidable enemy than a live and healthy one. They had to find a way that would look like an accident—or his own fault.

La compañía peered into Winston's past with a microscope and found many instances of youthful wildness, but nothing that would discredit or disgrace him. It had looked hopeless until . . .

. . . until Carlos's mystery source came through with a bit of history that Winston had thought he'd destroyed. Some U.S. agency had unearthed it in a background check during his first run for office and filed it away.

Carlos had passed it on, attaching little importance to it.

But it had proved to be *very* important.

And so the two of them had sat here in this very safe room and devised a wonderful and terrible plan. . . .

"It's about drug decriminalization, isn't it?" Gold said.

Carlos bolted from his reverie. "What do you mean?"

"The kidnapping. You've had it poised to go for weeks. And then as soon as the President speaks last night, *boom!*—you're on the phone to MacLaglen. There's got to be a connection."

Was I that obvious? Carlos wondered as he hoisted his bulk out of the chair and waddled around the office.

Or was Gold simply too bright? That was why Carlos had brought him in. He knew Allen would not be shocked by a plan against his President, but the fewer who knew, the better. An old *paisa* saying went: Three can keep a secret—if two are dead.

He stopped before a framed autographed photo of Richard Nixon. It was inscribed to someone else, but that didn't matter. The *man* was what mattered.

"I am not worried about a pipsqueak like Thomas Winston. He has no courage." He pointed to Nixon's photo. "How does he have the gall to sit in the same office as this man? *Here* was a president!"

"Nixon?" Gold said, his voice jumping an octave. "He was a jerk."

Carlos turned as quickly as his girth would allow and pointed his finger in Gold's face.

"When you speak of this man, you will show respect. He is the president who first declared war on drugs in 1972. You would not be standing here if he had not. You would not be wearing that fancy suit or driving that German sports car you prize so much. You owe this man everything—him and all the presidents who continued the war after him. They were *men!*"

Carlos turned back to his photo of Nixon and stared at that smiling face.

"Why can't Thomas Winston be like the others and follow in their footsteps? But no. He is a cowardly *hijo de puta* who will ruin everything!"

"He hasn't got a chance," Gold said. "The only thing he'll ruin is his political career."

If only you knew what I know, Carlos thought.

He returned to his desk and dropped into his chair. The automatic massager was still on. He adjusted his back against it for full effect but it gave him only minimal relief. He'd have to call that Chinese girl—Tree Flower, or whatever her name was. She was the only one who could soothe his pain. When she walked up and down his spine with her little feet and massaged him with her toes, he found the closest thing to heaven . . . next to his wife.

The thought of Maria saddened him. He had met her on a visit home. A girl then, barely out of her teens, pure *paisa* like him, no native blood, able to trace her family all the way back to Spain. For the first time in his life Carlos had known love. He wooed her, married her, and brought her to the United States. For ten years he knew bliss.

And then Maria began to change. She became moody, unhappy. She moved to another bedroom. And then three weeks ago, she rented a townhouse in Georgetown and moved out.

Carlos had never thought he could be so devastated by a woman. . . .

But he hadn't lost her. This was a temporary thing. She'd come back. He could *bring* her back, of course, but what good was that? He didn't want to be her jailer. But he *was* her watchdog, keeping her under round-the-clock surveillance.

"What is the latest from P Street?" he asked Gold.

Gold shrugged. "She shops. Goes to museums. Shops some more. Goes to the library. Shops. She's enrolled in a course at G.U. She—"

"What course?"

"Something in the Women's Studies program. I have the exact name in the report. Want me to—?"

"Never mind." He sighed. "No other man?"

Allen shook his head. "Or woman. It's like she's become some sort of female monk . . . with an AmEx card."

Carlos knotted his fists in frustration. *La perra!* He did not understand her.

Yes, he did. He knew what the problem was: the United States. She was being corrupted. Becoming . . . *American.* He had to get her away from the talk shows and soap operas and magazines that put crazy ideas into her head. He had to get her back home—to Colombia—whether she liked it or not. When he was finished with this business here, when he was a billionaire, he would build an estate bigger than Jorge Ochoa's Hacienda Veracruz, where he would raise magnificent *caballos de paso*, just as Maria's father had done. And there, back in her homeland, she would regain her senses. She would become his Maria again.

But all that was dependent on bringing down President Winston.

Everything depended on getting rid of that *cabron.*

Carlos picked up the TV remote. The sixty-inch rear-projection screen buzzed to life. He saw two vaguely familiar politicians, one white, one black, standing behind a podium at what looked like a press conference.

"Talk about politics making strange bedfellows," Gold said. "Good Lord, it's Jessup and Wagner side by side. Stay here."

The banners at the bottom of the screen identified the black man as REP. FLOYD JESSUP (D–NY) and the white man as REP. QUINCY WAGNER (R–SC). Each was outdoing the other in flogging the President. Congressman Jessup was shouting about "genocide on a level that will make Adolph Hitler look like a piker!" while Wagner was warning about "the unraveling of the very moral fiber of America!"

Gold was laughing. "First time I've ever seen those two agree on anything! This is awesome!"

"Allen," Carlos said. "I wish you to find the addresses of these fellows' re-election campaign funds and write out a check to each for two thousand dollars with a note to keep up the good work and *escalate* the war on drugs."

Gold nodded, grinning. "I love it! I'll draw them from the restaurant's account. Not that we need to contribute a dime—I mean, they can't fail—but I love the irony."

"And I love insurance."

Carlos cruised the channels, not sure of what he was looking for. Something, anything, to help him get a feel for the mood of the country. *La compañía*'s projections had predicted this initial angry reaction, but said it would be followed by a general cooling of emotions as the spin doctors in the media and the administration began to work their spell on the public and congress.

He stopped at a channel that showed a man standing on a stage before a sign with the word DRUGS in a red circle with a red line drawn through it. An 800 number flashed at the bottom of the screen. He recognized the Reverend Bobby Whitcomb. Everybody knew the reverend. In the past few years he had become increasingly influential in Christian Fundamentalism. At the rear of the stage, behind the no-drugs sign, sat three tiers of phone banks and busy operators.

"Looks like a telethon," Gold said.

The Reverend Whitcomb stood teetering on the edge of his stage, his microphone pressed to his lips, his free hand clawing the air, as he—literally—foamed at the mouth.

" . . . and I say to you now that we will not be able to live, work, or play in the sight of the Lord if we allow this to happen! We will not be able to hold our heads up when we enter the house of the Lord. In fact, the Lord will turn a deaf ear on all our prayers if we do not *cast* out this evil man from the White House! If we do not *disown* this man as the leader of our nation!"

The studio audience was on their feet, cheering, waving their arms.

"And so you must give *now!* Give whatever you can so that we can get these petitions moving, so that we can send our deacons into every city and town in the nation for signatures calling for the *impeachment* of President Thomas Winston!"

During the next burst of wild cheering, Gold turned to Carlos.

"An impeach-a-thon! You've got to let me call in a pledge. A big one. I've got to do this."

"How big?"

"Ten. You want to buy insurance, here's a good way."

Carlos was taken aback. "Ten grand? What for?"

"I need five figures to get his attention. You'll see. It'll be a killer."

"Very well. Go ahead."

On the screen, a long-robed choir was singing "The Battle Hymn of the Republic" as Carlos watched Gold dial the 800 number. When he started speaking he suddenly had a thick southern accent.

"Hello? Is this the Reverend Whitcomb? Well, Ah want to speak to the Reverend Whitcomb his own self. Don't tell me what ain't possible, darlin.' A'course it's possible. Ah got ten grand says it's possible. That's raht. Ten grand to donate to gettin' that Satan-speakin', coke-snortin', dope-smokin', drug injectin' heathen outta the White House, but you ain't a-gonna git it unless Ah speak to the reverend real personal lahk. That's raht. It's Sinus . . . Billy Bob Sinus. All raht. All raht. Ah'll do that."

Grinning and giggling like a school boy, he put his hand over the mouthpiece and turned to Carlos.

"It's working! I'm on hold while they go get him!"

Carlos wondered if his young financial whiz had been sampling the product.

Gold snatched his hand away and spoke into the receiver. "Yes? Turn down mah TV? Okay." He covered it again and spoke to Carlos. "They must be on delay. I'll go into the next room. You watch the TV."

As Gold left, Carlos noticed that he hit the record button on the VCR.

A moment later, on the screen, the choir suddenly broke off in mid-chorus as the camera cut to Reverend Whitcomb. The rage of a moment ago seemed forgotten as he beamed from the screen.

"Praise the Lord! We have a righteous soul on the line willing to give it all for the cause." He lifted a receiver to his ear. "Hello. To whom am I speaking?"

Carlos barely recognized Gold's voice coming over the line.

"Reverend Whitcomb, is that really you? Praise the Lord! What a thrill this is! This is Billy Bob Sinus from Washington, D.C., and Ah watch your show all the tahm. Truly you are the voice of the Lord!"

"Thank you, Billy Bob."

"And Ah want to help you in your faht agin that Satan in the Waht House."

"That's very good of you, Billy. What did you have in mind?"

"Ah want to contribute ten thousand dollars."

The audience erupted into frenzied cheering as Whitcomb raised his arms and gazed heavenward.

"Praise the *Lord!*"

"Faht him, Reverend Whitcomb," Gold could be heard saying over the cheering. *"Faht him till he's cast back into the fahrs of hell whence he came from!"*

"I will, Billy Bob!" the reverend said. "And with the generous help of righteous people like you, we *will* win!"

"Stomp him, Reverend Whitcomb. Stomp that Satan president into the earth and sow the land with salt so that he'll never rahse again!"

"Thank you, Billy Bob. That will—"

"Chew him up, Reverend. Chew up that Anti-Chrahst and spit him out and then—"

The camera cut back to the choir, which picked up right where it had left off as Gold stumbled back into the room. He collapsed on the sofa, kicking his feet, laughing so hard he could barely breathe.

Carlos allowed himself a laugh as well, a brief respite from the tension that so relentlessly knotted the muscles of his back. So much riding on this . . . so much. . . .

When Gold finally stopped laughing, he sat up and wiped his eyes.

"Oh, man! I can't remember the last time I had so much fun!"

"The stakes are rather high for 'fun,' no? Will you still be laughing if your President succeeds?"

"Not a snowball's chance in hell of that."

"I hope so," Carlos said.

But I cannot sit back and rely on telethons, he thought.

22　John drove around for an extra half hour before heading home. His surroundings were a blur. He drove on autopilot, unable to think of anything but Katie and was she alive and how were they treating her. If asked later where he'd gone, he doubted he'd be able to say.

Finally he forced himself to think, to focus. He had to pull himself together and come up with cover stories for his mother as to why he'd left his office early and why she wouldn't be picking up Katie from the bus stop this afternoon.

They had to be damn good. One look at him and his mother would know something was wrong.

By the time he pulled into the driveway, he had an explanation for why he was home. But as for Katie's whereabouts . . .

If only he could *think!*

Nana hit him with questions as soon as he walked in. She stood in the door to her bedroom dressed in her yoga outfit—he would never get used to the sight of his mother in a black leotard and white tights.

"John? You're home? Is something wrong?"

He rubbed his stomach. "A little gastroenteritis. It's a bug that's been going through the whole department. Hit me just after I got in."

"You look terrible," she said, her dark eyes searching his face.

"Believe me, I feel worse than I look."

"Can I get you anything? Some soup?"

"Thanks, but I couldn't eat a thing." That at least was true. "I think I'll just sip some 7UP and lie down."

"You go upstairs. I'll bring you some."

"That's okay. I'll bring it up with me."

He went to the kitchen and poured himself half a glass from the two-liter bottle in the refrigerator. His mother hovered over him every step of the way.

"I'll be fine, Ma. These things only last about twenty-four hours; then they're gone like they never were."

He left her standing at the bottom of the stairs, staring up after him, anxiously rubbing her hands together.

"I know some yoga positions that might help," she said.

"That's okay, Mom."

What was he going to tell her about Katie? She was no dummy. Having her around to help with Katie every day had been such a blessing. Now he wished she were back in Atlanta.

A thought occurred to him He turned at the top of the stairs.

"I think I'll lie down on the couch in the study," he told her. "There's this Senate hearing I want to follow and I can catch it on C-SPAN."

"I hope you'll be all right," she said, still rubbing her hands together.

"I'll be fine, Ma."

John closed the door to the study and went directly to his computer. His old Dell 486 was no longer up to the minute in speed and power but was still more than adequate for his needs at home. Soon after assuming his post at HHS, he'd arranged for a remote link to the department's network so he could access his files from home. He hadn't used it much, but now it would be a godsend.

As soon his machine was up and running, he logged into HHS, plugged in his ID number, and waited for the e-mail icon to appear.

No e-mail.

Just as well. He'd thought of a number of things he hadn't included in his first message.

For cover, he turned on the TV and switched it to C-SPAN; then he began typing.

What he needed most was proof that Katie was alive. Devastating enough that she was gone, but the fear that she might be dead . . . that was crippling him.

He had to *know*.

And the only way was to speak to her. How hard could that be to arrange? Get her to a phone, have her speak a few words, and that was that. He'd know she was alive and then he could concentrate on getting her back.

He decided on a tough, businesslike tone.

> *Snake—*
>
> *Addendum to previous e-mail: I must have proof that Katie's alive. You say you want a "service" from me, fine. But in return for that service I want my daughter back—alive and well. For all I know right now, she could be dead and buried somewhere.*

He had to lean back and take a deep, shuddering breath. Please, God, don't let that be true.

I will perform =no= service of any sort unless I have conclusive
proof that my daughter is alive. If you cannot supply that proof I
will have to assume that you've murdered Katie. I will go immedi-
ately to the FBI.

He wanted to add that he would drop everything else in his life and
personally pursue whoever was behind this to the ends of time and
space, but that would be too provocative.

It was a fact, though.

He had to soften his tone now, and try again to humanize Katie to
this monster.

But if Katie is alive and well as you say, please treat her gently.
She's a fussy eater but likes Lucky Charms cereal and Doritos and
McDonald's cheeseburgers. You can imagine what an awful ex-
perience this is for her. I know she's terrified. Please don't be
angry if she cries a lot. She didn't ask to be kidnapped. Be gentle.
=Please= be gentle.

That was it. That was all he could write without breaking down
again. He forwarded the e-mail to Snake's return address.

If only he could call the FBI. He wondered if they could trace the e-
mail back to Snake's hole in the ground.

But he didn't dare. If Snake had access to his phone line, what else did
he know? He might have somebody watching him. He couldn't risk it . . .
not with Katie's life at stake.

He stood at his window and stared out at his quiet neighborhood,
at people going out for lunch, coming back from shopping, walking
their dogs, playing with their toddlers, going about their normal,
everyday lives while his had been turned upside down and ripped inside
out.

Don't they know? Can't they sense it? Katie is gone!

She's all right, he told himself over and over in a prayerful litany. She
has to be all right.

Behind him, as C-SPAN broadcast the current doings in Congress,
John stayed at the window, trying to numb his feelings, trying to think,
trying to keep from screaming.

23 "You hear that?" Poppy said.

She sat across the kitchen table from Paulie, the remains of a turkey sub between them. She was still furious at him, but also wishing he'd shave off his beard and dye his hair back to black, so he'd start looking like his old self again.

"Hear what?" Paulie said.

"Shhh!" She got up and turned off the TV. "Listen."

She heard it, softly, coming through the front room from the master bedroom. The sound she'd known would come, the sound she'd dreaded hearing.

Muffled crying.

"The kid's awake."

"Better go check on her," Paulie said.

"Why me? This was your idea."

"C'mon, Poppy," he said. "You're not gonna be like this the whole gig, are you?"

"I'm not taking care of no kid," she told him. "That wasn't part of the deal."

"Fine," he said. "We'll let her cry."

He took a bite of his sub and started flipping through the copy of *Blue Blood* he'd brought along.

If that was the way he wanted to be, she'd do the same. She picked up *The Star* and opened it. She tried to concentrate on the page-three continuation of the cover story on Sharon Stone but gave up after reading the same paragraph half a dozen times.

The muffled sobs filled her brain.

"Damn it!" she said. She stood and threw the paper across the table at Paulie. "And damn *you!*"

Paulie looked up at her and smiled but said nothing.

Poppy stomped out of the kitchen and went straight to the master bedroom. She retrieved the Roseanne mask from the couch and slipped it over her face.

But she hesitated at the door. A crying kid. What was she like going to do with a frightened, crying kid?

More than Paulie, that was for sure, but that wasn't saying much.

Oh, hell. Let's get this over with.

She pushed the door open and poked her head inside. The kid was lying on her back on the bed, both hands tied to the bed frame above her head. The blindfold and gag were in place, but her beret had fallen off and she'd kicked off the blanket.

What skinny little legs she had.

And she was crying.

This totally sucked, frightening a little kid like this.

She stepped inside and closed the door behind her.

The crying stopped as the kid stiffened, listening.

Better not scare her anymore than she already is. Better say something.

"Don't be afraid. . . ." Hell, she didn't even know her name. "It's okay. You're all right. No one's gonna hurt you."

Poppy moved closer until she was standing over her. Even in the dim light of the darkened room, Poppy could see tears glistening on the cheeks below the black sleep mask they used as a blindfold.

"Listen, if you promise not to yell, I'll like take that gag out of your mouth. Is that a deal?"

The kid nodded.

"Promise not to yell, now."

Another nod.

Poppy removed the gag.

"Where am I?" the kid said, her voice wavering through a sob. "Who are you? Why am I tied up? Where's my daddy?"

"You're going to be staying here awhile."

"I want my daddy. Why isn't he here?"

Might as well lay it out for her: "He doesn't know where you are."

She started crying again, the sobs becoming progressively louder. More tears flooded from under the blindfold.

"I want to go home!"

"Remember our deal about not yelling. I'll have to put that gag back in if you yell."

The kid bit her lower lip in an attempt to muffle her sobs. The sound was so pitiful, it damn near tore Poppy's heart out. She knelt beside the bed.

"Hey, look," she said softly. "Don't be afraid. I'm not going to hurt you. No one's going to hurt you. You're just going to be visiting with us for a few days."

"I wuh-want my daddy!"

Poppy had to get her off that subject. "What's your name, kid?"

"Kuh-katie."

"Kuh-katie, huh? I never heard a name like Kuh-katie before."

"No. *Kay*-tie."

"Oh. Katie. I've heard of that. That's a cute name. Look, Katie . . . are you hungry?"

She shook her head.

"Have to go to the bathroom?"

A nod. "Your voice sounds funny."

"That's because I'm wearing a mask."

"Why?"

"Because I don't want you to see my face."

"I can't see *anything*."

"I know. But just in case the blindfold slips. We're like very careful about that here."

The kid shrugged—either she didn't understand or didn't care. She'd better care. It was important.

"Okay. Here's how we're gonna work this. I'll untie your hands and take you to the bathroom. You go in there and like do your business; then knock when you want to come out. Got it?"

Another nod.

"Okay, then."

Poppy began untying the cords around her wrists. Bathroom detail was usually Paulie's job, mainly because up till now all their packages had been totally guys. She'd never like actually done this, but she knew the procedure. Paulie had a handcuff routine he used with the guys—in case they got any wise ideas. Poppy didn't think that would be necessary now.

"Here's how this works, Katie. Your blindfold comes off only in the bathroom. Once you're finished up in there, you put it back on and like knock on the door. I'll let you out then. You understand? *You never take the blindfold off unless we tell you to.*"

"Why not?"

Poppy was taken aback by the question. No one had ever asked that before. Of course, all the other packages knew the answer.

"Because I don't want you to see my face."

"I thought you were wearing a mask."

What is she? Poppy thought. A lawyer?

"I am. But I don't want you to see that, either."

"Why not?"

"Because . . . because I don't, that's why," Poppy said as she undid the last knot. "There. Now you can sit up."

She grabbed the kid's shoulders and pulled her up. Through the fabric of her blazer and her uniform, Poppy could feel her bony little body trembling.

And she remembered feeling just like that at times when some guy she'd been with suddenly turned mean and began beating on her. She remembered that trapped, terrified feeling, with nobody to turn to for help. Probably the worst feeling in the world . . . and probably just what this kid was feeling.

She had a sudden urge to wrap her arms around Katie, to hug her close and absorb those tremors. No way. Keep her totally at arm's length. No telling what a scared kid might try.

But a little reassurance couldn't hurt.

"Don't be scared, Katie. You'll be fine. Think of this as a little vacation with some like really weird relatives." Yeah, Poppy thought: an Appleton vacation. She shuddered. "And after it's over, you'll be going home."

"I wanna go home now."

"Not now. But soon, okay?"

An unhappy nod, then, "What's *your* name?"

Another question that caught her by surprise. No package she'd baby-sat before had asked that. But she had an answer.

"Jane," Poppy said. "Jane Doe. And I'm here with my husband John Doe." She and Paulie always called each other Jane and John when they were baby-sitting a package. "You can call me Jane, okay?"

A nod. "Okay."

"Good. Now, let's get you to that bathroom. Stand up and I'll be behind you with my hands on your shoulders. I'll steer you right to it. Remember: Go inside, do your business, and knock when you're ready to come out."

Poppy guided the kid to the john and closed her in.

"And remember," she said through the door. "Have that blindfold on when I let you out. Got it?"

On the far side of the door she heard the kid start to cry again.

"I want my daddy!"

"Don't worry, Katie. You'll get your daddy. You just have to be patient."

Shit, this was a rotten thing to do to a kid.

And how come she never asked for her mommy?

24 Snake situated himself in front of a Dataphone 2000 in the lobby of the Hyatt this time. He had the instructions for getting the package's medicine all typed out and ready to upload from his Thinkpad. But when he logged onto Eric Garter's IDT account he was startled to find e-mail waiting.

Only one person that could be from.

He didn't like this. The way it was supposed to run was Snake telling VanDuyne what the situation was and VanDuyne acknowledging it; then Snake telling VanDuyne what to do, and VanDuyne agreeing, and so forth: Snake, VanDuyne . . . Snake, VanDuyne—none of this ad lib bullshit with VanDuyne dropping him a line whenever he felt like it.

Who does this guy think he is? He speaks when he's spoken to and that's that.

Snake glanced around. Checking the new e-mail was going to increase his time of exposure here, and that meant more chances of something going wrong. But no one seemed to be paying any attention to him.

Quickly he downloaded the message. He angled his Thinkpad's screen away from the lobby and called up the file.

Sure enough, VanDuyne had sent another message, now forwarded by the remailer. And it was an ultimatum! A fucking *ultimatum!* Where did this guy get his balls?

Snake reined in his fury. Hell, the guy was just doing what anybody would do: making sure Snake really had the goods he said he was holding.

I've got the goods, pal. And try to imagine how little I care if she likes Lucky Charms or whatever. *I'm* in charge. Get used to that. And get used to something else real quick: There's no way in hell you're going to talk to her.

What's this guy thinking? I'm going to drag a blindfolded kid out to a safe pay phone for a little chat with her daddy? Right.

He popped his own message onto the screen and added a couple of lines to the end; then he uploaded it to e-mail and sent it off into the Internet.

He disconnected and hurried for the exit. He was getting a bad feeling about this gig. First the epilepsy foul-up, and now the snatch wasn't a day old and already this VanDuyne was becoming a royal pain in the ass.

Any more trouble and Snake would have to send the doc a persuader.

25

Finally!

John had been sneaking in and out of the study all day, avoiding Nana, checking his e-mail, riding a roller coaster from hell as he downloaded one message after another, only to find each one was routine HHS business.

Why wasn't Snake answering? He had to get Katie her Tegretol—before tonight.

But now his heart began pounding as he saw *anon.nonet.uk* in the heading . . . the anonymous remailer. All the moisture left his mouth and collected in his palms as he began reading.

Phone in a prescription for a couple weeks' supply of your kid's pills to the CVS on 17th and K downtown in the District and it will be picked up. This pickup is a good faith gesture on our part. Don't try to fuck us up. Any sign that the store is being watched, there will be no pickup and your kid will suffer. Anyone follows me or stops me, she dies in minutes. As said before, we've got nothing against you or the kid, but we're not playing games. Cooperate and you'll have her back good as new.

As for speaking to her, no can do. Too inconvenient. Don't push us on this, Doc. We're not big in the patience department. Trust us and this will all work out fine.

Snake

Suddenly weak, John sat and stared at the screen, reading it over and over. The phrases *your kid will suffer* and *she dies in minutes* kept popping out at him.

He felt his stomach heave. Fearing he was going to be sick, he lurched out of his chair and rushed across the hall to the bathroom. He hung over the toilet, gasping, but nothing came up.

Finally the nausea passed. As he was bending over the sink, splashing water on his face, John heard a high-pitched cry. He straightened and heard it again. A wail this time . . . from across the hall.

Oh, no. "Ma!"

He rushed back into his study and found her standing before his computer, her thin hands locked in a white-knuckled grip on the back of his chair as she stared at the monitor. She swiveled her head toward him, her expression stricken, her eyes wide, her skin ashen.

"Johnny . . ." Her voice cracked and fell away. "Johnny, tell me this is a cruel joke!"

His first impulse was to lie, but what good was that? When Katie didn't come home from school later . . .

He stepped to her side and put an arm around her, gently guiding her toward the couch.

"Here . . . sit down."

"Oh, dear Lord, it's true, then! Someone's kidnapped Katie! Why? Oh, Lord, why?"

"I don't know, Ma."

John explained all that had happened, and why he was afraid to call in the FBI. His mother seemed to get a grip on herself as the story unfolded. She'd never been one for hysterics. She asked all the questions he'd been asking himself over and over: Why Katie? And what "service" did they want from him?

"But they *are* arranging to get Katie her medicine," she said. "I am thinking this is a good sign, yes? It means she's alive and they want to keep her so."

Or they just want me to think she's alive, John thought, but he didn't say it. They could pick up the pills and simply dump them in the garbage.

"I want—I *need*—more than a sign," he said. "I've got to *know*, Ma."

She clutched his arm. "Don't make them angry, John. They may take it out on Katie."

Yeah, they might—if she's still alive.

He nodded. "I'll be careful. I'll be polite. I'll kiss their butts, but I've *got* to know."

"John . . . ," his mother said slowly. "You don't think this could be . . . Marnie's doing?"

He stared at her. "Marnie?"

"Well, she *is* crazy, you know."

"She's very crazy." John was intimately familiar with his ex-wife's history of bizarre behavior, but this was too wild even for her, and far beyond her scope. And besides, Marnie was confined to Georgia, in deep therapy. "But I guarantee you Marnie's got nothing to do with this."

"Then what are we going to do?"

"First, call in that prescription."

He called information, got the number of the CVS at K and 17th, and told them to have fifty Tegretol 100mg. chewables ready for Katie VanDuyne ASAP. Since they'd never heard of him, he had to supply his office address and phone number, plus his DEA number.

"Now I'm going to get back to Snake."

"Please be careful."

"I'm just going to tell him that the prescription is ready and waiting. But I'm also going to ask for the answer to a question only Katie can give. And I'll tell them that as long as I know Katie's alive, I'll do anything to keep her that way. I'll perform any 'service' they want."

"I am hoping you can do this."

"I'm hoping, too, Ma."

But then what do I do? Sit around and wait? Call the pharmacy every five minutes to see if the prescription's been picked up?

He realized he was starting to fall apart. He'd be a gibbering basket case soon if he didn't do *something*.

26 Paulie parked the panel truck in a lot on DeSales Street and walked over to the Mayflower Hotel. He stood in the entrance to the bar and searched the late-afternoon crowd for Mac.

Some crowd—only half full and mostly suits. They called this a bar?

Cushioned seats and a polished floor and hardly anybody smoking. This wasn't a bar—it was a goddamn cocktail party.

Mac had called saying he had an errand for Paulie. That got Paulie nervous. Usually they never left the package once they started baby-sitting. Maybe Mac was making an exception because it was a kid. Still, Mac had sounded a little weird. He'd wanted Paulie to ask the kid if she knew how to swallow pills, and who was her favorite character on TV.

Poppy had got the answers out of her, no problem. But what was going on?

Paulie saw someone waving from a corner and went over. He noticed the suits gawking his leathers. He stuck out here. Usually he didn't mind that, but considering the circumstances, he'd have preferred to be some-where else.

Mac sat with his back to the room. He was wearing a white shirt and a blue blazer with a Spiderman pin in the left lapel. He was drinking something clear on the rocks.

"How come we always meet in hotels?" Paulie whispered as he took a seat opposite him. "There's gotta be less public places."

"Where would you prefer?" Mac said, a sneer playing about his thin lips. "Some low-life dive that's being watched by the fuzz twenty-four hours a day, where we'd stick out among the regulars?"

"Well, no, but—"

"Look, Paulie. I meet you in places where an unfamiliar face is the rule rather than the exception. If that doesn't make sense to you, then you've got a real big problem."

"All right," Paulie said grudgingly. Mac was right as usual. He or-dered a Heineken when the waiter came by.

Mac said, "You get the answers I wanted?"

Paulie nodded. "Yeah. She says she swallows pills real good. Does it all the time. And she likes Maggie Simpson the best of all. So what's this errand you need?"

"The package needs medicine."

"Oh, fuck!" Bad enough a kid. Now a sick kid. That explained about swallowing pills.

"Relax. Just a pill she's got to take twice a day. No biggee."

"Easy for you to say. Where's this medicine?"

"In a drugstore a few blocks from here."

"And you want me to pick it up."

"You got it."

Paulie said nothing as the waiter delivered his beer. He was pissed—and worried—but tried to show just the pissed part.

"What do I get for sticking my ass out like this?"

"Nothing," Mac said. "It's part of the job."

"No it ain't."

"Look, Paulie," Mac said, eyes blazing as he leaned forward and lowered his voice even further, "I don't like this anymore than you do. I learned about this after the pickup, so it's news to me too. I'm not getting extra because the package is sick, and so neither are you."

Paulie didn't feel like backing down this time.

"And what if I don't pick up the pills?"

"Then she starts flopping around on the floor like a break dancer OD'd on ice, and pretty soon she dies, and you and Poppy'll have to find a way to dump the body. Plus you'll have a murder rap hanging over you. But not for long."

"Why not?"

The look in Mac's stone eyes told him the answer.

Paulie drummed his fingers on the table. "I don't like this, man."

"Just do it and get it over with. You've still got your beard. You put on those shades, dump the leather, get yourself a hooded sweatshirt—*bam*—you're in and out and it's a done deal. I'll have you covered."

"Oh, well, then," Paulie said, letting the acid flow, "I don't have a goddamn thing to worry about, do I?"

27 Seemed like an eon since John had slipped into the CVS. He'd examined every Easter card at least twice, checked out all the chocolate eggs and baskets, and read the ingredients on all the over-the-counter medications. He could have hung out at the magazine rack but that was too far toward the front. He needed to stay within earshot of the pharmacy counter.

All the reading was eye exercise and nothing more. None of the information penetrated. And if it had, he wouldn't have been able to make sense of it. He was too keyed up to concentrate on anything except the names people gave at the prescription counter.

This is insane, he kept telling himself. Why am I doing this? I'm endangering Katie's life just by being here.

Why *was* he here? He was never impulsive. His style was to take the long view. Get the facts, act if necessary, but otherwise stand ready and see how things played out—traits that made for a lousy surgeon but an excellent internist.

But what kind of father had that made him? Katie would have been spared so much if he'd acted sooner as he saw Marnie decompensating. But he'd loved Marnie. And he'd thought he could keep an eye on her.

Wrong. He'd never dreamed she'd do what she did.

Maybe that was why he was lurking about this pharmacy. Maybe he'd learned that watchful waiting didn't always cut it. Especially where Katie was involved.

No "maybe" that he wasn't cut out for this sort of thing. The waiting had reduced him to a trembling mass of raw nerves. He—

And then a devastating thought struck him.

Snake knows what I look like. He has to. He's been watching us, waiting for his chance to snatch Katie.

What if Snake had already spotted him and ducked back out, saying to hell with VanDuyne's brat.

He nearly dropped the Easter egg coloring kit he was holding as a dull roar grew in his ears.

Oh, Christ, what have I done?

He had to get out of here. Maybe it wasn't too late.

And then through the roar he heard the counter girl's voice.

"VanDuyne? I'll check."

John grabbed the shelf to steady himself. It was him! Snake was here! He was picking up the pills.

He fought the urge to peek over the display to get a look at him . . . but his need overwhelmed him. Just one look. He had to know what this bastard looked like.

He turned his head just enough to frame the prescription counter between a pair of Easter baskets atop the display. Two people stood there—an elderly, blue-haired woman, and a stocky guy in a hooded jogging suit. John doubted Snake was an old lady.

As he watched, the girl at the counter handed a white paper bag to the jogger. John noticed he was wearing gloves.

Snake . . . that was him. He could have been Elvis for all that was visible between the beard, the sunglasses, and the hood. But that was Snake. Had to be.

John felt his weakness of a moment ago fade as hammer blows of rage began to pound through him. The son of a bitch who'd kidnapped Katie was twenty feet away. If he could get his hands on him, even if only for a few minutes, he knew he could make him talk. Oh, yes, a couple of minutes with John and Mr. Snake would tell him everything . . . *everything. . . .*

A small part of him was appalled at the savagery surging through him, but mostly he reveled in the fantasy.

Which was all it was. Snake wouldn't be working alone. Couldn't be. He'd have at least one accomplice, maybe more. If John harmed so much as a hair on this guy's head, the consequences to Katie could be horrific.

So was this all he could do? Stand here and watch this monster waltz out the door onto K Street and vanish into the afternoon?

Christ, he ached for someone to turn to, someone who'd know what to do. He wanted to call Bob Decker and ask him—kidnapping wasn't Secret Service business, but Decker had to know a helluva lot more than John.

He watched the jogger take his change and head for the door. Before John could think it over, he found himself following him.

What am I doing? a voice screamed inside his head.

Good question.

No heroics, he told himself. No chase. No cat and mouse. Just want to see where he's going. I'll stay way back, out of sight. He'll never know I'm behind him. If he gets in a car and drives off, I want to see the color, make, and model, want to memorize the license plate. But that's it. I'm not going to hop into my own car and trail him.

But if he walks, I *will* follow him. This particular drugstore was his choice. Why? Because he's holding Katie nearby? If that's the case, I want to know. I've *got* to know.

He followed the jogger out to the sidewalk and watched him stroll toward 17th Street. The rage was still roiling within, the savage just under the skin struggling to break free, but John was keeping himself under control.

He gave the jogger thirty yards, then followed.

28

What the *hell?*

Snake stood across the street from the CVS and gaped at the guy who came out after Paulie.

He'd watched the drugstore for a while before Paulie arrived and saw no signs of surveillance. No signs of activity after Paulie went in. That would be the giveaway—if the place was wired for a trap, things would start happening when Paulie asked for the VanDuyne prescription.

But nothing. Paulie came out and took off on a prearranged route while Snake hung back and watched to see if anyone tailed him.

And goddamn, somebody did.

VanDuyne.

"Shit!" The word hissed through his clenched teeth. Was the guy stupid? What did he think he was *doing?*

And then Snake relaxed. If nothing else, VanDuyne's presence proved that he hadn't called in the Feds. No way they'd let him near that drugstore if they were involved.

So . . . he was out here on his own. What a fucking cowboy. What was he going to do, follow Paulie home and rescue his little darling?

Fat chance.

Snake knew Paulie's route would take him around Farragut Square, and then to the Farragut North Metro station. He hurried to a bus stop at the top of the square and hung there until Paulie came by. He saw Paulie's eyes flick his way but he gave no sign that he recognized Snake.

Fifteen seconds later, VanDuyne came by. His eyes were fixed straight ahead on Paulie's back like he was the only other person on the street. Snake got a good look at those eyes and didn't like what he saw.

He was going to have to do something about the doc. Now.

But what?

His mind racing furiously, he gave VanDuyne a few yards, then fell into step behind him. As planned, Paulie entered the Metro station. VanDuyne followed, and Snake brought up the rear. The rush hour hadn't hit yet, so it was still fairly empty. As VanDuyne hung back, hugging a wall, watching Paulie buy a ticket, Snake came up close behind him.

He had to make his move now. And he had to be careful. No telling what kind of shape VanDuyne might be in—physically or emotionally. A guy who showed up at that drugstore could be capable of anything. He might go off like a screaming bomb. And the last thing Snake wanted was a scene in a downtown Metro station.

He reached out toward VanDuyne. Careful . . . careful . . .

29

John almost cried out when he felt the fingers close on the back of his neck and the voice whisper from somewhere behind his left ear.

"Freeze, asshole. Don't even *think* about turning around. You see my face, you're dead. And so's your brat."

John reached out a wildly trembling hand and slapped it palm open against the nearby wall for support. To passersby they probably looked like a pair of friends, one sick, the other comforting him. If they only knew.

Oh, Christ, he'd done it now. He'd screwed up everything! Poor Katie! They were going to kill her and it was all his fault!

He tried to speak but his throat was locked. All he managed was a hoarse croak. He tried again.

"Please . . . listen—"

"*No!*" The hand squeezed the back of his neck, the whisper grew harsher. "*You* listen! You're one fucking idiot, you know that? You want your kid dead? Is that what you want?"

"No! Oh, please, no!"

"Then why were you following my man?" The pressure on the back of his neck increased. "*Why?*"

. . . *my man* . . .

This was Snake, not the guy in the jogging get up. *This* was the one he had to convince to take good care of Katie.

John squeezed his eyes shut and concentrated everything on his words. He had to get through to this . . . this animal.

"Because she means so much to me. She's all I have in this world that matters. She's my *child*. Can you understand that? She's my daughter and she's little and she's defenseless and I'm responsible for her. If anything happens to her, it's my fault. And if anything . . . really bad happens to her . . . I don't think I can go on living. Do you see? Does that make any sense to you?"

"Not a bit, Doc," said Snake.

The utter flatness of the voice sent a blast of cold despair through John. The emotions he'd expressed were incomprehensible to this man. He might as well have been speaking Swahili.

"And you know what else doesn't make sense to me?" Snake said. "You disobeying and spying on my man. You know what that means, don't you?"

Panic surged through John. He didn't know and didn't want to know.

"I haven't called anyone or told anyone!" He began babbling. "Not a soul! Just as you said! But I have to *know*, don't you understand? Coming down here was a crazy thing to do, but that's what not knowing if Katie's alive or dead is doing to me! It's making me *crazy!* You've got to believe that!"

A long pause followed. John held his breath, waiting. Finally Snake spoke.

"Well, we don't want you going crazy, now, do we. We wouldn't want that." The hand released John's neck. "You freeze there, Doc. You stay facing that wall and the only thing you look at is your watch. You wait here ten minutes before you so much as turn your head."

"But Katie—"

A sharp jab in his back cut him off.

"Not another fucking word, you hear?"

Miserable, John nodded. He felt so helpless. Christ, if only he had the guts to turn around and grab this guy and throttle Katie's whereabouts out of him. But that might spell the end of Katie . . . if she wasn't already—

He heard footsteps moving away from him, heading back toward the escalator. He pushed back his jacket sleeve and looked at his watch: 4:11. He'd have to stand here until 4:21 while Snake and his accomplice got away.

And then he heard a voice shout two words from over by the escalator: "Maggie Simpson!"

At first they didn't register. Was that Snake or someone else looking for—

Maggie Simpson! The little pacifier-sucking girl from Katie's favorite TV show. Katie loved her! That could only mean . . . the only way they could have found out . . .

She's alive! Katie's alive!

John clamped his hands over his eyes and wept with relief.

30

Snake listened to VanDuyne's sobs, watched his shoulders quake as he leaned against the wall and bawled, then he stepped onto the escalator and rode it to street level.

Snake hadn't wanted to tell him, had wanted to let him suffer for being such a jerk, but then he'd reconsidered. If not knowing about his kid was really making VanDuyne nuts, then it was good business to tell him. Otherwise, the guy was a loose cannon. Who knew what crazy thing he'd try next?

And this guy had a crazy streak a mile wide. Sure, he was back there crying like a baby now, but Snake had an uneasy feeling he'd be making a big mistake if he wrote off that guy as a wimp. He'd sensed something dangerous at the bus stop as VanDuyne had passed by on Paulie's tail. Something in his eyes. Feral. Like some sort of predator. Hard to match that up with the sob sister downstairs, but the guy's eyes hadn't been lying.

Snake slammed his fist against the escalator's rubber hand rail.

That's why you never snatch a kid. Adult to adult, it's one thing . . . a snatch is the cost of doing a certain kind of business, a price they pay for not being careful. The packages lick their wounds and slink away, poorer but wiser.

But involve a kid and you're on a whole other level. You tap into something primal. You wind up dealing from a different deck. Suddenly everybody's taking it personally. And that's when people became unpredictable . . . *dangerous.*

Snake didn't understand it but recognized it when he saw it. And he sure as hell had seen it in VanDuyne's eyes.

So he'd told him about Maggie Simpson. To calm him down. Make him more predictable. He starts thinking his kid is dead, pretty soon he decides he's got nothing to lose—a very *bad* situation all the way around.

Up on the sidewalk he checked his watch. He'd wasted too much time jerking around with VanDuyne. He'd left his car at the Mayflower, so he started jogging up Connecticut Avenue. He'd have to hustle if he was going to make the meeting with Salinas.

He thought about VanDuyne again. Before this was over, he was going to need a persuader.

31 As planned, Paulie stepped onto the Metro train and waited until the platform emptied; then he stepped off again. And watched.

No one else got off.

He watched the doors close and the train slide away into the dark gullet of the tunnel.

All *right!* Nobody following him.

He headed back up to street level. He'd been twitchy as a strung-out crackhead since he'd walked into that drugstore, half-expecting a gang of feds to jump him as soon as he asked for those pills.

He checked his pocket to make sure he had the drugstore bag. A lot of risk to get that little vial.

But things had worked out okay. Better than okay. He'd hit Snake up for some cash to cover the jogging suit and the prescription, and a little extra to keep the home fires burning.

He checked his beeper in the other pocket. The read-out said no calls. Which reconfirmed that he hadn't been followed—Snake was to have beeped him if he'd spotted anyone on his tail.

So everything was cool.

He felt the tension ooze out of him.

He passed a guy leaning against a wall, looking for all the world like he was crying. Maybe he was sick. Or drunk.

Which gave Paulie an idea. Why not pick up a little bubbly as a gift for Poppy? She was all strung out baby-sitting the kid. She liked champagne and a bottle might get her to lighten up a little.

Yeah. Great idea. Buy her a goddamn magnum. Buy her *two*.

32

It took Snake a while, but he finally found a parking spot off M Street within half a block of Il Giardinello—he needed his car close by. He opened the glove compartment and started the tape recorder, then snapped his fingers in front of his chest. The mike in his shirt button picked up the sound and the needle on the receiver jumped.

All right. All systems go—as long as he didn't get too far away.

Snake walked around Georgetown a little before approaching the restaurant—just to be sure no one was tailing him.

What's the big attraction in owning a restaurant? he wondered as he approached the kitchen door. Actors, comedians, jocks, TV geeks—they all seemed to want one. Why? Looked like a royal pain in the ass.

He checked his jacket buttons and his lapel pin, then knocked.

One of Salinas's guards, a beefy guy named Llosa with dark skin and thick, Indian features, let him in. Snake handed him his .45 but the guy patted him down anyway. Satisfied that Snake wasn't going to murder his boss, he led him to the back office.

"Miguel!" Salinas said, from his recliner. His beige silk suit was wrinkled where it bunched around his rolls of fat, and his gold-toothed smile was humorless. "You're late!"

Mr. Fatso Drug Lord didn't like to be kept waiting? Tough. Snake wasn't about to incite Salinas, but he wasn't going to kiss his ass either.

"Had to arrange to get some medicine for the kid," Snake said pointedly. "You know, the kid no one knew was sick? Took me longer than I'd anticipated."

"But it is all taken care of, no?"

"Yeah. All taken care of."

"Excellent!" Now his smile was genuine. "Allen, pour our friend a drink. Scotch, right?"

"Right. A little soda."

"Give him the good stuff."

Salinas's financial butt boy hopped to the task. "We've got some beautiful sixty-year-old Maccallan single malt here," Allen Gold said. "Cost Carlos thirteen big ones at auction."

Thirteen grand for a bottle of Scotch? Now *that* was conspicuous consumption. Snake glanced around. Just like the rest of this dive. Look at the furniture, all dark and heavy and intricately carved, with real Tiffany lamps and Persian rugs; the walls were worse, hung with heavy burgundy drapes and all shades of garish Colombian art. And in among the paintings, a signed photo of Tricky Dick.

Very weird.

Gold handed Snake his Scotch, neat. "I held off on the club soda," he said. "You don't want bubbles getting in the way of the taste of this stuff."

Snake bit back a sharp retort. No profit in being ungracious, but he wondered about a guy with an MBA acting as gofer.

"To the success of the project," Salinas said, raising a glass of red wine.

They all drank. Snake smacked his lips around the sixty-year-old Scotch. Pretty good, but not worth five hundred bucks a pop.

"Allen," Salinas said, wiping off his mustache, "give Miguel his next installment."

Gold bent and lifted a leather attaché case. He handed it to Snake.

"You want to count it?"

"Not now," Snake said. "I'll count it later." He smiled to make it clear he was joking.

Salinas chuckled and his gut shook like the proverbial bowl full of jelly. A round man, Salinas—a round face with a round mouth on a round body. His smile was all white and gold except for the space between his upper front teeth—a gap big enough to shoot watermelon pits through.

Always polite, soft-spoken, almost formal. Yet Snake knew that behind that jolly exterior hid a diamond-hard, laser-sharp mind. An obsessively security-conscious mind. He'd realized that the first time they'd met here. Snake had recorded the conversation—he admitted to his own security hang-up—with a standard transmitter mike, but when he'd checked the tape, all he heard was thirty minutes of hiss. Which meant Salinas had a bug jammer in his office. A good one—randomly varying frequency and amplitude.

But there were ways around that. . . .

Snake took another sip of Scotch and dropped into a chair.

"All right. I've got the kid. I've got her daddy dangling on a string. What's this service he's supposed to do?"

Salinas looked at Gold. "Allen, will you please excuse us?"

Gold looked hurt. "You don't think you can trust me with this?"

"I think you can be trusted with anything, Allen. But I do not think you *want* to be trusted with this. *Comprende?*"

Gold stared at him a moment, glanced at Snake, then shrugged. "Okay. If that's the way you want it." He started for the door.

"It is not a burden you wish, Allen," Salinas said, smiling solicitously.

"Fine. I'll be at the bar."

As the door closed, Salinas said, "He is upset. He thinks he should know everything about my business. And perhaps he is right. But in this matter, I am not so sure."

Snake was beginning to get an uneasy feeling about "this matter."

"I believe your question," Salinas said, "was what service do I expect Dr. John VanDuyne to perform?" He took another sip of his wine. After he swallowed, his smile was gone. His voice was coldly matter of fact. "I expect Dr. John VanDuyne to remove his old friend Thomas Winston from the White House."

Snake felt the Scotch glass begin to slip from his fingers.

"The P-President?" He'd never stuttered before in his life. "The President of the United States?"

Salinas nodded.

Snake had a strange, floating sensation. He closed his eyes and took a deep breath. All along he'd known that the stakes in this job would be high—nobody offered you that kind of money just to put the screws to a doctor-bureaucrat in HHS. He'd tried to figure the angle but couldn't come up with any reason why VanDuyne would be so valuable.

The stakes were high, all right. Too high.

He opened his eyes. "Winston's legalization thing . . . that's what this is all about, right?"

Salinas nodded again. "This coward wants to ruin our business. Fifty billion dollars a year—gone." He snapped his fingers. "Just like that! You can understand why we cannot allow such a thing."

"Yeah, sure," Snake said. Fifty billion a year justified just about anything. What had he got himself *into?* "But how's this VanDuyne going to solve your problem?"

Salinas smiled. "VanDuyne is President Winston's personal physician. We will instruct him to administer a dose of chloramphenicol to his old friend."

"Chloram—what?"

Salinas gestured to the pad on the table to Snake's right. "Write it down."

Snake spelled it out phonetically as Salinas repeated it. *Klor . . . am . . . PHEN . . . uh . . . call,* then got the proper spelling from Salinas.

"What's that? A poison?"

"No. That is the beauty of it. Chloramphenicol is an antibiotic. An old one that is rarely used anymore."

Snake stared at the word on the sheet of paper in his hand. "I don't get it."

"One of the reasons chloramphenicol is rarely used is its effect on the bone marrow of a small percentage of patients."

"What's that?" Snake said.

"Like the atomic bomb on Hiroshima: The bone marrow stops producing blood cells. The condition is called aplastic anemia. I have never heard of it, but then, what do I know about medicine? However, I have educated myself over the past few months . . . ever since a certain source informed me that Thomas Winston almost died from aplastic anemia at age three. The cause was chloramphenicol."

"So?"

"So, if he gets another dose, the same thing will happen: His bone marrow will go on strike. He will sicken. He may well die."

"*May* die? What if he doesn't?"

Salinas shrugged. "He does not need to die. I would prefer that he did, but at the very least he will be gravely ill, much too sick to attend the drug summit in The Hague. And if he survives, he will have a long recovery. Too long to continue in office. He will have to resign."

"Which puts Robert Baldwin in the White House. What if he decides to push legalization too?"

Salinas smiled and shook his head. "We know Vice President Baldwin. We have him . . . ." He made an elaborate gesture of slipping his hand into his jacket pocket.

"So why not just plug Winston?" Snake said. "Be a helluva lot easier and more efficient than this 'may die' crap. Then you *know* he's out of office."

"No-no," Salinas said, for the first time leaning forward. He explained why *la compañía* had discarded that idea.

Snake nodded, only half listening. Already he could see problems.

"Okay. Whacking him wouldn't work. But what happens when Van-Duyne gets his kid back and tells the world he was forced to give Winston the chlor-whatever-it's-called? Same result: Winston's a martyr and you're out of business."

Salinas smiled. "But he will not get his child back. At least not for long. Immediately after their joyous reunion, they will have a terrible accident."

Snake went cold. "That's not my thing."

"I know it is not. I will arrange for that."

"All right. But won't whoever's treating Winston put two and two together and figure he's been dosed with this stuff?"

"Not unless VanDuyne tells them. The chloramphenicol will be long out of his system, and his doctors will not know about his previous bout of aplastic anemia."

"Why not?"

"Because he himself removed it from his medical records years ago. Thomas Winston wanted a spotless medical history when he presented himself to the American public."

"Then how do you—?"

Salinas smiled. "My dear Miguel, should it surprise you that I have excellent sources?"

"No," he said slowly. "Not at all."

Snake was just beginning to grasp Salinas's reach. The President's announcement was only last night, yet he and Salinas had been planning this snatch for two months. Salinas had *known* all along and had been ready to pounce as soon as Winston publicly committed himself. And he even knew what Winston had wiped from his medical history years ago.

This guy had a dedicated T-3 line into the government—he was *connected.*

Salinas leaned back again. "So you see? Everything is arranged. It's a perfect plan."

The reassurances rolled off Snake like a used car salesman's promises, and the cold within him grew as he took stock.

Allen Gold, who knew all the intricacies of Salinas's empire, had been sent from the room. That told Snake that Salinas was playing this hand *very* close to his ample vest. Maybe only he and his bosses in Colombia knew the real target. The only other people who'd know would be Snake and VanDuyne himself.

And afterward, they planned to eliminate VanDuyne and his kid.

Which would leave only one loose end: "Miguel" MacLaglen and his two hirelings.

How do you measure the lifespan of three people who know enough to bring down the Cali cartel?

Nanoseconds sounded generous.

And who would be the first to go? The know-nothing hirelings, or the guy who had worked out all the details with Salinas?

Snake tossed off the rest of the Scotch. He needed some antifreeze against the ice forming in his veins.

He glanced down at his shirt-button mile. *I hope you're working today.*

First thing tomorrow, he'd be back with a little present for the big man—he hoped.

But right now he had to concentrate on his next steps. This gig was going to be a real balancing act. Everything would have to go down by the numbers. If he screwed up, his insurance wouldn't mean diddly.

He cleared his throat. "All right. What's the next step?"

"That should be obvious, I think. First thing tomorrow you contact the honorable doctor and tell him that if he wishes to see his precious child again, he must give his friend and patient a hefty dose of chloramphenicol."

"How's he supposed to do that?"

"We will leave that up to him. He is a devoted father who wants his child back: He will find a way."

"And what if—Let's just say he refuses. What then?"

"You will tell him that if President Winston shows up at the Hague conference next week—"

"What's so important about this conference?"

"As a symbol, it is of immense importance. It is there that he will place his legalization plan before the world community as U.S. official international policy. That must not happen. And so you will tell the doctor that if Winston arrives at the conference, you will kill his little girl . . . but not before you do some very nasty things to her. And as proof, you start returning his daughter one piece at a time. I believe you have used that method before."

Snake nodded. "It's very persuasive. I've never had to send more than one piece."

Antsy as VanDuyne was, he was so wrapped up in his kid he probably wouldn't need a persuader. Or maybe he'd need one just to keep him in line.

"Good. Then you know what to do. Contact me tomorrow after you have spoken to Dr. VanDuyne."

"I'll come by personally," Snake said. "It may not be something I want to discuss over the phone." But he intended to deliver more than just a report on VanDuyne.

"If you wish," Salinas said. "Llosa will show you out. Good night."

Snake guessed that meant the meeting was over. Fine. He'd had enough of Salinas for the evening.

On the way out he retrieved his pistol from Llosa and figured the beefy bodyguard would probably get the assignment to whack "Miguel" and his people.

Except Salinas would have to change that part of his plans.

Once out in the night air, the enormity of what he was involved in bodyslammed Snake full force. He staggered out of the alley and looked up and down M Street.

I'm going to put the President—the President of the United fucking States—out of business. Maybe even off him. I'm going to be changing the course of history. Me!

But not only did he have to keep a close eye on what was going on in front of him, he had to watch his back as well. Much as he loved adrenaline, this might be too much of a good thing.

But dammit, he *loved* this feeling.

And tomorrow it would get even better. Tomorrow he'd put it to the doc that he was going to have to choose between his daughter and his old friend . . . his kid and the leader of the free world. How cool was *that?*

Yeah, if he could come through it all in one piece, this gig might just ruin him for anything else. Where could he play again for stakes this high? This was it: the mother of all buzzes. He had to soak up every last drop.

33

"That poor child!"

John held his mother and let her sob against his shoulder. The reversal of roles—the parent crying on the child's shoulder—unsettled him. He'd never seen her like this, not even when his dad died.

"Don't worry, Ma. Katie's going to be fine. We know she's alive. That's the important thing. She's alive and we'll keep her that way. I'll find out what they want from me, and whatever it is, I'll do it. Then we'll get her back."

"Oh, that poor child," she said. "That poor, poor child."

She'd been repeating the phrase endlessly. She was beginning to sound like a stuck record and that worried John. He couldn't have her going off the deep end now, not when he needed to focus every fiber of his being on getting Katie back.

"She's tougher than we realize, Ma. We all are. We got through everything else, we can get through this. They picked up her Tegretol, so at least we know she's getting her medication."

He hoped that was true, prayed they hadn't picked up the pills simply for show.

Please, he thought, whoever you are, follow the directions on that bottle. She's got to have her Tegretol twice a day. If she doesn't get it—

"That poor, poor child!"

34

Paulie lay on his back and stared into the darkness of the second bedroom as Poppy dozed with her head on his shoulder. Had this been a great night or what?

He'd come back from the drugstore run with two pizzas and a couple of magnums of Cook's champagne. So it wasn't imported and it wasn't expensive—so what? He'd guzzled both ends of the price range and got just as looped either way.

The goodies had worked their magic. Poppy really lightened up when she saw that he'd brought her a sauteed broccoli and eggplant pizza. She was into vegetables these days and that was her favorite combo. He'd bought a pepperoni pie for himself.

She fed some pizza to the kid, who requested pepperoni—good choice, kid—then they went to work on their own pies and started killing those magnums.

All of which had the desired effect: Poppy damn near fucked his brains out—once on the living room floor, and then again here in the bed.

Did it get any better than this? What more did he need beyond food, drink, a roof over his head, and Poppy in his bed? And soon they'd have a humongous wad of cash that, if they were smart about it, could last them a long, long time.

As he yawned he remembered the pills for the kid. They were still in his coat pocket. He'd forgot to tell Poppy about them. Something about giving the kid one twice a day.

He closed his eyes and let himself drift into sleep. He'd tell her tomorrow . . . tell her all about the pills in the morning. . . .

THURSDAY

"The United states now has over one million one hundred thousand prisoners in its jails. We have a greater percentage of our population behind bars than any other civilized nation in the world. And a good half of them are there for drug-related offenses. Think about it: five hundred thousand people in jail for using drugs, each costing us an average of thirty thousand dollars a year to house them—fifteen billion dollars a year, every year, and rising. Some of them are in for life—life for growing marijuana. The average murderer only serves nine years. And we're setting more and more of those murderers free to make room for pot smokers. Half a million Americans, most of whom have never harmed anyone but themselves, locked up—for what? For wanting to get high."

John opened his eyes in the darkness. Had he been asleep? Heather Brent was on the TV in a replay of some of her remarks on *The Larry King Show* last night. He saw light seeping around the shades. He searched for the clock. The glowing red numbers said 7:02.

He sat up, massaging his eyes, his face. He must have fallen asleep watching the TV. The last time he'd looked, the clock had said 5:30. God knew, he needed sleep—physically and emotionally. Any respite from this incessant sick dread. He was exhausted, yet his mind wouldn't quit. He'd tried to numb it with the early-morning parade of infomercials.

He staggered out of bed and down the hall. He stopped at Katie's door for the dozenth time since he'd gone to bed, and looked in, praying he'd see her there. It had all been a bad dream, right?

Wrong. Katie's bed was empty.

He continued down the hall to the guest room and—again, for the dozenth time since he'd gone to bed—logged into the HHS network.

"Come on," he whispered as the software wended its way toward his electronic mailbox. "Come on . . . *be* there."

He stood and stared at the screen. Why bother to sit? He wouldn't be staying. Every other time he'd checked for e-mail he'd come up empty, and he expected nothing this time either. Too early. He didn't see kidnappers as early risers.

And then he heard the chime from the computer's speakers: He had mail.

Mail!

Slowly, shakily, John eased himself into the chair. He chose the READ NOW? option and waited as the message was downloaded to his screen. His heart picked up tempo as he recognized the anonymous remailer heading. He jumped down to the message.

Go to the phone booth at the northwest corner of Franklin Square.
Be there at 9:00 A.M. sharp.
Snake

That's it?

John hit PAGE DOWN a couple of times to see if there was more, but found nothing. He stared at the message. Where the hell was Franklin Square? He'd never heard of it.

He rifled through the bottom drawer of the desk and pulled out the map of Washington he'd bought when he first came to town. The index guided him to a small park with its northwest corner at K Street and 14th—just a few blocks from the pharmacy that had filled Katie's prescription yesterday.

Why couldn't Snake simply have said K and 14th? What was he doing? Playing games? Toying with him?

Yeah, probably. Maybe that was how he got his kicks.

But why a phone? Up to now Snake had done everything by e-mail. What was different about today? What did he have to relate by voice rather than print?

No doubt the "service" he was to perform. A queasy feeling rippled through John's gut. What in hell could they want from him?

He glanced at his watch. Plenty of time. A quick shower, force down a little food, and he'd head for downtown. He wanted to be at that phone booth well ahead of the call.

Before leaving the study he erased the message. No use letting Nana see it. The fewer details she knew, the better.

He felt his fatigue slipping away. The endless night of waiting was over. He was in motion again. But in what direction? He shrugged off the cold dread enclosing him in its grip. Whatever it was, he'd handle it. The important thing was the sense that he was one step closer to getting Katie back.

2

Paulie! PAULIEEEE!

As Paulie rolled out of bed, his left foot tangled in the sheets and he landed hard on the floor. Half stunned, he shook the cobwebs out of his head and looked around. He didn't know where he was. All he knew was that Poppy was screaming his name like someone had taken a cattle prod to her. But she wasn't here. She was somewhere else in the house.

What house? Oh, yeah—the Falls Church place.

Poppy screamed again and Paulie was on his feet, hurtling into the front room. Empty. He lunged into the guest room and found her standing over the package's bed, whimpering and crying.

She turned and threw herself against him. "She's having a fit, Paulie! What's *wrong?*"

Paulie stared at the kid. Her hands were still tied to the bed frame, just as they'd left her, but the rest of her was flopping around on the bed like a beached fish. Her breath was hissing in and out between her clenched teeth and her eyes were rolled back into her head, leaving only the whites showing. He'd never seen anything like this.

"Make her stop, Paulie!" Poppy was saying, her voice going from a whimper to a scream. "Please make her *stop!*"

And then it was like something out of *The Exorcist*—the kid gave out this high-pitched sound somewhere between a growl and a scream and arched her back until only her heels and the back of her head were touching the bed. She stayed that way for God knew how long, until Paulie was afraid she was either going to float off the bed or break in two.

And then suddenly she dropped flat and lay still.

"Oh, God!" Poppy whispered. "Oh, God, Paulie, is she dead?"

She sure as hell looked dead—pale as a ghost, not moving, not even breathing. He was almost afraid to get near her, but someone had to check her.

As he stepped forward he was pushed aside by Poppy who dropped down on her knees next to the bed. She had her hands up in the air, waving them around like some holy roller at a prayer meeting. She looked afraid to touch her.

Finally, she brought her hands down and touched the kid. She grabbed her shoulders and began shaking her.

"Katie! Katie! Wake up!" Then she pounded on the kid's chest. "Breathe, dammit!"

The kid shuddered, coughed, then took a breath.

"Thank God!" Poppy said. "Here. Help me untie her." As she leaned across the kid, she stopped and felt around. "Oh, Jesus. She's wet herself."

Paulie loosened the cord around one wrist while Poppy worked on the other. The skin was bruised and scratched from all that violent yanking. Poppy massaged the wrist she'd untied.

"What happened, Katie?" she said. "Are you okay?"

But the kid only stared blankly past Poppy. She looked looped.

Poppy looked up at him. "She's not gonna start again, is she, Paulie? Tell me she's not gonna start again."

Paulie watched Poppy, stunned. He'd never seen her like this. Usually she was so cool, except when she got mad. But now . . . man, she was a freaking basket case.

"Easy, Poppy," he said, speaking slowly, softly. "Just calm down. She's going to be all right."

"How do you know that?" she said, her voice rising. "What's wrong with this kid, Paulie? Did Mac tell you anything?"

Christ, the pills! He felt like a total asshole.

"Yeah," Paulie said. "As a matter of fact, that's why he called me out yesterday. To get her some pills. She's got epilepsy."

"*What?*" She rose to her feet, and faced him, her face as pale now as the kid's. And her eyes wide . . . and very strange. "She's got epilepsy and you didn't tell me?"

"Hey, I only found out about it yesterday afternoon. Snake didn't find out himself until yesterday. But it's okay. I got pills for her."

"Why didn't you tell me?" She was talking through her teeth now. "Why didn't you give her any?"

"Hey, well, you know how it was last night. I came home and we ate and drank, then we got it on and I forgot."

Poppy closed her eyes. She looked ready to explode. "Get them. Give them to me now!"

"Hey, listen—"

"*NOW!*"

Paulie hurried into the front room for his jacket. He knew he was in a bad position here. Not a leg to stand on. Not even a freaking toe. He'd fucked up royally. Bad enough Poppy was doing a number on him, but if Mac found out . . .

He got the bottle and handed it to her, then watched her face go from white to red as she read the label.

"It says one tablet twice a day, Paulie! She was supposed to have one last night, goddammit!"

Suddenly she was on him, flailing away at him with her fists, pounding on his chest like it was a conga drum.

"You bastard! You stupid goddamn son of a bitch! You lousy—!"

He grabbed her wrists and shook her. "Cool it, Poppy! You're acting like a nut! What the hell's wrong with you?"

She pulled free of him and turned back to the kid. "Because she could start in like that again. And again and again and again and never stop! And then she'll die! All because you're so goddamn stupid!"

"Hey, look. I didn't think—"

"We've got to get one of these into her," she said.

"All right, then. Let's do it."

She glanced at him and nodded. She looked sane again. At least for the moment.

Turned out the pills were chewable, but so what? The kid was out cold. She wasn't going to be chewing anything.

Poppy took the bottle into the kitchen and tried to crush a pill with the flat of a butter knife, but her hands were too shaky.

"Gimme," Paulie said after she messed up a third time.

He crushed the sucker on the first try and looked up at her, hoping for a little smile, or maybe a nod of approval. But her stare was still icy, with no sign of a thaw.

"Do another," she said.

"Bottle says she's only supposed to get one."

"I'm making up for the one she *didn't* get last night."

Shit. Bad enough being in the doghouse, but worse when you know you belong there. He crushed the second. Poppy half filled a shot glass with water and dissolved the powder.

But getting the mixture into the kid was another story. She wouldn't wake up.

Finally they got the kid situated with Poppy cradling her head in her lap. Paulie pried her jaw open while Poppy dribbled the mixture into her. The kid coughed and gagged but Poppy held her head until she'd swallowed.

Paulie breathed a sigh of relief. "All right! She's gonna be okay now. No harm done."

Poppy glared at him. "You don't know that."

"Sure. She's got the medicine—"

"Go away," Poppy said. "Just leave me with her."

Paulie wanted to tell her off, tell her she couldn't talk to him that way, but it was like he wasn't even there, like he'd vanished in a puff of smoke. Poppy had pulled the kid onto her lap and started rocking her back and forth, cooing in her ear like she was a little baby. She seemed to be in her own world with that kid.

He wandered into the front room. This was way too weird. He couldn't have Poppy going off the deep end in the middle of a job. They had to pull together on this—at least till it was over.

I don't get it, he thought, staring back into the guest room as Poppy began to hum to the kid. She always said she hated kids, and now she's acting like she's the kid's mother or something.

3 John arrived at the northwest corner of Franklin Square at quarter to nine. No one was using the phone, but who knew how long that would last. Any minute now, one of the local pushers might commandeer it for the day.

To forestall that, John picked up the handset—it smelled like vomit—and pretended to punch in a call. Then he stood there with the greasy receiver to his ear, pretending to be in animated conversation while keeping the switch hook depressed with his free hand.

Around him, workers were spewing from the Metro's MacPherson Square stop, and the homeless were beginning to shuffle from their hidey holes to begin the day's panhandling chores. The sun climbed through the hazy air, warming the park and enhancing the rancid smell from the handset. John's stomach turned. The aftertaste of his quick cup of coffee sat on his tongue like swamp scum.

God, how long could he stand here and pretend to be in earnest conversation with nobody? Seemed like he'd been here all morning.

And then the phone rang, startling his hand off the switch hook.

"Hello!" he said. "This is VanDuyne."

"Hey, that was quick."

John recognized the voice: the one from the Metro station yesterday.

"I've been waiting. I promised to cooperate. I got your e-mail. You said to be here at nine, so here I am."

"Tears all dried up?"

The mocking tone made John want to lunge through the receiver, but he set his jaw. Why give Snake the satisfaction. "Yes. What do you want to tell me?"

"Let's not be in too big a hurry here. I'm going to send you to another phone."

"Is this a game?"

A cold laugh. "Don't worry. I've seen those movies too. No, just taking precautions. I'm sending you to another park—Lafayette Square. Know where that is?"

That one John did know. "Across from the White House."

"That's it. Northeast corner across from the VA Building. A mere four blocks from where you stand. Be there in five minutes."

The line went dead.

John checked his watch: 9:02. Four blocks in five minutes. He could do that walking backward, but he broke into a jog anyway. No sense in taking chances.

He reached Lafayette Square and found the phone in two minutes, but his heart sank when he spotted someone using it. A heavy woman in beige polyester slacks with a JUST SAY NO!/WINSTON MUST GO! button on her white polyester turtleneck was yakking away, one of the horde of protesters still thronging the square and marching up and down before the White House.

He waited an agonizing minute and a half, watching the time tick toward 9:07. And still she talked.

"Excuse me, ma'am," he said, "but I'm expecting a very important call on that phone in a couple of seconds."

She glanced at him but said nothing.

"Please, ma'am. It's very important."

She covered the receiver and glared at him. "Yeah?" she said in a New York accent. "What's this? Your office? Find another phone. They're all over the place."

"You don't understand. I can't go to another phone. I'm receiving the call on *this* phone."

"Stop bothering me or I'll call a cop."

That was the last thing he needed—but he *had* to get her off the phone. As she waved him off and started to turn away, he had an idea.

"Look," he said, digging into his pocket. "I'll pay you for that phone."

Now he had her interest. "You kidding me?"

He pulled out some of the cash he'd grabbed on his way out the door, found two fives, and waved them in her face. He watched her eyes narrow. She wasn't thinking of holding him up for more, was she? He didn't have *time*, dammit.

"Ten bucks for the phone, lady. Now or never."

As she stared at the bills, John thought, Take them, lady, before I rip that phone out of your pudgy little fingers and drop-kick you onto the White House lawn.

"You got a deal," she said.

With those words, John reached past her and slammed his hand down on the switch hook.

"Hey!" she cried. "I didn't say good-bye!"

"Deal's a deal." He snatched the receiver from her hand and replaced it with the two fives. "Thank you very much." Then he elbowed her out of the way and took over the booth.

She waddled off, muttering about "men." John didn't care if she thought he was Attila the Hun—he had the phone.

Ten seconds later it rang.

"VanDuyne."

"So, you made it. All right. Let's get down to business. This is all very simple. We need you to perform a small service for us. You do that, you get your kid back."

"A service. Yes. But *what* service?"

"Again, very simple. Nothing the least bit criminal. All you have to do is give a dose of medication to one of your patients."

John leaned against the booth. "Patients? I'm not in practice. I think you've got the wrong man."

Could it be? Could this all be a horrible mistake?

"Really? How's your sense of direction, Doc?"

"What do you mean?"

"I want you to face south. Can you do that?"

John glanced around. "I'm already facing south."

"Good. What do you see?"

He saw the telephone. The booth was facing north, and he was facing the booth. He couldn't mean—

A chill of foreboding inched through him.

He stepped to his right and saw it. Beyond the square and the promenade, behind its wrought iron fence . . .

"The White House?" He had to force the words past his throat.

"You got it."

"But . . ." The words and thoughts ground to a halt in his brain, frozen in the freon blasting through his arteries.

"No buts about it, Doc. You're the President's personal physician and you're gonna give him a dose of antibiotic before the week is done."

John still could not speak. He could only stand and stare at the White House.

"You listening, Doc? If you don't—"

"Yes, I know!" he blurted. He knew the ultimatum. He didn't need to hear the details.

God, they're after Tom.

He felt as if he were drowning. He groped for something, anything to keep him afloat. And one of Snake's words popped to the surface.

"Antibiotic? Did you say antibiotic?"

"That's right. Chloramphenicol." He said it carefully. "You got that, Doc? Chloramphenicol."

"Yes," John said dully. "I got it."

"You've heard of it?"

"Of course." Chloramphenicol . . . an old-time antibiotic rarely used anymore except for typhoid fever and maybe an occasional meningitis. "But why . . . ?"

And then he remembered . . . maybe a dozen years ago, when Tom began setting his sights on the presidency, asking his old buddy John to comb his entire medical history for anything that might someday be used against him. While going through Tom's pediatric records he'd found "NO CHLORAMPHENICOL" written in big red letters across the top of each sheet. He'd searched back and learned that little Tommy Winston had almost died of aplastic anemia at age three. The culprit: chloramphenicol.

John had mentioned it in his summary but did not consider it of any consequence. Tom's campaign strategists thought otherwise. They said any sign of physical impairment—even *potential* impairment—could be damaging. John thought it was ridiculous, and so did Tom, but he was paying for their expertise so he took their advice: Those old pediatric records became "lost."

Or so they'd all thought. How on earth had Snake or whoever he was working for unearthed them?

God, who cared? What mattered was what would happen to Tom if he had another dose of chloramphenicol. His immune system was still carrying the antibodies that had caused all the trouble when he was three. They were like sleeping guard dogs now, penned up, quiet, forgotten. But they'd awaken and burst free the instant they sniffed a chloramphenicol molecule. Trouble was, these were mistrained antibodies. They attacked their master last time—blitzkrieging his bone marrow and shutting it down—and they'd do the same again if set free. Maybe worse this time.

Probably Tom would survive. Hematology and immunology had come a long way in the four decades and more since Tom's first reaction—new drugs, bone marrow grafts, so many more treatment options were available.

But people still died from aplastic anemia.

Tom could die.

He moved his mouth but no words formed. This was monstrous. They couldn't ask him to choose between Katie and Tom, couldn't expect him to—

"You still there, Doc?"

"No!" he said. The word exploded from him and he was aware of people nearby glancing his way. He lowered his voice. "I won't do it."

"Then you'll never see your kid again."

Snake's cold, matter-of-fact tone rocked John. He sagged against the phone booth.

"No. Wait. Please. He might die."

"That's the whole idea, Doc."

"Yes-yes. But on the other hand, he might *not* die." John's mind was suddenly in high gear, looking for an angle, a way out, anything so he wouldn't have to do this. "It didn't kill him the first time, so there's a good chance it won't kill him this time."

"Then you'll have to give him another dose. And another. And another. Until he's either dead or so sick he has to resign. One way or another, we want him out of office."

"You can't ask me to do this."

"I already have."

"I need some time."

"Sure." The word dripped with sarcasm. "Take all you want. Just make sure he's too sick to make the drug summit next week."

The Hague meeting . . . that was when legalization would become official U.S. policy.

"So that's what this is all about."

John looked around at the antilegalization protesters swarming around him. Were they involved? Were some of them watching him right now?

"Yeah, Doc. That's what it's all about. Your old pal President Winston shows up at The Hague, you can forget about ever seeing your kid again."

"Oh, God!"

"And don't think of trying anything cute, like having your buddy play sick. Believe me: We're very connected. We'll *know*. And that will end it for your little girl."

"Please. I'll pay you. I'll sell everything I own and give you every penny, just don't hurt Katie."

"This isn't *Let's Make a Deal*, Doc. You either dose your pal or you don't. What's it going to be?"

John stood there paralyzed, staring at the C&P insignia on the phone while his numbed mind tried to formulate an answer. He had to say yes. If he didn't Katie would die. But how was he going to deliver? How could he poison Tom?

As he was trying to frame a replay, a hand flashed in front of him and depressed the switch hook.

"*What?*" John jerked around and saw the polyester fat lady from before. He ripped her hand off the switch hook and began shouting into the receiver. "Hello? Hello are you there? Hello?"

All he heard was a dial tone. He slammed the handset down on the hook and turned to the woman. He fought the rage swelling inside him. He wanted to scream, he wanted to cry, he wanted to rip her head off.

"Do you know what you just did?"

"I want my phone back," she said, waving a bill in front of her and chattering like a machine gun. "Every other phone around here's taken, so I want mine back."

"You cut off my call!"

"So? You cut off mine. Fair's fair. Now here's five bucks back. I figure I should keep half the money because I let you use the phone but—"

John felt his lips pulling back from his clenched teeth. If half of him wasn't praying for Snake to call back, he'd be grabbing the handset and shoving it down her throat.

"Get out of here," he said in a low voice.

Her chatter cut off. She took a faltering step back. "Hey. What's eating *you?*"

He leaned toward her, still speaking through his teeth, enunciating with slow precision. "Get away from me or I will kill you."

He'd never threatened anyone with harm before, let alone death. But right now he meant it.

She must have sensed that. She backed up another step, then hurried away. "I'm calling a cop!"

John turned back to the phone. "Please ring," he whispered. "Please call back." He slammed his fist against the side of the booth. *"Please!"*

But the phone remained silent. John waited in the morning sun, amid the milling people, clinging to the booth, a hand on each side, guarding it as if it were his personal property.

After five minutes he began losing hope. When fifteen minutes had passed, he knew Snake wasn't going to call back, but still he hung on, waiting. He couldn't leave.

He looked up and saw the polyester lady walking his way with a cop in tow. He couldn't get involved with the police right now. What if Snake had someone watching him? If Snake got a report that he was seen talking to a cop, no telling what he might do.

John released his grip on the booth, turned, and forced himself to walk away, to get lost in the crowd.

He told himself it was useless to stay by the phone. Snake wasn't calling back. John's best bet was to get to his computer and send Snake an e-mail explaining what had happened. The sooner, the better.

Still, in his soul, he felt as if he'd just abandoned his daughter in Lafayette Square.

4 *He hung up!*
Snake, sitting in traffic on Pennsylvania Avenue, still couldn't believe it. John VanDuyne, M.D., supposedly this loving, devoted father, and he hangs up on the guy who's holding his daughter. What the hell was he up to?

Snake had to admit he'd been rattled for a moment after the line went dead. He'd told him, *Either you dose your pal or you don't. What's it going to be?* And VanDuyne went and hung up on him.

After being so high last night, barely able to sleep, that had brought him down. He'd known this guy was going to be a problem.

Maybe it had been some sort of a reflex. After all, he'd verbally pole-axed VanDuyne with what he had to do to get his kid back.

He had to smile. Hell of a choice, wasn't it. Here was the stuff myths were made of: Choose between your old buddy, the leader of the free world, and your kid.

Something almost cosmic about that. And Snake was calling the cosmic tune.

Except VanDuyne wasn't dancing the right steps. Another example of the guy's instability. He was a wild card. But Snake knew just the thing to get him in line. He'd have Paulie take care of that. . . .

Right after he met with Salinas.

Snake patted the audio cassette in his jacket pocket and swallowed. He'd be walking a very thin line in the next hour or so. This meeting had to be handled just right.

5   "And so, Miguel, how did the good doctor take the news?"

Carlos Salinas sat behind his desk, leaning back in his enormous leather chair. His suit was charcoal gray this morning. A small, amused smile curved under his mustache.

"Not well," Snake said. He felt like pacing but forced himself to remain seated. He and Salinas had the office to themselves. No sign of Gold this trip. "We shook him up pretty good."

"And you did not have to explain to him about his friend's previous reaction?"

"Nope. He seemed to know all about it."

"*Bueno*. So, how do things stand at this moment? He has agreed to our ultimatum?"

Snake debated telling Salinas the whole truth—about VanDuyne hanging up on him—but held back. He didn't want Salinas to have the slightest doubt that he was in complete control.

"He'll do it, but he's a bit shell-shocked right now. I've decided to send him a little persuader to get him focused. By tomorrow morning he'll be falling all over himself to get some of that chloramphenicol into Winston."

"Excellent!" Salinas slapped his weighty thighs. He was grinning now. "Miguel, I am so very glad I put you in charge of this matter."

You may not be so very glad in a minute, Snake thought. He cleared his throat. Here goes.

"Speaking of 'this matter,'" he said, "it's much bigger than I'd ever imagined."

Salinas's eyes narrowed. "I hope you are not going to ask for more money. We have a deal—"

Snake raised his hands, palms out. "Absolutely not. A deal is a deal. No. What I'm saying is, this matter is *so* big that you might not want me around after it's over and done with."

"Yes," Salinas said slowly, nodding and smoothing his mustache. "I can see how you might fear such a thing. But it is not my way."

"Trouble is, I don't know your ways. We haven't known each other that long."

"Miguel, if I killed everyone who did a job for me, I would have been out of business a long time ago."

"Right, but this isn't some routine pick-up-and-deliver gig. This is major league. This is the biggest thing you'll ever do in your life, or I'll ever do in mine. I just don't want it to be the *last* thing I do in mine."

"It is not you I am concerned about. Paul DiCastro and Poppy Mulliner, however . . ."

It didn't surprise him that Salinas knew their names—he seemed to know everything—but it bothered him.

"I can see how they'd be considered a liability. I just don't want to be lumped in with them."

Salinas was staring at him—like a cobra eyeing a mongoose. "I have a feeling that all this is leading somewhere."

Snake reached into his pocket and pulled out the cassette. He leaned forward and placed it on Salinas's desk.

"What is this?"

"Recordings of some of our conversations."

Salinas's smile was tight and grim. "That is impossible."

"Because you have a bug jammer?" Snake said. "It worked on the tape I made of our first meeting—I got nothing but hiss. So I went out and found a filter that eliminated the interference." He pointed to the tape. "I believe you'll find your voice quite recognizable. Especially during last night's conversation, when you explained the ultimate purpose of this endeavor."

"*Mierda!*" Salinas turned a deep red as he slammed his fist on the desk and let loose with a string of curses in Spanish.

He won't kill me, Snake told himself. I've got the kid, I'm hooked into VanDuyne. He needs me. He *won't* kill me.

Across the desk, Salinas closed his eyes and calmed himself. Then he opened them and glared at Snake.

"I am insulted. We made a deal."

"And I made a deal with my people that I'm probably not going to be able to hold to. Things change, right?"

"And you intend to blackmail me?"

"Absolutely not. I'm on that tape too, you know. *I'm* the guy who did the snatch and told VanDuyne what the ransom was going to be. The last thing in the world I want is for anyone to hear that tape. What I *do* want is to make sure that you have an ongoing interest in my good health. I've got a dozen copies and I've—"

"Twelve tapes! *Chingate!*"

Actually only four more: another in his jacket, one hidden in his house, one in his safe-deposit box, and one with a lawyer. If Salinas found those, Snake wanted him to go crazy looking for the rest.

"They're all safe. But if something happens to me, they go to the FBI, the DEA, the Secret Service, and so on. I know you folks own a lot of people, but when this shit hits the fan, *nobody's* going to want to be downwind."

Salinas continued to glare, saying nothing. Snake was sure he knew how difficult it would be for the feds to get a conviction on the basis of an audio tape, but at the very least they'd shut down his money-laundering business and make his life a nightmare. So Snake tried to mollify him. Even though he was protected now, this was not a man he wanted pissed at him.

"Hey, look. I can understand how you feel. You took all these elaborate, state-of-the-art precautions against anyone eavesdropping or bugging you, and you wind up on tape anyway. But this could save you in the future. Technology's always changing. You've got to stay on the cutting edge if you don't want someone to get the drop on you."

Salinas said nothing, but he seemed to be cooling.

"And look at it this way: Knowing I've got this kind of life insurance will let me do a better job. I mean, I'm already juggling the kid and VanDuyne, and soon I'll be dodging the entire federal government. I don't want to have to keep looking over my shoulder wondering what you're planning for me too. That could be very distracting."

Salinas continued to stare. But no question, the rage was fading from his eyes.

Snake leaned forward and put on a smile. "And tell me the truth: If positions were reversed, wouldn't you do the same thing?"

A little smile from Salinas now, and then a nod. Snake felt his muscles relax. *You silver-tongued devil, you.*

"I suppose you are right," Salinas said with a sigh. "I cannot hold it against a man that he protects himself. And you are right. I will learn from this." And then he frowned. "But I am hoping that you do not wish to extend the coverage of life insurance to your two helpers."

Snake thought about that. Here was a chance to save Paulie and Poppy. He'd be pushing it, but he had Salinas over the proverbial barrel.

And then he thought about the aftermath. Paulie and Poppy rich and getting stoked every day. One of them sees the story about VanDuyne and his kid getting wasted, how he was our dead or deathly ill President's personal physician . . . wouldn't take a rocket scientist to put it all together.

Could you trust a couple of loadies with something like that? Yeah, right. They'd be racing to see who could babble about it first.

No, Salinas's approach made the most sense.

Snake held Salinas's gaze and shook his head. "No. This is just a personal policy. No group coverage."

6 If Snake had felt high after leaving Il Giardinello last night, he was stratospheric now. He'd done it! He'd stared down the goddamn Colombian cartel.

They blinked!

Or at least Salinas did. But that was enough. He'd sent the message and it had been received loud and clear: You don't fuck with Snake.

He began punching the air—left-right-left—as he made his way to his car. He was Ali, he was Tyson. Float like a butterfly, sting like a cruise missile. When he reached the car he knew he was too wired to sit behind the wheel.

A car? A *car?* Even a fucking Concorde would be too slow right now!

He grabbed his laptop from the trunk and set off walking through Georgetown like he owned it. Up Wisconsin, then left toward G.U. along the cobblestone streets with their obsolete trolley tracks, past the brick-fronted town houses, and up to the campus.

The walk burned off enough adrenaline to allow him to seat himself in the library and plug into one of the computer jacks. He logged onto his account and checked his e-mail.

He grinned when he saw the letter from VanDuyne, a rush of pleading, whining, moaning how it was all a mistake and how they got cut off by accident and to contact him again right away and please-please-please don't take it out on his dear little Katie.

Yeah, well, maybe it was an accident and maybe not. Maybe this was a game VanDuyne was playing. But Snake was boss. Even the Colombians knew that now. And Snake didn't allow games, or even accidents.

He began typing a reply that would tell VanDuyne just that, then stopped.

Nah. No reply. Let the pussy stew. Let him go crazy waiting for a reply.

He'd get his reply.

Tomorrow morning.

In his mailbox—his *real* mailbox.

7 Poppy watched through the eyeholes of her mask as Katie drained the glass of milk.

"Want some more?"

Katie shook her head. Poppy glanced at her watch. Three hours since the fit. The kid had woke up about an hour ago but still didn't seem to be all there. Her color was better but her fine dark hair was all like tangled.

At least she hadn't had another fit, thank God. And she wouldn't, either, as long as Poppy had something to say about it.

"Aren't you hungry?"

Another shake of the head, then a sob. "I just want to go home."

Poppy slipped her arms around Katie and hugged her close. "I know you do, honeybunch. And you'll be going home real soon, I promise you."

"But when?"

"I don't know exactly, but it won't be too long."

"That's what my Daddy always says."

"When's that?"

"When we're in the car and I ask him how long till we get there, and he always says the same thing: 'It won't be too long now.' Even if we just started out, he says, 'It won't be too long now.'"

Poppy laughed. "Yeah, my Daddy used to say something like that, only he'd go, 'Not much further now.' I guess all daddies are alike."

Except mine's dead.

She thought about Dad, how she'd heard about his heart attack six months after he was buried. And she still remembered Uncle Luke's voice on the phone: "That wasn't no heart attack. Your father died of a *broken* heart. And we both know who broke it, don't we."

Yeah, she knew. Totally.

Katie pulled away and stared at her. "Why are you wearing a Minnie Mouse mask?"

"I told you how I can't let you see my face, but I thought you'd like this one better than the Roseanne mask. You do, don't you?"

"Yes."

"And how about your new clothes?"

Katie looked down at her plaid shirt and Oshkosh overalls. "They're okay, I guess."

She's right, Poppy thought. They're okay. *Barely* okay. She'd sent Paulie out for new masks and dry clothes and underwear. She'd given him the size and that was about it. He'd done good with the masks—Minnie for her and Mickey for him—but the clothes . . .

"At least they're dry."

She reddened and looked away. "I'm sorry."

Poppy grabbed her and hugged her again. "Don't you be sorry! Don't you dare be sorry! That wasn't your fault. It was ours. We forgot to give you your medicine. That won't happen again."

What's up with me? she wondered as she pressed that skinny little body close against her. She hated kids. Never wanted any, but now all she wanted to do was like hold and protect this one. It's like I'm a different person.

She remembered waking up with a headache, and hearing this rattling and thumping coming from somewhere in the house. She'd tried to wake Paulie but he was like dead to the world. So she got up and went to see . . .

. . . and went to pieces when she found the kid in the middle of a fit.

Not the first time she'd seen a fit. God, no. She'd seen far more than her fair share and had hoped and prayed she'd never see one again.

"I promise you, Glory," she whispered into her hair. "It'll never happen again."

Katie said, "My name's not Glory."

Poppy stiffened. Glory? Had she really called her *Glory?*

"You're right," she said quickly. "Of course it isn't. What was I thinking?"

Was that what this was all about? Glory? Was Katie the kid Glory might have been?

If she'd lived?

She repressed a shudder. That was scary. And yet . . .

The phone rang in the other room. She left Katie on the bed and opened the door enough to poke her head through just as Paulie picked it up and said, "Yeah?"

Had to be Mac.

"Yeah, she's fine. . . . Nope. No problems. Got the pill into her just like the directions said. . . ."

Poppy caught his eye and glared at him through the mask. He shrugged, like, *What else am I supposed to say?*

Better say nothing, Paulie. Mac finds out you almost messed up his little package and he'll be like all over you.

She was still pissed at Paulie. Really, how could one man be so *stupid?* He had the pills in his goddamn pocket. All he had to do was—

She cut off the train. She got crazy every time she thought about it. Better to leave it alone.

But she was still royally pissed.

"What?" Paulie was saying. "Aw, come *on!* You gotta be shitting me, man!"

Uh-oh. What else had gone wrong?

She saw Paulie glance at her but his gaze skittered away. He turned his back and lowered his voice, but she could see his shoulder muscles bunching up and knew he was arguing. He stole a second gun-shy look her way, then took the phone into the bedroom.

Obviously, Paulie and Mac weren't seeing eye to eye about something. She wondered what it was. No matter. She'd find out soon enough. She closed the door and returned to Katie.

Took a long time, maybe fifteen minutes, before Paulie knocked on the door.

"You wanna come out here a minute?"

She slipped out the door, closed it behind her, and immediately pulled off the mask. Cool air felt great on her face. Hot and humid inside that plastic. She blotted the moisture off her face with her sleeve, then looked at Paulie.

Jesus, he looked totally spooked. His eyes were darting all around the room, anywhere but at her.

"What's wrong?" she said.

"That was Mac."

"Who else would it be. What'd he want?"

"He says the package's father ain't cooperating."

"Ain't cooperating? You mean he don't want her back?"

"I don't know exactly. Mac says he's giving him a hard time."

Poppy looked at the bedroom door. Jesus! Somebody steals your little girl and you haggle over the price? Like what kind of father does that?

"The son of a bitch."

"Yeah. So . . ." Paulie was staring real hard at the floor. "So Mac wants us to send the guy a persuader."

Poppy froze, staring at Paulie, who was still looking at the floor. She'd been gut punched once, and that was how she felt right now. She thought she was going to puke.

But she controlled it. And she controlled the urge to launch herself at Paulie and start screaming like a banshee. She controlled everything.

And slowly she turned to ice.

Then steel.

No one was going to hurt that little girl.

"Uh-uh," she said softly. She kept her voice low, even. "Not a chance."

Paulie's head jerked up like he'd been slapped. He stared at her like she was a stranger. Obviously he'd expected a different reaction.

"Hey, Poppy, we gotta do it."

"Really? Says who?"

"Mac. I told you—"

"Mac says, 'Jump,' and you say, 'How high?' That how it goes?"

"You think I want to do this? You think I want to hurt a kid? Christ, gimme a break! But this is Mac's gig."

"I don't care if this is *God's* gig—no one's touching that kid."

She started to turn away but he grabbed her arm.

"Look. Mac wanted us to send the guy one of her fingers. I talked him down to a toe. A *toe*, Poppy! A freaking little toe! She'll never miss it!"

Poppy wrenched her arm free. "Not a *fingernail*, Paulie! Not a *hair!* You got that?"

"It's got to be done, Poppy!"

She went to the guest room door, turned, and faced him.

"Over my dead body."

She could see that Paulie didn't really believe her. How was she going to convince him? How could she stop him?

He took a step toward her. "With or without you, it's gotta be done."

"Through me first, Paulie. You're gonna have to beat me to a total pulp before you get to her. I know you *can* do it. But *will* you do it? I hope not. I don't think it's in you. But if you do, you better kill me. That's all I can say, Paulie—you better kill me. 'Cause if you don't, and you hurt that little girl, I'll kill *you*. Some night when you're sleeping, I'll put a knife through your heart. That's my promise: You hurt that kid and some morning real soon you're gonna wake up dead."

He stood and stared at her, his hands opening and closing at his sides.

"Christ! You're really serious!"

She nodded. Yeah, she was. And that amazed her. She barely knew this little Katie and yet she was ready to die for her. What the hell was going on?

"You're forgetting Mac, aren't you?" he said. "We don't do what he wants, we could *all* wake up dead. And then he can take any damn part of her he feels like."

That shook her. Paulie was right. Mac wanted what he wanted. He was paying you, he expected you to take orders. Who knew what he'd do if they told him to shove his persuader.

Paulie ran both hands through his hair. "This is just great! I do what Mac wants, you'll kill me. I do what you want, Mac kills me. How the fuck did I get into this?"

Poppy felt sorry for him. She was putting him in a real jam. She didn't want to see Katie *or* Paulie hurt.

"There's got to be like some way out of this," she said.

"Yeah?" Paulie said. "Like how? Mac wants a piece of her to send to her father. He's not going to settle for anything less."

Poppy didn't know where the idea came from—she just blurted it out: "All right. Send one of my toes."

Paulie gaped at her. "Are you nuts? That's not only crazy, that's stupid. Like her father ain't gonna know the difference. What's happened to you, Poppy? What is it with you and this kid? I thought you hated kids."

"I . . . I do," she said. "But not this one."

Poppy leaned back against the door. Suddenly she felt miserable. Her ice and steel were melting away. She was all shaky inside.

"Can we call a truce?" she said.

"Sure." Paulie had his hands on his hips and was walking around in circles. "But that's not gonna help us when Mac calls back with the address of where I'm supposed to deliver his persuader. What do I tell him then?"

"We'll think of something."

He stopped and stared at her. He looked worried—real worried. "Don't be so sure."

"I think I need a hug," she said, taking a small step toward him.

He continued to stare at her, then shook his head and opened his arms. He wasn't smiling—she could tell he was a long way from that—but she really did need a hug. She fell against him and clutched him to her.

"Don't let's not fight, Paulie. We're in this together, and together we're bigger and better than Mac."

"I ain't so sure of that. One thing's for sure, we ain't meaner. And that's gonna get us in trouble."

"We'll think of something."

"We'd better." He kissed the top of her head. "You make me crazy, you know that? You'll be the death of me yet."

Poppy clutched him tighter. Dear God, she hoped not.

8 Daniel Keane watched his grandson swing from rung to rung on the jungle gym and felt a little sick. Not because he feared he might fall. No, in this upscale McLean, Virginia, playground, the ground under the slides and swings and jungle gym was padded. Danny had already fallen twice and bounced right back up again.

Little Danny—five years old, named after his grandpa, and full of boundless energy. A regular little monkey on those bars. But thinking of Danny and how precious he was to everyone who knew him led to thoughts of John VanDuyne's little girl. And thus the nausea.

Dan knew her name . . . Katie . . . knew everything about her and her father. And he'd fed all that information to Carlos Salinas.

Who used it to kidnap her.

Dan didn't know for sure that it had been done, but he'd checked on VanDuyne yesterday and learned that he'd left his office almost immediately after arriving, and hadn't been heard from since. Dan had a pretty good—and pretty sickening—idea what that meant.

That poor man. What he must be feeling.

Dan tried to imagine what it would be like to hear that someone had kidnapped Danny. He found it beyond comprehension.

And that little girl . . . the terror of being snatched from the street or wherever it was and kept prisoner by strangers.

He swallowed back a surge of bile.

God, he hoped they were treating her all right, that they'd let her go unharmed when this was all over.

But he had no control over any of it. He'd fed the stuff to that human slug, Salinas, and that was it. Dan had made suggestions as to how to best put it to use, but the final decision was up to Salinas.

He tried to concentrate on Danny. This was a sort of farewell trip to his favorite park. Carmella was taking their daughter and the grandchildren to their Florida condo for a couple of weeks. Dan would have loved to go along, to sit in the purifying rays of the sun and try to forget what was happening here. But he had to stay. Especially now that Winston had dropped his decriminalization bomb.

And now, when the wheels were in motion and he couldn't reverse them, he had to ask himself whether he'd do the same if he could go back and relive the past couple of months.

Yes. He doubted he'd change a thing. Because too much hung in the balance. This was so much bigger than the well-being of one little girl. A whole nation was at stake, a nation *full* of little girls like Katie Van-Duyne . . . and little boys like Danny.

"Don't blame me," he whispered to no one.

Blame that lousy, spineless excuse for a president. The country was already in the toilet, but legalizing drugs would pull the plunger. Tom Winston couldn't be *talked* out of this mad crusade—God knew how many people had tried—so he had to be *taken* out.

Even if it meant colluding with people Dan despised more than the President. It was, quite literally, a deal with the Devil, and if he burned in hell for it, so be it. *Somebody* had to stop Winston.

Daniel Keane sent up a prayer—not for himself, but for that little girl. He prayed that this crazy, brass-balled scheme would work out with no one getting hurt. . . .

Except the President.

9   The computer screen said NO MAIL.
     John pounded his fist on his thigh. He'd have much preferred to slam it on the desk, but that would bring his mother running, asking, *"What's wrong? Has there been any word? Do you think she's all right? Why aren't they telling you what they want?"* And a million other questions.

He'd lied to her on his return from Lafayette Square, telling her the kidnappers hadn't phoned him, that he'd stood around looking stupid, waiting for the phone to ring.

A good lie. It kept Nana's anxiety at its current, just-bearable level.

And it explained why he'd rushed in and gone straight to his computer to send off e-mail to the kidnappers. As far as Nana knew, it was to ask why they hadn't called. In reality, it was to explain why they'd been cut off and to arrange another call.

A lie was the only way. How could he tell Nana what they wanted him to do? And worse, that the call had been interrupted by some imbecilic woman in the park? She'd go to pieces.

The phone rang.

John stared at it. Who was it this time? Phyllis again? He'd called in sick this morning, telling her he had a bad case of gastroenteritis and didn't dare get far from a toilet. Highly unlikely he'd be in tomorrow either. See you Monday.

But that hadn't stopped her from calling about confirming this meeting with that committee and luncheons with various advocacy groups and a number of speaking engagements. Somehow he'd managed to sound coherent, though he didn't know how long he could keep it up. If this was Phyllis again he'd have to tell her whatever it was would have to wait. He was too sick to think.

He picked up, but instead of Phyllis he heard Terri's voice.

"You don't sound too sick."

He had to think a minute. Had he told her about it? He was new to this lying thing. Had to keep his stories straight.

And keep his voice light.

"You should be here listening to my intestines rumble. But how'd you know?"

"I called your office. Phyllis said you were out with an intestinal flu. Anything serious?"

"I don't think so. Probably one of those two- or three-day viruses.

"Then I suppose our date's off tonight, huh?"

John fumbled for a reply. Date? What date? Oh, God. He was supposed to have dinner with Terri tonight. He'd completely forgot.

"Food? Don't even mention it. I've been holding off on calling you, hoping the symptoms would ease up, but they haven't. I was just about to pick up the phone."

"Want me to come over and pat your hand and put cold compresses on your head?"

"That sounds great, but I'm going to try the sleep cure. And besides,

I don't want to expose you to this. Believe me, you don't want what I've got."

No one in the world wants what's ailing me.

But he wished to God he could sit her down and open up to her. He wished he could share this crushing burden with *somebody*. If he could bounce a few ideas off Terri, and get some feedback, maybe he could come up with a way out of this.

But how safe would it be to burden her with this? With Terri knowing the President was a target and her seeing Bob Decker or other Secret Service agents a dozen times a day, how long could he expect her to keep mum?

No. He had to keep this to himself—all to himself.

He fended off her offer of chicken soup and rescheduled their dinner for next Tuesday, then got off the phone.

Next Tuesday. How would he get out of that? This virus story would carry him through the weekend. Come Monday morning, he'd have to come up with something new.

He checked for e-mail again. And again, nothing. Damn!

He glanced at his watch. When had he got back this morning? 10:30, maybe? Here it was 4:30. Six hours since he'd e-mailed Snake and still no reply. Had he received the message? Why wasn't he replying? Was it over? Had they decided John wasn't going to do what they wanted and so they were disposing of Katie?

He couldn't think about that. No, that couldn't be. And that *wouldn't* be. Snake was playing games. Letting him twist in the wind awhile before he made contact again.

Well, he was twisting, all right. And damn near strangling with worry.

But when Snake did make contact, what would John tell him? Could he agree to poison Tom?

Yes. What choice did he have but to tell Snake what he wanted to hear? Say all the right things, then find a way to fake it.

But how, dammit? Snake had already warned him: "Don't try any tricks. We'll know." John had to respect that. Anyone who could ferret out Tom's reaction to chloramphenicol had world-class sources.

But there had to be a way. If John could relax just long enough to get his thoughts together, he knew he could come up with a way to save Katie *and* Tom.

10 "Yes!" Poppy said.

She circled the article and pulled the sheet free of the rest of the newspaper. As she rose from the kitchen table she felt her spirits lifting. She'd spent the day in some kind of long dark tunnel, and now she'd spotted a light at the end.

She stepped into the front room and found Paulie sitting and watching the phone. He'd stationed himself on the inside end of the couch in the corner, as far as possible from the phone, like he was afraid it was going to come to life and bite him or something.

"You finally finished with your reading?" he said. Snarled was more like it. "You up to date on all the local news now?"

She'd sent him out for all the local papers—the Washington *Times*, the *Post*, the *Banner*, everything available in the 7-Eleven. And then she'd begun combing them.

"Yeah, I'm finished," she said.

She had to bite the inside of her cheek to keep from grinning like an Appleton. She'd found the solution to all their problems. Okay, maybe not all, but at least the major one that was dogging them right now. She was so damn proud of herself she wanted to dance. But first she wanted to have some fun with Paulie. He'd been no help at all, so he totally had it coming.

"Good," he said. "Now maybe you can think of something I can tell Mac when he calls. And he's gonna call any minute, you can bet your sweet dimpled ass on that."

"Oh, I've got no doubt at all he'll call."

"So what do I tell him? 'Sorry, Mac. No persuader on this one. Poppy won't let me.' Right. Next thing you know he'll be busting down that door."

"You just tell him everything's under control and the persuader's ready for delivery."

He made that sour face he did every time he thought he heard something stupid. "Oh, right. And when it's *not* delivered? What then?"

"Oh, don't worry. You'll deliver it. Right on schedule."

He sat and stared at her a second or two, eyes bugged, jaw dropped. Oh, this was good. It was all she could do to keep from busting out laughing. Then he jumped to his feet, arms spread.

"How, Poppy? For Chrissake, have you gone crazy? Where am I gonna get a little girl's toe?"

Okay. Enough was enough. She shoved the paper toward him.

"Here." As he grabbed it and stared at it, she said, "I circled what you want."

He read some, then looked up at her. "But this is . . . I'll have to . . ."

She shrugged. "Who's the best B-and-E guy around if it ain't you, Paulie?"

He didn't seem to want to argue about that, so he kept on reading. Finally he looked up at her and the half-angry, half-worried look he'd worn all day had changed. He actually smiled—just a little.

"You know something, Poppy. I think this might work."

"I know it will."

He was grinning at her now—staring, nodding, and grinning. "You're pretty smart for a girl."

She punched him on the arm. "Smart? I'm totally brilliant!"

He hugged her and they laughed. He seemed proud of her, and to tell the truth, she was pretty damn proud herself. When was the last time she'd felt this way?

Then he pushed her to arm's length, suddenly serious.

"But Mac can never know. Even after this is all over, we can never let Mac even suspect what we did."

"After this is all over, we're never gonna see Mac again. Right?"

"Right. When he calls, we ain't home."

Poppy hugged him. She felt like the weight of the world had been lifted from her shoulders. She put her lips against his ear.

"Better get going."

It took Paulie longer than he'd figured to find the place. After all, he didn't know diddly about Arlington, Virginia, but people were pretty helpful when he asked for directions, and he only got lost twice. He passed a Home Depot along the way and picked up a sturdy pair of pruning shears. The sweet young thing at the check-out counter set him on the right course for the final leg of his journey to the Lynch-MacDougal Funeral Home.

Two wakes were in progress. Paulie figured he was pretty much dressed for mourning, being all in black. He wandered in, looking appropriately somber, and checked out the place's security system—or, like they said in the movies, "cased da joint."

He felt very much at home looking for electric eyes, motion detectors, window magnets. Breaking and entering used to be his bread and butter before he started baby-sitting for Mac. Still came in handy when the till ran low between gigs. Clean work. You get in when the place is empty, boost whatever's lying around, and get the hell out. In and out. No fuss, no muss. You go in empty, you come out with some cash and jewelry.

This time he'd be coming out with a toe.

Weird, man.

He found the control panel near the back door and it looked like a single-zone setup. The whole security system was pretty basic: windows, doors, and that was about it. Nothing that would keep him out if he'd had his tool kit—but that was back in Brooklyn. He needed an edge here.

He checked the name in the newspaper Poppy had given him. Edward Hadley, age seven. According to the obit, little Eddie was here "as a result of injuries sustained in a motor vehicle accident."

Sorry about that, kid. Let's just hope they didn't run over your feet.

He saw the Hadley sign so he stepped inside for a quick look-see. A bad scene. Lots of weepy parents and confused-looking grade-school kids. He did a fly-by on the coffin. Little Eddie—at least the front of his top half that was visible—looked pretty good.

He moved to one of the windows and checked it out. Just wired at the sill. Christ, all he needed was a glass cutter and a suction cut and he'd be in. He glanced through at the parking lot. Nah. Too many lights and too many buildings around. He'd be exposed for too long. And besides, he wanted to get in and out with no one being the wiser.

He slipped back out the door into the hallway where he saw this suit with a big red Irish face directing mourner traffic. That gave Paulie an idea. He stepped up to the guy and saw the name tag on his lapel: MICHAEL L. MACDOUGAL. One of the owners. He should be able to answer Paulie's question.

"Wonderful job you're doing," Paulie said.

"Thank you. We try. We try. But it's so difficult when they're so young."

"I can imagine. Say, where's—?"

"So many dying so young these days." Michael L. MacDougal was shaking his head. "We just received a new beloved only hours ago. Barely out of her teens. They're all so young. What's happening?"

"I wish I knew." *And I wish you'd let me get a word in.* "Where's the men's room, by the way?"

MacDougal pointed past the Hadley sign. "Make your first left and it's right at the bottom of the steps."

"Downstairs?" Paulie said, moving off. *Outstanding!*

On his way, Paulie passed a horse-faced woman in a tweed suit and a frilly blouse. Her name tag said EILEEN LYNCH. The other owner. Husband and wife? he wondered. Or maybe a brother-and-sister act. Like, who'd want to be married to that?

He hurried down the stairs and found a small paneled room with a couple of worn couches. Half a dozen people were sitting around, puffing on cigarettes. A fan in the ceiling sucked off the smoke.

A smoking lounge. How thoughtful.

Ahead were two rest room doors and a third marked PRIVATE. He stepped inside the men's room and found he had it all to himself. Over the toilet in the stall was a small casement window with no sign that it was connected to the security system. Beyond it, the rear parking lot stretched away at eye level.

How *very* thoughtful.

He undid the latch and yanked on the handle. It gave a little, then stuck. Hadn't been opened in years, but he couldn't see anything blocking it. All it needed was a little muscle from the other side and it would swing all the way up.

He stuck a piece of toilet tissue in the latch, left it in the open position, and stepped over to the sink to wash his hands. He smiled at himself in the mirror.

Piece of cake.

And then he frowned, remembering Poppy alone at the house with that kid. He hoped to hell Mac didn't decide to pop in for a personal visit to check out the persuader.

That could be big trouble.

12 Poppy adjusted her Minnie Mouse mask and then untied Katie's hands and removed her blindfold.

"You have to go to the bathroom, Katie?"

She shook her head and said nothing. She looked so down, poor kid. Poppy sat beside her on the bed and massaged her wrists.

"There. How's that? That feel better?"

Katie looked at her with those big blue eyes and nodded glumly, then looked back at Poppy's hands.

"How come your fingernails are all black?"

"'Cause I paint them that way."

"Oh. When am I going to see my daddy?"

"Soon. Real soon."

Again she wondered why she didn't ask for her mommy. Of course, Poppy had always been real close to her dad too. Mom had the regular job, working a register at Kmart, so she wasn't around most days. Dad did seasonal work and sometimes he'd be home for weeks at a time. Since he loved basketball and she was his only kid, he'd taught her the game early. They'd spent countless afternoons going one-on-one.

Dad . . . I didn't even know you were sick.

She looked at Katie and saw that her fine, dark hair was all tangled. A case of terminal bed head. But what'd you expect when the kid was tied to her bed all the time?

"How about I fix your braids?" Poppy said.

Katie brightened. "Could you do a French braid? My Nana never lets me have a French braid."

"Nothing to it. One French braid, coming right up."

Katie's smile—missing tooth and all—sent a shiver of pleasure through Poppy. If that's all it takes to make you happy, little girl, you'll get a million French braids.

And then the smile faded.

"You're not going to make my hair like yours, are you?"

Poppy felt her hair where it fell from behind the mask. "What's wrong with it?"

"The color's weird."

"Weird?" Poppy had to laugh. "That's Deadly Nightshade, honeybunch. The coolest color around. You rinse it into dark hair like mine and it comes out looking like red wine."

"I still don't want it on my hair."

"Don't worry. We won't change your color, just your braids. Now, turn around and let me brush it out."

As she worked with Katie's hair, Poppy couldn't help thinking about Glory, and wondering if this is what might have been. . . .

"What's your name again?" Katie said.

Before she could give it a thought, her real name slipped out.

"Poppy."

Damn me! What an Appleton thing to do! Jesus, what am I gonna do now? The kid knows my name.

"That's a pretty name," Katie said. "Isn't a poppy a flower?'

Oh, well. The damage was done. But maybe it wasn't so bad. Anybody asking her would like figure Katie's kidnappers would use fake names, so they'd pay no mind to "Poppy." She hoped.

"Yep. It's a little flower. That's what my daddy used to call me. His little flower. Until I got tall. Then he called me his sunflower."

"Where's your daddy now?"

Poppy's eyes misted for an instant. "He's far away."

"Is that where you grew up? Far away?"

"No. I grew up right around here."

Now that was like a total lie but it ought to throw off anybody coming around later looking for a Poppy who grew up in northern Virginia. No worry about her real home popping out. Poppy never told anyone her real home town.

Really, how could you tell someone you grew up on Sooy's Boot, New Jersey? *Sooy's Boot!* How could you let those words past your lips?

"I grew up far away," Katie said. "In Georgia."

"I figured you were from somewhere down South."

"How come?"

"Yo' axent, hunny," she said, mimicking Katie's drawl. "Lahk Joe-jah."

"I don't have an accent."

"Oh, yes, you—" Poppy stopped as her hand found a depression in Katie's scalp on the left side of her head—in her *skull.* "Hey, what's this dent in your head?"

"I . . . I had a accident."

"What sort of accident?"

"I broke my head."

Poppy's stomach turned. "Shit! I mean, shoot! When did that happen?"

"When I was little."

"When you were—?" Poppy had to laugh. "You're not so big now. At least you weren't born that way. If you were I might think you were an Appleton."

"What's a Appleton?"

"They're some weird folks from back around where I grew up. Lots of them got weird-shaped heads."

"I thought you said you grew up around here."

"Yeah," Poppy said quickly. "Yeah, well, somewhere not far from here."

Not far in miles, she thought. Probably less than two hundred. But so very far in every other way it might as well be like Mars or someplace.

Sooy's Boot . . . a hiccup on one of the roads running through the heart of the New Jersey Pine Barrens. She was born and raised there, which made her like a full-fledged Piney. Which meant "poor hick" to most people. But she didn't remember feeling poor when she was growing up. Mom had the Kmart job in May's Landing, and Dad worked the pineland's annual cycle: He cut sphagnum moss in the spring, picked blueberries and huckleberries in the summer, then cranberries toward fall, and cut cordwood through the winter. They had everything they needed.

Until Mom died. She'd been bothered by the veins in her legs forever, and one day one of her legs got red and sore. She should have seen a doctor, but she put it off and put it off, and then one day at work she grabbed her chest and keeled over. She died on the way to the hospital. Coroner said a giant clot had come loose from one of the veins in her leg and clogged her heart. Or something like that.

That left Poppy and Dad. She was all he had, and he doted on her. And no doubt Poppy would like still be living in the pines, would have grown up to be another Piney girl married to a Piney guy, raising a bunch of little Pineys . . . if it hadn't been for basketball.

Still brushing Katie's hair, Poppy smiled. Jesus, she'd been good. Dad had drilled all the fundamentals into her before she was ten, and by middle school she was playing with the boys at recess and giving them a run for their money.

The coach at the regional high school took one look at her in tryouts and put her in the starting five of his varsity squad. She had to put up with some heavy resentment until they started winning like they'd never won before.

All because of me, she thought.

No brag. Truth. She'd been totally awesome in the paint—could dribble circles around anyone who got in her way. And when they walled up to block her out, she hung back and dropped in three pointers. And when they got so frustrated that they started fouling her, she'd sink two for two on her free throws—ninety-five percent from the line.

By junior year she'd already been offered a full ride at Rutgers. Dad had been ecstatic: Not only was his little flower All State, but she was going to college. That big round ball was going to be her ticket out of poverty and the pines.

Then she did a real Appleton thing: She fell in love. With Charlie Pilgrim, of all people.

Even now she couldn't help wincing at the whole thing. How could she have been so totally stupid?

Well, one thing leading to another, as it so often does, Poppy had found herself pregnant. And since there was no way she'd have an abortion—after all, this was Charlie's baby and they were in love—she had to quit basketball. Dad was crushed, of course. And seeing his face every day when she came home right after school instead of practicing with the team became a total torture that finally got to be too much to take.

So she and Charlie had run off to New York City where Charlie was going to find a job and they were going to get married. Except Charlie never did find steady work and they never got around to like getting married. They wound up on welfare, sharing a filthy Lower East Side apartment with two other couples.

And then the baby had been born. She was beautiful, she was glorious, and so that was what they named her: Glory.

But soon Glory had started having fits, and the doctors at NYU Medical Center said she had a brain defect, something wrong in her head that gave her epilepsy. They tried all sorts of medications but she kept on having fit after fit after fit—the doctors called them seizures—

until her eighty-ninth day of life when she went into a final unstoppable fit that lasted until she died.

All the doctors had been sorry; some of the nurses even cried. They all said they didn't know why she had all those fits, but Poppy knew. It was Appleton blood. Some of it was in her. Dad had always said there wasn't, but what had happened to Glory was proof. Poppy had bad blood. Appleton blood.

She hadn't been too easy to be with after that. She totally hated the doctors, hated everyone around her, hated Charlie for getting her pregnant, but like hated herself most of all. Charlie couldn't take it anymore. He wanted to take her back to Sooy's Boot but no way could she face Dad again. Not after losing the baby because of Appleton blood.

So Charlie had left without her. Probably told all sorts of tales about her when he got back. Poppy hadn't cared. She totally wanted to die. And she damn well might have killed herself if she hadn't discovered the unholy trinity: grass, speed, and coke. They hadn't killed the pain, but they'd eased it, made it like bearable.

Some long, dark years had followed, years that were mostly a blur now. She tried not to think about the things she did to get by. She fell in with some bad people, even turned tricks when she was desperate, OD'd a couple times, got beat up more than a couple times, and just might be dead by now if she hadn't found Paulie.

Paulie had changed her life, and she liked to think she like changed Paulie's—for the better, of course.

Her only regret was that she hadn't gone back home, just for a visit. She'd been so wrapped up in herself, she never imagined something could have been wrong with Dad . . . that he wouldn't always be there.

And then . . . he wasn't there . . . would never be there again . . . and she never knew until he was six months in the ground.

Maybe that's what I'll do when this is over, she thought as she finished weaving Katie's French braid. Tending to Katie had awakened a longing in her. She'd thought she never wanted to see Sooy's Boot again, but now . . .

She felt like going home.

She still had family in the pines. Maybe she could like reconnect . . . if any of them would speak to her.

"I have to go to the bathroom," Katie said.

"Sure thing, honeybunch. And you can check out your braid in the mirror while you're at it.

She had her halfway there when the phone rang. Poppy hurried her into the bathroom.

"Now, you stay in there till I come and get you," she told her, then dashed for the phone.

She picked up on the fourth ring and slipped her Minnie Mouse mask to the top of her head.

"Hello?"

"What took you so long?"

She knew that voice: Mac.

"I was taking the 'package'" —Jesus, she hated that word— "to the bathroom."

"Put him on," Mac said.

Him. That meant Paulie. Poppy knew how paranoid Mac was about mentioning names or being specific about anything on the phone. Talking to him was all about *not* saying things. Maybe she could see his point, but how about a Hello or How's it going? Jesus, she hated this guy. The sooner they were rid of him, the better. She couldn't wait.

"He's not here."

"Where the hell is he?"

"Out." He wants info, she thought, let him scratch for it.

"Don't give me this shit, girl. Where is he?"

"Shopping. Getting some tools."

"Tools? What are you giving me? Did he get the persuader? Is it packed up and ready to go?"

"Not yet."

Silence on the other end, then a tone so totally low and cold she almost dropped the phone. "You'd better explain."

She was ready for that. She'd been rehearsing.

"It's gonna get done. It's just that this one's a lot trickier than the last. We got a smaller area to work with, if you know what I'm saying."

"Then go back to the original—like last time."

Right, Mac, she thought. Her finger. Sure. On a cold day in hell.

She said, "Either way, it's a different situation. We can't exactly get this package liquored up like the last one." What an absolute total nightmare that had been.

"So use something else. Or maybe I ought to come over and supervise."

Oh, Jesus, no. No-no-no-no!

"That's okay, Mac. We're handling it. It'll get done as soon as he gets back."

"Yeah? What tool's he out buying?"

"A meat cleaver."

Another silence on Mac's end, shorter this time. His voice was lighter when he spoke again. "Yeah. That oughta do it."

"Quick and neat," she said, forcing the words. She couldn't resist adding, "But no matter how you look at it, it's like pretty goddamn ugly. I mean, she's only—"

"Watch it! Watch what you say."

"All right, but—"

"No buts. And don't get all soft and fuzzy on me. A little persuader will make things run much smoother, and get this over quicker. And besides, she'll never miss it."

And she'll never forget what two strangers did to her in a back room when she was six years old, Poppy thought. But I'll see to it she doesn't have to forget.

Poppy sighed with all the regret she could muster. "I suppose you're right."

"Suppose? You'd better *know* I'm right. Have him call my voice mail if there's a problem; otherwise he knows where to deliver it."

Mac hung up right in the middle of her "Yeah."

Jesus, she hated him.

She got her Minnie Mouse mask back on and went to retrieve Katie from the bathroom. She needed a dose of that little girl to clear away the bad aftertaste of Mac.

13 Paulie stood in a clump of trees across from the Lynch-MacDougal Funeral Home and watched all the mourners trail away. He waited while all windows went dark one by one, then groaned as he saw Michael and Lydia appear at the back door.

"The parking lot lights, schmuck! Don't leave 'em on. It's a waste of energy."

The pair didn't seem to care. They locked up and headed for separate cars—MacDougal to a Buick Riviera and Lynch to a little Beamer—then drove off in the same direction. He still hadn't figured out how those two were related, and didn't really care. He had a problem: the sodium lamps didn't leave a single goddamn shadow near the building. This was going to be like breaking in at noon.

But it had to be done.

At least the bathroom window was around back. That gave him some cover.

He checked his pockets: penlight, pruning shears, the leather driving gloves from his chauffeur stint the other day—all present and accounted for. He checked the street. When no cars were in sight, he dashed across and pelted straight through the parking lot to the back of the funeral home. He stood there panting, looking innocent, while he waited to see if he'd attracted any attention.

Nothing stirred. He crouched, spotted the white of the toilet tissue he'd left to mark the right window, and gave it a shove. The window swung in easily.

Paulie rolled onto his belly, pushed his legs into the opening, and slid through the window. A tight squeeze for his shoulders, but he managed to wriggle through and wound up standing on the toilet. He pushed the window closed and turned on the penlight.

Moving out to the dark smoking lounge, he looked around for the PRIVATE door. He'd been thinking about what might be on the other side and had an idea. He stepped inside and flashed the light around. Just what he'd suspected: polished wooden boxes in tight neat rows. This was where they stored the coffins.

Holding the penlight in his mouth, he moved along the rows, going from coffin to coffin, finding the latches on each, unhooking them, and lifting the lids. Nothing to it. They were all pretty much the same. Good. He'd been worried that he'd have trouble with the Eddie Hadley coffin upstairs. He always made a point of keeping flashlight use to an absolute minimum if windows were involved. None down here, but he'd seen plenty of glass upstairs.

As he turned to leave, the light caught a silvery reflection in a rear corner of the room. Looked like stainless steel sinks and counters. Must be where Lynch and MacDougal did their embalming. He spotted a white-sheeted figure on a table. The next customer?

Paulie knew he should be heading upstairs for his date with Eddie Hadley's toe, but he found himself irresistibly drawn to that table. Just for a look. Only take a second . . .

As he neared, he figured which end was the head. He lifted the sheet and flashed the beam on the face of a young girl with long brown hair. Pale as the sheet, but with her eyes closed she looked like she was sleeping, like one shake of her shoulder and she'd open up and look at him. This must have been the young "beloved" MacDougal had mentioned.

Paulie lifted the sheet farther—nude as a lap dancer underneath and very nicely built. He stared at her, wondering what she'd died of. Too bad. She was a looker.

He dropped the sheet and headed upstairs. He found the Hadley room and stepped inside. A quick flash of the light showed him the path through the chairs. He reached the coffin and found someone had closed it.

Fine with me, he thought. He didn't feature having the kid watching while he crunched on his toe.

He felt along under the cover lip until he found the latch for the lower half, unhooked it, and lifted. Another quick flash to orient himself and—

"I'll be damned!"

The kid wasn't wearing pants or shoes or socks. This made it easier for Paulie, sure, but it was something of a shock. You figure if they dress the top half, they dress the rest of you too.

"All right, Eddie boy," he said, "time for your contribution to the cause."

No way around using his light now, but at least he'd have the coffin cover between him and the window. He pulled the pruning shears from his pocket, stuck the light in his mouth and bent over the kid's feet. He found the little toe on the right foot, fitted the shears around it, and squeezed. Nowhere near the resistance he'd expected. A little pressure, a soft *crunch*, and there it was: one persuader, made to order.

He pocketed the shears and picked up the toe. Tiny little thing—half the size of a cigarette filter, and about as white but heavier. As he took a closer look he saw that the cut end was wet and reddish, but it wasn't bloody. That might be a problem, but he'd worry about it later. Now that he had what he'd come for, he wanted out of here.

He glanced at his watch. Not bad: door to door—make that window to window—in ten minutes.

He pulled out the Ziploc sandwich bag he'd brought along. As he went to drop the toe inside, he felt it slip from his fingers.

"Fuck!"

He checked the bag. No, it hadn't fallen in there. That meant it was on the floor. Christ, he had to find it.

Paulie dropped to his knees and began flashing the light along the floor. Great . . . the carpet was beige . . . and thick—just his luck.

Easiest thing to do would be to just cut off the other toe and forget about this one. But sure as hell someone would find it tomorrow and want to know where it came from. And when they found out he'd bet his ass the papers and the TV news would start shouting about someone chopping off little kids' toes, and then for sure Mac would come gunning for him.

Nope. Had to find this one.

At least he was below window level where the penlight wouldn't be seen from the street. But where *was* the goddamn thing?

He didn't know how long he was down there on the floor, kneeling, crouching, crawling, lying flat on his belly, shining the light at all different angles—seemed like forever—until he spotted this slightly paler lump nestled in the carpet fibers four feet from the coffin. Was that—?

Yes. He almost sobbed with relief. How the hell did it get over there? Damn thing must have bounced and rolled. Who cared? He had it and he wasn't losing it. Still lying on the floor, he carefully sealed the toe in the baggie and stuffed that deep into the front pocket of his jeans.

Then he rose and closed and latched the lower half of Eddie's coffin.

"Thanks, buddy. You've been a real—"

The words choked in his throat. Outside the window . . . sitting in the parking lot . . .

A car.

Christ! Where'd that come from? Must have pulled in while he was on the floor. But who—?

Out in the hall, he heard the faint clack of a dead bolt snapping open. He made like a statue and listened. The rear door swung open with a creak. He heard the alarm panel begin to beep, then shut off as some-one punched in the security code. He heard someone humming—a guy. MacDougal? Yeah. The car outside was a Riv, just like he'd seen Mac-Dougal driving. As a light came on down the hall, Paulie crouched behind the coffin, but instead of coming this way, MacDougal headed downstairs.

At first Paulie cursed—that was his way out. He was stuck here until MacDougal left, and who knew how long that would be?

All right, he thought. I know the who. What's the why?

Only one reason he could figure for MacDougal to come back at this hour and head downstairs: He had to be embalming the babe on the table.

Shit, that could take hours, and Paulie didn't exactly have all night. Mac wanted a call when the persuader was delivered. He didn't get that call soon, he'd start getting antsy . . . might decide to pay the package a personal visit.

Then Paulie realized something: The alarm was off. He could sneak out the rear door—walk instead of crawl. He allowed himself a smile. When someone hands you a lemon, make lemonade.

He stepped out into the hall and headed toward the rear, moving carefully, hugging the wall where the flooring was less likely to creak. But as he passed the security panel he stopped and suppressed a groan. The indicator light was red—MacDougal had rearmed the system.

Okay. Only one thing to do. If MacDougal was in that back room doing whatever it was undertakers did to "beloveds," he'd probably never hear Paulie sneak downstairs and slip out the bathroom window. A risky move but doable—if you had the balls.

He *had* to get out of here.

He headed downstairs, taking every step as carefully as he could. The carpeting helped. When he reached bottom he peeked into the lounge and found it empty.

Excellent.

The door to the PRIVATE room was half open and he heard Mac-Dougal's voice coming from inside, talking now instead of humming.

Even better. Paulie's worst-case scenario on his way down the stairs had been sneaking into the bathroom and finding MacDougal taking a dump.

He skittered over to the bathroom door and was easing it open when he heard MacDougal's voice change. He was groaning now, making weird noises. Paulie knew he should stay on course but he had to see what was going on.

He crept to the PRIVATE door, put his nose against its outer surface, then eased his head to the side until he could peek around the edge.

At the far end of the room, MacDougal's fat naked body was bobbing atop the dead girl on the embalming table. Fascinated and repulsed, Paulie watched for a few seconds, then tore himself away. The growling animal noises coming from MacDougal now were the perfect cover for his escape.

Shaking his head, Paulie headed back to the bathroom. Weirdos—the world was full of them, man.

14 Poppy heard the garage door go up. She peeked out and saw the panel truck pulling in.

Finally! Jesus he'd been gone so long she thought something had happened to him. The extra time could only mean one thing: trouble. At least now she knew he hadn't got caught. But what if he hadn't been able to get that toe? He *had* to have it. She couldn't think of any other way out of this mess.

She could like barely breathe as she waited for him to come through the door. And when he did she totally jumped on him.

"Did you get it? Please say yes. *Please!*"

He gave her this innocent look. "Get what? Was I supposed to get something?"

"Paulie! Don't do this to me!"

Finally he smiled. "Of course I got it."

She sagged against him. "Oh, thank God! I was so worried."

"Nothing to it. Want to see?"

"No, thanks. I'll pass."

"Maybe you better take a look."

She backed up a step and looked at him. "Why? Don't tell me the dead kid was black or something."

"Nah. White as the package. But there's something missing, something we'll need if we're gonna pull this off."

"What's that?"

"Blood. The persuader ain't gonna be too persuasive if we send it like it is. We need to smear some fresh blood around the edge."

Poppy swallowed. He was right. She hadn't thought about that.

"Okay. We can use some of mine. I'll . . ."

He was shaking his head slowly. "What if dear old dad gets the blood typed, just to be sure, it's his kid's? We can't risk that. We need hers."

"Uh-uh," she said, backing up another step. "No way."

"Poppy," he said slowly. "I went to hell and back to save your little friend's toe. All we need to make this work—to really get away with it— is a few drops of her blood. A pin prick, f'Chrissake. Otherwise, you want to be responsible for what happens when Mac shows up with the news that the package's father says it ain't his kid's toe?"

He had a point—a very scary point. She hated it, but it was the only way. A little stick was like a small price to pay to save a whole toe.

She sighed. "All right. But let me talk to her first."

She was pretty sure she could make Katie understand. They'd got pretty tight tonight. What did the guys call it? Bonding? Yeah. That was it.

Katie and me bonded pretty good tonight.

FRIDAY

1 "*Marijuana's full name is cannabis hemp and it is one very useful plant. It produces the toughest known natural fiber. The first denim and most of the world's sailcloth used to be made from cannabis hemp. As a matter of fact, the Dutch word for cannabis is canvass.*

"*Did you know it takes four acres of twenty-year-old trees to make the same amount of paper as a single acre of hemp? And without using bleaches and dioxin? You can make methanol, cooking oil, vegetable protein, medications . . . the list goes on and on. Cannabis is a cash crop that won't need a single subsidy. It's silly to keep it illegal.*"

John turned down the volume on the TV, muffling Heather Brent's latest interview.

Was that a beep he'd just heard? It seemed to have come from down the hall, in the direction of the study . . . and the computer.

A real beep, or just wishful thinking? Probably his imagination.

He sat up on the edge of the bed and rubbed his face.

Another sleepless night. Another series of fruitless trips to the computer in search of Snake-mail. He'd been praying all night to hear from the kidnappers. Now he was hearing things.

But he had to check. He'd left the computer logged in to the HHS network. If e-mail arrived, it would beep.

The bastard, John thought as he stumbled down the hall for one more look. He's really punishing me for that hang up. Probably thinks I'll be so tortured by a whole day of not hearing anything that I'll be as compliant as a used examination glove and do everything he tells me.

Well, he's not far from wrong.

John had decided to agree—verbally—without question or reservation to everything Snake demanded. But all the while he'd be looking for a way around actually poisoning Tom. He didn't know how yet, but something would come up, he was sure.

He stepped into the study and blinked at the screen. Was that—? He stepped closer. Yes. The mail icon was blinking in the corner. He downloaded the letter to his screen.

From the anonymous remailer—thank you, God—but only eight words:

Check your snail mail, then e-mail your response.

Snail mail? But the mailman didn't come by until—

The mailbox.

John pulled on the first pair of pants he could find and ran out to the curb. He opened the mailbox door and found one of those padded mailers stuffed inside. He reached for it, then hesitated as thoughts of bombs and booby traps raced through his brain. He dismissed them, but found himself more than a little unsettled by the realization that Snake or one of his people—the guy in the sweatsuit in the CVS, maybe—had stood on this very spot not long ago. If he'd been looking out the window, he might have seen them.

Gingerly, he reached in and removed the envelope. Light. Couldn't be much more than paper inside. *Check your snail mail; then e-mail your response.* That could only mean printed instructions. Or maybe some new demand.

Taking a deep breath, he grabbed the PULL HERE tab and yanked. He reached inside but found no paper. Only a small plastic bag. He pulled it out and stared at it. At first he thought it was empty, then he spotted something stuck in the corner. Little. No bigger than one of his fingernails. White . . . and red . . . and the red was smeared along the inner surface of the bag.

His heart began to pound . . . the bag trembled in his fingers as he leaned closer for a better look. And when he realized what it was his legs seemed to dissolve and he dropped to his knees and let out an agonized howl of grief and despair so long and loud that it set the neighborhood dogs to barking.

2 Snake hurried up the front walk to the house. He would have preferred to limit all his contact with Paulie to phones and hotel bars, but he always made a point of visiting at least once to inspect the arrangements.

What he didn't like was someone remembering him or his car here in the unlikely event the place was ever connected to the snatch. Which was why he was wearing an Orioles cap and had his collar pulled up. The Virginia plates on the Jeep were borrowed and would be tossed in the Potomac as soon as this was over.

All those precautions, and still he felt buck naked out here.

But that didn't blunt his good mood. He'd heard from VanDuyne this morning and everything was under control.

As he approached the front door he made a quick check of the yard. The butter-colored blossoms on the scraggly forsythia along the foundation did little to offset the house's generally disheveled appearance. Not much of a lawn, but it looked like it was waking up from winter. Yard maintenance had been part of the one-year lease, but they'd all be long gone before it needed its first mowing.

He knocked on the door. "It's me. Everybody where they should be?"

He'd phoned earlier to let them know he was coming. He wanted the package safely tucked out of sight when he arrived.

Paulie opened the door. "Yeah. Everything's fine. C'mon in."

As the door closed behind him, Snake reached out and grabbed Paulie's hand. "Good job with the persuader, my man. Worked like a charm."

Always a good policy to lavish a little praise on the peons when it was well deserved. A few strokes cost nothing and sometimes were better than money. Sometimes.

He spotted Poppy on the couch, reading a magazine. She didn't look up and he didn't bother acknowledging her. The bitch was one major pain in the ass.

"Yeah?" Paulie said, smiling through his beard. "How do you know?"

"Got a message from him this morning. Guy's practically falling all over himself to cooperate."

"So he bought it, huh?"

Snake spotted a quick look pass between him and Poppy. What was going on here?

"Bought it?" Snake said. "What's to buy? It's his kid's toe."

"Yeah, I know. But he could've thought she was already dead and we just cut her toe off, or something like that. But then, with fresh blood on the toe, I guess he'd have to believe she was still alive."

Snake had never heard Paulie babble like this . . . and he didn't like it.

"Something wrong, Paulie?"

"Wrong?" His eyes got a funny, guarded look. "No. Why should anything be wrong."

"Because you're not acting like yourself."

"Maybe because he never had to molest a child before," Poppy said.

Snake didn't bother looking at her. "Nobody molested anyone. And who asked you anyway?"

"What do *you* call chopping off a six-year-old's toe?" she said. "Not exactly a walk in the park. And we're damn lucky she didn't take one of her fits."

Now he had no choice but to face Poppy, and he was shocked by the naked anger and revulsion in her expression—as if she were looking at something that had just crawled out from under a rock. He fought an urge to step over there and wipe that look off her face.

"Fits?"

"Yeah. The fits she takes those pills for."

Now he got it. "Oh. You mean *convulsions*." He let the words drip acid. "You need to work on your vocabulary, honey."

"And you need to work on your research. How come you didn't know she took *fits?*"

Snake had had just about enough of this bitch. He turned to Paulie.

"Tell your girlfriend not to speak unless spoken to."

"She's got a right to her opinion."

"When I want the opinion of someone with purple hair, I'll ask for it."

Paulie held up his hands. "All right, all right. The point she's trying to make is it was pretty goddamn dicey getting that toe. I hope to hell it was worth it."

Snake gave himself a few seconds to cool.

"Yeah. It was worth it. You should have seen her father's message. Frantic as hell. If it had been on paper it would have been covered with tear stains."

Snake smiled. As he'd read those pleading words he could almost hear VanDuyne's sobs. *Please oh please oh please oh PLEASE don't hurt her again!*

"I guess you're real proud of yourself," Poppy said.

She was asking for it . . . really asking for it. . . .

"C'mon, Poppy," Paulie said, giving her a hard look.

"Yeah," Snake continued, ignoring her. "No more arguments from Daddy. He's ready to do *anything* we want."

"And just what is it we want Daddy to do?" Paulie said.

"That's between me and the other people involved. Better you don't know."

No way in hell was he telling these two.

"So, where's the little package?" he said to Paulie.

He jerked his head toward one of the doors leading off the living room. "In there."

"Well, I'll just take a look, and that will complete my inspection tour."

"She's sleeping," Poppy said.

Didn't this bitch know when to shut up?

"Blindfolded?" he said to Paulie.

"Sure. That's SOP."

"Good." He started toward the door. "Then I'll just take a peek."

Poppy was up and standing by the door, her worried eyes flicking from Paulie, to the door, to Snake, and around again.

"Don't. You'll wake her up. You don't know what a time we had getting her to sleep."

"That's what baby-sitters get paid for."

He breezed past her and opened the door. The light was out so he found the switch and flicked it.

Poppy slipped past him and stood by the foot of the bed—no, *hovered* was more like it. She looked nervous as a cat, biting her lip, rubbing her hands together. Looking at her you'd have bet half your net worth the package was her own kid.

But Snake had to admit that everything looked okay: The package was blindfolded and tied to the bed frame, just as she should be. She wore a plaid shirt and overalls of some sort, a sneaker on her left foot, and a big gauze bandage on her right.

He nodded and walked out, leaving Poppy behind. Out in the front room, Paulie still didn't look right. And that worried Snake. He didn't want these two to get cold feet on him. The game still had a way to go before it was finished.

"Hey," he said with a smile, "she looks pretty damn good. No worse for wear, as far as I can see. And she'll never miss that toe."

"I'm real glad it worked," Paulie said. "'Cause I don't know if I could go through that again."

"What's the matter with you, Paulie? You going soft?"

"No. I just—"

Snake felt his rage flare. Time to lay down the law to these assholes.

"You just *nothing!* You're working for me. I tell you to cut off her fucking *hand*, you say, 'Which one?' Or you're out of this!"

But Paulie was shaking his head. He was looking at the floor, but he was hanging tough.

"All right," he said. "Then we're out of it. Find someone else to do your dirty work. But we ain't cutting up a kid. It ain't right."

The words shook Snake. Find someone else? Where the hell would he find another baby-sitter at this stage of the game?

This whole gig was going to hell. First he had to take out an insurance policy with Salinas, and then he had to deal with that unpredictable VanDuyne, and now the peasants were threatening revolt. What next?

"You threatening me?"

Paulie shook his head. "No threat. Just telling you the way it is. We'll play this thing through just like you want it, but no more persuaders."

Snake couldn't think of anything to say that wouldn't make him look bad. And since he couldn't do what he really felt like doing—put a .38-caliber hole in Paulie's face—he decided to make his exit.

Yeah. Leave them wondering what his next move would be.

"I'll be in touch," he said, and headed out the front door.

He fumed on the way across the yard. And to think he'd been feeling guilty about throwing Paulie and Poppy to Salinas's wolves when this was over. Just went to show how useless an emotion guilt was. Getting rid of these two was a great idea. He'd had it up to *here* with Paulie and his bitch.

3 As soon as the door closed behind Mac, Poppy threw her arms around Paulie.

"Paulie! You were awesome! The way you stood up to him . . . totally awesome!"

She could feel him shaking but wouldn't mention it—not for a million dollars.

"Yeah, well, I just didn't like him talking to you like that. Know what I mean? I mean, enough is enough."

She looked up at his face and realized something was different about him.

He'd started getting quiet last night after taking the blood from Katie. Poppy had held her while Paulie jabbed the corner of a razor blade into the pad of her little toe. They figured they were going to have to bandage her foot anyway to make it look like she'd had her toe cut off, so why not like get the blood from that spot. And Katie had been so good about it, a real champ. She'd winced and whimpered, but that was about it. She said she was used to getting stuck because of the regular blood tests she had to get as long as she was taking her medicine.

And after Paulie came back from delivering the persuader, he'd been quieter still, and had continued that way this morning. She'd thought he was still ticked at her for making him go out to that funeral home last night, but now she realized it was something else. Something deeper.

"What's up, Paulie? What's bothering you?"

He pulled away and went to the window. He stood there with his hands jammed into his pockets and stared out at the front yard.

"I don't know," he said. "I didn't sleep much last night. I got to thinking—I don't do much of that, but last night I couldn't turn it off. I kept thinking about how you stood up to me yesterday. I mean, Mac says, 'Cut off her finger,' I haggle him down to a toe, and I'm ready to do it. But you say no—this was something you weren't going to do, weren't going to allow to happen. You were ready to put everything on the line to stop it. I was pissed, as you know, but later on it hit me like a ton of fucking bricks: You drew a line and said, 'That's it. That's where I stop. I don't cross that line and neither does anybody else when I'm around.' And so I laid there last night thinking, Where's *my* line? I mean, do I even *have* a line? Or do I just wait for someone like Mac to tell me what to do, then go ahead like some fucking robot and do it? What kind of man is that? I couldn't turn it off."

Poppy stepped over to the window and slipped her arms around him, pressing her face against his upper back. She felt as if she were about to totally burst. She didn't dare speak because she knew she'd start bawling. So amazing . . . the feelings Paulie was talking about, they were the same ones that had been growing in her since the last baby-sitting job. But hers had been creeping up on her—at least until she'd seen Katie having a fit; then it all like came together. Paulie had got hit all at once.

"I'm gonna be thirty in November," he said. "And man, I laid there and looked back over my life and you know what I saw? Nothing. Not a goddamn thing. I mean, if I died now, is there any trace of me anywhere? Is there anything to say Paulie DiCastro was even *here?* No. There ain't. So last night I decided I was gonna start drawing lines. Gonna learn to say 'Stop, I don't go past this point.' I mean, you gotta stand for something in your life, and I never really stood up for anything, but that's gonna change. I'm not saying this good. Am I making any sense at all?"

Poppy hugged him tighter. "Truckloads. Maybe this is a turning point for us, Paulie. Maybe we can make something good out of his whole ugly scene. We take the money we get and like go off somewhere and use it to build something."

"Yeah, but what? I don't know anything legal. What am I good for except taking orders?"

"Don't worry. We'll find something. We're not *total* jerks. But the important thing is we'll draw another kind of line—between the old life and the new life. And we'll like never look back, Paulie."

"Yeah," he said, turning around and looking at her. His eyes searched her face. "You and me. We can do that."

Poppy pressed her face against Paulie's shoulder. She'd never felt this close to him.

4 "You will be able to come up with so much money?" Nana said. John looked up at his mother from where he sat before the computer and worried. She didn't know the half of it—a *tenth* of it— and already she looked like she was falling apart. Her hair was carelessly combed, her clothes wrinkled, her once rosy cheeks now pale and

pinched. And she kept digging her fingertips into the sides of her throat as if she were having trouble breathing.

No way he could tell her the truth—about the "service" he was to perform, about . . . Katie's toe. So he'd lied to her. He'd told her the kidnappers didn't really want a service from him, they wanted money—a million dollars.

"Yeah," John said softly. "It's in the works. I have calls out to some people who owe me favors, and a bunch of loan officers at the bank are working on it. I should be able to get it all together in a couple of days."

"A couple of days? But Katie will be a prisoner all that time. How can you—?"

He flared. Before he could stop it, his voice jumped to a shout. "Don't you think I want her back too? Today? This minute? It's not like I can just sit down and write a check!" He saw her flinch and that doused his anger. He reached out and grasped her hand. "Sorry, Mom. I'm just on edge. I'm doing the best that I can as fast as I can."

She patted his hand. "I know you are, Johnny. I never should have said . . . it is just that I cannot bear the thought of Katie being held prisoner by these people a single minute longer than absolutely necessary."

Prisoner, he thought, feeling sick again. If only that were the worst of it.

"I am going to lie down. Those pills you gave me make me so sleepy. I am too tired even for my yoga."

He'd started her on a tranquilizer last night. He wished he could pop a few himself, but he had to stay alert, had to stay on top of things.

"Do that, Mom. Lie down, close your eyes, try to sleep. It'll make the time go faster."

When she was gone, he got up and went downstairs to the kitchen. He opened the refrigerator door and looked inside. He knew he had to eat something, but his appetite was gone, maybe forever. He closed the door but didn't move away. His eyes were drawn to the freezer compartment.

He could almost see it through the door, still in the plastic bag, sealed in a white envelope tucked away behind the ice cube trays: Katie's little toe.

He had no delusions about reattaching it, and if he had, freezing would not be the way to preserve it. But what else could he do?

After dragging himself in from the mailbox and vomiting, he'd taken the Baggie and its contents down to the basement where he could cry without his mother hearing. He remembered shaking, sweating, and sobbing for only a few minutes, and then it was as if a circuit somewhere inside of him overloaded and tripped a breaker. He went numb. He'd sat there with the Baggie in his hand, not looking at it, staring off into space instead.

Finally he stood and began moving about, in circles at first, trying to focus. He couldn't wallow. He had decisions to make. Katie's life depended on those decisions.

But first, the toe . . . that horrid, precious, bloody little toe. He couldn't let Nana see it, and he couldn't bear the thought of letting it rot. He'd had to do *something*, and the freezer was all he could think of.

Thinking . . . God, that was such a problem. Trying to force his thoughts to get in line and make sense—it took such effort.

But after hiding the toe, he managed to sit down at the computer and tap out a reply to Snake. It wasn't all that coherent, but John didn't care. All he wanted to do was let this monster know that he would do any-thing—*anything*—he was asked, just please don't hurt Katie any more.

And he meant that. Snake had made his point: He held all the high cards. He was in charge. John had been tortured by the choice between his best friend and his daughter. But Katie's toe had dissolved the conflict. Katie. He chose Katie.

Katie would live.

And Tom would have to find some way to survive.

Snake's blood-freezing reply had reinforced that resolve.

NOW we understand each other! You know what you have to do. Do it soon. VERY soon. Or we'll start testing your jigsaw puzzle skills.

John dragged himself away from the refrigerator and went to the phone. He blocked all questions, all speculation as he narrowed his focus to the task at hand. He pulled out the yellow pages and searched the physician listings. He found a Dr. Adelson, an internist way up in Friendship Heights, and copied down his address and phone number. As Dr. Adelson, he began dialing the downtown pharmacies until he found one that had a small stock of chloramphenicol.

In the most matter-of-fact tone he could muster, he called in a prescription for someone named Henry Johnson: "Give him Chlormycetin 250, twenty caps, one Q-I-D, No refill, and generic's okay." When the pharmacist asked for his address and office phone number, John supplied Adelson's. Fine . . . Mr. Johnson could pick up his pills in about thirty minutes.

John leaned back in the chair and closed his eyes. Step one completed. Now for step two.

But as he picked up the phone, the doorbell rang. He jumped and almost dropped the phone.

Not a delivery man . . . oh, please, God, not another piece of Katie!

John hung up and forced himself toward the door that loomed ahead of him like the portals of hell. Clenching his teeth he grabbed the knob and yanked it open.

An attractive, fortyish woman stood on the front step. She wore a mink coat and high heels. Her long, glossy black hair was tied back with a gold clasp. Her face was perfectly made up. She was smiling, but her dark eyes challenged him.

John nearly staggered back at the sight of her. This was impossible.

"Hello, John." Her voice . . . so smooth, so cool, so perfectly modulated.

"Marnie!" His own voice sounded like steel dragging across concrete. "What are you doing here?"

"I've come to see my daughter."

"You-you're supposed to be in Georgia!"

"I was released."

"I don't believe that!"

"It's true, John. I'm cured. I'm on medication, and as long as I maintain my dosage, I'm fine. As a matter of fact, if I keep doing this well, Dr. Schuyler says he might try tapering my dose in the fall. Isn't that wonderful?"

John's mind reeled. This couldn't be. Marnie was supposed to be at the Marietta Psychiatric Center. What was she doing in D.C.? And why now? Of all times, why did she have to appear *now?*

"I don't care what Schuyler or anyone else says, the court said you're not supposed to leave Georgia."

Her smile held. "Dr. Schuyler worked it out for me. I'm well enough to travel now. And I want to see Katie."

"No," John said, shaking his head as vehemently as he could. "Not a chance. Not a chance in hell."

"I'm her mother, John." The smile wavered. "I have a right to—"

"You have *no* rights!" he said, feeling his anger rise—and loving it. So good to feel something other than sickness and dread. "You gave them up, remember? That was the deal: No prison for you, sole custody for me. And that's the way it's going to be."

Finally the smile vanished. "I *want* to see Katie. You can't keep me from seeing my own daughter."

"I can and will. And if you don't get away from here, I'll call the police and tell them you're a fugitive from a Georgia psychiatric hospital."

"That's not—"

"And I'll also tell them about the standing court order that forbids you from going anywhere near her. Do I call now, or do you leave?"

Marnie backed up a step. And now her lips trembled. "This isn't fair, John."

"That won't work on me, Marnie. And I don't want to hear about fair. Do us all a favor and go back to Georgia. Now."

"I hope you're taking better care of her than you are of yourself. You look terrible."

"Good-bye, Marnie."

He shut the door and leaned his forehead against the inner surface. *Please go away. I already have more than I can handle. I can't deal with you too.*

God he hated her, loathed the very sight of her. As an enlightened man of the nineties—and a physician to boot—he knew you couldn't hold the mentally ill responsible for their acts. But that didn't mean he had to forgive them.

And John would never forgive Marnie for what she had done. No matter what army of psychiatrists she assembled to proclaim her mentally and emotionally stable and perfectly fit to return to society, he would never allow Marnie back into Katie's life.

He stood on tiptoe and peeked through the miniature fanlight in the upper panel of the door. The front yard was empty. Marnie was gone. And she'd better stay gone or she'd screw up everything.

But he didn't doubt for a moment that she'd be back.

"John?" His mother's voice, coming from upstairs.

"Yeah, Mom?"

"Was someone at the door?"

"Just a salesman, Mom. Go get some rest. I'll let you know as soon as anything happens."

Katie, Tom, Mom, Snake, Marnie—how long could he keep all the balls in the air without dropping one?

Feeling as if he were about to explode, John returned to the kitchen and settled down to the task of arranging to poison the President of the United States.

Steeling himself, he punched in the direct line to Betty Kenny. Betty had started out as a clerk-typist in Tom's office when he was a lowly congressman. She'd moved with him to the Senate and was now his personal secretary, controlling his all-important appointment book. To get to Tom you had to get past Battleship Betty. But she knew John and liked him; and he knew how she worried about her boss's health.

"Hi, Betty," he said, trying to sound light and carefree with no idea if he was succeeding. "It's John VanDuyne. I need a few moments with your boss tomorrow to check his blood pressure. Will he be around?"

He crossed his fingers. *Please say yes.*

"Hi, John. Let me check. Weren't you here for that just the other day?"

"Yeah. Wednesday. And I didn't like what I found."

Her voice dropped. "Really? Was it bad?"

"I probably shouldn't have said that. Forget what you just heard, okay?"

"I won't say a word. You know that. But I want to know: Should I be worried?"

He played on her concern. "His pressure was borderline high, but I want to keep an eye on it. Especially if he's traveling to The Hague next week."

"I understand. Let's see . . . he's got a meeting in the Oval Office at ten . . . this won't take long, will it?"

"Ten minutes, fifteen at most."

"Okay. Why don't I keep that half hour between nine-thirty and ten o'clock clear? How's that?"

"Perfect." The word was bitter in his mouth.

A little small talk and he was off the phone again, leaning back, trembling.

Stage two completed.

He'd been so cool on the phone, on autopilot, but now the weight of what he was planning crept back to him.

Especially if he's traveling to The Hague next week . . .

But I'll be doing my damnedest to make sure he doesn't get to The Hague next week, John thought. If he shows up there, Katie dies.

I'm just going to make him sick, he told himself for the thousandth time since opening the mailbox this morning. He won't die. He may *almost* die, but the cutting-edge medical care available to the President of the United States will pull him through.

But what if the chloramphenicol didn't have any effect on Tom's marrow? It was a possibility. What then? Or what if there was a delayed reaction that didn't kick in for weeks? Would Snake believe he'd dosed Tom as instructed?

Not for a minute.

John wanted to scream, but that would wake up his mother.

Time to go on autopilot again.

He glanced at his watch. He had to get down to the pharmacy and pretend to be Henry Johnson picking up his pills.

I'm becoming a master of deception, he thought. I've lied to my mother, Terri, my office, a pharmacist, Tom's secretary, and tomorrow, my best friend.

He realized with a sick, sinking feeling that the only one he'd been truthful with all day was Snake.

SATURDAY

"John?"

He recognized the voice and stiffened. He'd been standing here, waiting for the elevator to the White House's first floor, silently screaming at it to hurry before he ran into anyone he knew.

Too late. He turned and saw Terri coming down the hall. He forced a smile.

"Terri. I didn't think you worked weekends."

"There are no weekends in a PR crisis of this magnitude." Her welcoming smile faded as she neared. "Are you all right?"

"I think so," he said. "Why?"

"Because you look awful."

I'll bet I don't look a tenth as bad as I feel.

"Gee, thanks."

"No, seriously." Her brow was furrowed as she peered at him. "That must have been some virus."

Virus? What—? Oh, yes. The virus lie. Had to keep all these stories straight.

Another forced smile. "Hey, you don't think I'd pass up an evening with you for anything minor, do you."

"I didn't realize . . . are you sure you should be up and about yet? You look completely washed out."

"I'm tired but that's about it. Another day of pushing fluids and I should be back to normal."

The elevator doors opened then and he quickly stepped inside, praying she wasn't on her way upstairs too. Thankfully, she held back. She smiled but her expression was concerned.

"Take care of yourself, John."

"I will. I'll call you to find out when you're free. We'll set something up."

The doors closed, separating them. He leaned back. God, how awkward was that? At least she believed he'd been sick. He didn't have to fake his malaise.

He patted the side pocket of his sport coat and felt the cylindrical bulge of the pill bottle. The chloramphenicol. He'd peeled off the label. The capsules inside were now anonymous . . . tiny masked assassins.

He still couldn't believe he was going through with this.

Only for Katie . . .

In the first floor hall he ran into Bob Decker, the last person he wanted to meet this morning.

All those years of training and experience . . . he'll know something's wrong the instant he sees me.

The big Secret Service agent did a double take and suddenly the pill bottle in John's pocket seemed to quadruple in size and weight. It felt like a can of baked beans, bulging the fabric for all to see.

"Hey, Doc. You don't look so hot."

"A virus, Bob. But I'm getting over it." He started to point to the door of the Oval Office and noticed his hand shaking. He dropped it and gestured with his head. "He in there?"

"Yeah. Said he was expecting you. How's he doing?"

"That's what I'm here to find out."

John waved and hurried to the end of the hall. He stepped up to the door, then stopped.

I can't do this.

But he could. He'd found a way to get himself through the act: Blame it all on Tom. It was Tom's fault. If he hadn't put forth this idiotic decriminalization program, Katie would never have been kidnapped. Katie would be safe at home right now watching her Saturday morning cartoons. *Katie would still have ten toes!*

That's right, Tom. Your godchild, the little girl who calls you "Uncle Tom," has been mutilated. Not because of something she did but because of something you did.

He stared at the presidential seal on the door and thought, *Whatever happens to you is your own fault, Tom. This is not my doing . . . it's yours. You set all this in motion. What goes around, comes around, and you can't escape the consequences.*

That was how he'd do it. Get angry. Stoke that rage to the point where he was capable of anything.

Setting his jaw, he knocked on the door, then stepped through. And stopped.

He'd been in the Oval Office before, and every time it was the same. Seeing Tom there behind that desk with the light filtering through the tall windows behind him, the royal blue rug with its huge presidential seal, the flags of the U.S., the presidency, and the armed services arrayed around him, never failed to awe John, move him. Seeing him here, he could truly believe that Tommy Winston was president of the United States.

Tom glanced up, smiled, then frowned. "Hey, Johnny boy. You look like shit."

And it's all your fault.

John stumbled through the virus explanation again but he could tell Tom was barely listening.

"Guess who's crowding in here at noon," Tom said, tapping a sheet of paper on his desk. He seemed excited, wound up, full of barely contained enthusiasm.

"Floyd Jessup and the Reverend Whitcolm to offer their support."

He laughed. "No, but almost as good." He tapped the paper again. "Almost the entire southern delegation—at least those from the tobacco states."

"What are they afraid of—marijuana hurting cigarette sales?"

"You kidding? They want to *grow* it—although they insist on referring to it as 'hemp.' No, they see the writing on the wall. With tobacco consumption falling steadily, they need a new crop, and 'hemp' fills the bill."

Do you see? Do you see? This is why Katie was stolen from me and mutilated! Because of your wrongheaded, egomaniacal plan!

"So they want to sell reefers instead of coffin nails. Great."

"To tell you the truth," Tom said, "I think they'd be just as happy if someone developed a flowerless hybrid that produced nothing smokable. We've been trying our damnedest to educate them on the commercial uses of cannabis hemp. Looks like they've finally come around to seeing that it's in their interest to support a change in the laws. They're just the first. It's going to happen, John. The snowball is starting to roll."

I hope you're proud and happy that Katie's suffering because of you.

Tom kept rattling on as John inserted the stethoscope's earpieces, muffling him. He inflated the cuff, watched the needle sweep up, then begin to bounce down. He listened to the blood forcing its way back into the artery beneath the diaphragm, and it seemed so loud, so vital, each whispery *thump* driving home the consequences of what he had to do and how it would effect that blood, cutting off its supply of platelets and red and white corpuscles, thinning it, wasting it, choking it to a trickle that could no longer supply the tissues it served.

He cut off the thought, cut off *all* thought. He couldn't allow himself to think, to be himself, to feel anything but anger. For the next ten minutes he had to be an empty shell, an automaton following a hardwired program: Take the blood pressure, lie about it, give him the pills, and then get the hell out.

Tom's blood pressure now was 140/88. Better than Wednesday. High normal.

"Well, how'm I doing?" Tom said as John unwrapped the cuff.

"It's higher."

A lie. See that? You've made me a liar.

"Higher? I'm surprised. I'm so much less stressed than last time. I thought for sure it would be better."

"Let me try the other arm, just to double check."

John went through the motions, and got 138/88 on the opposite side. He shook his head. "Nope. Even higher over here."

Another lie.

"Damn," Tom said. "I'm watching the salt. What else can I do?"

"I think maybe I should start you on a medication."

"Aw, John, I'd rather not. You know that."

Don't fight me on this.

"Yeah, but you're going to that international conference next week and you know it's going to be a pressure cooker. I don't want your BP going through the roof while you're over there."

He shook his head. "I don't know. . . ."

Do it! Take your medicine like a man!

"I'll put you on a small dose of an ACF inhibitor, something so mild you won't even know you're taking anything."

Tom hesitated, then shrugged. "All right. If you say so. I'll trust your judgment. If I can't trust you, who the hell *can* I trust?"

Please don't say that.

John didn't trust himself to look at Tom. He covered by reaching into his jacket pocket.

"I was afraid it might come to this, so I came prepared."

Tom laughed. "Like the Boy Scout you never were."

"Yeah. Right."

His fingers were so sweaty and shaky he had difficulty grasping the pill bottle. Finally he got it out and fumbled off the lid.

"Hold out your hand."

"Here?" Tom said. "Now?"

John somehow maneuvered a grin to his face. "I know you, Tom. I'll write out a prescription and you'll get it filled, and then you'll put off taking it. 'I'll start next week.' Am I right?"

"You know me too well."

"Yes, I do. And I know next week never comes." Somehow he managed to shake two capsules into Tom's palm. *Don't think. Don't feel anything but rage.* "So here you go. I figure once I get you started, you'll keep going. So I want to watch you take both of these right now."

John stepped over to a side table where a pitcher of water and glasses sat, and managed to half fill a tumbler. He turned and handed it to Tom.

Tom took the glass and stared at him. "You sure you're all right? You're shaking like a moonshiner with DTs."

"The virus. I guess I'm not over it yet."

Fearing he might vomit, John turned away and stared out the windows at the south lawn. He couldn't watch. In half a minute it would be done. The gelatin capsules would be dissolving in Tom's stomach acid, releasing their contents. The antibiotic within would begin making its way into his bloodstream, triggering the suicidal antibodies, releasing them to begin their kamikaze run on Tom's bone marrow. And soon it would begin to die. Soon—

"No!" John spun and leaped toward Tom. "Stop! Don't take those!"

But Tom already had the glass to his lips. John knocked it from his hand and sent it flying across the room to smash on the floor. He clutched at Tom's throat.

"Spit those out! For God's sake, don't swallow!"

Tom's eyes bulged in shock. He staggered back, knocking over the chair, but John stayed with him.

"Spit them out, dammit! Spit them *out!*"

Tom wrenched free, turned, and spat on the floor. John saw both capsules on the carpet, then felt himself grabbed roughly from behind.

"Mr. President! Are you all right?"

John recognized the voice: Bob Decker.

Tom leaned against his desk, rubbing his throat, and staring wide-eyed at John.

"I'm all right. But he isn't. In God's name, John, what's wrong with you?"

The Oval Office seemed to shrink around him. Decker was here . . . the Secret Service was involved now . . . and Snake said he'd kill Katie. . . .

And suddenly he could pretend no longer. Three nights with no sleep, slowly dying inside as he tried to shoulder the entire burden on his own—he slumped in Decker's grasp.

"Katie . . . they've got Katie!"

Suddenly Tom was in front of him, gripping his shoulders.

"Katie? Who's got Katie?"

John shook his head. "I don't know. They took her Wednesday morning."

"Kidnapped?" Tom said. "Oh, shit! Oh, Christ! Not Katie!"

John felt Decker's grip loosen. "If this is a kidnapping I'd better—"

"No!" John cried. "No, please! They'll kill her."

"Shut the door, Bob," Tom said, "and let's find out what this is all about."

"But—"

"This is my godchild we're talking about." There was a sudden sharp edge on Tom's voice. "Shut the goddamn door."

"Yes, sir."

2 "Her toe?" Tom slammed his fist on his desk. His face had gone pasty white. "They sent you her *toe?*"

John nodded. He'd told them the whole story. A disjointed telling, but he didn't think he'd missed anything important.

He glanced up from his seat at Decker, who stood to the side, hands behind his back, impassive, then back to Tom.

"Tom, I'm sorry. I didn't . . . I don't know what I was thinking . . . but I didn't see that I had a choice. . . ."

I've doomed Katie. The thought kept hammering at him. Why couldn't I have let Tom swallow those pills? What kind of a father am I? Snake will find out. And then he'll . . .

"You *didn't* have a choice," Tom said, "but you still couldn't go through with it. Even with poor Katie's life at stake you couldn't. Honestly, John, if positions were reversed, I'd have done the same." He slammed his fist on the desk again. "The soulless *bastards!* I can't believe this has happened." He looked at Decker. "What do we do first, Bob?"

Decker rubbed his jaw, looking uncomfortable. "Well, the first thing I think we need to deal with is the crime that was committed a few moments ago."

"What?"

"An attempt on the life of the President of the United States. That's—"

Tom held up a hand. "Stop right there. As far as I'm concerned, nothing happened."

"I'm sorry, sir, but I'm not permitted to ignore an—"

"Ignore what? Did you see anyone do anything to me, or attempt to do anything to me?"

"I heard his own statement about giving you those pills."

"And you now have my statement that he didn't. And without corroboration from the alleged victim, you don't have a case. So we will drop that subject and move on. What do we do now?"

Decker sighed. "All right, first thing is to call in the FBI. They're the kidnap experts and we'll need access to their crime lab. Next—"

"No!" John said, rising from his chair. "You can't do that. Once I'm exposed, I'm of no use to them. And if I'm of no value, neither is Katie. They'll kill her!"

"We can keep it all under wraps," Decker said. "We'll—"

"No!" John could hear his voice rising but he didn't care. He had to make them see. "They'll *know!* They've got someone inside. Maybe right here in the White House." He turned to Tom. "If they can find out about your chloramphenicol reaction, they can sure as hell find out that I didn't give you those pills and I've told you what's going on! Please! There's got to be another way!"

"He's right, Bob," Tom said. "They must have one hell of an information pipeline. And by the way, any ideas about this 'they' we're talking about?"

"Well, we know it's drugs," Decker said. "They told Dr. VanDuyne flat out they don't want you showing up at The Hague conference. It's probably Colombians, or maybe Mexicans." He rubbed his jaw. "And I think you're right about that high-level leak. They picked up the little girl the morning after your speech."

Tom nodded. "Which means they knew what I was going to say and had the plan in place, ready to go." He swiveled in his chair and spoke toward the windows. "Who is the son of a bitch? I swear, if I ever find out . . ." He swung back. "We'll find him eventually. Question is, what do we do now?"

Decker said, "Let me think."

John watched the Secret Service man wander around the Oval Office, staring at the floor, at his shiny brown wingtips, then at the ceiling. John wished he could come up with his own plan, but his mind was numb, dead, empty.

Finally Decker returned to Tom's desk.

"All right. Here's an idea. It's not perfect, but it's the best I can do on such short notice. Why don't we try a two-tier approach? Only three people know for sure you didn't take those pills. Let's keep it that way. We three will make up that first tier."

"Who's on the second tier?" Tom said.

"A small task force"—he glanced quickly at John—"a *tiny* task force consisting of select members of the Secret Service, the FBI, and the DEA that will—"

"They're going to find out!" John said, feeling close to panic. "As soon as they find out there's a task force, Katie's dead!"

"Not if I limit it strictly to people I've known for a long time, and not if the President himself puts them on special assignment and forbids them to discuss the details with anyone, even their superiors."

"Consider that done," Tom said.

John didn't know what to say. Did Decker know people who were absolutely trustworthy? Was *anyone* absolutely trustworthy? Maybe it could work. *Maybe.* But if it didn't . . .

"But there's one big point you haven't covered," John told Tom. "They're expecting you to get sick. If you don't . . ."

"I think we can cover that," Decker said. He turned to Tom. "But it will involve you admitting yourself to Bethesda Naval Hospital. Your office will say you're in for a check-up but the people behind this will read that as a sign that you're ill."

Tom pressed his fingertips together and leaned back, musing. "Well, Bethesda's got the presidential suite . . . I can conduct business from there for a few days . . . Not a good time for this . . . not a good time at all . . ." He glanced up and his eyes met John's. "But that's what we'll do."

John felt his throat constrict. "Thanks, Tom. You don't know what this—"

"It's Katie. And she's been kidnapped and hurt because of our friendship. That makes me part of this. Don't you worry. We'll get her back."

John leaned back and closed his eyes. He wanted to believe that. He *had* to believe that.

3 Bob Decker saw Dr. VanDuyne out to the elevator, then headed back to the Oval Office.

He had to admit he was pumped up. That had been one goddamn close call in the Oval Office. A catastrophe had been averted, but the Service could take no credit for it. Yet if VanDuyne had let Razor swallow those pills, even though he was Razor's best friend, the Service would have taken all the heat. A no-win situation all around.

But that was past. Razor was safe, the conspiracy had been exposed, now came the fun part: tracking down these sons of bitches.

Maybe not that much fun. The leak bothered the hell out of him. Directly beneath the Oval Office lay W-16, the Secret Service command post. Was the mole among the select one hundred agents on the White House detail who worked out of there? Decker hated to think so, but he had to consider the possibility. Had to be very careful who he brought in on this.

But the first step had been taken. He'd sent VanDuyne home to e-mail the kidnappers that he'd dosed the President with whatever it was that was supposed to kill him—Decker still didn't understand that part—and then he was to return with hard copies of all the e-mail he'd received from the kidnappers . . . plus his daughter's toe and whatever packaging had come with it. Who knew? Maybe they'd get lucky and find a fingerprint or something else to help narrow the search.

He stepped back through the door into the Oval Office. Razor was standing at the windows, gazing out at the morning. He turned as Decker closed the door behind him.

"I want this settled quickly, Bob." His eyes were blazing. "I want these bastards. I want them to resist arrest, and I want the shit kicked out of them. I want them hurt real bad, *real* bad before they're brought in."

Decker had never seen Razor this angry; he realized it was the emotions speaking and figured the best course was simply to agree.

"Yes, sir."

"But I can't emphasize *quickly* enough. I want that little girl returned before The Hague conference."

"We'll do our best, but without a full mobilization—"

Razor nodded. "I understand. You've got one hand tied behind your back. But what's your plan? Who are you bringing in?"

"Well, I figure I can limit the second tier to one each from FBI and DEA. Get them up to speed on everything except the fact that you didn't swallow the pills."

"Why DEA?"

"Because of the drug connection. We'll need some backgrounding on the possible players behind this. I may want to tap into the CIA too—"

"Good God, why?"

"This anonymous remailer in the UK. If we can locate the guy who's running it, we may be able to backtrack from his computer to this Snake character."

"All right. But keep them in the dark as much as possible. What about the tier-two people? Got anybody in mind?"

"Yes, sir. Gerry Canney over at the Bureau. He helped break the Duncan Lathram case, if you remember."

Razor allowed a chagrined smile. "How can I forget?"

"He just got moved up to a supervisory position. He's as straight and sharp as they come. Knows how to keep his mouth shut too."

"Perfect. Who from DEA?"

"I've got a few possibilities there. I was thinking of Dan Keane. He's with the Washington office."

"I know him. Good man."

"Right. I've known him for years and can't think of anybody who knows more about the drug trade and hates the dealers as much as Dan."

"All right. Canney and Keane. Get them. I want to meet with them personally. I want to make it very clear that even though kidnapping is FBI business and drug dealers are DEA, *you* are in charge. I don't want any interagency turf war here. I want them to hear it straight from me before I head for Bethesda."

Decker had to admire Razor's grasp of all the practical problems facing his mini task force. He remembered the infighting between Justice and Treasury back in 1994 when someone took a few pot shots at the White House. The jockeying for control between the Secret Service, FBI, and ATF had been embarrassing.

But with the chief laying out the chain of command at the outset, Decker was sure the operation would run smoothly.

"When are you going in?"

"This afternoon, right after I meet with your team." He lowered his voice. "Get this done, Bob. Get it done by Tuesday. Because no matter what, that's when I'm leaving for The Hague for the international drug conference."

Decker swallowed. He felt as if he'd been punched. "Three days, sir? That's not much time. Can't we—?"

"It's all I can give you. I love John. He's the best friend I'll ever have. And I love his daughter like my own. Hell, I'm her godfather. But I'm also the guy who occupies this office. As President I can't be influenced by terror and blackmail, and I sure as hell won't allow some slimy drug lord to dictate U.S. government policy. I'm leaving for The Hague Tuesday, and I want to step on Air Force One knowing that Katie Van-Duyne is back with her father. Am I making myself clear, Bob?"

"Perfectly, sir."

"Then let's get moving."

Bob Decker's intestines began to wind themselves into slow knots as he left the Oval Office and hurried down to W-16.

Tuesday! How the hell was he going to get this done in three days?

4 *"I've been talking practicalities, but let me get philosophical for a moment. Can we all agree that you own your own body? That seems to me to be the cornerstone of all human rights. If we can agree on that, then where does another person get the right to dictate what substances—food, liquids, whatever—you are allowed to put into your body? This is a completely personal decision on your part. And if one person has no right to so dictate, then neither do two . . . or ten or a hundred or a million or a hundred million. It's still your body. I think taking drugs is very stupid, but I also think it is a human right."*

Paulie turned down the radio volume. Had he just heard the kid giggling in the living room?

He leaned his chair back and edged his head past the jamb of the kitchen door for a peek. Some kind of weird scene in there, what with Poppy in a Minnie Mouse mask and the kid with a fake bandage on her foot, and the two of them playing Chutes and Ladders on the couch.

Paulie had retreated to the kitchen to get out of that damn Mickey Mouse mask he had to wear in front of the kid. Probably wasn't all that necessary, seeing as the kid had already seen him as the limo driver, and he still wore the beard that would come off as soon as this was over, but why risk her getting a better look at him than absolutely necessary?

Poppy glanced up and saw him. "Wanna play?"

He couldn't see her face through the Minnie mask, but something told him she was smiling.

"Nah. Not unless you switch to poker."

"Hey, we might," she said. "We just might do that. We'll let you know."

He grinned and shook his head. Standing up to Mac yesterday had broken the ice between them. They were back to being a team again, and that felt good.

He watched them for a little while longer. Poppy was a different person when she was with that kid. Softer, bouncier, happier than she ever was with him.

So what am I? he thought. Jealous?

Maybe. He wasn't exactly crazy about the idea of sharing Poppy with anyone, even for a week. But how could he be jealous of a little kid? Besides, it was one of those girl things, the way two gals who just met somehow start sharing all these secrets about things one guy would never tell another even if he knew him for a million years.

But this looked like more than that. This seemed to go pretty deep.

Well, whatever it was, it would be over in a week or so when the kid went back to her folks.

And suddenly Paulie had a bad feeling about what that scene might be like.

He waved his arm in the doorway and gave a low whistle. When Poppy looked up, he said, "Can I see you a minute?"

Poppy nodded behind her mask, then turned to the kid. "I'll be right back. You stay here . . . and don't move any of those pieces."

The kid giggled. "I won't."

Poppy stepped into the kitchen and dropped into the seat across the table from him. She pulled off her mask and wiped her face. Her cheeks were flushed with heat.

"Hot in there, ain't it," Paulie said.

She nodded and smiled. "It's worth it. What'd you want to see me about?"

Paulie hesitated, not exactly sure how to say this. "It's about you and the kid."

"She's got a name, you know. You can call her Katie."

"I don't want to call her Katie. I don't want to know anything about her."

"Why not? She's a sweet kid."

"I'm sure she is, Poppy. And you're getting too close to her."

"What do you mean, too close?"

Uh-oh. He could see her back getting up. "I mean—"

"Look, Paulie, she's a scared little girl. This has gotta be like the worst thing that's ever happened to her. I'm trying to make it as pleasant as possible for her while she's here. What's wrong with that?"

"You're getting attached."

"So?"

"*Too* attached. Like you're her mother or something."

"Yeah, well, I don't think she *has* a mother."

"That may be, but you can't start thinking *you* can be her mother. You're gonna have to say good-bye next week, or the week after at the latest."

She leaned back and her gaze shifted down toward the table top. "I know."

"And if you keep on like this, you're gonna be hurting. Bad."

"I'll be okay."

Paulie didn't believe that for a minute. He had visions of Poppy crying and hanging onto the kid and not wanting to let her go, not wanting to leave her alone at the drop-off point. The snatch itself was far and away the diciest part of these gigs, but returning the package wasn't far behind. The last thing you needed was someone going all mushy and emotional at a critical moment.

And on top of all that, he didn't want to see Poppy all torn up when this was over.

"I ain't so sure about that." He reached across and touched her hand. "I'm seeing someone with a broken heart when it comes time to wave bye-bye."

She looked up and smiled. "I'll be all right. I just don't want to see her scared, that's all."

She stood and came around the table. She sat on his lap and kissed him on the mouth.

"That's for worrying about me."

Then she adjusted her Minnie Mouse mask and returned to the living room.

Paulie watched her sit down with the kid and get back to their game. He had a sudden nightmare vision of Poppy doing something crazy after this was over, like finding out where the kid lives and driving by to get a look at her—"just to see how she's doing . . . make sure she's all right. . . ."

Paulie shuddered at the thought. That was death-wish behavior.

And on the subject of death wishes, what if Mac walked in now? What if he popped through the door and saw his "package" unwrapped and playing a board game in the living room? He'd hit the ceiling.

And if he ever found out the kid still had ten toes?

Forget about it.

Paulie had stood his ground yesterday, but he wondered how he'd do if Mac went berserk. Which was just what he'd do if he knew the chances they'd took to get some other kid's toe to use as the persuader.

If he ever does find out, Paulie thought uneasily, let's just hope it's long after this gig is over and done with.

5 Snake glanced around the lobby of the Sheraton. No one around with a line of sight to his laptop. He reread VanDuyne's latest e-mail.

It's done. Two capsules of chloramphenicol (250mg each) administered at 10 this morning. I've done my part. When do I get Katie back?

Administered, ay? How professional sounding.

And: *When do I get Katie back?* Never, dude.

But he couldn't tell VanDuyne that. Mac checked around again, still nobody near, so he pulled up his prewritten reply and made a few changes, but all in all, he'd been pretty much on the mark as to what he'd have to say.

We've been over this before, but I guess you weren't listening. So here it is again. How soon you get your kid back depends on how sick your buddy gets. The sicker, the better. If he's back on his feet in a couple of days, you'll have to do something else. In no case will your kid be released in less than two weeks.

Let me lay this out for you so there's no misunderstanding: We want this guy out of office. If we can't get that, we want him sick for a long time. If that doesn't work out, at the very least we want him to miss the drug summit. Simply put, if your pal makes it to the drug summit, you'll never see the rest of your kid again.

Snake smiled. He especially liked the part that went, *the rest of your kid*. That was driving the nail home.

He uploaded it through the Eric Garter account to the remailer, then logged off. He unplugged and dialed up Salinas.

"Hello." Gold's voice.

Snake didn't feel like speaking to Salinas, so why not let Gold play messenger boy.

"Tell your boss the deed is done as of ten this morning. Now we wait."

He hung up and smiled. That felt good. He wanted to keep reminding Salinas that he wasn't in complete control. Snake was not a hireling at his beck and call. Snake was an independent contractor.

He felt the slim rectangle of the audio cassette in his jacket pocket that he'd made a point of keeping on him at all times. That little baby was what was going to help him remain independent—and on the right side of the grass.

He walked out to the front of the hotel and watched the midday traffic on Connecticut Avenue. Light for a sunny Saturday. All the good suburbanites were probably home tending their gardens and fertilizing their lawns.

So what do I do with the rest of the day? he wondered. Maybe take a cruise over to Falls Church, ostensibly to check on the package, but mainly to lean on Paulie a little. Because Paulie *was* a hireling . . . and he'd begun acting like an independent contractor. Snake was still pissed about yesterday. The goddamn nerve—telling him there'd be no more persuaders from this package. Who the hell did he think he was?

Well . . . Snake had his pistol locked away in the Jeep. This might be a good time to wave it under Paulie's nose. No shooting, no overt threats, just let them see it stuck in his belt, let them know it was there, loaded and ready.

Time to reestablish the pecking order.

Not that it would have any practical value in the long run—seeing as how Paulie and his babe didn't *have* a long run—but simply as a matter of principle.

Marnie sat in her rented car and watched John's house through the windshield. Yes, she was stiff and uncomfortable from the long vigil, but it would all be worth it to see her Katie again.

Where is my daughter, John?

She was puzzled. She'd watched the house all yesterday afternoon and hadn't seen Katie come home from school. John must have sneaked her inside somehow. And no doubt Katie had been a willing participant in that sneaking. Always plotting, those two, always keeping secrets and not letting her in on them.

You don't deserve her, John. I have more right to her than you. *You* didn't carry her inside you through nine months of sickness and bulging discomfort. *You* didn't go through hours of screaming agony to deliver her into this world. *You* weren't left with extra pounds and ugly red stretch marks. *You* didn't have to stay home with her day after day and listen to her incessant crying.

She's mine. I *earned* her. You've no right to keep her from me.

And if it weren't for your crackpot "medical expert" cronies and that pet judge, Katie would be with me. Where she should be.

You aren't good for her, John. Always too easy on her. You can destroy a child with leniency. She needs me, John—now more than ever. I know you've probably turned Katie completely against me, but I can change that. All I need is—

She ducked as she saw John's car coming down the street. This was his second trip out today. Where had he gone? To see Katie? To bring her home?

Cautiously she raised her head and watched him pull into the driveway.

7   John spotted the car as he was heading into the house. A brand new white Taurus. He thought he'd seen it parked near the corner when he left to bring Katie's toe down to Bob Decker at the White House—a surreal trip, riding through downtown D.C. traffic with his daughter's little toe packed in ice in the six-pack cooler next to him on the front seat. But he was almost beyond reacting at this point.

Now he thought he saw the same white Taurus parked across the street. And at least one person in it. Maybe two. FBI? Secret Service? Or one of the kidnappers?

Better not to know.

Nana was waiting for him when he stepped inside. She stood in the hall in a tartan robe—Dad's old robe—looking older and more disheveled than he'd ever seen her, with her fingertips pulling at her throat . . . pulling at her throat. . . .

"Has there been any word?" she said.

John had debated whether or not to let her in on the fact that federal agencies were getting involved. He'd finally decided that she'd only worry more about the kidnappers' threats against Katie if the feds were brought in. So, for the time being, he'd stick to the ransom story.

"None yet, but I think I can have the money together by late this afternoon."

"Oh, thank God! And then Katie will be coming home?"

"Soon after I deliver it. Or so I hope. I've been following their instructions to the letter, but they haven't told me yet what to do with the money once I get it."

"So much money," she said, her fingers digging deeper. "How will you ever pay it back?"

He shrugged and said what he would have said if the kidnappers really had wanted only money. "I'm not going to worry about that right now. I'll have plenty of time to figure that out after we get Katie back."

"Yes, yes," she said. "Getting Katie back. That is what we must worry about."

"Why don't you try some of your yoga," he said. "Maybe it will relax you."

She shook her head. "No . . . no yoga. I can't do yoga with Katie gone."

As she turned and shuffled toward the kitchen, John stepped into the living room and sneaked a peek through one of the front windows.

The white Taurus still sat across the street.

And suddenly he had to see who was in it. Not to speak to them, not to confront them or get their names . . . just to look.

He hurried through the kitchen, past his mother with her cup of coffee, and out the rear door. He cut through a neighboring backyard, then dashed into the front and across the tree-lined street.

There . . . he now was on the same side as the Taurus. He began walking toward it, approaching from the rear. As he neared he saw the National sticker on the bumper. A rental.

Closer now . . . coming abreast of the rear door . . . the front door— passenger seat's empty—now by the hood . . . a quick glance over the shoulder to see—

"Marnie!"

Fury took him then. She could ruin everything! He ran around to the driver's door and yanked it open. It took all his control to keep from dragging her out of the car and throttling her.

"What the hell are you *doing* here?"

She cowered back, her hand to her mouth. "John! I—"

"What? Tell me! What do you think you're going to accomplish sitting out here?"

"John . . . you're out of control."

He wanted to say, *You should know—you wrote the book on out of control,* but he bit it back. She was right. His whole *life* was out of control. He stepped back, took a deep breath.

"Go away."

"I want to see my daughter. You won't let me talk to her, so I thought if I waited here I might at least get a glimpse of her."

"She's not your daughter anymore."

"She'll *always* be my daughter! And I want to know what you've done with her?"

"Done with her? What are you—?"

"She didn't come home from school yesterday. I was watching."

"Oh, no!" What was he going to do with this woman? She was going to ruin everything.

"Oh, *yes!* Where are you hiding her? What have you done with my daughter?"

John couldn't answer that, couldn't come up with another lie to cover everything. He stared at her for a few heartbeats, then went on the offensive.

"You're stalking her, aren't you," he said.

Marnie's eyes widened. "What?"

"I should have guessed you'd do something like this. You're going to try to kidnap her." He pulled a pen and a slip of note paper from his breast pocket. "Well, you won't get away with it."

He walked to the rear of the car and began writing. Marnie leaned out the open door and stared at him.

"What do you think you're doing?"

"I'm going to call the FBI and give them this license plate number. I'm going to tell them that not only have you violated a standing court order to stay away from your daughter, but you've crossed state lines to stalk her and kidnap her. That makes it a federal matter."

"You're bluffing."

"Why should I bluff? The court order is real; I've got witnesses that you've been lurking out here. And then all the Dr. Schuylers in the world won't be able to keep you out of the slammer."

Her mouth twisted into a snarl. "You son of a bitch!"

She slammed the door, started the car, and roared off.

John looked down at his note paper. Why not do as he'd threatened? Give the number to Decker and maybe let him get the FBI on her. Scare her away. The situation was at a delicate juncture. The last thing they needed was a loose cannon like Marnie blundering into the middle of everything and maybe getting Katie killed.

She'd already damn near killed Katie once. She wasn't going to get a second chance.

But even if Katie were safely inside with Nana, Marnie would still be a menace. What the hell was she doing roaming around D.C. in the first place?

John jammed the paper into his pocket and hurried inside. He knew just the man to answer that question. Dr. William Schuyler of Marietta, Georgia. It might be Saturday, and Schuyler might have the weekend off, but John had his home phone number.

He crept up to his study, closed the door, found the number, and dialed.

Schuyler's wife answered. John mumbled his name as Dr. So-and-so and said he had to speak to "Bill" right away. He sat there, seething, grinding his teeth. William Schuyler, M.D., Ph.D., a pompous ass who thought he had the magic touch. No one was so deranged that he or she would not respond to Dr. Schuyler's unique ministrations.

"Hello?"

"This is John VanDuyne."

"Oh."

"Yes. 'Oh.' Want to know who's been skulking around my neighborhood?"

"Oh, come now, John. 'Skulking' is such a loaded term."

The mellifluous tone, the precise diction, the haughty demeanor. It all came back to John in a flash, the sight of him sitting in the witness chair, bald head gleaming in the overhead lights, pudgy hands resting on his ample abdomen as he spewed his inexhaustible stream of psycho-babble until the courtroom was awash in empty, self-serving opinions that sounded for all the world like facts.

"You think 'skulking' is loaded? How about *stalking*? That's right. She's stalking Katie. And she says you said it was all right."

"That is absurd, John, and you know it. I did tell her, however, that I think she's recovered to the point where supervised visits might be equally beneficial to both mother and child. Now, if she's misinterpreted that to mean—"

"Always have your ass covered, don't you. But this time you're out on a limb. You had no right to say that to a deranged patient. You—"

"'Deranged' is such a—"

"Keep quiet and listen! You know the terms of the deal. No criminal prosecution if I got sole custody of Katie and Marnie stayed in intense psychotherapy for ten years. That was the deal. There were no maybes. She doesn't get near Katie for ten years."

"But that's so unreasonable."

"And damn near killing her daughter *isn't?* You know her history almost as well as I do. She damn near stove in Katie's skull with that fireplace poker. She's hated Katie since the day she was born. I—"

"'Hate' is such a vague—"

"Shut up, dammit! I don't know why she hates her and neither do you. We may never know. I don't care to know. All I care about is Katie. And if anything happens to my little girl because of your negligence, you will pay, Schuyler."

"If you think you can sue me—"

"Sue?" John heard himself laugh and it was an awful sound. "Oh, no, Schuyler. You won't pay with your money, or even your license. You'll pay the way Katie pays. Because anything—*anything*—that happens to her will happen to you. Double. Got that? *Got* that?"

Amazing. William Schuyler, M.D., Ph.D., was speechless.

John hung up and stared out the window at the tree branches. He'd meant every word he'd just said. Somehow, sometime, somewhere in the past twenty-four hours he'd decided to devote the rest of his life to finding the people who had amputated Katie's toe. He had fantasies of the feds being baffled but the relentless John VanDuyne somehow tracking them down . . . and cornering them . . . and then wading in with a chainsaw.

And now he'd add the esteemed Dr. Schuyler to the list. If Katie came to more harm because of Marnie, he'd see to it that Schuyler experienced it all first hand.

John folded his arms on his desk and rested his head atop them. He made a sound halfway between a laugh and a sob.

Marnie's not the only one who needs a psychiatrist.

8 "What I want to know is why this lunatic is still running around loose?"

Bob Decker looked up from his notes. Dan Keane of DEA was doing the asking; trim, silver haired, in his mid-fifties, his usually florid complexion had grown progressively paler since Bob began explaining why they were here. He sat between blond, handsome Gerry Canney of the FBI and balding, red-headed Jim Lewis from CIA.

"A number of reasons," Bob said. "The primary one being that the President wants it that way. You heard it from the Man himself just a few minutes ago."

He was still amazed that he'd been able to assemble this mini task force so quickly. Wonderful what could be accomplished when you had the full authority of the Executive Office behind you.

The four of them were crammed into a corner office in W-16. Bob had drawn the shades, locked the door, and stationed two uniformed agents in the hall with orders not to let anyone within ten feet of the door.

He'd briefed his team on the situation, describing everything pretty much as it had gone down. He'd diverged from fact only when he'd told them that Razor had swallowed the pills, and that VanDuyne, overcome by guilt, had confessed. Since it had been too late to pump Razor's stomach—Bob didn't know if that was true but expected them to buy it—the President was admitting himself to Bethesda for observation.

Bob didn't think it was necessary to con these men; he knew them all and would trust each of them with his life. But Razor wanted it this way, so that was how it was going to be.

"The other reasons," Bob added, "are that VanDuyne is the link to whoever's behind this. We need him out there, trading messages with these guys. And the third is that we're trying to save a little girl's life. Katie VanDuyne is Razor's godchild and he wants the rest of her back alive and in one piece."

Bob viewed the last objective as of secondary importance; his primary concern was protecting Razor from any more attempts on his life.

"The rest of her?" Canney said.

Bob turned and put the cooler on the desk. "Yeah. The kidnappers sent her little toe to her father to convince him they meant business. It's in here."

Canney winced. The grimace emphasized the fine scars left after a car accident half a dozen years ago; Gerry survived, his wife didn't. Bob knew he had a daughter somewhere around Katie VanDuyne's age.

"Oh, God," Keane whispered. He suddenly looked pale and sweaty. Bob knew he had grandchildren; probably imagining one of them in a similar situation.

Only Jim Lewis seemed unaffected. But then, nothing seemed to affect Lewis.

"I'll get this into the lab ASAP," Canney said. "But what do I say about it? I've got to attribute it to a specific case."

"I'll have the case number before you leave. Razor's talking to your director right now."

"What do you need from my people?" Jim Lewis said.

"That anonymous remailer in the U.K." Bob handed him a manila folder. "These are printouts of all his e-mail to VanDuyne. You find that remailer, find out who 'Snake' is, and this case will be on the home stretch."

"Snake?" Canney said. "Did you say Snake?"

"Sound familiar?"

"Yeah. I've heard that name before . . . connected to a couple of kidnappings . . . I think I heard of one where he sent a finger when things weren't moving fast enough to suit him."

"Got to be the same guy." Bob clapped his hands and rubbed them together. This was great. The team hadn't been together half an hour and already they were rolling. "Okay. Pull your file on him and we'll—"

"Sorry. No file. The information's been tangential—you know, the kind of stuff you pick up when you're looking for something else. We don't know diddly about the guy except that he seems to specialize in snatching the kind of people who won't holler for a cop."

"So we're dealing with an experienced team," Bob said.

Not good news. It meant this guy Snake had probably perfected his technique before snatching the VanDuyne girl. He turned to Keane.

"We figure this has got to be drug related, Dan. Who's most likely to be behind it?"

"Hmm?" Keane seemed mesmerized by the cooler. Bob wondered what was bugging him. He repeated the question.

"I can only guess," Keane said slowly, as if choosing his words carefully. "The Cali cartel—and that pretty much means Emilio Rojas these days—has the most money, but the Mexican traffickers have the most Stateside contacts now. Could be Rojas working through the Mexicans, or the Mexicans acting on their own."

Bob hid his annoyance. He'd hoped for a little more in-depth analysis from the assistant director of the DEA.

"What's your best guess?"

"Best guess? I'd say Mexicans. Kidnapping is an art form in Colombia; they'd bring in their own people. But I can see the Mexicans hiring local talent. We keep tabs on Carillo, Garcia, Esparragosa, and the other big shots. I'll run a check and see if any of them have been crossing the border lately."

That was better. "Good. All right. We all know what we have to do. Don't waste any time. This is top priority." He wished he could tell them they only had till Tuesday, but only he and Razor knew that. "I say we meet back here at six P.M.—sooner if something breaks." As they began to rise, Bob said. "I know I don't need to repeat what the President said when you all first got here, but I will anyway. Nothing said here goes beyond these walls. Doesn't matter who asks, whether it's the director of your agency or a senator or a cabinet member, you say nothing. Razor has signed an executive order to that effect, so you're off the hook. It's not that you don't *want* to discuss it, you are *forbidden* to discuss it. And I want to know immediately the name of anyone who presses you about it."

Dan Keane was the first out—seemed in a big hurry to leave— followed by Jim Lewis. Gerry Canney hung back, the cooler dangling in his hand.

"Thanks for calling me in, Bob. I appreciate the confidence."

Bob smiled and thought of the close call they'd had with a certain Dr. Lathram a few years back. "Not the first time we've worked together on a plot against a president. Except you may never get a chance to talk about this one."

Canney shrugged. "I'll save it for my memoirs. But more than anything I want to get that little girl back alive."

"Thinking of Martha?" Bob said.

"How can I not? Katie VanDuyne is only a couple of years younger." He glanced down at the cooler. "I don't know what I'd do if someone ever . . ." He shuddered.

"I know," Bob said. His own boys were teenagers, but it seemed only yesterday that they'd been small and so much more vulnerable.

When Canney was gone, Bob sat down and began making notes and organizing his information. He couldn't have a secretary in on this, so he had to do it himself.

Not a bad start. Dan Keane tracking from the drug lords toward Snake. Jim Lewis tracking from the anonymous remailer toward Snake. Gerry Canney tracking from Katie VanDuyne's toe toward Snake.

Snake, my man, whoever you are, wherever you are, you're the key.

And you're in deep shit. Because we're going to find you. And when we find you, we squeeze you. We squeeze you like no one's ever been squeezed before. We squeeze until you cough up who you're working for. And then we find them and squeeze again. And pretty soon we get to the guy who started it all.

By Tuesday, please God.

9   After a quick stop at his office to pick up his briefcase, Dan Keane hurried along Sixth Street toward the Mall. The chances of his running into someone he knew downtown on a Saturday were slim to none, but he kept watch, kept glancing around, unable to escape the feeling that someone was following him.

Just paranoia, he knew. And well deserved. The plan was unraveling before his eyes. The weak link had always been VanDuyne, and he'd broken.

But not before dosing Winston with that antibiotic, thank God. That was all that mattered: taking Winston out.

And making sure nothing linked the plot to the drug cartels. Because if that was ever established, it would advance the decriminalization cause— precisely the opposite effect Dan wanted.

Dan was in the clear, at least. Nothing to link him to VanDuyne, the kidnappers, or Salinas.

And to lessen the possibility of linking Salinas to the plot, the whole kidnap apparatus had to be immediately dismantled and its components scattered.

But what about the child? What happened to her?

He tried not to think about that little girl. Yes, she had a name, but he kept it far to the rear of his thoughts, kept telling himself she'd be all right, but already he knew she was anything but.

Great God in heaven, what sort of monster can carve a toe off a child?

Dan knew exactly what kind. And this was simply further proof that these slimy bastards had to be eliminated—not by legalizing their filthy trade, but by hunting them down, rounding them up, locking them away from decent society and throwing away the key.

Dan knew his particular monster's name. He was going to speak to him today. Now.

The little girl would be all right. But even if she weren't—

He couldn't believe he was actually thinking this, but even if she weren't all right, even if it worked out that she never made it back to her home, she was only one life. If she was the means that put an end to Winston and his decriminalization plans, her single life would be spent to save countless others.

Keep thinking about the big picture, he told himself. Don't let the minutiae swallow you up. What was one little life weighed against the unraveling of the moral fiber of an entire nation?

One little life . . .

He spotted a phone near the Air and Space Museum and stepped up to it. He removed the battery-operated voice distorter from his briefcase and glanced around. No one nearby. He attached the mechanism to the mouthpiece, dropped a quarter in the slot, and dialed. He had no doubt Salinas was recording these calls, and doing his damnedest to trace them. Good luck. Dan used a different phone every time, and in the highly unlikely event that the tapes ever got to court, the distorter would confound any attempt at voiceprint analysis.

When someone on the other end answered, Dan said, "Put Salinas on."

The first few times he'd called there'd been some argument about calling him back. Dan had always refused. Those days were gone. Now when they heard his distorted voice, they put him right through.

"Yes?" he heard Salinas say. "Who's calling?"

He pictured the fat slob sitting in a chair or on a sofa, his belly drooping between his spread thighs. *When was the last time you saw your dick, pig?* Dear God, he hated his type. That was why he'd joined DEA—to rid the earth of them.

But Salinas was no dummy. Dan had to hand him that. He, too, assumed the calls were being recorded, so he always played dumb. No one was going to entrap Carlos Salinas.

And so they began their verbal dance.

"You know damn well who it is," Dan said.

"Sorry, I don't recognize the voice. Must be a bad connection."

"Right. The worst ever. Here's what you need to know: The target is being admitted to the hospital later today."

"That is too bad for Mr. Target, but I don't believe I know him."

"Maybe you know his doctor. Shortly after treating the target, the doctor confessed to his mistake. A number of agencies are involved in trying to unravel the matter."

A long pause on the other end. Dan was sure this was the last thing Salinas wanted to hear.

"But Mr. Target is sick?"

"Not yet, but he expects to be. The doctor, obviously, is of no further use, therefore the apparatus you assembled to put pressure on him must be dismantled immediately, and his valuables returned to him."

"Valuables?"

"Yes. The valuable thing you took from him."

"No," Salinas said. "I do not think that will happen. You see, he did not fulfill the terms of the arrangement, therefore he cannot expect the return of his possession. Besides, it is more . . . how do I say? . . . discreet if the possession is never seen again."

Dan closed his eyes and repeated his mantra: *The big picture . . . forget the details . . . always look at the big picture. . . .*

He swallowed. "Will you be as thorough regarding the other components of the apparatus?"

"Of course. It is a small apparatus. No one will miss the parts."

"No one must connect you or your business with it."

"There will be no trace. How can I be connected with something that never existed?"

How indeed?

Dan hung up and retched.

. . . forget the details . . . always look at the big picture. . . .

How the hell did he get himself involved in this?

He had to ask himself how many people at DEA hated Winston and his plan. Easy answer: Everyone. How else do you react to someone who has condemned your career, your life's work to extinction?

But how many had considered conspiring with the enemy to put a stop to Winston? Maybe a few. But he knew of only one with the guts, only one who cared enough about his duty and his country to follow through with it.

Daniel J. Keane.

But were his reasons so purely idealistic? He wanted to think so, but in his most honest moments, at 3:00 A.M. when he found himself wide awake and staring at the clock, his mind taunted him, whispering that he was motivated not so much by principle as by self-preservation.

He'd devoted most of his working life to the DEA. And now that he was finally in line to be administrator, Winston was planning to render the agency obsolete, and Dan's entire career irrelevant. The DEA might continue to exist, but only as a shell, a vestigial organ, of as much consequence as the human appendix.

Had he made a deal with the Devil merely to salvage his career? No. He couldn't accept that. He was better than that.

But then another question would arise: When you join forces with the enemy, don't you *become* the enemy?

But he hadn't *joined* the enemy, he was only *using* the enemy. He had a noble goal.

A goal so noble and lofty that he'd allow a child to die so that he could achieve it?

"I'll make up for it," he said softly. "I swear on the lives of my children and grandchildren that as soon as this is over, I will devote every waking moment of the rest of my life to hunting down Carlos Salinas and his kin and putting them away."

No doubt Salinas thought he had an ally high up in the government. He was wrong. Very wrong.

10

Carlos slammed down the handset and signaled to Llosa to turn off the tape recorder.

"Our contact has hung up. I believe I upset him. Did we get a good recording?"

Llosa pulled off his headphones and gave a thumbs up.

"Excellent. Now get hold of that *pendejo*, MacLaglen. Tell him I must speak to him immediately."

As Llosa crossed the room to the secure phone, Carlos leaned back and closed his eyes.

Mierda! This was what he had feared. MacLaglen had not frightened the doctor enough. The *federales* were now involved. Which meant it was time for a quick cleanup. Get rid of the child and MacLaglen's two helpers—kill them, bury their bodies deep where no one will ever find them. Carlos knew where a new parking lot was being paved in Alexandria. A perfect spot for disposal.

He wished he could include MacLaglen in the paved grave as originally planned, but the *cabrón* had outmaneuvered him.

He sighed. Ah well, not so bad. MacLaglen was a professional. He was a good risk.

And he'd pushed the doctor far enough to get the chloramphenicol into Thomas Winston. That was what mattered. The President was entering the hospital. When that news reached home, Emilio Rojas would be pleased.

Now Carlos had to hope the medicine would do its work. Whatever happened, it was out of his hands. The doctor's confession only meant that the cleanup would begin earlier than anticipated. This was no problem.

Llosa finished speaking into the phone and turned to face him. He spoke in Spanish. "I paged him and left a message on his voice mail. He should be getting back to us any minute."

"You told him to call back immediately?"

"Just as you directed."

"Very good. Follow the usual routine when he calls."

Llosa nodded and left.

And Carlos sat and wondered: Did the doctor really believe that we would not find out about him? Did he realize that he had ended his daughter's life when he confessed? What a reckless, foolish man.

11 Poppy sweated behind her Minnie Mouse mask, doing some curls with her dumbbells in the front room while Katie watched cartoons. When she heard a car door slam out front, she glanced out the window. Her heart suddenly twisted in her chest, then took off like she'd just snorted a gram of crank.

"Oh sweet Jesus! It's Mac!"

She heard a kitchen chair fall over as Paulie bolted into the room.

"What? Where?"

Panic chased her to the center of the room. "Outside! He's coming in!"

"Shit!" He pointed to Katie. "Get her out of here! I'll clean this up! *Move!*"

Poppy grabbed Katie under the arms, lifted her, and rushed her toward the guest room.

"What's wrong?" Katie said. "Why are you so scared?"

Poppy placed her on the bed and shut the guest-room door.

"It's our boss. We can't let him know that we let you walk around without your blindfold."

"Why not? I only—"

Poppy placed a finger over Katie's lips and lowered her voice to a whisper. "Shhh. Boss's rules. You gotta be real quiet while he's here. Quiet like a mouse. Okay?"

She stared at Poppy and matched her whisper. "Okay."

"Great."

Poppy hid those big blues behind the blindfold. Her shaky fingers fumbled the knot a couple of times, but finally she got it good and snug around Katie's head.

"Okay." She pulled off her Minnie Mouse mask. "Now lie back and let me tie up your arms."

Katie's lip pushed out and she sobbed. "I don't wanna be tied up."

Oh, Jesus, Katie, Poppy thought, biting her own lip. Don't give me a hard time now. Not with Mac about to come through the door.

"Shhh! Please, Katie, you gotta be quiet. Remember how I said you had to be quiet like a mouse? Well, you gotta be tied up too. Boss's rules. And he don't like his rules broken."

Katie sobbed again and her voice got louder. "But it *hurts!*"

And that was when she heard the front door open, and heard Mac's voice. She couldn't catch the words, but it was him.

Oh, Jesus, don't let him come in here yet. Just give me another half a minute.

"Okay, okay. I'll tie you real loose, okay? It won't hurt, I promise you, but you gotta *look* like you're tied up, see? Boss's rules, remember? You don't want to get me in trouble, do you?"

She shook her head. "No . . ."

"Okay, then. Quick now. Lie back and let me do what I gotta do, and I promise you, it won't hurt."

Katie sniffled a little, but stretched herself out on the bed and put her hands out to be tied.

"You're a good little soldier," Poppy whispered.

But now her bad case of fumble fingers had got even worse. She could barely hold the cord, but somehow she got it twisted into things that looked like knots.

"Okay. You're tied. Do they hurt?"

Katie shook her head.

"Great. Now I'll just—"

Poppy glanced at Katie's feet. Her heart had been racing since she spotted Mac's Jeep outside, but now it kicked up to light speed. Katie's left foot was in a little white sock, but the right one was . . .

. . . bare!

"Jesus, where's your bandage?"

Katie wiggled her five exposed toes. "I guess it fell off."

No! This couldn't be happening! Not with Mac just a dozen feet away!

Frantic, she checked the floor, checked in the covers, but no bandage. And Mac could be popping in here any moment.

"Okay, look," she said. "I'll just pull the covers over your bottom half. Don't kick them off. Even if it gets a little warm, keep your legs under the covers. Got that?"

Katie nodded.

"Good girl," Poppy said. She leaned over and kissed Katie's forehead above the blindfold. "Soon as the boss goes, we'll play another game of Chutes and Ladders. Okay?"

Katie smiled. "'Kay."

Poppy adjusted the covers, backed away for a last look. Everything seemed to be in place. All right. One last look at Katie . . . and it was time to face Mac the Monster.

She stepped out into the front room and closed the door behind her. She saw Paulie standing by the couch, and Mac wandering around the room, casually twirling his key ring on his finger. He wore jeans and an open Orioles baseball jacket. She could smell the tension.

Mac stopped wandering and smiled at her, but only with his lips. "Tending to our little asset?"

Poppy nodded. "Just put her . . . " Her mouth was so dry she had to clear her throat. "Just put her down for a nap."

"Good. I knew you'd come in handy on this job. A nice little mother hen for the package."

Poppy stole a few glances at the room. Looked like Paulie had done a good job cleaning things up. The Chutes and Ladders board and pieces were gone, as was his Mickey Mouse mask. He never picked up after himself. She never thought he could. She'd have to remind him of this sometime. Where had he stuffed all the stuff? Under the couch?

"Your boyfriend was just telling me that he hopes there's no hard feelings about our little contretemps yesterday."

Contra-what? What was Mac talking about? He had a funny look in his eyes. Was he looking to start a fight?

"We don't want no hard feelings with nobody," Poppy said. "We just want this thing over and done with."

She was going to say more but something white by the rear leg of the coffee table caught her eye. It lay between her two dumbbells. She didn't want to lean closer so she had to focus out of the corner of her eye. Something white with a little bit of red . . .

Oh, Jesus, the bandage! Katie's foot bandage! If Mac saw it he'd start asking questions, maybe want to see Katie's foot! Oh, Jesus, oh, Christ, oh, Mother of God, she couldn't let Mac spot it!

"I'm sure you do," Mac told her. He turned to Paulie. "But am I to take that as an apology?"

Poppy edged closer to the coffee table. If she could get herself between Mac and the bandage . . .

Paulie shrugged. "If you want. All I'm saying is you're the boss, you're calling the shots, but we got our limits."

She watched Mac shrug out of his Orioles jacket and toss it onto a chair. He tried to make it look casual, but as soon as Poppy saw the dark-brown pistol handle jutting from the little leather holster next to the beeper on his belt, she knew he wasn't being casual.

What's Mac up to? she wondered. Trying to scare us? I'm already plenty scared.

She saw that Paulie had noticed it too. Don't mention it, Paulie, she told him, wishing he could read her mind. Don't give him the satisfaction.

She edge closer to the bandage. More important now than ever to keep him from seeing it.

Mac said, "Let me get this straight: You're saying I'm the boss, but only up to a certain point. After that, *you're* the boss?"

"No, Mac," Paulie said, his voice easy. "It don't mean that at all. It means you hired me, you didn't buy me."

Mac stared at him, like he was thinking about what Paulie had said. Poppy used the lull to make it the rest of the way to the coffee table. The bandage was right near her foot. She wished she could simply step on it and keep it under her sneaker, but it was on the other side of the stretcher. All right, she'd just stay here and block it from Mac.

But then Mac started wandering around the room again. Cold dread seeped through Poppy. He was going to spot it, she just knew it.

"I think you've got a point there, Paulie," Mac was saying. "And maybe it's a good one."

Jesus, he was moving her way. He couldn't miss it.

Quickly Poppy put her right foot up on the coffee table and began fooling with her sneaker lace, like it was loose and she needed to retie it. Mac was about five feet away. With her heart thumping, she undid the knot, made a loud, "Tsk," then turned, sat on the edge of the table, and bent over to retie the sneaker. While her hands were down near the floor, she snatched the bandage and balled it up in her fist.

Got it!

"What's that?" Mac asked. He'd stopped twirling his key ring and was staring at her.

She glanced up at him, then at her hand.

"Hmmm?" What could she *say?* "Oh, just a tissue."

Mac looked like he was going to say something else when his beeper went off. As he angled it up to read the message, Poppy sniffed, made a quick swipe at her nose, then stuffed the gauze in her pocket. And held her breath.

Mac pressed a button and released the beeper. "'Immediately' might take a little while," he muttered, then began wandering again.

"Yeah, Paulie," he said, talking slow, like he didn't really have a point, like he was just killing time, "but a guy hires on to do a job, don't you think he should do that job?"

"Absolutely," Paulie said. "Take me and Poppy, for instance. We hired on to baby-sit. And that's cool. That's the job and that's what we do, and do it good. But we didn't hire on to slice and dice a kid. That wasn't in the job description, so to speak."

Poppy was barely listening. She just sat there, feeling weak, breathing deep while her muscles relaxed and her heartbeat wound down to a normal rate.

They were okay now. Long as Mac didn't go in there and check Katie's feet, they were home free.

And then she heard a click and looked up and thought her slowing heart was going to stop dead because there was Katie standing in the doorway to the guest room with no cords and no blindfold and no sock on her right foot.

Fighting through her panic, Poppy snapped around and saw that Mac had his back turned. But Paulie was facing this way and he looked like he'd just swallowed a couple of feet of razor wire. Poppy coiled to make a sprint for the door, to tackle Katie and carry her back into her room—

But then Katie spoke.

"I have to go to the bathroom."

Mac whirled and time seemed to stop, like the projector of her life's movie got stuck and all action screeched to a halt. All the air seemed to get sucked out of the room but that didn't matter because no one was breathing.

Her life became a photograph.

But only for a single, long, agonized instant. And then it all returned to horrific life.

Mac's eyes bulged and his face turned a dark, furious red as he gaped at Katie.

"What the fuck? She's . . . she's . . . !" He couldn't seem to believe what he was seeing. And then his eyes widened even further as he pointed to her bare foot. "Her toes! How come she's got all her fucking *toes?*"

"Hey, Mac," Paulie said. "It's not like you think."

But Mac was pulling the pistol from his belt. He thumbed back the hammer and aimed at Katie.

Poppy couldn't move. She seemed to be stuck to the table, the floor. But she could scream.

"Mac, no! Jesus, *NO!*"

Whether Mac heard her or not, she couldn't say. Maybe he was afraid of the noise a shot would make, and the attention it would attract. Whatever, he jammed the gun back into his belt, thank God.

"Goddamn!" he shouted and started looking around for something— what, Poppy couldn't guess. He kept saying it over and over. "Goddamn!"

"Easy, Mac," Paulie was saying.

"God*damn!*"

Mac couldn't seem to find what he was looking for in the living room so he stalked into the kitchen.

Finally Poppy could move. Paulie was looking in her direction with a stricken expression, motioning her to get Katie out of sight, but Poppy was already on her way. She was just dragging Katie back when Mac reappeared. His face was back to normal color but had lost all expression, and his eyes . . . his eyes were flat and cold, like everything human had gone out of them. He gripped something long and slim in his right hand. Sunlight flashed off its steely surface as he passed the window.

Oh, sweet Jesus, a knife—the big, foot-long Ginsu knife she'd seen in the utensil drawer.

Poppy whimpered as she pulled Katie close against her and cowered back into the room. Oh, no, he couldn't . . . he wasn't going to try and cut her toe off now, was he? This couldn't be happening.

"Paulie!" she cried. "Paulie, he's got a knife!"

But Paulie was way ahead of her. He stepped in front of the door and put his hands out.

"Stop right there, Mac. Don't do anything crazy now. It's not like it looks."

Mac slowed but didn't stop. "It's not?" he said in a voice as cold as his eyes.

"We sent the persuader just like you told us," Paulie said, rattling out the words like a machine gun. "A little kid's toe. Only it just wasn't this kid's toe. And it worked, didn't it? I mean, you said yourself the guy was ready to do anything after he opened that envelope. So there's no harm done. Everything worked out okay, right? So what's the point in cutting off her toe now? What's that gonna get you?"

Finally Mac stopped. He stared at Paulie with this look of complete disgust. "You fucking idiot. What the fuck do I care about her toe now. She *saw* me! She's seen us *all!*"

The words were spikes through Poppy's heart.

He's gonna kill her! He's gonna kill my little Katie!

"It'll be okay," Paulie said.

"Damn right it will," Mac said, starting to move again. "Just as soon as I'm finished with her."

He tried to get past but Paulie blocked his way.

"Hey, Mac. You can't be serious. You're not gonna off a little girl!"

"Out of the way, Paulie! I'm not getting sent up because some little brat can point the finger at me."

Paulie shoved him back. "Time out, Mac. You're not thinking."

Mac went wild then. His lips drew back from his teeth and he slashed with the knife.

Poppy screamed. "Paulie, look out!"

Paulie jumped back, holding his arm. His hand came away wet and red.

"You son of a bitch! You cut me!"

Poppy knew that tone. Now Paulie was pissed. He made a move toward Mac, dodged another slash, and then they were grappling, kicking, cursing, grunting, snorting like animals as each tried to get control of the knife.

Poppy pushed Katie back onto the bed. "You stay here! Don't move!"

She eased herself into the front room, pressing her back against the wall as Paulie and Mac rolled around on the floor. She had to find a way to stop Mac. But how? And then she spotted her dumbbells by the coffee table.

Yes!

She grabbed one and raised it just as Paulie rolled on top of Mac. She crept closer, looking for an opening, waiting for a clear shot at Mac's head.

And then she heard Paulie let out a loud, "*Uhn!*"—a cross between a strangled cry and an agonized grunt—and in that same awful, horror-filled instant saw the bright red point of the knife blade pop through the back of his shirt.

She screamed his name and rushed forward just as Mac was pushing Paulie off of him. She'd all but forgotten the dumbbell in her hand, but when she saw Mac getting up she let out a sound she'd never imagined she could make, a screech of rage and fear like a truck with bad brakes. Mac looked up, and for an instant she cherished the look of sudden terror that filled his eyes when he saw her and realized what she had raised over her head.

He shouted, "No!" and tried to get a hand up but he was too late.

Poppy smashed him square between his cold, rotten little eyes with the end of the dumbbell, flattening his nose and spraying blood all over his face. His head slammed back against the floor and he didn't move again.

Poppy immediately forgot about him and dropped the dumbbell. She turned to Paulie who was on his back now with the knife's black handle sticking out of his stomach, right under the breast bone. His black shirt wasn't showing the red of the blood, just looking blacker—and wet. And he was *all* wet. His face was sugar white and he looked like he was having trouble breathing and Poppy didn't want to think it, didn't want to believe it could happen, but she knew right then that her Paulie was dying.

"Paulie . . . ?"

His eyes focused on her, then down to the handle sticking up from his shirt. His fingers trembled as he touched it. He tried a smile as he spoke in a wheezy whisper.

"It's not as bad as it looks. I'll be okay."

Poppy tried to hold back the sobs but they broke through and she started crying. "Oh, Jesus, Paulie, it came out your back!"

He blinked. "It did? Oh." He looked down at the handle and touched it again. "Help me get it out."

"No! I can't!"

"Poppy, it hurts so much. You gotta get it out. Please."

"O-okay." The last thing in the world she wanted to do was touch that handle, but if it was hurting Paulie . . .

She forced the fingers of both hands around the black plastic, squeezed tight, and gave a little pull.

Paulie stiffened and groaned.

"It's stuck!" Her voice rose to a wail. "I can't do this, Paulie!"

"It's my only chance. Pull it out! Now!"

Shaking, sobbing, Poppy tightened her grip and yanked the handle with everything she had. After some initial resistance, it suddenly came free and she almost fell backward.

When she straightened, Paulie was even whiter than before but smiling at her.

"Oh, that feels better."

But when Poppy looked at the wound she saw blood gurgling from the slit and running down Paulie's sides. Suddenly his whole body twitched and he looked at her. She could barely hear his voice.

"Maybe we should have left it in."

And then he was gone. He didn't move, didn't make another sound; his eyes were still open and looking at her, but Paulie wasn't there anymore.

No . . . that couldn't be . . .

"Paulie?" she said. "Paulie?"

Poppy dropped the knife and leaned toward him, arms out to hug him when something moved against her leg. She turned. Mac was stirring.

His nose was smushed to the side and he looked like he'd been hit in the face with a ripe tomato, but his eyelids were fluttering. He was coming to.

And right then Poppy knew she had to kill him. She couldn't let the man who'd killed Paulie and wanted to kill Katie take another breath.

She looked around for her dumbbell and saw that it had rolled across the floor. She started to rise to retrieve it when she noticed the handle of the gun in Mac's belt.

Yeah. With his own gun.

But as she began to pull it free, a hand grabbed her wrist.

Mac looked at her groggily. "No way, bitch."

Poppy got her other hand on the gun and yanked it free, but Mac still had hold of her wrist. And now he brought both of his hands into play, trying to twist it away from her. But Poppy wasn't letting go. She knew her life and Katie's depended on keeping it away from Mac.

Suddenly the gun went off and Poppy felt something *whiz* past her cheek. The sound was so deafening at such close range she jumped and almost lost her grip.

She glanced down and saw Mac's finger against the trigger, then up to see him grinning at her, so sure he was going to win. Just to show him he wasn't, Poppy gave the gun a vicious twist and it discharged again, the bullet nipping a lock of his hair as it went by.

Suddenly he wasn't smiling. If he hadn't just been coming out of being knocked cold, and if he hadn't been struggling with someone who worked out a lot more than he did, he might have won already. But he was far from his peak and Poppy was right at hers, and she knew she had to get that gun fast before his bigger muscles and weight advantage wore her down.

She jammed her thumb inside the trigger guard, right on top of his, and pressed down hard while pushing the barrel toward him. Another shot, and this one nipped his shoulder before it smashed through the window. He winced and jumped as red began seeping through the hole in his shirt, and now his feet were kicking along the floor, looking for leverage against her. Poppy kept staring at him, not saying a word as they no longer fought for the gun, but for which way it would point, and he must have seen something in her eyes because now he was looking scared.

Finally his feet found something to push against and suddenly he was angling up, looking to topple her over and trap her under his weight. If he did that, he'd be in control. Poppy put all her strength into one last desperate twist of the barrel, lifting it and crunching down on the trigger.

The muzzle flash seared her chin as Mac gave a shout and lurched back with blood spurting from the right side of his head. His grip loosened and suddenly the gun was all Poppy's.

She scrabbled backward on her free hand and feet and butt, and then sprawled there gasping, pointing the gun at him, ready to drill him again. But he didn't move. He lay flat on his back, arms and legs splayed in all directions, his right eye all bloody, an expanding pool of red encircling his head.

Mac was dead. She'd killed a man, but that was okay. It wasn't really a man—it was Mac. And he'd killed Paulie. And was gonna kill—

Katie!

Dimly, through the ringing in her ears, she became aware that a child was screaming. Poppy dropped the gun and ran into the guest room where she found her crouched whitefaced in a corner, hands over her ears, eyes squeezed shut, and her mouth wide open. She lifted Katie and held her trembling, quaking little body against her.

"It's all right, baby," she said, putting her lips against Katie's ear and whispering. "It's all right. It's all over and no one's gonna hurt you. Poppy's gonna take care of you. You're safe now. You're safe."

Safe . . . Poppy realized that was the one thing they weren't. How many times had the gun gone off? Three? Four? She couldn't remember. But sure as hell someone was dialing 911 right now and saying Sylmar Street was turning into the OK Corral.

She had to get out of here.

But where to? She had no place to go. And she had no money. Paulie always took care of—

Paulie! Oh, Jesus, poor Paulie was dead in the next room. . . . She bit back a sob. She couldn't think about that. She had to get Katie and herself to safety.

"Here's what we're gonna do. We're gonna move to a new place, a brand new place where nobody gets hurt. Okay? First thing you have to do is close your eyes."

Katie didn't say anything, but when Poppy looked, her eyes were closed. Maybe they'd been closed all along. She carried her out through the living room, keeping her own eyes straight ahead and Katie's turned away from the blood-splattered floor. Once in the kitchen, she put her down on one of the chairs.

"Stay here, Katie. Don't move. I'll be right back."

Katie sat unmoving, her eyes still closed.

Poppy hurried back into the living room and fought the rising nausea as she approached the bodies. Blood everywhere. She couldn't think of anyplace she totally wanted less to be, but she needed money. And more than that, she needed the keys to the truck.

Without really looking at him—she couldn't bear to see his slack, white face—she sidled around to Paulie's body and knelt just outside the wet stain that encircled him. She reached toward him and pulled back.

Poor Paulie. She couldn't even look at him. How was she gonna touch him? But she had to. No time to kneel here wringing her hands. The cops were coming, dammit.

Steeling herself, and only looking out of the corner of her eye, she forced her hands to pat his pockets. The front ones were empty. Biting her lip, she rolled him half over—so heavy!—and found his wallet, but no truck keys.

The money in Paulie's wallet wouldn't take her far. She glanced across him at Mac. He always had lots of cash. She got up and approached Mac from the other side. Easier to go through his pockets. Only his head was bloody. And she didn't give a damn about Mac.

She yanked out his wallet and sighed with relief when she found it loaded with twenties and fifties, plus half a dozen Visa cards under as many names.

Okay. She and Katie had money. Now they needed wheels.

She spotted Mac's keys on the floor near the gun. She reached for them, then thought better of it. She knew she wasn't the brightest bulb in the box, but she did know that the Jeep had been sitting out front when the shots were fired. Someone might have taken down the plate number. The truck would be better. Except for a couple of quick trips, it had been kept in the garage all the time.

She jumped up and ran into her bedroom and spotted the keys on the dresser. She snatched them and her little purse, and ran back toward the kitchen. Halfway there she dropped everything. A gun, a purse, two wallets, and keys—too much to carry. And she'd probably have to carry Katie too. No time to consolidate. She needed—

She spotted Mac's baseball jacket on the chair. She didn't want anything that belonged to that slimeball but right now she couldn't be choosey. She pulled it on and stuffed everything into the pockets. Then she scooped up Katie and headed for the garage.

"Come on, baby," she cooed. "We're getting the hell outta here."

As she opened the door between the kitchen and the garage, she heard Mac's beeper go off again. Whoever wanted him was going to get old and gray waiting for a callback.

12

"You are sure you are calling the right numbers?" Carlos said. Llosa nodded vigorously. "¡Si!"

"I tried them myself," Allen Gold said.

"Then why isn't that *hijo de puta* answering? He has always called in before."

"Maybe his beeper's turned off," Allen said, "or broken. Maybe the battery died."

"But what about his voice mail?"

Gold shrugged. "Who knows how often he checks it?"

Carlos was getting worried. MacLaglen should not be out of touch at such a critical time. It was very careless of him, and if Carlos knew one thing about MacLaglen, he was not careless. A bad feeling was growing in his gut: Something was wrong.

He pointed to Gold. "I want you to take Llosa and drive past his house."

"Do we know where he lives?"

"I will give you the address. And I will give you another address, as well. But you must drive past and nothing more. Do not knock on the door, do not even stop the car. *Comprende?*"

"Sure."

"Call me immediately if you see anything."

He watched them go, then turned on his back massager. His muscles were very tight.

Something was wrong . . . he could smell it.

13 The sun sat high and bright in a cloudless sky, but Poppy drove through a fog. She could barely feel her hands on the wheel. Like numb all over.

She pushed the panel truck to its limit along 95 North through Maryland and got about sixty miles an hour out of it. She wished she could go like a hundred, *two* hundred, but the last thing she needed now was to get pulled over by a cop. Sixty would do just fine.

She glanced over at Katie, belted into the passenger seat. She'd been a talkative little thing the past few days, but Poppy had heard barely a peep out of her since they'd left the house. Poor kid . . . she'd seen stuff today that no adult should see, let alone a six-year-old girl.

Soon as we get somewhere, Poppy thought, I'll have to work on her. Bring her out. And figure out what to do with her.

Yeah. Soon as we get somewhere.

But where was she going? And what was she going to do when she got there?

My next move, she thought. Good question. What do I do now?

She wished Paulie was here. She wasn't good at this sort of stuff, but Paulie'd know what to do.

The thought of Paulie started an ache deep in her chest. She remembered his funny laugh, his crooked smile, always trying to be a hard guy when he didn't have a mean bone in his body. And now he was dead. She didn't want to remember him like that, all soaked with blood, his face so pale, his dead eyes staring. She wanted to remember him in bed, doing wonderful things to her. . . .

"Why are you crying?"

Katie's voice startled her. She wiped at her cheeks and her hand came away wet and stained with mascara.

Poppy sniffed and stifled the building sobs. Can't go to pieces now. Got to hold together for Katie.

"Because I'm sad, Katie." How did she say this? She didn't want to start answering questions about lovers and death. "I . . . I lost a very dear friend today."

She felt something touch her. She looked down and saw Katie's little hand patting her forearm.

"That's okay. I'll be your friend."

And that only made Poppy cry harder.

I'm a basket case, she thought. I'll kill us both if I don't get off the road and pull myself together.

Somewhere north of Baltimore she spotted a GAS-FOOD-LODGING sign before the Edgewood exit. She'd never heard of Edgewood and figured maybe that was good. Who'd look for her in Edgewood, Maryland?

She hit the Exit 77 ramp and the first place she came to was a Best Western. A Denny's and a McDonald's occupied the opposing corners. Perfect.

She pulled into the parking lot, turned off the engine, and sat there,unable to move, feeling like she suddenly weighed a couple of tons. She felt so totally alone, so unsure. Was stopping here the right thing?

What would Paulie do?

He'd probably say, Get off the road, park the truck around back, and hole up until you've made a plan. Don't go running around without a plan.

Okay. She'd make a plan. But first she'd have to like figure out how to pay for the room. Cash or credit?

She opened Mac's wallet and went through the credit cards. All those different names—James King, Eric Coral, Francis Black, Steven Garter, Jason Rattle, William Boa . . . stolen cards or real accounts with phony names?

Weird, she thought. All snake names. That couldn't be a coincidence. And she remembered what Paulie used to say about him—"a real detail guy." Not the type to get caught with hot plastic. Probably a good bet they were real accounts.

Good. She'd rotate them and save her cash. Mac sure as hell wouldn't be reporting them stolen.

"How come your face is all black?" Katie said.

Poppy glanced in the rearview mirror. Her cheeks were a mess of black smears.

"That's mascara. I kinda like to pile it on."

"How come? And how come your lips are all black too?"

"Because I use black lipstick, silly."

Poppy wondered at all the questions, then realized that Katie had never seen her without a mask until this morning.

"And how come you got earrings in your face?"

Poppy glanced in the mirror again. She barely noticed the diamond stud in her left nostril and the fine silver ring through her right eyebrow anymore. Nobody she hung out with gave them a second thought. Hell, most people she hung out with were pierced a lot more than her. A *lot* more.

But they did make her stick out in the straight world. She'd never minded that before. Liked to flaunt it, in fact. Thumbing her nose at all the uptights.

But the last thing she wanted now was to stick out. The rings had to go.

But not all of them.

"Want to see another?" She pulled up her shirt and showed Katie her pierced belly button. "What you think of that one?"

Katie made a face. "Eeeuuuuw! How come—?"

"That's enough questions for now. Let's go get us a room."

"We're staying here?" Her eyes lit up. "Oh, goody! I hope the bed's got Magic Fingers!"

And Poppy did something she'd thought she might never do again. She smiled.

14

"I think we've got trouble."

Allen Gold had said he was calling from a parking lot in Falls Church. His words made Carlos's back muscles bunch.

"Tell me."

"Nothing doing at his house. We drove by twice and didn't see anything unusual. But it looks like the shit's hit the fan at the second address."

The Falls Church house. Carlos squeezed his eyes shut. *I knew it!*

"What has happened?"

"Cops all over the place. Looks like it might have been a raid or something. Couldn't get a good look."

"Our friend's car . . . the Jeep?"

"Couldn't tell you. I mean, what with all the squad cars, the ambulances, the EMS trucks, who could see? We passed by and did a typical rubbernecking thing, but the cops on the street kept us moving. Did see a body, though."

"Was it—?"

"Couldn't tell. Wrapped head to toe in a sheet and rolling toward the meat wagon."

Mierda! This could be disastrous. But he could not let Gold or Llosa know he was upset.

"Return immediately. We must make plans."

He hung up and drummed his fingers on his belly. He had contacts down at D.C. police headquarters. He would contact them and find out exactly what had happened in the Falls Church house.

Worst case scenario was that MacLaglen was dead. That meant his treacherous little tape would soon be on its way to numerous federal agencies. And *that* meant that Carlos would be on his way to the private airport where he kept his new Gulfstream V.

MacLaglen alive and in custody would be almost as bad. MacLaglen had a lot of pride, but he would be facing grievous charges. How long before he struck a deal to give up the one who had hired him? Carlos guessed he'd last about a day.

MacLaglen in custody would also prompt a hurried trip to the airport.

But what about Maria? If Carlos had to run, he'd never be able to return. He might never see his Maria again.

So she'd have to come with him—like it or not. He'd have Llosa grab the *perra* and drag her out to the plane.

But where could he go? Colombia would be the safest as far as extradition was concerned, but extradition was only one of his worries. After all, he had failed. Either through his damned tape or his confession, MacLaglen would expose a plot by the drug cartel to assassinate President Winston. Attempts to put *la compañía* out of business, either by a frontal assault or by legalizing its product, would intensify.

Somehow he couldn't see Emilio Rojas welcoming him with open arms.

He might have to find a new home. He'd worry about where later.

He looked up the number to the airport. Best to call and make sure his jet was fueled and ready to go.

15

"Whoops, there's some news," Poppy said. "Leave it there for a minute."

"I don't like news," Katie said.

She had the remote pointed at the motel TV, her thumb poised over the button. She'd been in the middle of channel surfing when Poppy spotted the word HEADLINES on one of the D.C. stations.

"It's only for like a minute, honeybunch. I just want to hear something."

Poppy leaned forward, listening. The big story seemed to be President Winston's sudden admission to Bethesda Naval Hospital—*"for a check-up before leaving for Europe next week."*

"Look, it's Uncle Tom," Katie said.

"Right, honeybunch. Just let me listen a sec, okay."

This super-straight-looking babe—Heather Something—who looked like she'd never had a beer, let alone a joint, came on and started plugging legalized drugs.

"Look what we've done by educating people about the perils of smoking. In the 1950s the average American consumed thirteen pounds of tobacco per year. The per capita consumption is now down to seven pounds a year and falling. Yet tobacco is legally available. The exact opposite trend has occurred with illegal narcotics. The conclusion is obvious: We can address the problems and focus public education on a legal addictive substance far more effectively than on an illegal one. Using antismoking campaigns as a model, there's no reason we can't cut U.S. consumption of legalized drugs by an equal percentage."

Great, Poppy thought. Just when I'm like getting off the stuff.

The newswoman went on to read stories about protests against the President's drug decriminalization proposal and closed with a tape of the Reverend Bobby Whitcomb calling down Holy Fire upon the head of President Winston.

Damn. Not a word about a double murder in Falls Church.

Maybe she'd been wrong—maybe no one had called the cops. That meant Paulie could still be lying there, and would keep on lying there until the landlord came looking for his rent check or somebody reported the stink.

Poppy couldn't bear the thought of that. If she didn't hear something by tomorrow, she'd phone in a "tip" to the Falls Church fuzz.

Of course, maybe the murder of two nobodies couldn't like compete with all the stuff the President was doing.

"Okay," she said. "Hit that button to your heart's content."

But the channel didn't switch. Poppy looked over and saw big tears rolling down Katie's cheeks. She moved closer and put her arms around her.

"Whatsamatter, little Katie?"

"I want to go ho-home," she said.

Poppy held her tighter. "I know you do, honey."

But I don't want to let you go, she thought. Paulie's gone and you're all I've got now.

But she knew she had to. She just had to figure out a way to get her back where she belonged without like landing herself in a jail cell.

Poppy gave Katie another squeeze. But maybe she could keep her a little while longer. Just until—

She stiffened as a terrifying thought struck her. The cops wouldn't be the only ones looking for Katie. As soon as the people Mac had been working for found out he was dead and his precious "package" missing, they'd be out looking for Katie too.

And me.

No choice. For Katie's sake, Poppy was going to have to get her back home tonight.

Suddenly, Poppy wanted to cry.

She couldn't believe how attached she'd become to this little girl. Like she'd filled an empty place within her, an emptiness she never even knew she had. And when Katie was gone, Poppy knew she'd leave an even bigger empty place, so big it might swallow her up.

Dammit, she thought, stop thinking of yourself for once. Katie doesn't belong with you, and she'll only get hurt or killed if she stays. Whoever's after us will be looking for this pierced-up gal towing a little girl. We'll both be better off if we split up.

"You know what?" she said as brightly as she could. "We're gonna make your wish come true. We're gonna figure out a way to get you back to your Daddy."

Katie straightened and looked at her. "Really? I'm going home?"

"Yes, baby. You're going home."

Katie threw her arms around her and squeezed. "Oh, thank you, thank you!"

Poppy felt the tears start. "I'll miss you, little Katie," she said, sniffing.

"Don't cry," Katie said. "You can come visit me. We'll play Chutes and Ladders and I'll show you all my dolls."

"Right," she said dully. "That'll be great."

I'll never see you again, little Katie . . .

Poppy pulled free and stood up. She wiped her eyes and said, "Okay. First step is to get in touch with your dad. You wouldn't just happen to like know your phone number, would you?"

Katie rattled it off.

"You're one smart girl," Poppy told her.

"My Daddy made me memorize it, in case I got lost."

All right. But what next? She wondered if she was smart enough to figure out how to work this without getting caught. What would Paulie do . . . ?

16 John picked up on the first ring, almost knocking the receiver off the kitchen wall in his mad rush to get to it. He didn't want it waking Mom.

"Mr. VanDuyne?" A male voice, low-pitched, official sounding.

"Yes? Who's this?"

"This is Sergeant James Waltham, Falls Church Police Department. Sir, do you have a daughter named Katie?"

Oh, no. Oh, please, God, no!

He opened his mouth but couldn't speak. He reached out blindly with his free hand, found the back of a chair, and dropped into it.

Finally . . . "Yes?"

"We found a bottle of pills that seem to belong to her."

"Pills? What about Katie? Do you have Katie?"

"No, sir. Just her pills. Do you know where your daughter is?"

"She's been—" No. Don't tell him. "She's been on a trip. Where did you find them?"

"At a murder scene."

"A murder—? My God! She's not—?"

"No, sir. No child victim there. But we did find some children's clothing—a Holy Family school uniform and—"

"Oh, God!"

"Sir, just where is your daughter?"

"Look. I'll be right down. Just tell me where you're located and I'll be there in fifteen minutes."

Sgt. Waltham spelled his name and gave John the police department's address. John hung up and called Decker's private number. He repeated to Decker almost word for word what he'd been told.

"What's it mean, Bob?"

"I wouldn't even hazard a guess right now. But this might be a major break for us. You stay put. I'll go down there and see what—"

"Not on your life! I *know* her clothes! I can identify them!"

Didn't Decker realize that he had to see that blazer and jumper with his own eyes, touch them, bunch them in his hands?

"No. Stay there. You might get e-mail—"

"I gave you my password—*you* monitor my e-mail. I'm going to Falls Church. See you there!"

And he hung up.

As John stepped toward the hall closet to grab a jacket, his cellular phone began to trill. He snatched it off the counter.

"Is this Mr. VanDuyne?" A woman's voice this time—young but husky.

Two calls in a row with the same question. But who had his cellular number?

"Yes. Who's this?"

"Got someone who wants to talk to you."

A rustle, a rattle, and then a child's voice.

"Daddy?"

John knew that voice, but for an instant his mind refused to identify it. Wasn't possible, couldn't be . . . some sort of cruel trick . . .

"Daddy, it's me—Katie."

And then the kitchen swam around him. "Katie! Dear God, Katie, is that you?" He realized he was shouting but he couldn't help it. He thought he'd burst with joy. "Is this really you?"

"Uh-huh."

"Where are you—*how* are you?"

"Fine." *Fine* . . . she always said *fine*. The bastards had cut off her toe and she was *fine*. "I'm coming home."

John sagged against the wall and tried to keep from sobbing. "Oh, Katie, I've missed you so! Where are you? I'll come and get you right now!"

"Now's not a good time." The woman was back on the line. "You can get her tonight."

John's mind whirled in confusion. What was going on? Where was the catch?

"But how . . . why?"

"Let's just say the real kidnapper is dead and I've got Katie and I wanna give her back. But I don't like wanna get locked up, know what I'm saying?"

The real kidnapper is dead . . . ? She has to mean that murder scene in Falls Church where they found Katie's pills . . . what has that poor child gone through?

"You want money? I'll give you whatever I have. I'll—"

"Don't want your money, guy. I got a sweet little girl here who can't wait to get back to her daddy and I'm gonna like see to it she gets there. Come to the Maryland House on Ninety-five. Wait upstairs by the phones around nine o'clock. I'll meet you there with Katie. And no cops, okay? Let's do this so's we both walk away happy. See you at nine."

"Wait!"

Another rattle and then Katie's voice. "Bye, Daddy!"

A click and she was gone. He stood there, pressing the receiver against his ear, listening to the electric silence, searching for an echo of her voice, not knowing whether to laugh or cry.

Finally he turned to hang up and saw his mother standing in the doorway.

"Katie?" she said, digging at her neck. "That was Katie?"

He could only nod. He threw his arms around her.

"I heard you shouting," she said. "It sounded like you were talking to—"

"She's alive, Mom! That was her! She's alive and she's okay and I'm getting her back, Mom. Katie's coming home tonight!"

17

Agent Samson caught him in the White House parking lot. Bob Decker was just unlocking his car door when he spotted him running across the pavement, waving a sheet of paper.

"What is it, Rick?"

"The VanDuyne taps!" he said, puffing as he reached the car. "I thought you should see this."

Bob scanned the sheet and couldn't resist a tight smile. The whole plot was crumbling. Looked like there'd been a falling out among the kidnappers and someone wanted to cover her ass.

"Where was she calling from?"

"The place she mentions for the switch—the Maryland House?"

"What's that?"

"A traveler's stop on the median on Ninety-five. You know, tourist info, burgers, yogurt." He cleared his throat. "This sounds like a kidnapping. How come we're involved in—?"

"Friend of Razor's," Bob said.

Samson nodded. That was all Samson needed to know, all he'd ever know. He was monitoring a line tap and was to transcribe all conversations. Beyond that, he was in the dark.

"She called on his cell phone," Samson said. "Probably thought no one would be listening on that. Nobody seems to realize how unsecure they are."

Bob nodded, half listening. No use sending anyone out to the Maryland House now. The woman would be long gone by the time anyone got there. Better to wait for her tonight.

He wondered if VanDuyne would tell him about this call. He decided not to hold his breath. The woman had said no cops and the doc wanted his kid back.

All right. He'd get his kid back. And Bob would get the woman. Put her together with whatever went down in that Falls Church house where the child's pills were found, and he'd probably have this thing sewn up before the weekend was over.

He imagined how it would feel to stroll into Bethesda Naval Hospital tomorrow night and tell Razor his godchild is safe and the assassination conspirators are either locked up or on the run.

Sweet. Very sweet.

18

Poppy finally heard it on the six o'clock news.

"*. . . And in Falls Church today, a murder mystery. Neighbors on this quiet suburban street called police when they heard shots fired. Inside the house, a dead man. But the as-yet-unidentified victim died of* stab *wounds. Nearby, in Alexandria . . .*"

Somehow, hearing it on the news made it official. Paulie was dead. Poppy started to cry, then caught herself.

"*. . . the as-yet-unidentified* man . . . ?" What about *men?* She'd left *two* bodies in that house. Paulie had been stabbed to death, and Mac had a bullet in his brain. How come they were only talking about Paulie?

Unless . . .

A stab of fear, as sharp as the blade that had killed Paulie, knifed through her.

"Oh, Jesus!" she said aloud and leapt to her feet.

"Can I change the channel now?" Katie said.

"Sure," Poppy said without looking at her.

She went to the window and peeked around the edge of the curtain. The light drizzle outside made the parking lot shine. The Holiday Inn sign reflected from the wet surface.

A minute ago she'd felt so safe. She'd had everything planned. Tonight she and Katie would get back on Ninety-five, but they would *not* stop at the Maryland House. She'd copied down the numbers from a couple of the phones there when they'd called Katie's dad this afternoon. At nine o'clock sharp she'd place a call to one of those phones, tell her father that he'd find his daughter waiting in the Roy Rogers at the *next* rest stop up the freeway from the Maryland House. Then she'd leave Katie in a booth with a burger and fries.

If Katie's dad was like the rest of Mac's victims, he probably hadn't said word one about the snatch to the cops. And even if they were involved, they'd all be at the Maryland House. Poppy would be long gone by the time they reached Katie.

Poppy's heart would be broken but Katie would be safe and at home with her family, where she belonged.

But she wouldn't be safe if Mac was alive.

Poppy could still see his eyes as he came out of the kitchen with that knife, saying "She *saw* me!" Only two people could connect Mac with the kidnapping—and Paulie's murder—and both were in this room.

Even the slightest chance that Mac was still alive changed everything.

A whole new game, a completely different world if Mac had survived.

But how *could* he be alive? She'd like shot him in the head.

She had to know. Before she made another move, she had to be sure.

She turned to Katie. "I'm gonna run down the hall for like a soda. You want anything?"

"Can I have a Yoo-Hoo?"

"Sure."

"My daddy never lets me have Yoo-Hoo."

Her daddy, her daddy. Never her mommy. Poppy forced a smile. "Well, I'm not your daddy. Be right back."

This was risky, she knew, maybe even stupid, but it couldn't wait. She dashed through the drizzle to the Shell station on the far side of the parking lot and found the pay phone. A call to information got her the Falls Church Police Department, and pretty soon she was talking to a homicide detective. He kept trying to get her name and she suspected he was trying to like keep her on the phone.

"Look," she said, "I'll just say this once: I know the names of the dead guys in the house on Sylmar Street. The stabbed guy was Paulie Di-Castro. The shot guy was—"

"Wait, wait, wait," said the cop. "Nobody was shot. We've only got one victim."

Oh, no. Oh, sweet Jesus, no! He's gotta be lying!

"No. You know damn well there were two! All I can tell you about the shot guy is that his name was like Mac and he drove that blue Jeep out front."

"What blue Jeep? Do you know the tag number?"

Poppy hung up. The drizzle had suddenly become freezing and the night much darker. She shivered and looked around, feeling as if someone was watching her.

Mac was alive! But how? She'd seen him lying there on the floor with like a bullet in his head. Somehow he'd survived.

She dashed back across the parking lot, ducked back into the motel room, and locked the door behind her.

She saw Katie sitting there on the bed, eyes glued to the TV. How could she send that little girl back to her father with Mac alive and on the prowl? Her father wouldn't know how to protect her. Mac had known enough about Katie to kidnap her. How much would it take to get a rifle and put a bullet in her the next time she stepped out her front door?

Poppy shuddered. No way Katie could go home tonight. She hoped the information she'd given the Falls Church cops would set them hunting for Mac. But until they caught him, Katie would be safer with her.

Katie looked up. "Didn't they have any Yoo-Hoo?"

Damn! She'd forgotten all about the drinks.

"I didn't see any. Want me to get you something else?"

"That's okay. I'll take my pill with water."

Pill? Oh, Jesus! Do I have her pills?

Poppy ran over to the night stand where she'd left her pocket book and dumped it out on the bed. She had some Valium, her driver's license, some bills and change—but not Katie's medicine.

She ran to the closet and yanked Mac's jacket off the hanger. Maybe she'd stuffed the pill bottle in one of the pockets as she was leaving. She didn't believe that for a minute but she had to check. She emptied the pockets; Paulie's wallet, some loose change, and a cassette tape fell out. But no little amber bottle of pills for Katie.

Poppy slumped on the edge of the bed and wrung her hands. In the horror and confusion and panic back at the house, she'd forgot all about the pills.

Jesus, what else could go wrong?

She stood and paced the tiny room. Decision time. She had to get some medicine for Katie. She remembered the name on the bottle: Tegretol 100 mg. If she couldn't get hold of any, she'd have no choice: Katie would have to go back home. A possible threat from Mac was not as bad as the totally certain threat of fits if she missed a dose or two of those pills.

Poppy had to get hold of some.

But where? How?

She pulled out the phone book and began flipping through the yellow pages.

19 Carlos listened to the distorted voice barking from the receiver. "What kind of half-assed operation are you running there, Salinas? I just learned that a bottle of pills belonging to the little girl was found in a house in Falls Church where someone was murdered. What the hell is going on?"

Carlos stared at the ceiling. *Please, God, if you will ever do anything for me, do this for me now.*

"One dead man?" Carlos said. "Has he been identified?"

"Yes. They got a tip as to his name and confirmed his prints. A small-time hood named Paul DiCastro."

Thank you, God, Carlos thought. *I will make a large offering to the church.*

"No one else? No woman? No child?"

"No sign of anyone else, but they're looking. Looking hard, because this death is now linked to the other matter. Better clean house, Salinas. And fast."

The line went dead and Salinas hung up. He turned to Gold who was stuffing a valise with papers from a filing cabinet.

"I believe we can relax for a while, Allen."

"Relax?" Allen said. His face was unusually pale, even for him. "How can I relax?"

"Well, you insisted on knowing about my dealings with MacLaglen, and now you know." He smiled. "Don't you feel better?"

When Carlos had thought he would have to flee the country, he'd filled Gold in on the plan to remove Winston. After all, Gold had to know why they were running for the airport.

He did not return Carlos's smile. "You want to say, 'I told you so,' go ahead. But right now, if we don't get out of here—"

"Be calm. MacLaglen is not dead. He is still alive and free."

Allen stared at him. "You're sure of that?"

"My source."

Allen staggered to the nearest chair and dropped into it.

"What a relief! But why doesn't he call back?"

"That I do not know. Something happened. An argument, perhaps. He may be busy trying to find a new hiding place for the child. Or, even better, a place to dispose of her. Keep trying to reach him. Sooner or later he will call in."

Carlos agreed with the voice on the phone: Time to clean house.

20

"See, I got like this problem with my nephew," Poppy said to the pharmacist, keeping her voice so low that he had to lean forward to catch every word. "He's visiting and I found these pills in his room. Not that I don't trust him or nothing, but I'm like, 'What *are* these?' you know?"

The overhead fluorescents gleamed off the black of the pharmacist's balding scalp as he nodded and stared at her over the top of his reading glasses. The old dude couldn't seem to take his eyes off her eyebrow ring. Did he like live in a cave or something? Hadn't he ever seen one before?

For more than an hour she'd driven around with the yellow pages on her lap, checking out one drugstore after another. Finally she'd settled on Doc's Pharmacy in what looked like a black neighborhood. Kinda small but with a good-sized front window, and off the main drag in a building that looked like it had been built when dirt was new.

"I'll be happy to identify them for you," said the pharmacist, like he got asked this all the time. He might have been "Doc," but more than likely he was the original Doc's grandson. Kind of grumpy, but then, closing time was near and he looked like he wanted to go home. "Give me one and I'll look it up."

"That's just it. I ain't got any. He only had one in the bottle and I'm like, I can't take his last pill. But I saw the name on the bottle. It was Tegretol 100mg. Is that bad stuff? You know, like drugs?"

"Does your nephew have a seizure disorder?"

"You mean fits?"

"Yes, I suppose you could call them that. Tegretol is used for er, 'fits.'"

"I don't know. My sister never told me about that, and she's on a trip and I can't get hold of her to ask. If you could just let me see one . . ."

He sighed. "Sure. Wait right here."

Poppy watched him go to the rear shelves and return to the counter with a white plastic bottle. He shook a few pills into a plastic tray and handed her one.

"Is that it?"

Poppy held up the precious little pill to the light, but her eyes were on the bottle sitting a foot away on the counter. So close. So tempting. All she had to do was reach out, grab it, and run.

And maybe get caught.

Too many people around, too much traffic on the street outside. She couldn't risk it.

"Yeah," she said. "That's it. You think you could like sell me some of those?"

"Not without a prescription."

"But he's only got one left." Poppy slipped a twenty on the counter. "Just a couple to hold him until I can get in touch with my sister?"

The pharmacist shook his head. "I'd like to help, but it would be against the law."

They went 'round and 'round, but this old dude wasn't going to budge. He gave her all sorts of suggestions that would have worked out fine if her little story was true, but they didn't help Poppy one bit.

Just when she was getting desperate enough to make a grab for the bottle, he screwed the cap back on and held it in his hand.

"You can have that one," he said. "Maybe it'll give you a little extra time."

"Thanks," she said. "What do I owe you?"

"Forget it. I can't sell it once it's been touched anyway."

Poppy stood on tiptoe and watched where he went, mentally marking the section of the rear shelves where he placed it. Then she looked at the single pill in her hand. At least Katie wouldn't have to go through the night without her medicine.

Nice of the old grump to give it to her. Made her almost regret what she was going to have to do.

21 John pulled off 95 and coasted into the Maryland House parking lot. He found a space under a light and looked up at the big colonial-style brick building squatting on a rise about fifty yards away. Raindrops flickered through the light from its windows. With its wide brick chimneys and many-paned windows, it looked like a mansion that had fallen on hard times and was now tolerating tours to cover expenses—until you spotted the Bob's Big Boy, Roy Rogers, Sbarro, and TCBY signs.

He checked his watch: 8:35. He was early, but didn't see how he could be too early for this.

John sat and shivered. Not from the drizzle outside, because he was warm and dry here in the car. The cold came from within.

Something had gone terribly wrong in the Falls Church house where they'd been keeping Katie . . . wrong enough that a man had been stabbed to death.

What if something else goes wrong tonight and Katie winds up getting hurt?

John had identified her clothing at the police station. He'd have been sick with worry that someone had sexually molested her if he hadn't heard her voice an hour earlier. She'd sounded so normal, almost *happy*. He was glad of that, but for the life of him he couldn't understand it. She'd been kidnapped, her toe amputated—she should have sounded lost, shocked, disassociated; yet she'd been perky, bouncy, her old self. As Katie herself had said: "Fine." Like she'd been out on an overnight with her favorite aunt instead of her captor.

God, who *was* that woman who'd called?

He'd sensed something in her voice . . . genuine regard for Katie. He prayed he was right.

And he prayed he'd done the right thing by not telling Decker about Katie's call.

"I guess I'll know soon enough, won't I," he said aloud as he stepped out into the wet air and went looking for the phones.

22 "There he goes," Gerry Canney said.

Bob Decker had parked in the south lot. He squinted through the dripping windshield and watched VanDuyne trot through the rain toward the Maryland House. Plenty of light from the mercury bulbs overhead and the fluorescent backwash from the Exxon station behind them.

He yawned. A long, hard day, but he felt wired instead of tired. Excitement and apprehension burned inside him.

"Your people set up?"

Canny started to answer, then held a hand up as his walkie-talkie earpiece buzzed. He pulled out his handset.

"Good work, Trevor," he said. "Keep an eye on her."

Bob stiffened. "We've spotted her?"

"It's VanDuyne's wife. She followed him from his place. When I heard that, I put an agent named Trevor Hendricks on her. Used to be a stunt driver. As they got within a few miles of here, he boxed her in behind some slow-moving cars until VanDuyne was out of sight. She's still on Ninety-five, somewhere north of here, racing along, trying to catch up to him."

Bob smiled. "Smooth. I love it."

Earlier VanDuyne had told Canney about his wife and how she was asking all sorts of troublesome questions about Katie's whereabouts. VanDuyne's lawyer had faxed him selected sections of the court file on Marnie VanDuyne . . . one very messed-up lady. Bob had told Canney to put someone on her. Good thing too.

He glanced up at the glowing windows of the Maryland House. A *busy* place, with travelers of all ages, shapes, sizes, colors streaming in and out, tour buses disgorging hordes, even at his hour.

"Pretty amazing inside," Canney said. "The phones are up on the second floor, along with a bank, a copy machine, fax services. More like a business office than a rest stop."

"What'd you tell your people?"

Canney shrugged. "As much as they need to know and no more. They've all got pictures of Katie and VanDuyne. They know it's a kidnap situation and possibly—hopefully—a victim transfer."

"Right. *Hopefully*."

Canney turned to him. "You thinking what I'm thinking?"

Bob's turn to nod. "That this is some sort of trap? Yeah. Makes sense, especially after that corpse in Falls Church. DiCastro had to be involved. I mean, the kid's prints are all over the bedroom, bathroom, and living room. She was *there*. What I don't get is, we've been so sure this was a cartel operation, yet this DiCastro's got no drug connection."

"That we know of," Canney said.

"Right. But he's still not the sort I expected to run into. Maybe the cartel isn't involved. But with the President checking into Bethesda today, whoever's behind it must figure VanDuyne's done their dirty work. That makes him and his kid expendable."

"More than expendable," Canney said. "They're loose ends. DiCastro was probably a loose end, and look what they did to him."

"Yeah," Bob said, wishing VanDuyne didn't know him. He'd love to be up there, loitering around the Maryland House himself. "That's what I'm worried about."

23 Poppy drove past Doc's Pharmacy three times before she was satisfied that the streets were empty. She didn't even know the name of the town, but, hell, it was only 11:30 and it looked like everyone was asleep.

She parked the panel truck in the shadows around the corner from the store and gathered the "tools" she'd picked up earlier from a hardware store: a flashlight, two bricks, and a baseball bat. She left the sack of spray paint cans on the floor. Twisting in the seat, she shrugged into Mac's Orioles jacket and stuffed a brick in one pocket, the flashlight in the other. She pulled the leg she'd cut from a pair of pantyhose over her head, slipped into a pair of striped work gloves, then clutched the remaining brick in one hand and the bat in the other.

Ready.

But she couldn't move. Her heart was racing so fast it made her whole body feel like it was vibrating. She wished she was smarter; then she might be able to figure out a better way to do this. But hey, like what could she do? You make do with what you got.

Can't turn back now, she thought. Got to get in, get out, and back to Katie.

Poor Katie. Poppy had found her a Yoo-Hoo and crushed up a Valium in it. The little thing was sound asleep back at the motel. She hated leaving her alone like that, but she was locked in and safe . . . if anywhere was safe with Mac hunting them.

Katie would wake up dopey in the morning, and Poppy would have to lie and say she'd slept through the time she was supposed to go back to her daddy, but that was okay because soon they'd arrange another time.

Right. Soon. Poppy just wouldn't say like how soon.

At least she'd have Tegretol for her.

She hoped.

Do it now, she told herself.

Leaving the car running, she jumped out and ran around to the front of Doc's Pharmacy. Speed was everything. She hurled the first brick at the lower half of the display window, putting everything she had behind the toss. The glass shattered, leaving a gaping hold and setting off a deafening alarm bell. She had to fight the urge to run. Instead she pulled out the second brick. The first hole was big enough to crouch through, but just her luck, the rest of that glass would fall on her as she was going through. Probably cut her head off. So she tossed the next brick higher, and that brought down most of the center of the pane. She used the bat to knock off a couple of daggerlike pieces, then leaped through the opening.

Flashlight glowing ahead of her, she jumped to the floor, ran to the back, vaulted the counter, and fond the bottle of Tegretol right where

"Doc" had left it. Just to confuse things, she knocked everything she could reach off the drug shelves, then dashed back toward the window. She hit the sidewalk running, jumped into the truck and glided away with her lights out.

She was breathing hard, sweating, shaking with fear and excitement as she kept watch ahead and behind, looking for flashing red lights.

None.

So far, so good. Just give me a couple of minutes more before—

Red-and-blue flashing lights appeared way down the road ahead. She swung to the curb and ducked out of sight, trembling as she waited.

She began a mantra: *He didn't see me . . . he didn't see me. . . .*

Seconds later a squad car roared by, no siren. As soon as it passed, she popped up and waited till it screeched around the corner to Doc's. Then Poppy started moving again, lights still out, accelerating slowly so as not to attract any attention. Cruising.

Soon she was a mile, then two miles from the store. She put her headlights on.

How long had the whole thing took—from first brick to driving away? Like ninety seconds?

Paulie would of done it better, smoother, but what really mattered sat beside her on the seat: a whole stock bottle of Tegretol.

"Wasn't pretty," she said aloud, "but it worked." She pounded on the dashboard and laughed. "It *worked!*"

We're in business, Katie, she thought as she picked up speed back to the motel. We can stay together as long as we want now.

24

"Here he comes," Canney said.

Bob Decker looked at his watch: 1:28. He shifted in his seat to relieve the stiffness in his joints and watched VanDuyne shuffle down the ramp from the Maryland House. A different man from the one who'd trotted past them five hours ago.

"Poor bastard," Bob said.

"Yeah. I tell you, I'm glad I wasn't up there. Don't know if I could stand watching him wait all those hours for a call that's not coming. Rips your heart out."

Bob stared at him. "Identifying with him, Gerry?"

"How can I help it? If that was me and it was Martha I was waiting to hear about . . . " He shook his head. "And you know what's worse? We may be the reason he didn't get his daughter back."

Bob nodded. He'd already thought of that. "You think we were made?"

"Possible. Maybe whoever was returning the kid saw something and got spooked."

"Or maybe the hit team got spooked."

Canney didn't answer right away. They both watched VanDuyne's car pull out of the lot and head for 95 south.

"That's a good thought," Canney said. "I'll keep telling myself that. Over and over. Soon I may actually believe it."

Bob knew the feeling. For the past hour he'd been telling himself that they might have saved VanDuyne's life tonight.

So why did he still feel like a bum?

SUNDAY

"Another hidden cost of the war on drugs has been the accelerated spread of AIDS. Because we don't allow IV drug users to buy clean needles legally, they reuse old needles. That's why forty-four percent of newly reported AIDS cases last year were drug related. "Serves 'em right," some might say, but these people pass the virus on to their sexual contacts, who then spread HIV further into the heterosexual community, and on to any children resulting from these contacts. AIDS babies are the civilian casualties of the War on Drugs."

Look at us, John thought. We're a Hopper painting.

He imagined himself a stranger standing in the kitchen doorway, taking in the scene. Nana sat at one end of the rectangular table, half turned away from him, her eyes fixed on the TV. *Meet the Press* was on but he doubted she saw Tim Russert or heard a word Heather Brent was saying. John sat at the other end, staring out at the backyard as the morning sun poured through the windows, enveloping him without warming him. Two people in the same room, connected by ties of blood and nothing else. Bright light and estrangement. Edward Hopper would have jumped on the scene.

But that was only the surface.

In truth, he and his mother had commiserated for so long into the night, shared so much pain, that sheer emotional and physical exhaustion demanded they withdraw into themselves for a while.

Down time.

What had been the purpose of making him go to the Maryland House last night? A cruel joke? This whole nightmare had started out seeming purely political—get Tom out of the White House—but now it had taken on an almost personal tone. What had they accomplished besides torturing him?

And it had *been* torture, unremitting agony hanging around that rest stop, scrutinizing every traveler hurrying to the bathrooms or buying a yogurt, hating everyone who used a phone in case the kidnappers might be trying to call on one of them.

And with each passing hour, his hope fading, progressing from growing uncertainty to devastating conviction that Katie wasn't coming back to him.

And he'd been so sure. That woman who'd called had seemed genuinely concerned about Katie. Had she changed her mind? Or worse— one person connected with the plot was already dead . . . had something else gone wrong?

And even if something hadn't, even if Katie and this woman were sitting safe and sound in another house in another town, Katie had no Tegretol. The pill count from the bottle found in Falls Church showed only a few missing.

John sighed. One more thing he'd kept from Nana, but it yawned before him like a bottomless pit: Right now, as they sat here in their desolate cocoons, Katie could be having a seizure.

The phone rang and John leapt to get it. Good news? Bad news? No news? The phone had become a loaded weapon; answering it, placing it to his ear, a form of Russian roulette.

"Good news, Doc. I think."

Bob Decker's voice. John guessed he was supposed to ask who was talking if he didn't recognize it. Decker tended to be deficient in the social amenities, but John appreciated his no-nonsense approach.

"You 'think'?"

"Yeah. It's about the toe."

Decker seemed a little unsure, and that couldn't be good. John glanced at his mother who had straightened in her chair, listening. He waved off her questioning look and covered the receiver.

"Just an update," he told her. "Nothing new."

She still didn't know about the toe. He wanted to keep it than way.

As casually as he could, he stretched the phone cord and slipped around the corner into the hall. Then he leaned against the wall, bracing himself.

"What about it?"

"It's not your daughter's."

"*What?*" John didn't know whether to laugh or cry. "How . . . ? I don't . . . "

"Damnedest thing. I've already been on the phone twice to the Bureau crime lab. They say the toe you gave us is full of embalming fluid."

"Embalming?" He had to keep his voice low—a whisper. "But there was fresh blood. I saw it."

"That's right. And the type matches your daughter's, but—"

"Wait. How do you know her blood type?"

"Her hospital records—when she had that head injury."

"Oh. Right." Of course they'd have done an in-depth background check on Katie, trying to find out everything about her.

"Anyway, the lab is a hundred percent certain the blood *on* the toe didn't come *from* the toe. That toe's been dead for days."

John took a breath. Thank God he'd spoken to Katie yesterday. If he hadn't, he'd be convinced right now that she was dead.

"This makes no sense!"

"Tell me about it. But it gets weirder. The toe belongs to a little boy."

"A boy? How on earth did they figure that out?"

"Did some DNA thing. Found a Y chromosome."

John tried to slow his whirling thoughts, tried to snatch bits of co-herency from the maelstrom. A Y chromosome . . . females didn't have one, so the toe couldn't be Katie's.

"There's no mistake?" John said.

"That's what I'm told. The lab boys say they've checked and re-checked: double X on the blood, but the cells of the toe itself are XY."

John bit his lip. He wanted to pound the wall and shout. But confusion blunted his relief.

Why send a dead boy's toe? The kidnappers were obviously murder-ous thugs—the bloody corpse in the Falls Church house was testament to that—and yet they'd sent a bogus toe rather than cut off Katie's. . . .

"Any of this make sense to you, Doc?"

"No. I can't imagine. . . ."

"Neither can I. Are you *sure* you can't help us out on this?"

"What do you mean?"

"Anything you haven't told us?"

John stiffened. Did they suspect that he'd been contacted? Had they followed him last night? He was tempted to tell Decker about speaking to Katie yesterday, but the woman had been worried about being caught. Suppose someone on Decker's team *had* followed him and scared her off?

Damn you if that's true, he thought. I might not get another chance.

"No. I told you everything I knew. And I haven't heard a word from Snake." That much at least was true.

A pause before Decker responded. "All right. But let us know the instant you hear anything. Every little scrap is important."

"Of course. But what happens next?"

"I meet with our little task force in about an hour. I'll keep you informed."

As John hung up, he wondered: Was it just his imagination, or had Decker put extra emphasis on the "you?"

Who gave a good goddamn? He was worried about Katie. Where was she? What were they doing to her?

2 "But I want to go home! I want to see my Daddy!"

Poppy watched Katie's lower lip push out. She looked like she was going to cry. Poppy couldn't bear the thought that she'd caused that.

"You will, honey," she said, giving Katie a one-armed hug. "It's like I told you: You fell asleep last night and I didn't want to wake you. But you know what? We'll call him again today and you can talk to him. Okay?"

Katie nodded. "'Kay."

"Great. How you feeling?"

"Fine."

The poor little thing had had a bit of a Valium hangover this morning. Good thing Katie had been zonked out last night because after getting into bed beside her, Poppy had got to thinking about Paulie, and Katie would have had to listen to a ton of crying. Paulie was like the best thing that ever happened to her. And now he was dead. And it was her fault because she'd got him to break Mac's rules. If she'd kept her damn mouth shut . . .

But then what would have happened to Katie?

Why couldn't life be simple?

Yeah, well, maybe it could have been simple if they hadn't got involved with Mac.

She'd clung to Katie all night. Poppy didn't know how she'd have made it to the morning without her.

Dawn had broken gray and cloudy, but they'd both perked up after a stack of waffles at the Denny's across the highway. And now, back in the room, she wished she could find some cartoons to distract Katie, but the tube was like totally filled with talking heads, and if they weren't blabbing about legalized drugs they were speculating about like why the President was in the hospital. As if anybody cared.

"How come your hands are all red?" Katie said.

Poppy looked down at her hands. Black fingernails and blood-red fingers. Very weird.

She stood and stepped toward the window. "C'mere and I'll show you." She pulled back the curtain. "Check out the truck."

Katie pressed her face against the window. "It's red!"

"Sure is. Did it myself last night."

She'd pulled the truck around the back of the motel and parked near a storage shed. There, out of sight of pretty much the whole parking lot, she'd emptied like can after can of spray paint. Her fingers still ached from pressing those nozzles. Sure as hell wasn't pretty, but anyone scanning the freeways for a white panel truck would probably skip right over this one. She hoped.

Poppy dropped the curtain and turned back to the motel room. They couldn't stay here. She'd charged it on Mac's bogus plastic, thinking he was dead. But Mac *wasn't* dead. And what if he had a way to trace her through the card?

They had to get out of here.

But first they had to make some changes.

"Good," Poppy said. "Let's play a game, then. How about"—she made a show of trying to decide—"oh, I don't know . . . how about a game of let's pretend?"

Katie's pout of a moment ago seemed to be history. "What are we going to pretend?"

"Let's see . . . why don't we pretend we're boys? Won't that be fun?"

"Boys?" Katie didn't seem to be too sure about how much fun that would be. "How do we do that?"

"It's easy. We change our hair and change our clothes and we act dumb. You know . . . " Poppy made a face. *"Duh!"*

Katie laughed. "Duh! That's easy."

"But we gotta look like boys."

A wider grin. "You mean dress in boy clothes?"

"Right! And cutting our hair."

The smile vanished as Katie's hands darted to her hair. "Cut my hair? Oh, I don't—"

"Yeah, we'll cut it, color it, comb it different. This'll be the most fun we've ever had!"

But Katie still wasn't buying.

She *has* to buy it, Poppy thought. I've changed the color of the truck, and I'm going to change license plates and change motels, but if we're both going to get through this in one piece, I've got to change *us*. She'd stopped at a Giant Foods on the way back from Denny's and picked up all the necessary materials. Now she had to sell Katie.

"Look," she said, grabbing a pair of scissors. "I'll go first."

She grabbed a fistful of her own hair and began cutting.

3 Dan Keane sat stiffly in his chair in the cramped back office of W-16 and listened with growing horror as Gerry Canney updated the task force on the latest developments from the FBI Crime Lab.

"And here's the latest finding: two different types of blood on the carpet in the Falls Church house. Both fresh. One belongs to the dead man, DiCastro. The other is unidentified, but it is definitely not Katie VanDuyne's."

Everything's unraveling, he thought. He wanted to flee the room.

Decker took over. "Okay. Now, in the U.K. Jim says CIA's found the guy who runs the anonymous remailer Snake's been using."

Jim Lewis cleared his throat. "His name's Steve Fletcher but he refuses to tell us where he hides his computer. The easiest solution would be to follow him to it and steal it. Then we run through his hard drive to find Snake's e-mail address. Snake's got to have an account with an online service or a private server to get on the Internet, and we track him through that. But stealing the CPU would shut down the remailer service and cut off communication from Snake. So we're working with British Intelligence to pressure Fletcher into giving up the information. If it looks like there's going to be too much red tape, we have other options."

"Like what?" Decker said.

"I'll get into that when and if."

Dan steadied himself. *If they can trace this Snake to Salinas, we're screwed.*

Decker nodded. "Fair enough." He turned to Dan. "And finally, what's DEA got?"

Dan licked his dry lips. Truth was, he'd gone through some motions but hadn't done much of anything. But he couldn't tell Decker that.

"We've got all our ears open. I wasn't specific about kidnapping or assassination plots, but I put the word through to check all our informants and inside people about any rumors as to how the traffickers and the cartel are reacting to the threat of decriminalization."

"And?"

"And nothing yet."

Which was true. It was too early to hear much of substance, but the little that was filtering back was negative. Salinas had done a good job of keeping his operation under wraps, but it looked as if he'd hired a bunch of rank amateurs to pull it off.

"All right," Decker said. "That's where we stand. We've got lots of leads, lots of new information, but also the damnedest set of new questions. If the toe VanDuyne received isn't his daughter's, then whose is it? Or rather, whose *was* it? Why send someone else's toe? We know Katie was in the Falls Church house at one time, but where is she now? And why was she moved? Why was a small-time thug named Paul DiCastro murdered in that house? Was he part of the action from the outset or someone trying to horn in? Who does the other bloodstain on the carpet belong to? Another of the kidnappers or an outsider? And where is this wounded person? Is this a small-time or big-time operation? Did the kidnappers have a falling out? Is the conspiracy busted? Who was the woman that called VanDuyne and offered to return his daughter—for *no* ransom—and then never showed. *What the hell is going on?*"

"Damn straight," Canney said. "This one's got to be the most bizarre goddamn kidnapping I've ever seen or heard of. One moment it appears to be a highly sophisticated operation; the next—strictly amateur hour."

You've got that right, Dan thought. But Carlos Salinas is a pro. Some of the people he hired may have fucked up, but even as we sit here, he's tying up all those loose ends.

Dan forced himself to relax.

Everything will be all right. Salinas will have everything under control soon, if not already. He won't leave a trace.

4 "Where *is* he?" Carlos pounded the desk with both fists.

"He could be anywhere," Gold said. "We have his house staked out, so we know he's not there. We just have to wait until he calls in."

The MBA looked fidgety, and Carlos was glad of it. Let him be frightened of me. Let him fear not only for his future income, but for his physical well being. His *life*.

Because Carlos was afraid for all those things himself. MacLaglen might be alive, but he might be hurt and hiding somewhere, or even dying. Carlos was not concerned about the *cabrón*'s health so much as the fact that his very disappearance might trigger the release of that damned tape.

"I want him found!" He turned to Llosa. "Get some men together. We have a picture of MacLaglen—have copies made. We know he likes to call from hotels. Make the rounds. Go from hotel to hotel and look for him."

It was a long shot, but he couldn't simply sit here and wait for something to happen.

Llosa nodded and pulled out a pistol. "And when I find him, should I . . . ?"

"*Madre*, no!" He didn't want Gold or Llosa or anyone to know about the tape. "Bring him here, to me. He has much explaining to do, and a dead man cannot explain."

5 Poppy checked out her hair in the bathroom mirror.

"It'll grow back," she told herself for the hundredth time since she'd started hacking it off.

Her China doll bob was gone. So was the Deadly Nightshade rinse. Instead she now sported jet-black hair, close on the sides, spiked on top. Kind of retro and like eighties-ish, and normally she wouldn't be caught dead looking like this, but the whole idea of the makeover was staying alive.

She checked out the rest of her get-up: baggy jeans, oversized denim shirt, sneakers. She'd removed her earrings, eyebrow ring, and nostril stud. No makeup, no nail polish, and still no way she'd pass for a guy. But Mac would have to be looking pretty damn close to recognize the Poppy Mulliner he'd known.

Katie, however, was like a totally different story. Poppy stepped back into the sleeping area and admired her handiwork.

Katie sat on the bed, remote in hand, channel surfing. She'd been a little difficult during her makeover, but seemed to have forgotten it now. But it had been worth all the trouble. Katie really looked like a little boy.

A *red-haired* little boy. Poppy had tried to make her a blonde, but the bleaching solution had turned her dark hair red instead. Which was okay, she guessed. Blond would have been cooler, but with the short bowl cut Poppy had given her, her Jets T-shirt, and jeans and sneakers to match Poppy's, she looked ready for peewee football practice.

I hope this works, she thought. Just long enough for you to get to safety and me to disappear.

She put on a smile and clapped her hands. "Hey, bro. Let's go. How's a call to your daddy sound?"

Katie dropped the remote and ran to the phone.

"Can I dial?"

"You sure can. But let's find another phone, okay?"

Before leaving, Poppy scoured the room of every trace that they'd been here. Even if someone tracked them to this room, they'd have no notion that hair had been cut or dyed.

She stopped their newly red truck at a gas station, got a fistful of change ready, let Katie punch in her dad's cell phone number, then held the handset between them as her father answered.

"Hi, Daddy. It's me."

"Katie!" said a masculine voice. "Oh, Katie, thank God it's you! What happened? I thought I was going to see you last night. I waited and waited."

Poppy heard the voice crack and almost break with emotion. Damn me, she thought. I should've let him know I wasn't coming.

"I fell asleep," Katie said.

"Are you all right?"

"Sure. We're playing let's pretend and you know what we did?"

Poppy pulled the handset away. "Let me talk now, okay?"

No telling who might be listening. Maybe even Mac. Paulie said he was a genius. He might have tapped Katie's home line, but how could you tap a cellular phone? No wires.

"Sorry about last night," she said. "I had to like change plans."

"As long as Katie's all right. But she needs her medicine. She—"

"All taken care of," Poppy said.

A pause on the other end, then, "But the pills were left—"

"Don't worry about it. I'm taking good care of her. I ain't about to let her start having fits."

"Can I ask how you got them? I mean, is it the right dose?"

"Exactly the same as the ones in the bottle. I had to like knock over a drugstore to get them."

After another pause, longer this time. "You did that for Katie? You . . . you really do care about her, don't you."

"Sure. You got a great kid here." A *totally* great kid. "But how come she's got like this dent in her head?"

"An . . . accident. A fractured skull. It left her with the seizure disorder." He cleared his throat. "Listen . . . can I ask you . . . is she all there? I mean, her toes . . . ?"

"Yeah. She's still got all ten. How'd you figure out the one you got wasn't hers?"

"A laboratory. Were you the one responsible for—I mean, for not . . ."

"Not allowing her to get hurt? Yeah. Me and Paulie. And it got Paulie killed."

"The dead man in the house?"

Now it was Poppy's turn to get tight in the throat. She swallowed. "Yeah. He was a good guy. He died protecting her."

"I . . . I don't know how to thank you . . . I'll never be able to thank you enough . . . but I don't understand. . . ."

"It's like a long story and I don't have time to tell it. But what you gotta know is that the guy who killed Paulie is still alive. That's why I didn't bring Katie last night. I thought he was totally dead. I mean, like I put a bullet in his head. I—"

"You?"

"Well, yeah. He was trying to hurt Katie. She knows what he looks like, so he'll still be after her. If I give her back, you gotta get her protection."

"Oh, trust me, she'll have the best protection in the world. I guarantee as soon as she's back the FBI, the Secret Service, and DEA, even the CIA will be guarding her."

Poppy's stomach did a flip-flop. All those federal initials. What if they were looking for Katie now? That meant they were looking for her too. Suddenly she wanted this all over with.

"They'll protect you as well," Katie's father was saying.

"Oh, I don't know about that. My hands ain't so clean in this."

"Believe me, you bring Katie back and help them, all sorts of deals can be made."

"I think I'd just like to fade into the scenery, if you don't mind."

She kept thinking: *FBI, Secret Service, DEA, CIA.* She glanced at her watch. She'd been on the line *far* too long. Her mind raced. How could she get Katie safe back home? Couldn't do it back in the D.C. area, and she couldn't stay around here any longer. Where?

And then she knew.

"All right, look. Here's how it'll go down: I'll meet you in A.C. tomorrow and give Katie back."

"Aycee?"

"Atlantic City." Paulie liked blackjack; they used to hit the casinos regularly. "Register tonight in Bally's Park Place under your own name and I'll get in touch. You'll have Katie back like tomorrow for sure."

"Can't we do something today?"

"Sorry. Gotta be tomorrow. Bally's. Don't forget."

She hung up.

"You didn't let me say bye," Katie said.

"Oh, I'm sorry, honeybunch. But guess what? You're going back to him tomorrow for sure."

Katie's big smile and the light in her eyes were daggers through Poppy's heart. *Aren't you going to miss me? Just a little?*

6 Every time he thought things couldn't get worse, they did.

Dan Keane sat in on the task force update and tried to appear calm as Decker summarized the latest information. But it wasn't easy. Murphy's Law had taken over.

" . . . and so it appears that the actual kidnap operation is a bust. If we can trust this unidentified woman who's been calling VanDuyne, the kidnappers had a falling out over cutting off the child's toe. The disagreement left Paul DiCastro dead and someone named 'Mac' wounded. 'Mac' may or may not be 'Snake.' According to the woman, he's got a head wound. Consequently, we've got an APB out for a man with a gunshot head wound—officially listed as a suspect in the Falls Church killing. We're combing emergency rooms in a fifty-mile radius."

I've got to call Salinas, Keane thought. He's got to start his own ER sweep.

"We *want* this guy. We've got to get to him before he gets to Katie VanDuyne. Once we have him, we can tie him to the kidnapping and to the murder. With those counts against him, I know we can make him roll over and give up whoever put him up to this."

Canney spoke up. "But first we need Katie VanDuyne alive and well. We traced the last call to a pay phone in Edgewood, Maryland, but they could be anywhere between Maryland and Atlantic City now. We could clamp down on the A.C. Expressway and check every car, but that might frighten her off. We want this exchange to *happen*. We want Katie back. We'd also like the woman who has her, of course, but we'll settle for Katie. She can identify 'Mac.' She's the key right now."

"Right," Decker said. "That's why this will be our last face-to-face meeting for a while. Gerry and I are heading to Atlantic City tonight. That's where VanDuyne's supposed to get Katie back. We'll bug his phone and be in the wings making sure nothing goes wrong."

Why risk another call? Keane thought. I'm clean. No links. Let's keep it that way.

Right. Everything has already gone to hell. Let Salinas worry about it. Time for Dan Keane to wash his hands of the whole affair. Let the little girl get home to her father, let Decker and Canney catch this wounded kidnapper. It won't matter. He was certain Salinas had insulated himself from the plot. And if this missing guy does pose a threat, Salinas will see to it that he never gets a chance to talk.

What mattered was that the plan had worked. That fool Winston was in Bethesda Naval rather than on his way to The Hague. His decriminalization debacle was heading for derailment. Without him, it would never get back ontrack.

And I did it.

Dan headed straight home to Georgetown after the meeting. Still early on this Sunday afternoon, but he needed a drink. A stiff one. He wished Carmella and the kids hadn't gone to Florida. He didn't feel like being alone today.

The phone was ringing as he entered his townhouse. He hurried down the narrow front hall and snatched it up.

"Hello, Mr. Keane."

Dan nearly fell into a chair as he recognized the voice. He could not speak.

"Hello?" said Carlos Salinas. "Are you still there?"

His panicked mind whirled. How? How did he trace me? What do I do?

Play dumb.

"Who . . . who is this?"

A laugh. "You know very well who this is. And I know who *you* are."

Dan said nothing. His body had turned to stone . . . *cold* stone.

"I haven't heard from you since yesterday so I am calling to see if you are all right."

"I'm fine," Dan managed. This couldn't be happening. Salinas couldn't have traced him. It was impossible. He'd covered himself completely. "What do you want?"

"I would like some news. Our lost *amigo* is still missing. Has anyone found him?"

Play dumb!

"I don't know what you're talking about."

"Really? Tell me then, do you recognize this voice?"

Dan heard a click, then a recorded voice coming through the receiver: *"What kind of half-assed operation are you running there, Salinas? I just learned that a bottle of pills belonging to the little girl was found in a house in Falls Church where someone was murdered. What the hell is going on?"*

Dan felt his stomach heave. My voice!

Had the distorter failed?

"How?"

"A miraculous world we live in, no? What is hidden can be found. What is distorted can be made clear." Salinas's voice lost all its lightness. "Now tell me, señor, what are the latest developments?"

Dan raged—at himself, at this slimeball drug pusher—and thrashed about for a way out of this. He could speak—the chances of his home phone being monitored were near zero—but he loathed the idea of becoming a pawn to this creature.

"Hurry, señor. We do not have much time. This should be of equal concern to you because if I am taken into custody, my collection of tapes comes with me. Where is our friend?"

Dan sagged. He was trapped.

"No one knows. Supposedly he had a head wound. They're searching high and low for him. If you know what's good for you, you'll find him first."

"And the child?"

"Apparently she saw 'our friend' and can identify him. A woman is going to return her to her father in Atlantic City tomorrow."

"A woman . . . that is very interesting. I will look into this. And I hope to hear from you frequently. Remember, your freedom is tied to mine."

The line went dead. Dan sat with the silent handset dangling from his fingers. He felt dead inside. The only thing stirring was fear. No longer fear for his country and his career. Now he feared for his freedom, for his life.

What had he *done?*

MONDAY

"You're a mess," Snake muttered as he stood before the motel bath-room mirror and redressed his wounds. "But you're alive."

That alone was a miracle.

Most of Saturday was still a blur. He vaguely remembered coming to in that empty house—Paulie had been there, lying next to him, but he no longer counted—and climbing to his feet, unable to see out of his right eye. What he remembered best was the pain, the excruciating pain in his eye and the right side of his head. And the blood. Running down the side of his head, down his neck, under his shirt. He'd finally found a towel and tied it around his head.

Somehow he'd found his keys. He grabbed them and his revolver and staggered out to the Jeep. Somehow, he'd managed to drive away before the cops arrived.

And all the time his beeper going, each beep a spear of pain through his head.

He hadn't wanted to go home, but that bitch had stolen his wallet and his jacket and he needed cash. Lots of it. He knew a guy in Northeast D.C., an M.D. whose license had been yanked because of his fondness for Class II controlled substances, and his habit of selling prescriptions for the same. But that hadn't stopped him from practicing. His name was out: You got a reportable wound you don't want recorded, see Doc Moeller.

But he only took cash.

The doc stitched up the ragged furrow the bullet had torn from the corner of Snake's right eye, across his temple, to somewhere above his right ear, saying how lucky he was that the temporal artery had only been nicked. Straightened out his broken nose. That was the good news. Nothing he could do about that right eye, though. It was shot—literally and figuratively. The bullet had nicked it, causing intraocular hemorrhage, the muzzle flash had seared it, and it was completely out of order. Maybe an opthamologist could salvage it, but the doc doubted it.

At the very least the eye work would take days, and most likely a stay in a hospital, and Doc Moeller didn't know of an opthamologist who wouldn't report the bullet wound.

So that was out.

Call me Deadeye.

The bleeding had stopped, but the pain went on and on. A symphony of agony—deep throbbing basso aches inside his skull accompanied by tight steady whining jabs from his scalp and nose, highlighted by staccato bursts of glass-shard stabs in his eye socket. The Percodans he was popping like M&M's did next to nothing to mute the pain.

He squeezed a glob of antibiotic ointment onto a gauze eye pad and pressed it over the red horror that had once been his eye. Then he began winding a roll of two-inch gauze around his head.

But then he dropped the roll and grabbed the sink, hanging on as the bathroom suddenly spun around him. His head had been playing that trick for two days now. Doc Moeller had told him to expect it—post-concussion syndrome, or some such. Whatever it was called, it was scary. Didn't want something like that to happen when he was driving.

But he was going to have to drive today. Get out of this neighborhood and find a phone. He'd stopped at the first motel he'd seen after leaving Doc Moeller's—somewhere on Rhode Island Avenue. He had to be the only white man in a couple of miles. He sure as hell wasn't going to call from this room. Probably have to go into the Federal area to find a phone that worked or didn't have a pusher hogging it.

The room steadied and he straightened up from his death lock on the sink. He finished winding the fresh gauze around his head and stared at his handiwork. Gauze encircled his forehead, running down over his right eye and covering the whole right side of his head, including the ear. Not as neat as the doc's had been, but it would do.

He thought of Poppy and the hot surge of hate and rage made his pain recede a little. This was all her doing. What'd she think she was up to? Shooting him and running off with the kid. What was going on in her crazy head? When he got hold of her . . .

He could still see the look in her eyes as she'd pulled the trigger. She was crazy, that bitch. And she'd damn near killed him. A fucking broad had got the best of him. How the hell had he let that happen? Sure, he'd been groggy from that conk on the head, but still it wasn't something he'd ever talk about. He could barely face himself.

And Paulie. For the life of him, Snake couldn't figure out what had gone wrong with Paulie. Such a simple thing to chop off the package's toe and send it to the father. What was the big fucking deal? Why couldn't he have just done as he was told?

And why had he got in Snake's way when he went after the package? Didn't make any sense. Not at all like Paulie.

Only one explanation: Poppy. She'd done something to Paulie's head. Probably got into some mother thing with the package. Snake remembered the way she'd been cradling the kid when he'd come after her. Yeah. Had to be it. And she'd infected Paulie.

So *stupid!*

Poppy's fault. All of this.

His beeper went off again in the next room. Shit, didn't Salinas ever give up?

All right. He couldn't put it off any longer. He was going to have to call in.

Luckily, things didn't look near as bad as they really were. Unlikely that Salinas knew anything about the trouble at the Falls Church house. The story of the killing had been on the news, but nothing to connect it to a kidnapping. And no one had mentioned Paulie's name.

And the Pres was still in Bethesda. Salinas should be happy about that.

Sure. He could convince Salinas that he still had the kid and that everything was under control. They could go on stringing VanDuyne along while they waited for Winston to die.

And meanwhile Snake would be scouring the whole goddamn countryside for Poppy and that brat.

And when he found her . . . ohhhh, yes, when he found her . . .

He'd fantasize later. Right now he had to get to a phone.

2 Decker had been on his way out of W-16 when Razor called. He
updated him on the latest developments.

"So John's in Atlantic City now?"

"Yes, sir. He checked into Bally's last night. We bugged his room while
he was out to dinner. I'm on my way there now myself."

"Does he really think he can handle this better on his own?"

"Apparently. He hasn't told us about the phone calls."

"Well, keep an eye on him. I want you to make sure he gets Katie
back unharmed. And I want you to make that happen today. Let me
know the instant she's in safe hands. As soon as you call, I'm out of here.
I'm going buggy in this hospital."

"Yes, sir," Decker said, trying to sound neutral. He was remembering
VanDuyne's crushed, haunted look as he'd left the Maryland House
Friday night. Something must have come through.

"Don't think I don't appreciate what John's going through. Nor that
I'm not concerned about Katie. I am. But larger matters are involved
here. As soon as I know she's safe, I can get out in public again and let
whoever's behind this know that they've failed."

"Yes, sir. We'll do everything we can."

"And tell John to give me a call at the White House as soon as he gets
home with Katie."

"Will do, sir."

Decker hung up and called Gerry Canney, who was with the surveillance team in A.C.

"Any contact from the woman yet?"

"Nothing. He called his mother and that was it. But we do have a
problem."

"What?"

"His wife. She followed him here."

"I thought your man was going to box her out like last time."

"That was the plan. And he was following her when he got jammed
behind a truck-bus accident on the turnpike. She slipped past and he
was never able to catch up."

"Do we know where she is?"

"Not exactly, but she's got to be somewhere in the vicinity of Bally's.

We're keeping an eye out. If she shows up and looks like she's going to be trouble, we'll isolate her."

"Do that. I don't want anything to queer the transfer this time. And neither does Razor."

"You spoke to him?"

"Just got off the phone. He wants this settled *today*."

"I hear you."

Decker hung up and headed for Andrews Air Force Base to hop a copter. He'd be in A.C. in a couple of hours. The thought of VanDuyne's ex wandering around without a tail bothered him. Here it wasn't even nine A.M. and already something had gone wrong.

What next?

3 "Let me speak to the man."

"What?" A pause. "Is this . . . ?"

Snake recognized Gold's voice, but it sounded strange. Strained.

"Yeah. This is me. Here's where I am." Snake began to read off the hotel phone when Gold interrupted him.

"Wait, wait. Let me get a pen."

What was this? Gold always had a gold Mont Blanc stuck in his shirt pocket. While Snake waited, he took a quick look around the hotel lobby. The sudden movement brought on another spasm of vertigo. He clung to the phone to keep from rocking. Didn't want anyone to think he was drunk. They'd boot him out.

The lobby steadied and he saw that no one was paying any attention to him. The combination of a bulky sweatshirt with the hood up, and the largest pair of sunglasses he could find, hid ninety percent of his bandages. Still he felt as if he were carrying a blinking neon sign: *Look at me. . . . Look at me. . . .*

"Okay," Gold said. "Got it. Give it to me."

Snake read it off and was about to hang up when Gold spoke again.

"He's, um, indisposed at the moment, so it might take a little longer for him to get back to you. Be patient."

Snake had a sudden vision of Salinas on the crapper, his rolls of fat bulging over—

He banished the thought. "Okay, fine. I'll wait."

"So, um, where've you been?"

Small talk from Gold—the last thing he needed.

"Busy. What's it to you?"

"Well, we've been paging you for days."

"You have? Hmmph. Maybe I'd better get my beeper checked. Battery must be low. Haven't heard a thing."

"Yeah, you damn well better get it checked. The man has had some important things to discuss with you."

"Really? I can hardly wait."

Snake depressed the plunger, but kept the phone to his unbandaged ear while he waited for the call back.

The man has had some important things to discuss with you.

Snake didn't like the sound of that. Could Salinas know about the fuckup at the house?

He leaned against the edge of the booth. He wished Salinas would hurry up and call back. And he wished they had seats for these phones. He was feeling weak and shaky, and his head—his goddamn head was killing him.

Come on, Fatso! Let's get this over with!

And then the phone rang. Snake immediately released the plunger. "Yeah."

Salinas's voice: "Miguel. So good to speak to you. I was worried about you."

Something in the tone sent a chill down Snake's back. Too calm, too pleasant.

"Why would you be worried?"

"I was not able to find you. You were not answering your pages."

"Like I told your butt boy, I'll have to replace the battery."

"Please do. Now tell me, how is the package faring?"

"The package is fine."

"Everything is under control?"

He knows something, dammit!

"Why do you ask?"

"Because of stories I have heard."

Uh-oh. "Really?" Snake tried to keep his voice light while his stomach was filling with lead. "Like what?"

"Oh, that the doctor has spoken to the package on the phone and a woman has promised to return it to him . . ."

No!

" . . . and that a government laboratory discovered that a toe supposedly belonging to the package actually came from a little boy—an *embalmed* little boy.

Shit!

"Let's see . . . what else? Oh, yes, that a dead man discovered in Falls Church is linked to the package, and that a hunt is on for a man known as 'Snake' and a man known as 'Mac'—both possibly the same man—who was seriously wounded in that same house."

Now Snake *really* needed a seat. He was sweating and shaking—and not from fever. But even if he had one, he couldn't allow himself to sit. He had to get out of here.

"Do not hang up, Miguel," Salinas said, and now there was an edge to his voice. "We are not finished speaking. And if you look around, I am sure you will see a familiar face."

Snake turned—slowly this time—and stifled a gasp as he spotted Llosa standing half a dozen feet away, a smile on his pitted face, his right hand in his coat pocket.

Now he understood all the delays—Gold looking for a pen, Salinas "indisposed" so he couldn't call back right away. Delaying tactics so they could trace the call and give Llosa time to find him.

What a goddamn sucker!

Snake swallowed. "I see him. What's he doing here?"

"He was already out looking for you. Now he is going to escort you to a warehouse I lease. I am going to meet you there. And then we are going to have a very deep discussion, you and I. *Mano a mano.* I will want some answers."

Snake glanced at Llosa again and saw that he wasn't alone. Someone had joined him. Snake had never seen the new man before, but had little doubt from his coloring and dress that he was another Colombian.

"Don't forget the tapes," he told Salinas. "Remember the tapes."

"I remember them. They are among the things we will discuss."

Snake knew what kind of discussions Salinas had in mind—probably with meat hooks and cattle prods. Salinas would want to know the locations of all the tapes, and Snake knew he'd give them up—every one of them—before the first jab of pain. The thought of adding torture to the pain he'd already endured for the past two days made him feel even weaker than he already was.

He had to think fast. Do something, anything, to keep from taking a ride with Llosa and his pal.

Something rattling around in the back of his head, something bad . . . talk of the tape had shaken it loose. A tape . . . his missing jacket . . .

And then it hit him. Hit him hard, making him a little sick. He'd thought things were bad before. They'd suddenly got worse.

"The girl has one of the tapes," he said.

Salinas was silent. "I do not think I believe you, Miguel."

"I swear it's true. She got the drop on me. She took my jacket while I was out. I had a copy of the tape in one of the pockets. She's got it."

"Then we will have to find her."

"*I'll* find her. I've known her for years. I know her better than anyone you've got. If anyone can find her, I can."

Only marginally true. Everything he knew about Poppy-the-bitch-Mulliner was what he'd heard from Paulie, and that hadn't been a hell of a lot. Next to nothing, in fact. But Salinas didn't know that.

"*No me jodas!* Llosa will bring you in . . . where you will be safe. It is for your own protection."

"Look, man," Snake said, desperate now. He had to convince this greaseball. "I've got as big a stake as you in finding her. That tape was only supposed to be listened to if I was dead. *I'm on it too!* If that gets around, my ass is on the line with yours!"

Salinas let out a long stream of profanity in Spanish. Snake could catch only snippets, but he got the idea.

Finally Salinas ran out of steam and agreed to let Snake stay on the streets and search for Poppy. But he wanted Llosa to go with him. More arguing before Snake convinced him that not only would Llosa slow him down, but Salinas would be better served by having Llosa search separately.

"Very well. Search on your own. But no games when you find her. Finish it and let me know immediately."

"I'll send you her head."

"You will find her in Atlantic City. She will be contacting the doctor about returning the package today. He is staying at Bally's Park Place."

How does he *know* all this? Snake wondered, amazed as ever by Salinas's connections.

"I'm on my way." He eyed Llosa and his buddy, waiting expectantly. "But you'd better talk to your amigo here, so he knows his assignment's been changed."

Salinas sighed. "Put him on."

Snake held up the phone and called to Llosa. "Yo! The boss wants to talk to you."

And while Llosa got new orders, Snake reviewed what he knew about A.C., which was damn near nothing. He'd never been there. Gambling was for jerks.

Didn't matter. He'd haul ass up there this morning and learn about it. One way or another he'd find the bitch and the kid, grab the tape, and tie up the last loose ends.

Then he'd disappear. Forget the final payment. He wanted to get as far away as possible from Carlos Salinas.

Singapore sounded pretty good right now.

After Atlantic City.

4 Marnie watched the elevators over the top edge of her complimentary copy of *USA Today*. She'd followed John here in a different rental car—a red one this time. She'd even parked near him in the Bally's garage and followed him inside, watched him register.

She was tired, but she wasn't giving up. She'd positioned herself in the Bally's lobby first thing this morning and had been on sentry duty ever since.

Sooner or later, John would have to show. And then she'd follow him to Katie.

What are you up to, John?

Marnie was sure that Katie wasn't at John's house. She'd peeked in the windows a couple of times during the dinner hour and had only seen John and his battle-ax mother at the table. He must have hidden Katie away in another of his cruel attempts to keep them apart.

But if you're *not* here to see Katie, what *are* you doing? Gambling?

What kind of father hides his daughter from her natural mother—
God knows where he's stuck her—and goes traipsing off to a casino?

And he calls *me* a bad parent . . . and dangerous.

Probably here to see one of his whores. Marnie had never been able
to catch John at it, but she'd been sure he was sleeping around before
the divorce. Katie knew all about it, but she'd kept John's secrets . . . no
matter what.

Always hiding things from me, those two.

You've corrupted her, John, I know it. But she's still young. None of
the damage is permanent. I'll get her back. I'll save her. I'll straighten
her out.

5   The phone rang at 11:02. John knew because he'd been sitting on
the bed since 7:13 A.M., watching the red LED numerals climb
toward noon.

"Hi, Daddy."

Katie! John's heart soared. She sounded so close. And suddenly he
was sure that this time it would work. Today he'd get her back.

"Hi, honey. Where are you?"

"With Poppy."

Poppy . . . was that—?

Suddenly the woman was on the line. "Uh, you should like forget you
heard that, okay?"

"Heard what?" John said.

"That's the spirit."

He hoped they understood each other. If this woman truly had saved
Katie's toe and Katie's life and was truly returning her to him unharmed—she'd said she robbed a drugstore for the Tegretol—he would
forget anything he knew about her. No court in the world could get him
to remember her name or the sound of her voice.

"Are we set for today?"

"We are. Go down to the boardwalk at three and stand by the phones
between Boardwalk Rogers and Planet Hollywood."

"Where's that?"

"Just a little ways down from where you are. You can't miss Board-walk Rogers—looks like a little ceramic church or something. I'll call the first phone on the left and let you know where to pick up Katie."

Three o'clock . . . seemed like years away.

"Can't we make it earlier?"

"Three. I got some things to work out first. We don't want no screw-ups."

"No. We don't. Okay. First phone on the left. At three. Got it. But I'll be there well before that. Call me earlier if you want."

John planned to be at that phone around two. He didn't want a scene like the one in Lafayette Square last week. No arguments this time over whose phone it was. He'd claim it and hold on to it.

6   Bob Decker took Canney's call on the car phone on his way in from the A.C. heliport. He glanced at his watch.

"Three o'clock? Can you get someone over to that phone to hook up—?"

"Already on his way. But we need more manpower. We need people stretched all along the boardwalk, because sure as hell she's going to do the Hollywood thing."

"What's that?"

"You know. In the movies. You've seen it—where the kidnapper keeps someone running from phone to phone. It's been shown so many times, real kidnappers have come to assume that's the way it's done."

"This is my first kidnapping," Decker said. "I'll have to take your word for it."

"It's actually pretty effective, especially if the caller keeps switching phones as well."

"So I take it the last place we should concentrate our troops is around the phones."

"You got it. You can bet VanDuyne's going to be sent somewhere else. Oh, and we got a bonus out of the call: The woman's name is Poppy."

"Poppy . . . could be her real name, could just mean she's a junkie."

"I know. But we're running it through New York. That's where DiCastro lived. Maybe we'll get lucky."

"Okay. As for manpower, see how many people you can grab from the Bureau, and I'll call Keane to see what DEA can supply. I figure they should have a fair number of agents around fun city here."

Decker hung up and leaned back. Things looked good. This whole thing might be wrapped by four P.M.

7   "What a dump," Snake thought as he stood by a pay phone at New York and Atlantic Avenues and waited for Salinas to return his call.

This wasn't anything like the Atlantic City he'd seen on TV. Looked more like the Bronx. He didn't like even being out of his Jeep, but using his car phone was verboten.

He felt like crap. This headache wouldn't quit. He was ready to bang his head against the sidewalk—that might feel better than this deep relentless ache. And the drive up here had been pure hell. With only one eye, his depth perception was off and he'd damn near cracked up half a dozen times. And now the sun was so damn hot he was sweating and itching under the bandages, and so bright it hurt his bad eye even through the shades and the gauze eye pad,

Dizzy . . . sick . . . in pain . . . and suffocating inside this hooded sweatshirt. He wanted to kill somebody.

An emaciated-looking black guy shuffled toward Snake through the nearby vacant lot and offered him a flyer. Snake's first instinct was to wave him off—the last thing he was interested in now was an ad for some local grind house or escort service—but better to take the sheet than have some crackhead hanging around while he was trying to talk to Salinas.

But even after Snake took the flyer, the guy stood there staring at his face, at the bandages.

"What're you looking at?" Snake snapped.

"Nothin'." The burnout moved off. "Nothin' ay-tall."

Snake crumbled the flyer and was about to toss it into the gutter when he spotted the word REWARD. He flattened it out again and read

about the thousand bucks being offered for information as to the whereabouts of two runaways—an eighteen-year-old and her little sister. The
descriptions perfectly matched the ones Snake had supplied Salinas with
before leaving D.C. this morning.

Poppy was no eighteen-year-old, but the rest of the description fit.
Anybody who spotted her with that little girl wouldn't be put off by the
fact that she didn't look quite like a teenager. They'd drop a dime to the
local number listed at the bottom of the sheet.

A thousand bucks. That's all? Salinas should be willing to pay a million to get his hands on Poppy and the kid. Then Snake realized the fat
man couldn't let on how important they were. A grand sounded about
right for a couple of runaways—and it would buy somebody a lot of
crack.

He wondered how many of these flyers were floating around. Probably every junkie and pusher in A.C. had one. Had to be thousands of
junkies in town. Each one turning a daily profit for the traffickers. All
that money . . . millions and billions flowing from cities and towns all
over the map. No wonder Salinas and his bosses wanted to off a guy looking to legalize their trade.

The phone rang. Salinas was on, sounding like he was riding the edge
as he launched into a rapid-fire spiel.

"The doctor will be waiting for a call in front of Boardwalk Rogers.
You can be sure the delivery won't be there. His phone is not secure.
You will be called shortly after he is contacted, so keep your cell phone
at hand. Be careful. Very many feds around."

And that was it. The line went dead.

Salinas had to be feeling pretty desperate if he was talking about contacting him on his cell phone. But Snake could think of ways to endrun
the cellular's vulnerability to eavesdropping. The most obvious was to
relay the message to someone at a pay phone, and have him make a
short, cryptic call to the cell phone.

Whatever. Snake wasn't going to waste time worrying about it.
Salinas would be cool. He was pretty canny when it came to phone security.

What Snake wanted to know was what the hell he was going to do
with the info Salinas relayed to him, especially with the city crawling
with feds? Obviously he had a man inside, and that was fine for raw data.

But what if Snake needed a little assistance? What was he going to do—recruit a bunch of crackheads?

Sure.

Right now the best thing he could do was cruise the casino area and hope he got lucky.

Or hope Poppy got unlucky.

8   "Can I help you?"

Poppy nearly yelped in fright as she whirled to face the salesgirl. "N-no. We're just looking. Th-thanks."

Jesus, she thought, shaking inside as the salesgirl smiled down at Katie. I'm about ready to jump out of my skin.

Poppy and Katie had spent the last ten minutes standing at the rear of Peanut World—"The Boardwalk's Largest Gift, Nut & Candy Shop!"—first looking at the T-shirts, sweatshirts, caps, ashtrays, thimbles, every imaginable piece of junk, each imprinted with ATLANTIC CITY; then they oohed and ahhed at the elephants, alligators, cats, dogs, and other animals made of sea shells; then they moved to the candy counter, checking out the fudge, the jellies, and the salt-water taffy, pretending to be trying to decide which flavor to buy. At least Poppy was pretending. But they weren't here for taffy. The real attraction was the view of the phones on the boardwalk about fifty yards south of Peanut World's door.

"Tough to decide, huh?" the salesgirl told Katie, then glanced up at Poppy. "You think your little boy would like to try a sample?"

Poppy suppressed a smile—Katie really did look like a strawberry-blond boy. But Katie frowned and put her hands on her hips.

"I'm not—"

Poppy jumped in. "Yeah, he'd love some."

As the salesgirl turned to pick from the bins, Poppy nudged Katie and whispered, "Let's pretend—remember?"

The salesgirl picked out three different flavors and handed them to Katie.

"Here y'go, guy. Enjoy."

Then she moved off.

Poppy looked around the crowded store. Thank God it was a warm, sunny day. The whole boardwalk area was like mobbed with people getting out of their houses to take advantage of the summerlike day—after all, it was almost spring and they'd been cooped up all winter. The only bad thing was that they all seemed to be about a hundred years old, which made Poppy and Katie stick out more than she liked.

She hadn't dared even to glance at the phones as she'd hurried Katie inside, but now she felt it might be like safe to risk a peek. As Katie unwrapped a strawberry taffy stick and began to chew, Poppy stepped toward the front of the store; from within a cluster of people lined up to buy lottery tickets, she stared south along the boardwalk.

Bright sunlight from a robin's-egg sky glittered off the darker blue of the ocean. White sand, strewn with seaweed, stretched to the boardwalk where two people hung by the bank of four phones—one was a woman by a middle phone, the other a tall, dark-haired man standing by the last phone on the left. The Katie phone. And he looked a little like Katie.

No . . . he looked a *lot* like Katie.

And then it hit Poppy.

I'm gonna lose her.

Suddenly her throat was tight. She turned to look at Katie, happily chomping away as she began unwrapping another stick. She looked up at Poppy and waved, smiling around the huge wad of taffy bulging the side of her cheek.

Poppy felt her eyes fill with tears. Only like five days since she first laid eyes on that kid and yet right now she didn't know how she was going to live without her.

I can't let her go.

And yet she knew she had to. A little girl belonged with her Daddy. But still . . .

She rushed over and lifted Katie in her arms, hugging her tight against her.

"I love you, Katie."

Katie's arms went around her neck. "I love you too, Poppy. Can you come home and live with me?"

"Oh, I'd love that, honeybunch, but I can't right away. I've got a few places I gotta go."

"How about when you come back?"

"Sure. If it's all right with your daddy."

"I'll ask him, 'kay?"

"'Kay."

The plan was to call the phone where Katie's dad was waiting and tell him he could find her in the taffy shop to his left. She'd rented a cell phone earlier—on one of Snake's cards—just for that one call.

She'd made it pretty clear to Katie's dad that no one else was supposed to be involved in this. But she couldn't like count on that.

She had to assume that a whole lot of people were out there waiting for this to go down. And she figured everybody would be expecting her to act like a typical kidnapper, like in the movies where they called people and told them to race to another phone to get the next call, and then to another phone for still another call.

But what if she told Katie's daddy on the very first call where he could find her? Who'd be expecting that?

All right, maybe it was an Appleton scheme, but it was the best she could come up with. And Appleton or not, it *felt* right. She'd leave Katie here, chomping on taffy, and wander out of the store, off the boardwalk, down to the street, get into the truck, and call Daddy on her cell phone as she was like driving away. She didn't feature leaving Katie alone, but it would only be a few minutes before Daddy got there, with maybe like a zillion feds and cops swarming into the store behind him.

She'd dump the cell phone somewhere, and keep driving . . . and cry all the way home.

All the way home . . .

Where had that come from? She didn't have a home. Not anymore. And nobody in Sooy's Boot much wanted to see her again.

Home. Sooy's Boot wasn't all that far from here. Was that why she'd chosen Atlantic City? So she could run home afterward?

She shook off the questions. She'd worry about them later. Right now she had to get Katie back where she belonged.

Sweet Jesus, how am I going to do this? How am I doing to let you go?

As Poppy closed her eyes and fought back the tears, she felt Katie stiffen and whisper, "Mommy."

"I wish I was, honeybunch, but you've got—"

"No. That's my mommy."

Poppy froze. What the hell was Katie's mother doing here? In *this* store? Despite the hair and boy clothes, had she recognized Katie and followed them in? Poppy couldn't see how anyone could spot Katie unless they were right on top of her, but maybe mothers had like an instinct for their own child.

All right, she told herself, stay calm.

Still holding Katie against her pounding heart, she made a half turn, slow and casual like.

The store was filled with women. None of them seemed to be staring at her or Katie.

"Don't point," Poppy whispered. "Just tell me who it is."

"By the door," Katie said softly in her ear. "With the big hat."

Poppy saw her now: Big dark glasses, wide floppy straw sun hat, the kind you could buy anywhere along the boardwalk, worn over a silk scarf wrapped around her head. Either she was allergic to the sun or thought she was like in disguise.

And she didn't even know they were here, right behind her. She was too busy staring out the door, watching the man who had to be Katie's father.

That was it. Dear old Dad must have told Mom that they were getting their daughter back today and the poor woman just couldn't stay away.

That lump in her throat again: She absolutely had to give Katie back to her folks. It was the only right thing to do.

And suddenly Poppy realized she'd been presented with a totally golden opportunity to do just that.

"Look, honeybunch," she whispered, "I'm gonna put you down and let you go to your mother. You—"

"No!" Katie's arms tightened around her neck. "I don't want to!"

"You gotta, honeybunch," Poppy said, deeply moved that Katie wanted to stay with her. "You gotta go back. Your mom will take you back to your dad."

Katie straightened and looked around. "Daddy? Is my daddy here?"

Poppy wondered at the change in Katie at the mention of her father. This was definitely Daddy's little girl.

Like I was . . . once.

"Not right here. But he's close by. You go with your mom and soon you'll be with your dad too. Okay?

"'Kay."

Poppy put her down and straightened her Jets shirt. She bit her lip to keep from crying.

I gotta get out of here before I start blubbering.

"You be a good girl, now," she told Katie, crouching before her and smoothing her chopped hair. "And you have a good life. And maybe you think of me once in a while, okay?"

"'Kay."

Poppy gathered her in her arms again and held her tight, never wanting to let her go, but knowing if she didn't get out of here right now she'd explode.

"I love you, little girl."

"I love you too, Poppy."

She forced herself to release Katie.

"Why are you crying?"

"Because I'm going to miss you." She wiped her eyes on her flannel sleeve. "But here's what you do. Wait a second or two while I go outside, then go up to your mother and say, 'Hi, Mom.' Can you do that?"

Katie nodded, her blue eyes flicking back and forth between her mother and Poppy. "But where will you be?"

"I'll be outside." Not a lie. She *would* be outside—far outside, and getting farther every second. "Got that? Wait till I'm outside; then go up to her."

"'Kay."

Poppy straightened and took one last look into that little face. She touched her cheek, then somewhere found the strength to turn and hurry past Katie's mother—still fixated on the phones outside—and stumble into the afternoon sunlight.

Feeling as if she'd torn out her heart and left it behind among the souvenirs, she made a sharp right and kept her head down as she forced one foot in front of the other away from the boardwalk.

She made it down the ramp to street level, was vaguely aware of the mass of Bally's on her right and a vacant lot to her left, but then the building pressure in her chest wouldn't let her go any farther. She stumbled into the shadow of an empty loading dock, sagged against a wall, and began to sob.

9 "Hi, Mom."

Marnie started and turned. This little boy, this ragamuffin with orange hair was tugging on her skirt and looking up at her. She brushed his hand off.

"Get away," she said. "I'm not your—"

Those eyes . . . those blue, blue eyes . . .

She looked closer.

"Oh . . . my . . . God!" It was Katie! Feeling faint, she dropped to one knee and grasped both her shoulders. "What has he done to you? Your hair! Your clothes!"

"Poppy—"

"Is that what he has you calling him now? Poppy? What else does he have you doing?"

She wrapped Katie in her arms, but the child didn't return the embrace. She remained stiff, wooden. Almost as if she were afraid. John's work—no question about it. Here was proof positive of how he'd been filling the child's head with terrible lies about her mother.

Suddenly Marnie was furious. John was such an expert at twisting the truth. And now he was twisting Katie—in body as well as soul. Look at her! How could he do this to his own daughter? What sort of perversion was this? Coloring her hair and dressing her like a boy? She sensed sickness here. Deep sickness.

Sickness the courts should know about, should see with their own eyes. . . .

A wonderful idea leaped full blown into her mind.

"Katie," she said. "I'm going to take you home."

Suddenly Katie seemed to relax. "Goodie! I want to see Daddy!"

Poppy . . . Daddy . . . the poor child didn't know what to call her father.

Marnie glanced out at the boardwalk. John was still by the phones. The negligent bastard! Leaving poor Katie alone in here while he waits for a call. But from whom? Some bimbo? Or worse—someone who liked little girls dressed up to look like boys?

Her stomach turned. It was a sick, sick world out there, and little girls like Katie needed to be protected from exploiters—especially if their father was doing the exploiting.

John was staring out at the ocean. Now seemed like the best time to move. Marnie lifted Katie and carried her from the store, keeping Katie's face and her own averted from John.

A matter of fifteen seconds and they were down on the street and out of sight of the boardwalk.

Marnie breathed a sigh of relief and set Katie back on the ground. She took a firm grip on her hand and led her toward Bally's parking garage.

"Where are we going?" Katie said.

"To get the car."

"And then we're gonna see Daddy?"

"No. Then we're going to the airport. We're flying back home." *I've got a lawyer and a judge who'll be very interested in seeing you just as you are. And then they'll change their exalted opinion of Dr. John VanDuyne.*

Katie pulled her hand free. "No! I want to see Daddy!"

"You will. I promise you." *When he has to appear in court.*

"I want to see him now!"

Marnie grabbed Katie's upper arm and yanked her toward the garage's glass-enclosed elevator area.

"No arguing now. Come along."

"No!"

Marnie felt her anger rising. Out of the corner of her eye she noticed people standing nearby on the sidewalk. She didn't want a scene here. As she pulled Katie inside the glass enclosure, she raised her voice, yet kept it cloyingly sweet for the benefit of anyone within earshot.

"Come on, baby," she said. "You can press the button when we get into the elevator. It's three. You know three, don't you?"

An elevator stood open and Marnie gave Katie the bum's rush through the doors.

"No!" Katie cried. "I don't want to be with you! I want to be with Daddy!"

That did it. Before she knew what she was doing, Marnie jabbed the "3" button herself, then gave Katie a well-deserved slap across her whiny little face. The sound echoing harshly in the tiny elevator cab as the doors slid closed.

"That's just about enough," she said. She glanced down at Katie who was holding her face with her free hand and sobbing softly. "One thing you're going to learn and learn well is to do as you're told and keep a civil tongue in your head."

The car stopped on the third level, the door slid open; and Marnie stepped out, pulling the still-sobbing Katie after her. Another glass enclosure. She stepped through the doors into the parking area and looked around. Now . . . where had she left her car?

Suddenly a noise to her left as the EXIT door slammed open; a slim young woman in jeans and a plaid shirt was moving toward her, breathing hard as if she'd been running. She had short, jet-black hair, and red-rimmed eyes. She looked as if she'd been crying. Those eyes blazed as they found Katie. She never stopped moving as she spoke through clenched teeth, bared in a snarl.

"You bitch!"

And then Marnie's face exploded with pain as the woman smashed a fist into her nose.

10 Mommy dearest staggered back as blood began pouring from her nose. She let go of Katie and raised her hands to her face. She began to scream and so Poppy hit her again, right in the bread basket.

She grunted, doubled over and lurched away, like she was going to run. Poppy started after her, fists raised, itching to hit her again.

Poppy had been crouched in the loading bay, bawling, feeling sorry for herself, when she spotted the mother dragging Katie down the street toward Bally's garage. Immediately she'd sensed something wasn't right. Why hadn't Katie been reunited with her daddy?

Poppy had followed them into the garage and seen her slap Katie just as the elevator doors shut.

What followed was mostly a blur—running up the steps with murder in her heart, pacing the elevator, getting to level three and seeing Katie with tears on her face and a big red slap mark across her cheek.

Something snapped in Poppy then, and Jesus it had felt so good flattening that bitch's nose. She wanted to keep on pounding her, let her know how it felt.

And now the bitch was trying to run. Still bent over, she staggered away. But she didn't get far. She ran the top of her head dead on into a concrete support. Poppy heard a meaty smack and then the bitch was crumbling to the floor like an empty burlap sack.

She stood over her, waiting for her to get up, but she didn't move.

And as suddenly as it had come, the red rage was gone. Poppy turned and hurried back to Katie. She swept her up in her arms and carried her toward the stairs.

"C'mon honeybunch. We're getting out of here."

She'd parked the truck across the street in a church parking lot. The place was plastered with no parking signs but she'd left a note on the dashboard about engine trouble and how she'd gone to get a mechanic—*Please, please, PLEASE don't tow me!* Risky, yeah, but she hadn't wanted to get trapped in one of these multilevel garages if she had to make a fast exit. Like now.

Poppy belted Katie into the passenger seat and pulled out onto Pacific. Not sure yet where she was going, she gunned past the medical center and headed up to Atlantic. A sign said NO RIGHT ON RED there but she made one anyway, just to keep moving.

As she braked for a stoplight at Kentucky, she turned to Katie who was still sobbing softly.

"You mad at me for hitting your mother?"

Katie sniffed. "No. I'm glad. She hurt me," she said, holding her reddened cheek. "She always hurts me."

"Yeah? Well she ain't never hurting you again."

"That's what my daddy said, but she did."

Your daddy's not too good at keeping promises, is he, Poppy thought. If he was, this never would have happened.

But in a way she was kind of glad things had gone wrong. It was like a sign.

Poppy didn't believe much in signs and all that religious mumbo jumbo, but Jesus, if something was supposed to be a signal that Katie was better off with her than with her own folks, that little scene back there in the garage was it. A totally major-league sign.

And that's fine with me, she thought, glancing over at Katie. I'll keep you for the rest of my life. I'll raise you just like I'd've raised Glory. You'll never have a lonely moment, and you'll never *ever* have to worry about getting hurt.

Jesus, what was it with people? Kids were supposed to be precious. They were helpless. They depended on big folks for like everything— food, clothes, a roof over their heads. And safety. Big folks were here to protect little folks until they could protect themselves. That was what it was all about. So what kind of a world did a kid see when she had to be afraid of the very people who were supposed to like protect her.

She leaned over and ever so gently kissed Katie's cheek.

"There. Does that make it feel better?"

Katie stopped sobbing, but the tears looked ready to run again at any second.

"You still don't look too happy. What say we get a Happy Meal the first McDonald's we see? How's that sound?"

She nodded and—finally—a smile.

"And I think you could use a big hug too, Katie. How about it?"

Another nod. Poppy snapped Katie's seat belt open and gathered her into her arms.

"You'll never get hurt again, Katie. I promise you that. From now on you're gonna have a safe and happy home. Just like mine."

The truth of that struck her like a blow. She'd had a very happy home growing up. Things had been iffy in the money department sometimes, but she'd always felt safe and wanted. And with her dad having all those brothers, there'd like always been lots of family around.

And they were still there, still living in Sooy's Boot. Maybe they'd take her back. Maybe if she showed up with Katie and said, This is my little girl . . . this is your brother Mark's granddaughter—maybe they'd let bygones be bygones and welcome her back.

Yeah. Go back to the Pines. Nobody'd think to look for her there. And even if they did come looking, they'd never find her.

"Katie," she said. "How'd you like to see where I grew up? You want to meet all my uncles and aunts? I know they'd love to meet you. You wanna do that? We can—"

The car behind them honked. Poppy glanced up and saw the light was green. Quickly she belted Katie back in and started moving.

"Yeah," Poppy said, getting more psyched by the minute. "Let's do that."

Let's go home.

Snake was cruising Atlantic Avenue, mostly because it was big and wide and seemed to be A.C.'s main drag. He'd been up and down the side streets all afternoon, looking for a white panel truck, looking for a woman with a little girl. He'd seen plenty of those, but none of the women had burgundy hair, and none of the little girls looked like the package.

He had the Jeep's radio tuned to a local station, listening to A.C. news. He wasn't sure what he was listening for, but if something relevant happened, he wanted to hear it.

Instead, he heard the Reverend Whitcomb.

"*. . . and how do we know President Winston's really in the hospital for a checkup? How do we know he isn't in there to kick a drug habit of his own? Maybe that's why he's so hellfire bent on legalizing this poison!*"

Suddenly furious, Snake turned him off.

Idiot! Drugs didn't put Winston in the hospital! *Snake* put him there! He's not there for detox! He's there because of *me!*

He was crossing Kentucky then, and glanced left at the sound of a horn. A red panel truck had stalled at the light. Same model as he was looking for—too bad it wasn't white.

He slowed. Shitty paint job . . . almost as if it had been spray enameled. He checked out the driver. A punky brunette hugging a little boy with reddish hair. Nothing like what—

And then the brunette turned to check her side mirror and he saw more of her face.

Poppy!

Snake yanked the Jeep into a quick U-turn that earned him a couple of angry horns—fuck 'em—and gunned it back across Kentucky just as the light changed.

He started out three cars behind the panel truck, then two. He fondled the Cobra in the front pouch of his sweatshirt. Nothing he wanted to do more than pull up alongside that truck and Swiss cheese the cab with all six rounds in the cylinder. And if not for that goddamn tape, that was what he'd be doing right now, cherishing every pull of the trigger.

But he'd have to delay that pleasure. And maybe that wasn't so bad. Delay it until he could truly savor it. Get wired on the anticipation, then get her where he could look her in the eyes. Rip off his bandages and show her his wounds.

Look at what you did to me, bitch. Thought you killed me, didn't you. But Snake doesn't die easy. Snake rose from the dead. *You* won't.

And then he'd watch her head explode.

Oh, yes. It was going to be good. Very good.

But he had to get the tape first.

He focused on the panel truck ahead, keeping two cars between them. He had her in his sights—all he had to do now was be patient and wait for the right moment to make his move.

He noticed the Maryland plates had been switched for Jersey's and smiled.

A complete makeover, eh, Poppy? New paint job, new plates, new hair for you and the kid. Think you've got everybody fooled, don't you. And maybe you do. Everybody but me.

12

"It's for you."

Bob Decker stepped across the trailer office they'd set up as a coordinating center on a vacant lot off Indiana Avenue. Canney's voice came through.

"We found her."

Bob's heart leaped. Thank God!

"Katie?"

"Uh, no," Canney said. "Sorry. I guess I should have phrased that a little differently. I meant the woman. We know who she is."

"Oh." Bob tried to keep the disappointment out of his voice. For a moment there he'd thought this was over. "Who is she?"

"Poppy Mulliner. She was picked up twice in New York about three years ago. Once each on shoplifting and solicitation. Suspended sentences on both. Stayed pretty clean since then."

"Sure. She moved into kidnapping."

Bob had listened over and over to the tapes of this Poppy Mulliner's calls to VanDuyne, and he'd found it difficult to reconcile the caring in her voice with someone who'd kidnap a child.

"Looks that way. I got her photo faxed down and we're passing it out to everybody we've put on the boards. Unless she's changed her style, I don't think we'll have any trouble spotting her. A real looker, but weird."

"Great. Get one over to me here. Anything else?"

"We're trying to scrape up more on her. One thing I can say about her is she's pretty bad at keeping appointments."

Bob glanced at his watch. "Yeah, I know. It's three-ten and she hasn't called."

"You don't think she's just stringing this poor bastard along, do you?"

Poor bastard is right, Bob thought. VanDuyne must be going through hell on that boardwalk.

He imagined himself up there, hanging onto the phone, praying for it to ring. . . .

He was glad he'd joined the Secret Service instead of the Bureau. He wasn't cut out for kidnappings. He was getting emotionally involved.

"Somehow, I don't think she is," he told Canney. "You heard her on the tapes. She ripped off a drugstore to make sure Katie wouldn't be without her medication. Someone who cares that much for that little girl isn't going to torture her father."

"Maybe she cares *too* much."

Bob hadn't considered that. "You mean she can't let go?"

"Wouldn't be the first time."

"Or maybe she spotted us. I'd hate to think we kept that man from getting his little girl back today."

"We're pretty well camouflaged. The DEA guys Dan set up for us are good at blending in."

"Let's hope so."

Another glance at his watch: 3:12.

Come on, lady. Call. Let that poor bastard off the hook.

13

Snake followed the panel truck as it turned left on Delaware and hit the White Horse Pike.

She's leaving town, he thought. Perfect.

The thinner the population, the easier this would be.

He hung back for a few miles until she turned into a McDonald's in a town called Absecon. He pulled onto the shoulder across the highway and watched her get on the drive-thru line.

What do I do now?

His aching head crawled with questions and possibilities. Where was she headed? A motel? The tape could be in the truck now or back wherever she was staying. If she had a room somewhere, the best thing to do was follow her there and settle everything at once.

But what if she was heading back to D.C.? If she got on 95 and didn't make another stop, he might not get another chance at her. This could be his last best shot at retrieving that tape.

But how do I work this?

And then Snake realized that the mother thing Poppy seemed to have with the package—the thing that had screwed up this whole gig—could be used to his advantage.

He watched a car pull up behind the panel truck. With another in front of her, she was locked in the drive-thru lane.

Now or never.

Snake pulled the Cobra from his sweatshirt pouch, hit the gas, swerved into the McDonald's lot, and was already opening his door as he jerked to a stop. He leapt out, yanked open the truck's passenger door, and grabbed the kid. In one move he clapped a hand over her mouth as she started to scream, and pressed the muzzle of the pistol against her head, careful that no one in the other cars could see.

Then he looked at Poppy who sat frozen at the wheel, eyes wide, mouth hanging open, gaping at him. She looked stupid.

Even the mild exertion had made his head pound harder, but Snake forced a grin.

"Surprise, bitch! I'm still around!"

Poppy's mouth worked, but no sound emerged. She reached for the kid but Snake pulled her back.

"Don't even think about it. Just give me the tape."

"Tape?"

"*Don't* fuck with me! I'll blow her head off as soon as look at her. And you know it."

"I-I don't have it!"

She wasn't lying. Snake could see the terror in her eyes. She was damn near paralyzed with fear that he'd hurt the brat.

"Where the fuck is it?"

"I left it—" Her eyes seemed to unfocus, as if she was trying to remember.

"You got a room somewhere? You left it in some fucking *motel* room?"

How could she be so goddamn *stupid?*

And then he realized she probably had no idea what was on the tape. The truck had no tape player. Where would she get a chance to listen to it?

"Yes," she said, her voice a hoarse whisper. "I left it. . . ."

"Then we're gonna go *get* it!" Snake said. He pocketed the pistol but kept a stranglehold on the kid. "You lead the way. Me and the kid'll follow."

"No!" she cried, reaching for her. "Please!"

Snake yanked the kid out the door and carried her toward his Jeep. He glanced around—couldn't see much with only one eye—to check if anyone was paying much attention. Probably looked like a family spat. One thing he knew for sure: Poppy wasn't going to be calling the cops.

The Jeep door was open, the engine still running. As he lifted the kid to push her inside, a weight suddenly slammed against his back. A high, insane screech filled his ears as fingers reached around from behind, raking at his eyes, the good one and the bad one, yanking at the bandage.

Had to be Poppy—could *only* be Poppy—but it was like being mauled by some wild animal.

Snake shouted as bolts of pain spiked through his right eye socket. He forgot about the kid. Suddenly the most important thing in the universe was to get those fingers away from his eyes, from his head. And then something—a fist, an arm—whacked the right side of his head square on his sutured scalp wound. Not a powerful blow, but it might as well have been a sledgehammer.

The explosion of pain drove him to his knees, retching as the world rocked and spun.

Dimly through the roaring he heard a child crying, heard Poppy saying, "Come on, baby. I've got you," then retreating footsteps.

She was getting away, but it was difficult for Snake to care. He had to cling to the pavement, fearing he'd tumble off the whirling earth if he let go.

14   Panting, trembling, more afraid than she'd ever been in her life, Poppy dropped Katie in the passenger seat, slammed the door, then ran around to the driver's side. As soon as she got behind the wheel, she yanked it hard to the right, jumped the drive-thru curb, and roared out of the lot.

As she hit the highway she realized that maybe she should have taken the time to run over Mac and put him out of their lives for good.

Too late now. Just get away, go, put miles and miles between them.

Screw the seat belt—she hugged her sobbing, trembling Katie against her as she sped west along 30.

"We're getting out of here, honeybunch. Don't you worry about that man. We're going someplace safe. Someplace where no one'll ever bother us."

Jesus, that had been close!

Mac . . . here in A.C. How?

He wanted a tape! What tape? The only one she could think of was that cassette she'd tossed out in Maryland. What could be on it that—?

Aw, who cared? The reality was that she couldn't lead Mac to his tape, and that he'd do something hideous when he realized that.

She'd been paralyzed by the sight of that pistol against Katie's head. And she'd almost died when he pulled her out of the truck and started dragging her away. She'd known right then if he got Katie into his Jeep, she'd never see her again.

That was when she'd stopped thinking. Some blind, crazy instinct took over and she'd found herself racing from the car and leaping onto Mac's back, making animal sounds as she clawed and pummeled him with everything she had.

She still wasn't sure what had happened back there, but the important thing was she had Katie.

About a mile down the road she got a bad case of the shakes but didn't dare stop. Finally they passed, and suddenly she was exhausted. She wanted to cry. How much more of this could she take? How much longer could she keep this up?

But she couldn't cry right now. Not in front of Katie. Poor thing needed to feel safe, and how could a blubbering wimp make you feel safe?

Fine, she thought. But how do *I* feel safe?

Especially after Mac had found her here. He shouldn't have even *known* she was in A.C. She'd told only one person.

Katie's father.

The jerk. Who else had he told beside Katie's psycho mother? What a family! Good thing Katie was going to stay with her from now on. Poppy had a good mind to—

She glanced down and saw the rented cell phone on the seat.

Yeah . . . why not? She had the number of that pay phone. If Daddy was still waiting, she'd give him a well-deserved piece of her mind.

15 Bob Decker paced the cramped confines of the coordinating trailer. 3:42 and the woman hadn't called.

Bob was going stir crazy in here, but poor VanDuyne—he had to be going through hell up there on the boardwalk.

The door at the far end opened and Gerry Canney stepped in amid a blaze of afternoon sunlight. He wore bicycle pants and a tank top. With his blond hair and muscular arms, he looked like a surfer. Almost. He needed a tan.

"Don't you look comfortable."

Canney smiled. "I'm undercover, don't you know." He waved a sheet of paper. "More info on our friend Poppy. She's a Joisey goil. A native."

"That makes two of us."

"You're kidding."

"Nope. Grew up just this side of the George Washington Bridge in a place called Hackensack."

Canney shook his head. "Hackensack . . . Sooy's Boot. Weird names you've got here. But how come you don't sound like you're from Joisey?"

Canney's bad accent was beginning to get on Bob's nerves. "Because hardly any of us say 'Joisey'—unless they were transplanted from Brooklyn."

"If you say so. Our friend Poppy sounds like she was transplanted from the South. Instead, she was born in Sooy's Boot, En-Jay."

"Sooy's what?"

"Boot. Sooy's Boot.

"Never heard of it."

"Neither did any of the maps I checked out. Found a Sooy Place, but that's not the same. Finally had to call Trenton. Even they had a tough time, but they finally located it northwest of here. Closest town to it on any map is a place called Chatsworth."

"You got me there too."

"Somewhere north of Wharton State Forest. Looks like it's in the woods—*deep* in the woods."

Bob suddenly had a flash. "In the pines. I'll be damned—she's a Piney."

"What's that?"

"Means she grew up in the Pine Barrens, a huge forest that takes up most of the center of the state."

"A Piney, huh?"

"Yeah. Not always a compliment. Sometimes it's used as the New Jersey equivalent of redneck or hillbilly, which probably isn't too far off, from stories I've heard. Pineys have been connected with inbreeding, bootleg liquor stills, and—"

"Hey!" said Harris from his seat in the corner by the monitoring equipment. "The phone just rang." He pulled off his headphones. "She's on!"

"Put her on the speaker," Canney said. "And start that trace."

"Thank God," Bob muttered.

But his growing sense of relief was stalled by the angry tone that suddenly filled the trailer.

16

"You're a real jerk, you know that?"

The woman's words—John recognized her voice—hit him like a blow to the head. He struggled for something to say.

"Is . . . is something wrong?" That sounded so lame—of course something was wrong. "Is Katie—?"

"Yeah, Katie's fine—except for a slapped face. No thanks to you, *Daddy*." She spat the last word.

"A slapped face?" His stomach turned. "Oh, no. You didn't—"

"*Me?* You stupid Appleton! I wouldn't hurt a hair on her head! But your wife—now *that's* totally another story!"

"My wife? Marnie? Oh, God!" How'd she get involved in this? Had she got hold of Katie somehow? The very thought made him ill. "She . . . she's not my wife. We're divorced."

"But not so divorced that you don't tell her about our A.C. plans?"

"I didn't tell her. She—"

"Yeah, well, I thought it'd be safe to let Katie go with her mother, but then I see her clobbering the poor kid. So I let her have it. But Mommy was the least of Katie's problems today. Mac showed up."

"Mac?"

"The guy who snatched her in the first place. He tried to get her again."

"No!"

"Yes! You been talking when you weren't supposed to be, *Daddy*. And you been talking to all the wrong people. It's like you put up a billboard saying: 'I'm getting Katie back this afternoon in A.C.' Well, let me tell you something, *Daddy*. You ain't. I'm keeping her. She's better off with me than with you and that bitch who's supposed to be her mother. I sure as hell know she's safer."

John felt as if the boardwalk was crumbling beneath him.

"No, please! You don't understand! I—"

"Cut the broken-heart act, *Daddy*. You blew it. And you got no one to blame but yourself."

"Poppy, *please!* You've got it all wrong! Let me speak to Katie. Just once. I . . ." Something had changed on the line. "Hello? Hello?"

The line was dead. She'd hung up.

John leaned against the phone stand, feeling as if he were about to explode with grief. But another emotion was mixing in. . . .

"You been talking when you weren't supposed to be, Daddy. And you been talking to all the wrong people. . . ."

But that wasn't true. He hadn't told a soul.

But that didn't mean someone hadn't been listening.

"You blew it. And you got no one to blame but yourself."

No . . . not true. Someone else was to blame. And he had a pretty good idea who.

And now the new emotion—anger—began edging out the grief.

He still had a sweaty grip on the handset. He lifted it and spoke through teeth clenched so hard that his jaw ached.

"Did you get all that, Decker? Is it all on tape? Then get this: I'm going back to my room. I'm sure you know where it is. I want to see you there. If you don't show up, I'll come looking for you in D.C. Face me now or face me later, but one way or another, you're going to explain this."

He slammed the handset back into the cradle.

17

Bob Decker winced at the harsh *click* echoing through the trailer. Harris cut the speaker feed as Canney turned to him. "Ouch."

"Shit," Bob said. "What else can go wrong? We lost VanDuyne's ex—who somehow found Poppy Mulliner when we couldn't. We can't find this guy Mac or Snake or whoever he is, but apparently *he* managed to find Poppy too. We've got all these men running around and we haven't had so much as a glimpse of her. Dammit!"

A few minutes ago he'd been fantasizing a triumphant call to the presidential suite at Bethesda, informing Razor that his godchild was safe and he could head for The Hague free of guilt.

Now . . .

"How are you going to handle VanDuyne? Stonewall him?"

Bob shook his head. "No. He has a right to know. I'll go see him."

"You want me along?"

Bob smiled. "For protection?"

"Don't knock it." He pointed to the speaker. "That sounded like one angry man."

"Yeah. And he's got a right to be." Bob turned to Harris. "Anything on the trace?"

Harris said. "A cell phone. Used an Absecon tower, which means she's inland from here." He shrugged. "Sorry. Didn't have time to get closer than that."

"Heading for those Pine Barrens, I bet," Canney said. "If we only knew what she was driving, we—" He snapped his fingers. "VanDuyne's ex! She must have seen Poppy Mulliner. Maybe she saw her car too."

"Good thought," Bob said. "But let me ask you something. I'm a little bothered by this 'Mac' guy showing up here. How the hell did he know VanDuyne or Poppy or Katie was going to be in Atlantic City?"

Canney shrugged. "We know he wasn't tapping VanDuyne's phone—our equipment would have registered someone else on the line. Probably followed him here. Just like his ex."

"Yeah? That's possible, but somehow it doesn't sit right. I get this picture of VanDuyne being tailed by our mystery man as well as by his ex, and then your man tailing the ex . . . half the people on Ninety-five North are following VanDuyne to Atlantic City. I don't know, Gerry. . . ."

"Let me check with Trevor. He was on the road. We'll see what he says. But that has to be it. What else can it be? Only four people on our end knew what was going on."

"Three," Bob said. "Jim Lewis is in the U.K. I never got around to telling him about Atlantic City."

"There you go. Three of us. You didn't talk, I didn't talk, and Dan Keane sure as hell didn't. VanDuyne was followed."

"I guess you're right." He rose. "Okay. Time to face Dr. VanDuyne."

"Good luck." Canney glanced at his watch. "I'm going to take everyone off the boards and get them looking for Marnie VanDuyne. She may be the break we've been looking for."

"I hope so. We need one."

18

John didn't have to look through the peephole in his hotel room door to know who'd knocked. As he reached for the handle he made a promise to himself that he'd keep his rage in check. Yes, he was furious, but he was a grown man, a rational human being—a physician, for God's sake. He wouldn't do anything violent.

But when he yanked the door open and saw Decker standing there, confirming all his suspicions, he snapped. He heard a small cry—his own voice as he'd never heard it—and suddenly his right hand was balled into a fist and swinging at Decker's face.

The Secret Service agent jerked his head to the side and John hit only air. When Decker grabbed his right wrist, John swung at him with his left. Decker caught that too.

"I know you're hurting, Doc," he said levelly as John glared at him. "But you're out of your league."

John knew he was right. He wasn't a fighter. He couldn't recall ever hurting another creature in his entire life. He dropped his gaze, pulled back, and Decker released him.

Feeling utterly miserable—impotent, useless, helpless—he turned and stumbled back into the room. He had an urge to grab a lamp and smash it through the big picture window with its wide-angle view of the Atlantic. At least he'd have an effect on *something*, even if it was only a pane of glass.

"She's taken Katie," he said, trying desperately to keep his voice from breaking—not in front of Decker; please, God, he couldn't crack up in front of this man. "And it's your fault."

He heard the door click closed before Decker spoke.

"Not fair. We've kept this tightly confined. We—"

John whirled and jabbed a finger at him. "You tapped my phones! You knew all my plans, every move I was going to make. And so did the bastard who kidnapped Katie. He was *here*, dammit! Right here in town, waiting to get my Katie. You've got a *leak*, Decker! You've got a mole!"

Decker didn't flinch. "Did our mole tell your ex-wife too?"

The question jolted John. Decker had a point. How *had* Marnie found out?

"You were supposed to be watching her."

"We were," Decker said. "We watched her follow you on your trip to the Maryland House. We cut her out of that so she couldn't mess up the transfer."

"She followed me?" He'd had no idea. . . .

"And she followed you to A.C. An accident on the interstate prevented us from diverting her. So who's to say this Snake couldn't have done the same thing?"

John stared out the window at the surf. He was right, dammit.

"Dear God. How many people have been watching me?"

When Decker hesitated, John turned and looked at him. His brow was furrowed, his expression troubled . . . as if he'd just thought of something. Whatever it was, it passed.

"Your house is under surveillance right now," Decker said. "Just in case somebody targets your mother."

John dropped onto the edge of the bed, staring up at Decker. The horror of what he'd just said . . . Nana?

"My God! I never even imagined . . ."

"But we did. And truth is, Doc, you should have told us about those calls."

"Why?" John said, his anger flaring again. "You don't care about Katie. I know what your primary objective is and it's not getting Katie back. Is it?"

For the first time, Decker's eyes broke contact. And John felt a tiny surge of triumph.

Gotcha, you son of a bitch.

"I want to get her back, believe me. But no, you're right. My primary directive is to safeguard the President and bring in the people behind this plot. But don't ever say I don't care about your daughter. That isn't true."

John stared at Decker. Somehow, for some reason, he believed him.

The phone rang. John leapt to it. Could it be? Had Poppy had a change of heart?

But no . . . a male voice, asking for Decker. John handed it to him and went back to the window. Behind him he heard Decker say, "Tell you what. Come up here and tell me. Yeah, he's here, but I see no reason why he shouldn't know."

John turned as he hung up. "Shouldn't know what?"

"New information on Poppy and Snake. We'll both find out at the same time."

John realized Decker was making a gesture.

"Thanks," he said softly. "I appreciate that."

While they were waiting for the caller to ride up from the lobby, Decker filled him in on what they knew about Poppy Mulliner and their theory about the violence at the Falls Church house.

A blond-haired man who looked like he'd just come off the beach arrived and was introduced as Supervising Special Agent Gerry Canney of the FBI. He seemed hesitant about speaking in front of John, but finally relented at Decker's insistence.

"Okay," he said, looking at John. "We got this call from the A.C. Medical Center emergency room about some woman saying she was beaten up in a parking garage and her daughter kidnapped. We checked it out and guess who it was?"

"Marnie," John said.

"Right. Says she found her daughter wandering around alone in a souvenir shop."

John remembered a big souvenir shop north of the pay phone where he'd spent the better part of the afternoon.

"Not the one—?"

Canney nodded. "Yeah. Peanut World. About fifty yards from where you were standing."

"Aw, no." He felt sick. Katie had been so *close*.

"She said she was taking Katie to her car when this twenty-something woman with spiked hair starts beating on her. Broke her nose, knocked her out."

John closed his eyes. *Yes!* How many times had he wanted to do that? Give Marnie a taste of what she'd done to Katie. But he'd never raised a hand to her. Kept telling himself she was sick, couldn't help herself.

Thank you once again, Poppy Mulliner. . . .

"The fallout from all of this is we have a good description of Poppy—a lot different from her three-year-old mug shot, believe me— and the changes she made in Katie."

"Changes?"

Canney explained about Katie's new look: boy's clothes, short reddish hair.

"But here's the best part. We canvassed the parking garage and the area around it and came up with somebody who saw a woman and a child fitting Poppy and Katie's new descriptions climbing into a red panel truck. She noticed them because they were in an otherwise restricted church parking lot."

Decker smacked a fist into his palm. "Great! You put the description out?"

"Just before I came here. Jersey State cops have it, all the local munis. Every major road is being covered. But I'm willing to bet they won't come up with a damn thing."

"Why not?" John said.

"Because she's not on a major road. I'll bet next year's salary she's heading into the pines. Home . . . to Sooy's Boot."

Decker was on his feet. "All right, then. Let's go."

John rose too. "I'm going with you."

"No way," Canney said.

"Damn right, no way," John said. "No way you're leaving me behind. If this Sooy's Boot is where Katie is, then that's where I belong. You don't take me along, I'll go on my own."

"Look," Canney said. "I've got a little girl too. I understand. But we can't let you jeopardize a federal investigation."

But John was concentrating on Decker. "You owe me, Bob."

Decker hesitated, then nodded to Canney. "We'll bring him along."

Canney's eye went wide. "*What?* We can't—"

"We can discuss it later. Right now we've got some traveling to do." He turned to John. "Pack up and we'll—"

"To hell with packing. Nothing here I can't do without. Let's go."

The grief, the rage, the frustration of the past few hours had vanished. Suddenly John felt alive again.

Hang on, Katie. I'm on my way.

19 Poppy drove past the house three times before she had the nerve to stop.

"Is this where you grew up?" Katie said.

"No. This is my Uncle Luke's house. He's my father's brother. They were like real close."

So close, she thought, that he probably won't even speak to me.

She sat and stared at the mailbox: #528—LUKE MULLINER. Dad's name was Mark, and he'd had five brothers: Matthew, Luke, John, Peter, and Paul. Yeah, Grandma Mulliner had been like real heavy into the Bible. All the Mulliner boys had been close, but Dad had always found Uncle Luke the most simpatico. He saw the most of Luke, and so naturally, Luke was the uncle she'd known the best. And loved the best.

She knew Luke had been royally pissed that she went and got knocked up and had to quit the basketball team—not for himself, but for what it had done to Dad's dream's of her going to college. And if he'd been so mad about that, would he ever like forgive her for running away and leaving Daddy alone? And for not showing up at his funeral?

I didn't know he died!

But that probably wouldn't cut it. All the Mulliners tended to carry grudges to their grave. And Uncle Luke's temper was like legendary.

She checked out the yard. The grass looked kind of weedy and scraggly, and would need cutting soon. An old Ford pickup sat in the driveway. Beyond it stood the tiny two-bedroom ranch Uncle Luke had called home for longer than Poppy had been alive. As far as she was concerned, it had been here like forever, nestled amid the close-packed scrub pines. And in all these years, no other homes had joined it. Uncle Luke's was still the only house along this whole stretch of potholed and crumbling asphalt.

Even in the fading light she could see how the place needed some paint. So did the flaking propane tank peeking around the right rear corner. She noticed how the toolshed in the backyard leaned to the left.

And that made her kind of sad. Looked like Uncle Luke wasn't keeping things up the way he used to. Not that he was too old. He couldn't be fifty yet.

Maybe he was just lonely. His wife, Aunt Mary, had died not long after Mom, and his one son, Poppy's cousin Luke Jr—"little Luke," who surely wasn't little anymore—was probably married and living on his own. So who was around for him to keep the place neat for?

A light came on in the front room.

"He's home," she said aloud. She didn't see how she could put this off much longer. "Come on, honeybunch. Let's see if Uncle Luke will take us in."

She lifted Katie in her arms and carried her up to the front door. She put her down on the stoop, took her hand, and reached out to knock . . . and hesitated.

She sent up a little prayer. If he's gonna say no, please just let him say no. Don't let him start yelling and screaming. Katie's seen too much trouble already today. And I feel I'm about to break into like a million or two pieces.

She knocked. She waited but no one answered. As she was about to try again, the door swept open.

He was big, like her Dad had been, but older, heavier, grayer, with lots of new lines visible through the white three-day stubble on his cheeks. But his heavy red-and-black plaid shirt and green work pants were the same as they'd always been, and his blue eyes were as sharp as ever.

An ache started deep in her chest. Jesus, he reminded her of Dad.

He stared at her and said,"What do you want?"

"Uncle Luke? It's me. Poppy."

His expression never changed. "Poppy who?"

The ache grew as she wondered, Is this how he's gonna play it? Like I don't exist.

"Your . . . your niece. Poppy Mulliner. Mark's little girl."

He squinted at her. "You ain't little. And you don't look like no Poppy I ever knew."

The ache deepened. Don't do this to me, Uncle Luke. I got no place else to go.

"It's me, Uncle Luke. I . . . I like need a place to stay."

He didn't seem to hear her. "The Poppy I knew ran off and left her father alone. She as much as killed him. Then she didn't even bother to show up for his funeral."

"I didn't—"

"I hope you're not telling me you're that Poppy."

This wasn't working. She knew she should go now. No sense trying to say any more to this stone-faced man. But she had to tell him. . . .

"I guess I am that Poppy, and I guess I'm not. Not anymore. A lot's happened since I left. Most of it bad. I need some help now. I thought I could like come back here. I thought maybe you'd . . ."

The ache had moved up to her throat and was pulling it tight. Almost too tight to talk. He was turning her away . . . no more than she deserved. She should have known . . . shouldn't have even bothered coming here. . . .

She just couldn't believe how much this hurt.

She took one look last look at Uncle Luke before turning away, and thought she saw a softening in his eyes.

"That your kid?" he said, jutting his chin at Katie.

Poppy shook her head. *Don't ask me about Glory!* She felt the tears welling in her eyes, spilling over. Her voice sounded like a gasp.

"No. She died . . . when she was three months."

He looked stricken. "Dead?"

She couldn't talk about Glory. She had to get away from here before she made a complete Appleton of herself.

"Sorry to bother you, Uncle Luke."

She couldn't say any more. As she lifted Katie and took her first steps back to the truck, she heard a tortured sound. Almost like a . . . hiccup.

She looked back at Uncle Luke and saw him leaning against the doorjamb, his face all screwed up and his mouth turned way down at the corners. Through her blurred eyes he looked just like the sad mask she'd seen outside theaters.

His chest heaved and he made another sound—this was a sob.

And then he was motioning her toward him. She stepped back up on the stoop and he enfolded her in his arms, pressing her against him. She felt his chest begin to heave.

"Oh, Poppy," he said, his voice high and strange. "I miss him. Oh, God, you got no idea how much I miss your dad."

And then they were both crying—loud, wracking wails and sobs.

And for the first time in days, Poppy felt safe.

She was home.

20

"I don't get it," VanDuyne said, packing back and forth in the Pineconer Motel parking lot. "Why are we waiting for tomorrow? We should be doing *something*."

Bob Decker saw Canney make a little "be my guest" gesture. Bob sighed. Maybe it had been a mistake bringing VanDuyne along, but he did feel he owed the guy something. And besides, this was the best way of keeping the doc under control.

"We *are* doing something, Doc," Bob said. "We've got men checking out Sooy's Boot right now, getting the lay of the land."

"They should be doing more than that. And why aren't *we* there instead of way the hell out here in Tuckerton or whatever this place is called?"

"First of all," Bob said, "do you have any idea how many Mulliners there are in these parts? Take a look at the phone book later—and those are just the ones with phones. We have to get census records to find the others, and even then we won't have all of them. Second, they don't have a motel in Sooy's Boot, or anywhere near it. And third . . ." Bob gestured at the pine woods that surrounded the motel, seeming to grow thicker by the minute as the light faded. "Look around you, Doc. This may be New Jersey, and you may be just thirty or forty miles from Philadelphia and the northeast corridor, but you are on the edge of very deep woods. *Thousands* of square miles of scrub pine. No streetlights out there. No street *signs*. Most of the roads are unpaved, and the ones that are don't even have lines down the middle. People get lost out there in broad daylight. What do you think we're going to accomplish in the dark? Poppy Mulliner could be hiding anywhere."

"So we just give up?"

"You know damn well we're not giving up. We—" He capped his anger; the guy was half crazy worrying about his kid. "While we're questioning all the Mulliners we can find, a pair of helicopters from Lakehurst Naval Air Station will be flying a grid pattern over the area looking for that red panel truck." Bob wished he could set up a full-scale search—bring in state cops, the county sheriff, the National Guard—but he still had a mandate to keep a low profile. "But we need light. When that sun comes up, you'll see plenty of action. We're going to run a fine-tooth comb through these woods tomorrow. We'll find her."

"*If* she's here," VanDuyne said.

"Oh, she's here," Canney said. "We would have caught her if she tried running north or south. She knows these woods, and she knows she can hide here. But not for long."

"So get some sleep," Bob told VanDuyne. "We're up and moving at the crack of dawn."

VanDuyne hesitated, as if he wanted to say more, then shrugged and headed for his room.

"Finally," Canney said. "And I thought my little Martha was tough to get to bed."

"Let's get back in the car," Bob said. "I heard from Jim Lewis."

Canney's expression brightened. "He got to the remailer?"

Bob nodded but didn't speak until they were safely cocooned in the car.

"I don't know how he did it and I didn't ask, but I suspect he had somebody sneak in and copy the database from the remailer's server. Whatever, they found a 'Snake' account with an IDT return address. IDT was very cooperative. Turns out 'Snake' is the handle of an 'Eric Garter' who pays for his Internet services with his Visa card. The Visa bills go to a mail drop. The house address in the Visa computer is a fake. 'Eric Garter' doesn't exist."

"'Garter?'" Canney said. "As in 'Snake?' Shit." He rubbed his face. "My news isn't so good either. I had a long talk with Trevor. He says the only one who trailed VanDuyne to Atlantic City was his ex."

"He's got to be wrong."

"That's what I said, but he told me there were times when he and VanDuyne and the ex were the only cars on the road. No way anybody else followed. He was pretty adamant about that. And Trevor's damn good."

A worm wriggled through Bob's gut. "You know what you're saying."

"Yeah. Someone's rotten."

"But only three of us knew."

"All right. Let's look at that. Let me ask you a question: Is the Secret Service going to be hurt by decriminalization?"

"Hell, no. We'll probably have to beef up to provide extra security."

"Right. And as far as the Bureau is concerned, drugs are mostly a sideline. So our appropriations won't be much affected."

"Stop," Bob said. "I know where you're going and—?"

"Who in federal law enforcement gets hurt the most, Bob?"

"You're talking about Dan Keane—"

"All right, I'll answer my own questions: DEA gets *gutted* by decriminalization."

Bob felt his anger rising. This was groundless, unfair.

"I've known Dan for a dozen years. Nobody hates the drug trade more. Nobody has fought harder against the traffickers."

"Right. And maybe he hates them so much that he doesn't want to stop fighting them."

The simple logic of the conclusion struck Bob dumb for a moment.

But logic wasn't always the truth. He'd spoken to Dan not thirty minutes ago. It was unthinkable. . . .

"It just can't be. I won't buy it."

"All right," Canney said. "You know the guy. I'll go with your judgment."

"There's another explanation," Bob said. "We just haven't thought of it yet."

Another explanation . . . had to be . . .

But what? Who?

21   "I've looked all over town and can't find her," Snake told Salinas. He'd used the phone in his motel's parking lot for the call. Not the best section of A.C., but his appearance attracted less attention here.

"That is because she is not *in* town," Salinas said. "She has fled into the big woods in the center of the state."

Snake winced as another stab of pain shot through his head and eye. The pills had eased the agony since this afternoon, but these stabs were still frequent enough and severe enough to keep him on edge.

Poppy pain . . . all because of that bitch. What the hell was the matter with her? The damn kid belonged to someone else, yet she'd attacked him like a mother lion protecting one of her own cubs . . . hadn't even sounded human, screeching like that.

Crazy bitch.

"'Big' woods? This is Jersey. There's *nothing* big here."

"The others who are looking for her disagree. They are launching a wide search for her tomorrow. And they expect to *find* her and the package. *Tomorrow.*"

Salinas left the words hanging, and the emphasis was not lost on Snake.

Tomorrow . . .

Snake closed his good eye and tried to organize his thoughts. If they found Poppy, they'd find the tape. Maybe she hadn't had the tape with her this afternoon, but after the big scene he'd made about it, he was willing to bet the rest of his life that she'd gone back and got it and listened to it, and knew what a bargaining chip she had.

The tape would land him in a federal prison and force Salinas to close up shop and leave the country. Salinas would be gone, but he wouldn't forget. No matter what the prison, no matter what the security, Salinas would see to it that somebody got to him.

And even if Poppy had lost the tape, she could still finger him as the guy who set up the kidnapping. And then, as the only guy who could link Salinas to the plot, how long would he last?

Either way, betting the rest of his life didn't seem a particularly heavy risk.

So tomorrow it was do or die—literally.

But he was Snake. He could do it.

And not just to save his skin. Poppy had hurt him twice now—*twice.* Both times she'd taken him by surprise. No third time. No messing around with threats. He'd pop her as soon as he saw her and search her body and the truck. And if he didn't find the tape, then so be it. But no games this time: Poppy was dead.

"I think you'd better come in," Salinas said. "We need to make contingency plans should this tape be found."

Snake knew what that meant. Fat chance.

"I've still got tomorrow. Plenty of time."

"You are one man. They are many, with helicopters. You cannot hope—"

"If I can get a little goddamn support, I can get to her first, dammit!"

He wanted to scream at Salinas. Didn't he know who he was dealing with?

This is Snake talking here. I can turn the tables on the feds and stupid greaseballs like you any day. I can take this big-ass search and turn it to my advantage.

"What sort of support do you need?"

"Mostly information. You've got a pipeline. Here's what I need."

Snake began reeling off his list.

22

"That was *you?*" Katie said, pointing to the photo in the scrapbook.

Poppy sat on the sofa in Uncle Luke's front room and stared at her seventeen-year-old self, dressed in her old number 23 basketball uniform, hair pulled back into a ponytail that trailed halfway down her back, long legs bare, knobby knees bent, poised at the foul line to make a free throw.

Only ten years ago . . . yet it totally seemed like someone else, like a photo from another century.

She looked at that fresh face, those clear eyes that had a whole different future planned out . . . no idea at all what the next ten years would hold.

"Yeah, that was me." *The other me.*

She glanced at her Uncle Luke. "I can't believe you like saved all this stuff."

"What else was I going to do? After your father died, I couldn't just throw it out. And besides . . . " He turned his head away.

"Besides what?"

"He asked me to keep your scrapbooks and trophies. He said he . . . he knew you'd come back some day."

Poppy closed her eyes and tilted her head back. She didn't want to cry again.

All the pain she'd caused in her life. What was wrong with her? She'd been around for like a quarter century. . . .

Jesus, you'd think I'd be able to get *something* right by now.

"Uncle Luke—"

An urgent-sounding knock on the door interrupted her. In a surge of panic, she wrapped her arms around Katie.

"Wait!" she said in a fierce whisper. "Don't answer that!"

But then a voice called from the other side.

"Luke! It's me—Matt!"

Poppy relaxed, but only a little. Uncle Matt. That was okay—she hoped.

Uncle Luke gave her a strange look, then opened the door. Uncle Matt, a thinner, bearded version of Uncle Luke, stepped in, all excited and talking a blue streak.

"Luke, there's been men in town asking about—" His voice cut off as he spotted Poppy and Katie.

"Hi, Uncle Matt."

His eyes widened. "Is that you, Poppy?"

She nodded.

He gulped. "Then it's true. People are looking for you. They say they're from the government and that you—"

"Don't believe them," she said, quickly overcoming her shock. How could anyone—Mac, the feds, *anyone*—know to look for her here? "Not even about being from the government."

She gave them a slightly cleaned-up version of events, something to the effect that she and Katie had witnessed a crime and the bad guys were trying to shut them up. She was trying to get Katie back home to her dad but her plans kept getting messed up.

"So those guys who're saying they're feds might not be the real thing?" Uncle Luke said.

Poppy nodded and hid a smile. Announcing you were from the federal government—or *any* government, for that matter—was one sure way to get people in these parts to clam up.

"You always were trouble, Poppy," Uncle Matt said. "You went and broke your father's heart. You know that, don't you."

"Easy, Matt," Uncle Luke said, putting a hand on his shoulder. "We been through all that. What we got to do now is put her someplace where no one'll find her till we straighten out who's who."

"That's easy enough," Uncle Matt said. "Hide her with the Appletons."

Poppy would have leaped off the sofa if Katie hadn't been on her lap. "Oh, no! Not them!"

"Where else you gonna stay, girl?" Uncle Matt said. "They'll be checking every Mulliner in the pines. But *nobody*'ll be checking the Appletons, even if they could find them."

Oh, Jesus, she thought. Not the Appletons.

"He's right, Poppy," Uncle Luke said. "I'll lead you out there come first light. Soon as I can see the road. Don't worry. They won't turn you away. You're kin."

She knew. And the thought made her queasy. She'd almost rather face Mac again than move in with the Appletons.

23 Bob Decker lay in his creaky motel bed and glanced again at the glowing numerals on the clock radio. Almost midnight.

He needed sleep, dammit. They'd all be up and moving in five hours or so.

But Gerry Canney's suspicions about Dan Keane kept echoing off the inner walls of his skull.

And maybe he hates them so much that he doesn't want to stop fighting them. . . .

What was the one thing all his years in the Secret Service had taught him? *Never take anything for granted.*

Which meant he couldn't take Dan Keane for granted.

As much as he doubted—loathed—the possibility, he'd worked out a plan to check out Keane. But he couldn't do it alone.

He reached for the phone and dialed Canney's room.

TUESDAY

1 "Where *are* we?" Katie said, staring out the panel truck's side window.

"We're in the woods, honeybunch. Like *deep* in the woods."

Poppy squinted through the windshield into the dim predawn light as she followed her uncle's pickup along a narrow, winding back road. Weeds growing in the mound between the sandy ruts scraped along the undercarriage. The forty-foot scrub pines crowded close to the road, leaning over it, seeming to open ahead as she approached, and close in behind as she passed.

She'd been out here a number of times as a girl with her dad when he'd make a run to bring the Appletons some Christmas pies or stock up on their applejack, but she'd never learned the way. Never wanted to. She'd been a passenger those times and had never noticed how one stretch of road looked pretty much like every other, almost as if they were driving in circles.

She wished she could like turn on her headlights or something, but Uncle Luke had said it was safest to keep them off—otherwise he would have brought her out here last night.

Thank God for little favors. Appletons by day were bad enough, but Appletons by night . . .

She shuddered.

"It makes me feel lonely out here," Katie said.

"It *is* lonely. But some folks don't get lonely like us. And some folks don't like to have much to do with other folks, so they like it out here."

And some folk shouldn't be seen by the rest of us.

At least no one would find Katie and her out here—not in a million years. But that cut both ways. She was just as lost out here as anyone else—safe but trapped.

Uncle Luke finally made a sharp right turn and pulled to a stop in a small clearing. Four other pickups in various stages of rust rot were parked any which way in the sand. Poppy's truck brought the total to six.

"All right now," Uncle Luke said as he helped her and Katie from the truck. In his free hand he held a gallon jug and the sleeping bag he was lending them. "Stick close to me until they know who we are."

"They don't know we're coming?"

Poppy's stomach was cinched into a double granny knot as she looked around. Trees. Nothing but trees and sand and scrub brush . . . and a path leading away through the brush.

"How was I supposed to let them know?"

"You didn't—?" She stopped herself. She'd been about to say something about calling them, but remembered there were like no phone lines out here. No electricity, no running water, either. "Never mind."

She carried Katie along the path, keeping close behind her uncle. At least the light was better now. The cloudless sky was turning a pale blue as the path moved onto an upslope. Going to be another beautiful sunny day.

"Are these more uncles we're visiting?" Katie said.

"Oh, no," Poppy told her. "I'm not related to—"

"'Course you are," Uncle Luke said.

"Well, sure," she said, wishing her uncle would shut up. "Everybody in the pines is related one way or another. I meant—"

"No, these are real kin. My great-grandfather Samuel—your great-*great*-grandfather—married off his sister Anna to Jacob Appleton way back when. These folk are your cousins."

Poppy wanted to kick her uncle in the butt. Damn! Why'd he have to go and say that sort of stuff in front of Katie? She didn't want the little thing to know she shared blood with the Appletons.

Suddenly Uncle Luke stopped and Poppy bumped into his back.

"Hello to the house!" he called.

Poppy jumped as a voice shouted from no more than ten feet to their left.

"Who the hell's out here so goddamn early in the mornin'?"

"It's me—Luke Mulliner. I got my niece Poppy with me, and she's got a little one with her."

A grizzled-looking guy who could have been sixty or could have been eighty, skinny as the scrub pine he'd been hiding behind, stepped into the open. He held his shotgun ready while he gave them the once over.

And Poppy gave him her own once-over. His overalls were worn through in spots—so fashionable in SoHo, but this was the real thing. He wore worn sneakers with no socks, and his ankles were filthy. His hands weren't much better. His left eye seemed to be stuck looking at his nose while his gray hair shot from his scalp in tufts. His back was bent and twisted, which made him lean forward and to the right.

She remembered this Appleton from when she was a little girl, even though almost everything about him had changed. Everything except his tongue. He kept licking his lips. Every two or three seconds his beefy red tongue would zip out and run along his lips, then disappear.

Poppy remembered that tongue.

"Yeah," he said finally. "You look like a Mulliner."

"And you're Lester, aren't you?" Uncle Luke said. "I haven't been out here for a while."

"That's right," Lester said, lowering the shotgun. He didn't offer to shake. "C'mon. I'll take you up the house." He eyed the jug dangling from Uncle Luke's finger. "Here for some jack?"

"Yep. Been a while since I had some and I miss it."

"It's awfully good, ain't it."

"That it is."

Poppy remembered stealing some of her dad's stock of applejack when she was a teenager. Powerful stuff—Jersey lightning. And no one made better applejack than the Appletons. Matter of fact, she'd been high on Appleton applejack when she and Charlie did it and conceived Glory.

But that wasn't the Appletons' fault.

Another hundred yards uphill and they came to a large clearing hazed with blue-white woodsmoke, and sprawled in its center . . . the house.

Poppy stopped and stared as it all came back to her. The house . . . the crazy Appleton house.

It looked like it might have started out as like a one-room shack. Then somebody must have added a shed to one end, and then maybe an extra room to the other, then an extension on to the shed, and so on . . . and so on. . . .

That was because as the Appleton kids grew up, they didn't move away, they just like added a section for themselves. Poppy guessed that if the Appletons had been some rich and respectable clan like the Kennedys, this sort of thing would be called a compound.

But this was no compound—this was a . . . *sprawl*. A sprawl with lots of galvanized pipe acting as chimneys, and all those chimneys smoking.

The place looked like they'd built it out of whatever scrap material they could find with little or no thought to matching it with what they'd used before. No section looked like it was any kin to any of the other sections nuzzling up against it. Corrugated metal nailed to marine plywood abutting particle board and cedar shakes. Roofs of genuine shingles, vinyl siding, sheet metal, or old rugs and linoleum tacked over wooden slats.

The hide of a deer was tacked to one wall; and over to the right, three dead rabbits hung head down from a clothesline. She turned Katie slightly so she wouldn't see them and ask what had happened to Bambi and Peter Cottontail.

The Appletons had lived here as long as anyone could remember. All of them. Nobody left, and nobody new was allowed in. And that meant that with no outsiders to choose from, you had to like pair off with somebody who was a pretty damn close relation.

Which was why a lot of the Appletons tended to be soft in the head and look the way they did.

"Company, everybody!" Lester shouted. "Companeeee!"

And then they started coming out. The men in dirty shirts and jeans or work pants, the women in stained housedresses, hardly any shoes on anyone, and the bare feet as tough as shoe leather and just as brown. Some folks with no hair and misshapen skulls, some heads too big, some way too small, some with pure white skin and hair and pink eyes, some looking pretty normal at first glance, but a second look telling you that not all the circuits were making contact inside. And the kids . . . some of them were running in endless circles while others sat and rocked . . . and rocked . . . and others just stared.

Poppy felt Katie's arms tighten around her neck in a fearful stranglehold.

"I want to go h-home," she whimpered. "I want my Daddy."

And deep in her breaking heart Poppy knew that had to be. Katie couldn't stay here—couldn't stay *anywhere* with Poppy. Maybe it had been all the fear and stress and near panic, maybe it had been the heat, but for a crazy time yesterday she'd really thought she could keep Katie. Now she knew that was impossible. Too many people were looking for them. She wanted what was best for Katie, and a life on the run wasn't it.

"I know you do, honeybunch. And I'll see that you get back to him. As soon as it's safe."

They'd stay here today—just today, but not overnight. No way overnight. Maybe Uncle Luke could go back to Sooy's Boot and find the feds . . . make sure they were *real* feds, and help her like cut a deal.

Yeah. That could work. She'd saved Katie's life—two, maybe three times—and took good care of her. Why couldn't she get a suspended sentence and like some sort of protective custody in return?

Hell, even a short jolt in a federal joint would be better than moving in with the Appletons.

2

Dan Keane had barely seated himself behind his desk when Decker called.

Please let this be good news, he thought, knowing that good news for him would be quite different than for Decker.

Dan so desperately wanted this nightmare over. Another call had come from Salinas last night, telling him about a tape that Poppy Mulliner had, a tape that would topple the entire house of cards. And then he was demanding phone numbers and call frequencies, and when Dan asked why, he was told not to worry about it, just do as he was told.

"*Just do as you're told.* . . ."

Carlos Salinas speaking that way to *him!* Giving Dan Keane orders. Just two days ago that would have been *unthinkable!*

"We found Poppy Mulliner," Decker said.

"Alive?" Dan's heart and lungs suspended operations while he waited for an answer.

Please say dead.

"Very much alive."

He almost sobbed as his heart and lungs kicked back into action in triple time. Oh God oh shit oh Christ!

"Is she talking?"

"I said we found her—we don't *have* her."

"I don't understand."

"She's in a motel in a town called Tuckerton—the Adamston Motel. She's got the little girl with her. We could pick her up now, but since they both seem pretty safe and healthy, we decided to wait and see what she does. We've got her phone tapped. Maybe we'll get lucky and she'll call one of her accomplices. We'll give her the day. If nothing shakes out by tonight—or it looks like she's moving out—we'll pick her up."

Dan's mind screamed: It's over! They've got the woman, they'll get the tape. What do I do now?

"Dan?"

Dan cleared his throat and managed to keep his voice calm. "Great work. Has she called anyone yet?"

"Nope. But it's still early."

"That it is. Keep me informed, will you?"

"Want to come up here and be on the scene?"

"I'd love to, Bob." That was the *last* place he wanted to be right now. "But you guys are doing such a great job, I'd feel redundant. I'll hold the fort here. By the way, any word on how the patient's doing?"

Dan had tried every avenue he knew to ferret out details on Winston's condition, but it was as if a wall had been erected around the presidential suite at Bethesda, and only one message filtered through: "The President's fine. Nothing but routine tests that should be finished soon."

Which told him nothing. Winston could be sick as a dog right now and the message would be the same.

"All I hear is that he's doing fine. How about you?"

"Same thing. I hope that's true."

"We're all praying for him," Decker said.

Not all of us, Dan thought as he hung up.

He dropped his head into his trembling hands and squeezed his eyes shut. Only a matter of six or eight hours—maybe less—before Decker got that tape. He wanted to run, but where? He had no place to go. He had to stick this out.

He took a deep breath. All right. Six or eight hours. Maybe that was time enough for Salinas to do something. His fat ass was on the line too. What was the name of that motel. . . ?

Pulling on his jacket, he hurried down to ground level and out onto Sixth Street. He'd already called Salinas once today—to give him those phone numbers and frequencies he'd demanded. Now he was calling again, but this time he wouldn't be Salinas's fucking errand boy.

He chose a different phone from last time—this one on Maryland Avenue—and scanned the area to make sure no one was too close. All clear. Only a guy with a soft-pretzel cart heading for the Mall.

He dropped the quarter, spoke to someone, then hung up. As he waited for the return call, Dan glanced at the sky. Another hot one. The pretzel guy was still down the block, fiddling with his cart. Looked like one of the wheels had jammed. On a day like today he'd set up shop near the Smithsonian and make out like a bandit—and probably declare only a small portion of it.

The phone rang.

"Yes?" said Salinas's voice.

Dan jumped to the heart of his message. He didn't want to spend a second more than necessary on the line with this toad.

"The woman's been located—the Adamston Motel in Tuckerton, New Jersey. They're watching her to see who she contacts. If you can do something, better do it now. Your fate is in your own hands."

And then he hung up. There. Done.

My fate is in your hands as well, Salinas. *Do* something, dammit!

And then he stopped.

Listen to me. I want Salinas to kill someone. And if he succeeds, he'll probably kill that little girl too. For what? To save my worthless ass.

But I did start off with the right intentions. I got involved for a *good* reason, a *just* cause. I did it for the country, dammit. That should count for something.

Maybe it did. Somewhere. But it did nothing for the cold, sick weight sitting in his chest.

As Dan walked away, the pretzel man started kicking at his jammed wheel. What a life when the worst thing you had to deal with was a jammed wheel. For a moment, Dan wished they could trade places.

I'll push the cart and let him swim this river of shit I've got myself into.

3 "Was that an Esso sign we just passed?" Bob Decker said as he drove toward Sooy's Boot.

"Yeah," said Canney from the passenger seat. "It's like we've hit a time warp."

Some kind of warp, Decker thought. A Pine Barrens town seemed to consist of a gas pump, a canoe rental place, and half a dozen plywood boxes on cement slabs that they called homes. Here they were on a county road with no shoulder and only an occasional isolated house, usually with a sign offering decoys for sale. A graveyard tended to have half a dozen headstones and no more. He saw lots of signs for rod and gun clubs, hunting clubs, even a muzzle-loaders club. He got the feeling there might be more guns per capita here than anywhere else in the country.

Bob glanced in the rearview mirror at VanDuyne in the big rear seat of the rented Buick Roadmaster. He'd said little since they'd picked him up for breakfast an hour ago. He looked terrible—pale face, sunken eyes, sloppy shaving job, wrinkled clothes.

"I picked this up by the registration desk," Canney said, holding up a pamphlet. "All about the Pine Barrens. You know it's as big as Yosemite Park? A *million* acres of scrub pine. And we're in one of its least populated areas—averages only one person per eight square miles around here. And it says here there's places in the pinelands that no human eye has ever seen. Can you imagine that?"

"Seems hopeless," VanDuyne said from the back, finally showing signs of life.

"That's why we need those helicopters," Bob said.

"You think they'll help?"

"They can cover a helluva lot more ground than we can. They'll start their search pattern from Sooy's Boot and move outward. They'll call in anything that looks remotely like a red panel truck, and we'll check it out from the ground. We'll—"

A cell phone chirped. Decker checked to see if it was his but it turned out to be Canney's.

"He did?" Canney said. He looked at Bob and nodded significantly.

Oh, shit, Bob thought. Oh, no.

Canney was peering through the windshield as he spoke into the phone. "Wait. Let me get to a pay phone and—" He glanced out at the woods and shook his head. "What am I—crazy? All right. Give me the barest details and no names. This is a cell phone, remember."

As Canney went through a series of nods and uh-huhs, Bob silently cursed himself. He hadn't believed it could possibly be Dan Keane. If he had, he would have come up with better disinformation—chosen a real motel and watched it in the hope that whoever Keane was feeding would make a move and reveal themselves.

Finally Canney ended the call.

"All right," Bob said, knowing what was coming. "Give it to me."

"It's him, all right. We have these vendor carts rigged with minicams and parabolic mikes. One of them got within a hundred feet of him at a pay phone. That was close enough. We don't know who he called but we know he mentioned Tuckerton and the Adamston Motel."

"Aw, no." Bob felt sick. Dan Keane . . . what on earth could have possessed him? "There's got to be an explanation."

"What's wrong?" VanDuyne said.

"Nothing," Canney said.

"Might as well tell him," Bob said. "We found our leak."

VanDuyne was leaning forward now. "Son of a bitch! Who is he?"

"That's not for publication."

"I've got a right to know! I'd have Katie back by now if it wasn't for him. The bastard almost had her killed!"

"And you almost killed the President!" Bob said, flaring.

"They had my daughter."

"And how do you know they don't have this man's wife? Or one of his grandkids?"

VanDuyne leaned back again, slowly. "If they do, then my heart goes out to him. There's nothing . . . absolutely nothing worse than having the life of someone you love hinge on your doing something vile."

"Have your people check that out," Bob told Canney. "But discreetly . . . very discreetly."

And while Canney called, Bob continued down the road to Sooy's Boot, almost hoping that Dan Keane had been forced into this treachery by a threat to his family rather than a threat to his career.

And yet—the prospect of all those billions in appropriations being diverted from your agency to another . . . who knew what that could do to a man?

4   Snake finished reprogramming the third cell phone and stretched. All set.

His head and eye still hurt, but not so bad this morning. He was a long way from feeling *good*, but the dizziness seemed to have receded, and the pills were managing the pain better.

He went to the bathroom to check himself out. After going on his electronics shopping spree last night, he'd removed all his bandages except the eye patch, and had slept that way. Turned out to have been a good move. His scalp lacerations had dried out; some crusting remained around the sutures, but in general they looked pretty clean.

He peeled off the eye patch and studied himself in the mirror.

Pretty fucking frightening.

With his half-shaven head, the crisscrossing stitches, and his ruined right eye, he looked like the Terminator after a bad day.

And he *liked* it.

Not that he wanted to look like this for the rest of his life, but it just might come in handy today. He'd been planning to do the mummy thing with his head and the hooded sweatshirt. But this was better. This would scare the shit out of those Jersey hillbillies.

Scare Poppy too, he'd bet. He'd let her get a good look at him before he blew her away.

He buttoned up a denim shirt. Over his right eye he gently fitted the black eye patch he'd bought last night. And over that he slipped a pair of superdark sunglasses.

Humming the riff from "Bad to the Bone," he began to gather his equipment.

Time to hit the road.

5 "That is impossible," Carlos Salinas said. "It must be a new motel that is not listed yet."

"I'm telling you the place doesn't exist!" Allen Gold was flushed and sweaty as he stood on the far side of Carlos's desk, the phone in his hand. "I've called information and there's no listing—new *or* old—for an Adamston Motel in Tuckerton or anywhere else in Ocean County, or in any of the counties around it. I even called the Tuckerton town hall and they've never heard of the Adamston Hotel. You know what this means, don't you?"

Carlos knew exactly what it meant. *"Mierda!"*

"Right. Deep *mierda!* They're onto us!"

"Perhaps," Carlos said, keeping cool on the outside and trying to stay equally cool inside. Now was not the time to panic. Not yet. "And perhaps not. It means for certain that they are onto Señor Keane. This false information may be a lure to trick us into revealing ourselves.

"I say we get out of here," Gold said, breathing like he had just run up half a dozen flights of stairs. "Pack up shop and git!"

Carlos was tempted. His survival instincts urged him to run, but his *paisa* upbringing held him back. Do you flee your burning house if there is a chance you can put out the fire? Of course not. He had worked too long and hard to reach his present position. He would not abandon it so quickly.

"Not quite so fast, Allen. We are in no danger."

"The hell we aren't!"

"Think a moment. They do not know who we are, otherwise they would not have tried so clumsy a trick. This was not meant to lure us into the open—we would naturally check on the exact location of this motel before doing anything. No, my young friend, the more I think about it, the more I am sure that this was set up to confirm their suspicions about Señor Keane."

Gold did not seem soothed by this. "Okay, so we're not in the fire yet. But we're still in the frying pan. If they suspect Keane, it means we can't trust anything we get from him."

"That is obvious. We will accept no further calls from him."

"But what's worse," Gold said, "if they already know Keane is dirty, and can prove it, how long before they bargain him into revealing who he's been talking to?"

"Not long," Carlos said. "Not long at all."

He'd already thought of that. In the course of a single phone call, Señor Daniel Keane had dropped from valuable asset to dangerous liability.

Of course, what could Keane say beyond the fact that he'd had conversations with Carlos Salinas? And he had no proof that these alleged conversations ever took place.

But still, he was a liability. As was MacLaglen. They were the only two people out there who could connect the name Salinas with the kidnapping and the poisoning of the President. Carlos Salinas liked to remove liabilities from his balance sheet. MacLaglen was protected by his tape—but Keane . . .

"I must think on this," Carlos said. "Perhaps we will make one more call to Señor Keane."

6 "Yes, sir," Decker said, and held the cellular phone toward him. "It's for you."

John stared at the phone.

"Me?"

Who'd be calling him out here, in middle of nowhere, in Decker's car?

"Yeah. An old friend."

John took the phone. That could only mean . . .

"Johnny. It's me."

"Tom!"

"How are you, buddy?"

How the hell did he think? "I don't have Katie yet. But you know that."

"Yeah, I do. But they're closing in. Won't be long now. A couple of hours and she'll be safe home."

"From your lips to God's ear."

John wanted to ask why the call, here, just this side of noon, in the middle of nowhere. But he didn't. He let it hang.

Tom cleared his throat. "John . . . I'll be leaving Bethesda in a few minutes."

Even with the air conditioner running, the summerlike sun had kept the inside of the car uncomfortably warm. But now John felt a chill.

"What?"

"I've got to, Johnny. I've got to show up at the drug summit tomorrow morning. If I don't the whole program will sputter to a halt."

"But they've still got Katie! You said—"

"She's as good as back, John. She—"

"But she's *not* back! We're in the middle of the woods, Tom—the mother of all goddamn woods! They could hide her here for days, weeks!"

"You know if I thought there was the slightest danger to Katie I'd stay right here, but the plot, the conspiracy, whatever you want to call it, is a bust. This woman who's got Katie obviously cares for her and—"

"And no doubt cares for her own life too! The only thing we know for sure about this Poppy Mulliner is that she was born in the Jersey sticks, has a criminal record, and was a party to kidnapping my daughter. The rest is all talk. For all we know she could have been stringing us along since day one, feeding us a line to help her work out a deal with whoever she had a falling out with. One guy's already dead. She may be bargaining with Katie to save her own ass."

"John—"

"If you suddenly appear in public in perfect health, they'll know they've lost. They'll do whatever they can to cut their losses, eliminate anything that connects them to this plot. And Katie's one of those connections." He was so afraid . . . little Katie in the hands of those soulless animals. "Please, Tom. I'm begging you. Just one more day. You promised."

"John . . ." A long silence, then: "I've got to show up—on time, and in tip-top shape. You know what they've been saying about me: that I'm kicking my habit, that I'm in rehab, that I've had a breakdown . . . all rational explanations for my irrational ideas."

"Who cares what anybody says! This isn't talk, this isn't a reputation that's at stake—this is Katie's *life!*"

"I know that, John. Don't think I don't. And don't underestimate my love and concern for Katie. But this is bigger than you and me and Katie. This is a bunch of lowlifes trying to dictate the policy of the United States, John. My oath of office doesn't allow me to make a choice between the country and a little girl I dearly love. If I had my way . . ."

The cold sick fear was fading in the heat of his growing anger.

"Bullshit, Tom! *Bullshit!*"

John found the END button and hit it. He stared at the phone a moment, then looked over at Decker who was concentrating on navigating the twisty back road to the next Mulliner on the list.

"He's leaving the hospital," John said. "Going to The Hague."

"I know."

"How long have you known?"

Decker glanced at him, then back to the road. "You sure you want to know?"

"Of course I'm sure."

"Since Saturday."

John closed his eyes and pressed back against the headrest.

Saturday! That meant Tom had intended all along to go to the drug summit, whether Katie was safe or not.

Tom . . . Tom of all people. He'd held Katie at her baptism. How could he. . . ?

John felt as if he'd been spiked to his seat through the heart. Dear God, this hurt.

Still keeping his eyes closed he said, "How long before the kidnappers find out?"

"If they're listening to a radio or watching TV anywhere in the world—immediately. Bethesda Naval is under media siege. The instant he sets foot out the door it'll be on the satellites."

"You heard what I told him. What do you think?"

"That it's going to make a difference? I don't know, Doc. I wish I did, but I don't. It all comes down to this Poppy Mulliner, doesn't it. If she's been shooting straight, we should be okay. If she's been feeding us a line . . . well, we've got to hope we get there first."

7   Snake sat in his Jeep and stared at the cell phone in his hand. *Damn I'm fucking good!*
That had been the President of the U-S-of-fucking-A on the phone just now.

And he wasn't sick. Hadn't been sick at all. He'd been faking. The whole Bethesda Naval Hospital deal had been a smoke screen.

Damn good thing he'd thought of having Salinas get him the numbers and carriers of the cell phones the honchos in the search would be using. Also had him find out the VHF frequency the copters would be using. After that it was a simple matter of buying a couple of cell phones and reprogramming them to ring when the honchos' phones rang. As a precaution he'd disabled the receivers so no ambient noise from his end would taint the feed.

He'd been catching the calls of a guy named Canney and a guy named Decker all morning. Mostly nothing calls . . . until this one.

Wow.

Wait till Salinas found out. Shit, he'd be bouncing off the walls—and he had the blubber to do it.

Snake had to admit he was pretty pissed too. And embarrassed. The doc had screwed him—hadn't given the chloram-whatever and ratted out to the feds—all while he'd thought they'd cut off his kid's toe!

What kind of a father was that? Man, you couldn't trust anyone these days.

But the good news was that the feds didn't have any better idea of the whereabouts of Poppy and the kid than he did—which meant they didn't have his tape. Snake still had time. His options were still open. If he could reach Poppy first, get the tape, then off her and the kid, he'd be safe. And Salinas would be safe. And the two of them could both live happily every after.

Preferably on different continents.

He kept driving, mostly up and down 539, as he monitored the progress of the search—listening to the feds talk to each other via his hacked cellular phones, and following the reports from the search helicopters on his hand-held transceiver. If Poppy or her car were spotted, Snake would be among the first to know.

He just had to hope he could get there first.

8 Allen Gold rushed into the office, white as a flour tortilla. "Oh, God! Oh, my God! Where's the remote? You've got to see this! Quick!"

Carlos Salinas pointed to an outside corner of his desk and watched as Allen snatched up the TV remote and began frantically jabbing buttons. He almost dropped it twice before the screen came to life.

Carlos half rose from his chair as the picture came into focus . . . a picture of a very healthy-looking Thomas Winston, closely surrounded by Secret Service men, walking out of Bethesda Naval Hospital to his car.

Stunned, feeling as if someone had slammed the end of a two-by-four into his belly, Carlos could only stare as all the warmth drained from his body.

No! *Válgame Dios!* This cannot be!

He checked the words in the lower left corner of the screen—CNN–LIVE—as the reporter's words filtered faintly through the thickening air around him.

"As I said before, Bernard, this is a complete surprise. The President's press secretary announced only moments ago that he would be leaving the hospital today, and here he is. The lack of advance warning may be for security reasons.

As we all know, the President has received numerous death threats since his announcement a week ago tonight of his intent to decriminalize all drugs. And indeed, there seems to be more than the usual number of Secret Service agents in his personal escort today. I must say he looks hale and fit, and in an obvious attempt to squelch all the recent rumors to the contrary, the medical team here at Bethesda has issued a statement stating unequivocally that President Thomas Winston passed all his medical tests with flying colors and is in excellent health. Once again . . ."

"How did this happen?" Carlos said when he could finally speak.

"Isn't it obvious?" Gold's voice was so high now it almost squeaked. "He was never sick! He never took the fucking pills! He's been playing us for idiots all along! They know about Keane . . . they're going to catch MacLaglen next . . . and then it's going to be *our* turn!"

Carlos slumped back into his chair. No . . . this could not be happening. How could everything go so wrong? It was a perfect plan. How could it turn out so miserably?

Gold turned away from the TV and leaned over the desk. "We've got to get out of here, Carlos!"

Gold had been saying that for days. Finally, Carlos had to agree. The United States was no longer a good place to be.

But where could he go? Home?

A cold sick feeling engulfed Carlos like a truckload of wet sand as he realized that the silent scene here a few moments ago no doubt had been mirrored in another office . . . in Cali, Colombia. He was certain that Emilio Rojas had watched the smiling, waving President Winston with the same open-mouthed shock as Carlos. The major difference would be the other emotion tingeing the shock. Here it was dismay. In Colombia, it would be anger.

No, Colombia might be more dangerous than the U.S.

Really, he had money enough to live anywhere. All he had to do was spin a globe and pick a spot.

Why not Spain? Yes, the Motherland. He would return to the land of his ancestors.

He nodded. Spain . . . strangely enough, he found something deeply satisfying in that course, as if he were closing a circle, finishing a multi-generational voyage.

He glanced at his nervous, sweaty money manager. A liability or an asset? After a few heartbeats he decided that Allen Gold was still useful. Carlos would need help in moving his money between the Swiss and Cayman banks where he kept most of it.

"Pack your things," he told Gold. "But only the necessities."

Gold rolled his head heavenward. "Thank *God!*"

"And send me Llosa," Carlos said. "We have some loose ends to tie up before we leave."

9 "Are you my cousin?"

Poppy looked up at the Appleton standing before her—*towering* was more like it. She and Katie had been standing outside Lester's section of the house when the guy came up and like started staring.

He could have been in his late teens or as old as thirty and had to be six six, three hundred pounds. He rocked back and forth on his bare feet, hands behind his back. Thin, frizzy brown hair grew close to his scalp; he wore bib overalls over a flannel shirt, and she could smell him from here. But his face put her off even more. With his big, long head, wide-set brown eyes, and long, stretched-out nose, he reminded her of a horse . . . a fat horse, with half its teeth missing.

"Yes, I guess I am," Poppy said, forcing the words out. "I'm your cousin Poppy."

He laughed, and damn if it didn't sound like a bray. "And I'm *your* cousin Levon." He turned his attention to Katie. "And who's this cousin?"

Katie had been clinging to Poppy's thigh, and now she was pressing so hard against it she seemed to be trying to melt into it.

"This is Katie and she's not kin. She's just a very good friend. I'm keeping her for her daddy."

"That's nice," Levon said, still staring. "You both sure are pretty."

Don't get any ideas, Poppy thought. Her impression of the sexual practices of the Appletons was that they weren't like too picky. She didn't want to know any more.

Suddenly Levon's hands came out from behind him and he was thrusting something toward Katie.

"Here," he said. "This is for you."

Katie whimpered and cringed deeper into Poppy's thigh. It took Poppy a few seconds to figure out what Levon was offering. It was made of ragged, filthy cloth and seemed to be stuffed with something. In some bizarre way it looked vaguely human.

"It's my doll," Levon said. "I had it ever since I was little. I brought it so Katie could play with it."

"Thank you, Levon," Poppy said, touched. "That's real . . . sweet."

She looked up and saw him smiling, pushing the doll toward Katie. He really wanted her to have it, but Poppy knew there was no way Katie was going to touch it. And no way they could turn it down. Steeling herself, Poppy reached out and took the doll with her fingertips.

"Katie's a little scared right now with all these . . . new faces around." Jesus, she'd almost said *strange*.

"Why don't she come down and play with the kids. We—"

A sudden whirring noise interrupted him. An engine of some sort, with a low-pitched rhythmic beat, coming closer, filling the air with noise.

And then she saw it: a helicopter.

Levon started running about, shouting for Lester who came limping around a corner, moving as fast as his bent spine would let him.

"Guns!" he shouted. "It's the ATF come for the stills! Everybody get your guns!"

Poppy looked about, and saw Appletons running everywhere, ducking into the house and reappearing with rifles and pistols.

"Better get back inside," Lester said as he hobbled up to her. "This could be serious."

Poppy backed up under an overhang but didn't go inside. She was pretty sure that wasn't an ATF copter; most likely it was looking for her instead of bootleg stills. She didn't want to tell Lester that, but she couldn't let all the Appletons get into federal-level hot water for her.

"Don't shoot," she told him. "You'll only get in trouble."

Lester stood staring at the copter which hadn't come overhead yet. It remained hovering at the base of the rise.

"We're not lookin' for trouble," he said, "but we'll surely provide it if someone starts it."

"No. You don't understand—"

The helicopter suddenly turned and roared off.

"Lucky for them," Lester said, spitting. "Damn lucky for them."

Yeah, but unlucky for me, I'll bet.

10

"Look!" VanDuyne said, pointing ahead through the windshield. "Tire tracks. And they look fresh."

Bob Decker hid his relief. Finally a sign of intelligent life. They'd turned off 563 about twenty-five miles ago. Somewhere along the way the pavement had disappeared but they'd kept going on the hard-packed sand. But going where? Not only had they not seen another human being for the past 25 miles, they hadn't seen a *trace* of civilization. Not even litter. Except for the ruts they were following, this was exactly how the area must have looked before Columbus. The sense of isolation was more than oppressive; Bob found it downright unsettling.

He'd been beginning to suspect they were hopelessly lost, but now these tire tracks suggested that civilization might not be too far away.

"Wait a minute!" VanDuyne said. "Stop."

Bob angled around the branches of a fallen tree that jutted onto the road, hit the brakes, and brought the big Roadmaster to a halt.

"What's up?"

"That fallen tree," VanDuyne said. "This is the second time we've passed it. These are *our* tire tracks. We've just come full circle." He slumped back. "This is hopeless! We're no closer to finding Katie now than we were this morning, and now—" He slammed his fist against the door.

Bob Decker kept his eyes on the narrow sandy path ahead and had to admit VanDuyne was right. They were very lost. They'd been taking forks this way and that, thinking the road eventually would loop them back around toward Sooy's Boot. But all they'd done was loop back on themselves.

How much was the poor bastard supposed to take before he detonated? VanDuyne's best and oldest friend had let him down when he needed him most—Bob perfectly understood that Razor had no choice, but he was sure that wasn't how VanDuyne saw it—and his daughter was still missing. Plus the two of them had been cooped up together in this sedan all day. And now they were lost.

Very lost.

Bob hid his own unease and frustration and tried to sound upbeat when he replied.

"Not true. We've covered a lot of ground, spoken to a *lot* of Mulliners—"

"But the afternoon's half gone and we still haven't got a clue to her whereabouts."

"We know where she's *not*. We—"

"You said we'd find her today, Bob. Be honest: Do you still believe that?"

Truthfully, the chances were dwindling with each passing hour. But that didn't mean it still couldn't happen.

"We've still got lots of light left."

How was that for a nonanswer?

"I'm not so sure of that," VanDuyne said, craning his neck and pointing past Decker. "See those clouds? They're thunderheads. We've got a storm coming. And it looks like a big one."

Bob glanced left at the massing clouds that had indeed taken control of most of the western sky. They'd started out white and billowy but turned dark and ominous after swallowing the sun.

Yeah. A storm would be a problem.

"I'll call Canney and see how he's doing," Decker said. The FBI man had split off to cover another area with a fellow FBI agent. "Maybe he's onto—"

Suddenly a staticky squawk filled the car. "*SSD, do you read? SSD, this is Search One.*"

Bob grabbed the transceiver. "Got you Search One. What've you got?"

"*We've got a vehicle similar to the object vehicle in sight below.*"

Since this was an open channel, and God knew who else was listening, "object vehicle" was the code they'd chosen for a red panel truck.

"Parked or on the move?"

"*It's stationary. Parked in a small clearing with four or five other vehicles . . . downhill from a very strange looking house.*"

"Great. Where are you?"

"*Over deep woods about five klicks southeast of Sooy's Boot. At thirty-eight degrees, forty-six minutes north, seventy-four degrees, thirty-three minutes west, to be exact.*"

Bob glanced at VanDuyne who'd been acting as navigator all day. "That any help?"

VanDuyne shook his head and pointed to an area of the local map that was mostly empty green. "There's nothing there—not even a road."

"How do I get there, Search One?"

"*Well, we've got a road in sight, but it's not on any of our maps. The only way you'll get here is to have someone lead you, and I guess that'll be us. Give us your present location and we'll find you. You can follow us here.*"

"We're lost, Search One."

VanDuyne was looking at the map again. "Tell him we're somewhere south of 532 and west of 563."

"*We copy,*" the transceiver said. "*Find a clearing and get ready to wave a shirt or something. We'll be overhead soon.*"

"I think this is it," VanDuyne said, still staring at the map. He seemed transformed, as if someone had hooked him up to a wire and was pumping juice into him. "I can feel it."

"Don't get your hopes up. Got to be a lot of red panel trucks out here."

VanDuyne shook his head. "We've only spotted three all day, and all of them were sitting out on the street. This is the first one tucked away deep in the woods. That's Poppy's truck. I know it. We're going to find Katie."

"If I may quote you from earlier: From your lips to God's ear." He slapped his hand against the dashboard as he thought of something. "You know what we could use right now? A GPS unit. Damn! Why didn't I think to bring one?"

"What's that?"

"A global positioning system. It would tell us exactly where we are."

VanDuyne shrugged. "As long as we've got the helicopter to follow, we don't need it."

Yeah, Bob thought, but I should have thought of it. Never even crossed my mind.

But VanDuyne was right. The helicopter would get them there. Besides, no one could think of everything.

11 Snake pulled his Jeep off 563 in a tiny place called Jenkins. He attached the suction cup of the GPS antenna to his roof, then got back in and fired up his laptop. The GPS card was already snapped into the PCMCIA slot. The grid appeared. He tapped a few keys and waited for the program to pick up the signals from the satellites miles above, run a triangulation on them, and pinpoint his exact position on the earth.

Snake loved this: Using the Department of Defense's thirteen billion dollar satellite system to outmaneuver its fellow federal agencies.

The laptop beeped softly as a blinking dot appeared in the center of the grid next to the coordinates.

"Okay," he said aloud. "There's me. Now let's see how far it is to this 'object vehicle.'"

Snake punched in the coordinates he'd copied from the copter conversation he'd monitored on his VHF transceiver. A few seconds later his dot jumped to the lower left of the screen as a blinking star appeared in the upper right. The readout said: *11.2 km—43° NE.*

Not far at all. About seven miles . . . as the crow flies. But out here, that might mean fifteen, twenty, thirty miles by road—*if* you could find the roads. His software had the capacity to link him up to a street map and lead him to his destination—but no software developer in the universe offered a package on the pinelands. Too bad his GPS program couldn't download a satellite photo of the area.

Maybe next year.

But he had the next best thing: He'd scanned a sectional map of Central Jersey into his hard drive. He fixed his blinking dot on the town of Jenkins, entered the scale, and *voila!*—he was in business.

Now he had to find a way to get his dot to that blinking star in the middle of nowhere before the feds. The 'object vehicle' might not be Poppy's truck, but he couldn't risk sitting here and doing nothing.

He heard a deep rumble and glanced at the sky. Thunder. That storm was coming on fast.

He threw the Jeep into gear and started moving. Not quite as good as having a helicopter to follow, but at least he'd know when he was heading in the right direction and when he wasn't.

And he'd be approaching the spot from the opposite direction. Maybe he was already closer than the feds. And who knew? Maybe the storm would help him get there first.

As he drove he passed through an area of burned-out trees. Lightning? A careless camper? Whatever, it looked like there'd been a helluva fire here. All the trunks had been scorched coal black, the smaller branches seared right off. But the trees weren't dead. Every trunk had little branchlets forcing their way through the charred crust of the bark and sprouting new bright-green needles.

Can't kill these damn things, he thought. Then he grinned. Maybe this is a good place for me. I like these pines. No matter what you do to them, they keep coming back.

I'm just like your pines, Poppy. You can't kill me, can't stop me. I keep coming. And I'm coming for *you*, bitch.

12 Dan Keane stared out his office window, wondering why he hadn't heard anything from Decker since this morning. He checked his watch. A little after three already. Had anything happened at that motel in Tuckerton? Should he call? Would that make him appear too interested? But how could you appear too interested in something like this? Yes, he should call. He was useless here, otherwise. Couldn't concentrate, couldn't think about anything else.

But as he reached for the phone, his intercom buzzed. That might be Decker now. He hit the button.

"Yes?"

"A restaurant just called," his secretary said.

"A restaurant?"

"Yes. Very rude. Said you were supposed to call them about confirming a reservation. Il Gia-something. They hung up before I could get the name straight."

Dan stiffened. Salinas's place. Calling here? Oh, Lord. It could only be bad news.

"I know the place."

"Want me to—?"

"No, thanks. I'll take care of it later. Hold my calls, Thelma. I'm going out for a short walk."

The heat on Sixth Street hit him as soon as he stepped onto the sidewalk. Like summer. He peeled off his wool suit coat and went searching for a phone.

Wild thoughts danced around him as he walked. What could Salinas possibly have to tell him? What was so important that he risked a call to the DEA offices?

He spotted a phone at the corner by NASA and picked up his pace toward it. As he fished for a quarter, he made his usual survey of the area to make sure no one was too close. Pretty clear. Not even a pretzel cart this time. Just a bicycle messenger speeding along in his direction. No problem there. Those guys could really move. He'd be past before Dan finished dialing.

He found the quarter and plunked it into the slot. As he waited for it to register, he glanced around again. The bike messenger was almost on top of him—racing helmet, dark sports glasses, skin-tight bicycle pants and top, riding a slim French street bike. But he seemed to have lost speed. As Dan watched, he pulled something metallic from his messenger pouch. It was pointed at him before he recognized it as a silenced automatic. He saw the tiny muzzle flashes light the dark hole of the silencer bore.

Before he could move, before he could scream, he felt the slugs hit him. No piercing pain—more like iron-fisted punches to his chest and abdomen, exploding through his back, lifting him off the ground and hurling him backward.

He saw the intense blue of the sky for an instant, and then it, the street, the city, the world all dimmed and went away.

13

"Move, you son of a bitch! *Move!*"

John VanDuyne felt as if his shoulder was about to pull out of the socket, but he wouldn't back off. Lightning flashed as he dug his feet into the sand and leaned everything he had against the Road-master's rear fender.

The tire spun, kicking up sand that was picked up by the rising wind and swirled into his face. Damn rear-wheel drives, anyway! Why the hell was anyone still making them?

He squeezed his eyes shut and pushed harder. The car rocked for-ward, the tire rising halfway out of the hole it had dug for itself.

"Keep going!" he shouted to Decker over the thunder and the whine of the engine. "We're almost there! We're—"

But then the car began to slip backward, and nothing he could do could keep it from sinking back into the sand.

John leaned against the bumper and pounded his fist on the trunk. He wanted to scream.

They'd been doing so well, making good time following the helicop-ter along the pair of sandy ruts that passed for a road out here when suddenly they'd rounded a corner and found a deer standing in their path. Decker'd slammed on the brakes, the deer bolted into the brush, and they hadn't moved an inch since.

And now it began to rain—huge drops splattering the car and his head and back. John looked at the gray, lowering sky and wondered how things could get worse. A slashing bolt of lightning gave him an answer of sorts, so he stumbled to the passenger door and dropped into the seat.

Decker was on the hand-held transceiver. "All right Special One. Safe home. And thanks."

John knew who he was talking to: the helicopter. "They've leaving?"

Decker nodded. "Heading back to base. This weather's getting too heavy for them."

John nodded silently. He'd been expecting that.

"Hey," Decker said, "they hung on as long as they could—maybe longer than they should have. I hope they don't have trouble getting back to Lakehurst."

"I know. It's just—"

The sky opened up then and the rain dropped in sheets.

"Hang in there," Decker said. "We're close. The rain ought to thicken up the sand and help us get out of this hole. As soon as it stops, we'll get moving again."

"But where? We'll have to wait for the copter to—"

"No. They gave me directions. There's a smaller road that cuts off to the right about half a mile ahead of us here. We take that for about a mile or so and look for another trail off to the right. The truck's in there."

The rain increased, bringing visibility down to zero. The pines disappeared. With the deafening tattoo on the car roof and the incessant roar of the thunder, they could have been sitting under Niagara Falls.

The world constricted to John and Decker and the car.

14   Snake smiled as he clicked off his transceiver—he wouldn't need that any more. He continued to inch through the rain. He wasn't making much progress, but he was doing a thousand percent better than VanDuyne and his fed buddies.

Mired in sand and no flyboys to lead them even if they got out. What a shame.

Snake realized he might be in the exact same spot as those two if not for his Jeep's four-wheel drive.

He checked his laptop again and saw that he was closer than ever. The GPS program told him that the blinking star of his destination was somewhere about a klick and a half to his left.

He shook his head in wonder at the irony of using all this high-tech equipment to search what had to be one of the low-tech capitals of the country.

He peered through the rain. Had to go slow here, look for a road, a path, a deer trail, anything that led off to the left. Damn near dark as night outside. Hard enough to see under these conditions with both eyes, but when you had only one . . .

And then he spotted something out his near side window and slammed on the brakes. He wiped away the condensation and peered through the downpour.

Two ruts in the sand, leading leftward. Good thing his wrecked eye was on the right and the lightning had flashed at the right moment, otherwise he'd have gone right past it.

Grinning, he backed up, then turned onto the path.

Almost there, Poppy-bitch. Hope you're enjoying your last hours on Earth.

15

"I'm scared," Katie said, clinging to Poppy as the thunder shook the ground and the wind rattled the walls.

"It's okay, honeybunch," Poppy said, sitting on the bedroll and rocking Katie back and forth. "The storm'll be over soon."

"Scared o' storms, is she?" Lester Appleton said, licking his lips as he positioned a tin can under a leak. That made twelve containers scattered around his floor. "So's most of the wimmins and kids. All probably hiding under their beds right now. Do it every time the thunder starts. That little girl'll do well to get used to 'em if she's a-gonna stay. We get some real doozies out here."

She ain't staying, Poppy wanted to say, but didn't want to be rude. All the Appletons had been kind to them today. Some of them said they remembered her stopping by with her daddy when she was a kid, but maybe they were just imagining it. The main thing was the way they'd welcomed her and Katie, sharing their home and their food . . . even their dolls, so to speak.

The Appleton ideas of what was clean and what was cooked, of what was edible and what tasted good were light-years from Poppy's, but they meant well. What they had was hers.

After all, she was kin. . . .

Lester had said they could sleep in his place for now. His place: a ten-by-fourteen space lit by two kerosene lamps—one on a crate that served as his dresser and the other hanging from the six-foot ceiling. The walls creaked and shuddered under the wind's attack, which set the hanging lamp to swaying. And the moving light did funny tricks with Lester Appleton's nose-gazing eye.

Another crash of thunder and Katie tightened her grip on Poppy.

"Hope them stills is all right," he said, swigging from a ceramic jug. "Wish my back was better—I should be out there helpin'." He shook his head. "First that heeliocopter, now the storm. Bad omens. I feel it in my bones—somethin' bad's gonna happen."

The sight of the "heeliocopter" earlier had spurred her to run down to the clearing and pull the panel truck under some trees. That might have been like closing the barn door after the proverbial horse was gone, but she did it anyway.

And then the storm had hit and all the able-bodied men—the overly attentive Levon among them, thank you very much—and some of the women had run off to make sure the stills didn't get damaged and the fires didn't get too wet. Applejack was their major asset. They sold it for cash and bartered it for goods.

Poppy wondered how her Uncle Luke was faring with the feds. He'd said he was going to try and make a deal for her. What was taking him so long?

16 Carlos Salinas took the photo of Nixon from the wall and tossed it into his valise, then looked around the room. Nothing remained that he couldn't part with, nothing that couldn't be replaced with a simple telephone call.

As for records, Allen Gold kept all sensitive information on the office computer—verbally coded and digitally encrypted. He'd copied the pertinent data onto a Zip Drive disk and erased the hard drive. That done, Carlos had Llosa fire a few 9mm rounds into the drive— just to be sure.

"All set?" Gold asked, popping into the room for the third time in as many minutes.

Carlos nodded. Too bad, he thought. Leaving the United States and this wonderful setup. But if decriminalization went through, he'd be out of business soon, anyway.

He regretted leaving Maria behind, but that was only temporary. He'd send for her later.

Llosa was waiting by the back door. Carlos nodded to him as he approached. Llosa stepped outside, then jumped back in.

Carlos skidded to a halt. "What is it?"

"A car! In the alley!"

"Oh, no!" Gold whimpered. "Oh, God! Oh, please, no!"

"Silence!" Carlos hissed as his heart began to thump. He turned back to Llosa. "Is anyone there?"

"I did not see anyone."

"Look again."

Llosa opened the door a crack and peeked through. He shook his head. "I see no one."

"It could be nothing," Carlos said.

"But it's blocking our way."

Carlos thought of his waiting Gulfstream, fully fueled and ready to go. If he could just get into the air. . . .

He turned to Gold. "Call a tow truck. Have someone come and move it. Pronto!"

Gold nodded. His smile was sickly. "Right. No way I'm going near that car."

In the single heartbeat it took Gold to reach for the phone, Carlos heard a roar, felt the floor tremble, saw the door shatter as an onrushing ball of orange flame swallowed Llosa and engulfed Carlos, but not before a million wooden daggers from the door ripped the silk suit and most of the flesh from his body.

17 When Snake reached the clearing, he saw four or five pickups but no panel truck. He began to curse and pound on his steering wheel in red-hazed fury. The nearer he'd gotten to this place, to this blinking star on his GPS map, the greater his anticipation of finding Poppy, getting his hands on her, hurting her like she'd hurt him. He *needed* that as much as he needed the tape, and the need had grown until he felt ready to burst.

But she wasn't *here!* She must have run off after seeing the copter overhead.

Still cursing, he began angling the Jeep to turn around, and that was when he spotted it, hidden behind one of the pickups at the very edge of the clearing.

Snake leapt from the Jeep and ran through the deluge to the truck. Yes! This was it. This was Poppy's. But where was she?

He moved along the perimeter of the clearing . . . had to be a way out of here.

And then he found it. A break in the underbrush. Using lightning flashes to guide him, Snake pulled the Cobra from his belt and started up the path, a path to the "strange-looking house" the copter pilot had mentioned. He headed for one of the few lit windows.

18

John had tuned the car radio to an all-news station, hoping for word of when the storm would break. Instead, he found himself listening to Heather Brent.

"Let me bore you with some more statistics. Federal, state, and local police made well over a million drug-related arrests last year. Seventy percent of those were for possession—not sale or manufacture, simple possession. But they're not even scratching the surface. Six and a half million people used cocaine last year. Twelve percent of Americans admit—admit—to illegal drug use. How many do not admit to it? If we pursue the stated goals of the war on drugs, we should be trying to jail all those tens of millions of Americans. Do we really want to do that? Wouldn't the resources and countless man- and woman-hours that went into last year's million-plus drug arrests be better directed toward muggers, rapists, murderers, wife beaters, and child abusers?"

"I wish we had some of those resources and man-hours at our disposal right now," Decker muttered.

John switched the station. He'd wanted weather, not Heather Brent.

"I'll be damned," Decker said, looking in the rearview mirror. "Someone's coming."

John VanDuyne twisted in his seat and looked through the fogged up rear window. Sure enough, two smeary blobs of light were bobbing their way through the downpour.

"Dear God, we haven't seen anybody for hours, and now—It's a miracle."

A big pickup with fat tires eased to a stop on their right. John rolled down the window and saw a weathered face grinning at him from the truck's cab. A similar and equally weathered face, this one bearded, peered over the driver's shoulder.

"Looks like you found yourself some sugar sand," the driver said.

"Can you help us out of it?" John said.

The driver shook his head. "That stuff's like soup now. Maybe after the water settles out a bit."

Desperate, John was about to ask him for a lift when he heard a door slam and saw another set of lights behind the truck. Someone holding a newspaper over his head was sloshing their way.

Good Lord—Gerry Canney the FBI agent.

"Come on!" Canney yelled to him as he jerked a thumb over his shoulder. "Get in our car!" He turned to the driver of the pickup. "They're with us."

The driver nodded and rolled up his window.

John didn't even bother checking with Decker. He jumped out and followed Canney. Seconds later a dripping Decker joined him in the back seat of the FBI man's sedan.

As the pickup pulled away, Canney introduced the driver as Special Agent Geary. He waved over his shoulder and began following the pickup.

"How come you're not stuck?" Decker asked, wiping the rain from his face.

Canney shrugged. "Front-wheel drive, I guess. Look. Those guys in the pickup are two of Poppy Mulliner's uncles. They're taking us to her."

John levered forward and gripped Canney's shoulder.

"They've seen her? Is Katie—?"

"Katie's fine. She and Poppy are hiding out with some deep-woods relatives of the Mulliners."

"And that's where they're taking us?" When Canney nodded, John wanted to hug him. "Thank God!"

Almost over, he thought. A few more minutes and Katie will be safe.

"They wanted to make a deal," Canney said. "If Poppy gave herself up, could we do anything for her? I said, Hell, yes. I even offered witness protection if she turned state's evidence. How's that sit with you, Bob?"

"I've no problem with that," Decker said. "She's an angel compared to some of the other people who've been offered that deal."

John felt a nudge from Decker.

"How about you, Doc? Will you squawk if we make a deal with Ms. Mulliner?"

"Absolutely not," John said, meaning it. "I have a feeling she's the only reason my little girl is still alive. Give me back my Katie and Poppy can walk, as far as I'm concerned."

"Good," Canney said, then turned to Decker again. "And you know that leak we were discussing?"

Now Decker was leaning forward. "What about him?"

"Plugged. With four 9mm hollow points."

Decker grimaced and lowered his head. "Where?"

"On the sidewalk near his office—making another telephone call. And another thing: I don't know if there's a direct connection, but an explosion on M Street this afternoon reduced a restaurant to dust. The owner, a very well-connected Colombian named Carlos Salinas, was inside."

Decker nodded. "They're covering their tracks, erasing all the links. We're not going to be able to pin this conspiracy on anyone."

A few hours ago, John would have been intensely interested in the identity of the "leak" and the names of the people behind Katie's abduction. Now he didn't care.

Just get me to Katie, he thought, wishing the car could fly.

19 Just when Poppy thought the storm couldn't get any worse, it did. The thunder was so loud, she was sure the house would get knocked flat by the sound waves.

So when the door smashed open, letting the wind and rain howl into the tiny room, she thought it was just the storm.

But then the lightning flashed and she saw somebody standing in the doorway. At first she thought it was the Frankenstein monster—with an eye patch. But then he smiled and she recognized him.

She screamed as Mac stepped into the room.

"Hello, Pop—"

But he never finished. Lester was suddenly in his face.

"Here! Who the hell do you think—?"

Mac's hand darted up and Poppy saw the pistol clutched in his fist. Lester grabbed at it and the gun went off, sounding like an explosion. A stream of water gushed through a new hole in the ceiling.

Poppy huddled with Katie, who wailed in terror as they watched the two men struggle for the gun. Lester was holding his own but Poppy wasn't going to leave anything to chance. She looked around for something to hit Mac with and spotted Lester's applejack jug against the wall. As she began to crawl toward it, another shot blasted through the room. She felt this one whiz past—right between her head and Katie's. Katie huddled on the floor, eyes closed, hands over her ears, screaming.

Without hesitation, she picked her up and ran for the open door. She had to get Katie outside—the next shot could hit either of them—then she'd come back to help out Lester.

She'd carried Katie maybe twenty feet through the almost night of the rain when she heard a third shot behind her, followed by a cry of pain. Poppy rounded the corner of the house, then stopped and peeked back, hoping, praying that Lester would appear in the lit doorway. It took a long time, but finally someone stepped through and looked around.

Mac.

With a small cry, she spun and dashed for the brush at the rear of the house. He hadn't seen her—or had he? Maybe he'd go the other way.

Still carrying Katie, she crashed through the bushes for a good dozen or so feet, then turned and crouched behind a tree, panting. She and Katie were soaked through to the skin. No shelter from this rain—the wind seemed to be driving it at them from all directions. Katie shivered against Poppy and began to cry.

"I want to go home! I want my Daddy!"

"Hush, honeybunch," she whispered frantically, placing her hand gently over Katie's mouth. "If that man hears you, he'll find us."

She rocked Katie, trying to soothe her. With the dark and the rain and the thunder, maybe they could survive here until the rest of the Appletons returned from their stills—if they kept quiet.

Katie seemed to be calming down until a bolt of lightning sizzled into a tree not a dozen feet to their left, and the simultaneous thunder clap knocked them flat.

Katie wailed in terror then, long and loud, lasting well after the thunder had faded, and Poppy knew Mac had heard it. How could he not have?

They had to move, but she couldn't cover any ground carrying Katie. She'd have to go without her.

"Katie," she said, peeling the dripping child off her, "I'm going for help. You stay here and keep quiet and I'll be right back." *I hope.*

Katie wailed again and grabbed for her. "No! Don't leave me!"

"I got to, honeybunch," she said, fending her off. "It's the only way. Just sit tight and don't make a sound."

Poppy gave her a quick kiss on the forehead and resisted the impulse to hug her—she might never get free. Then she turned and slipped away.

She felt like such a creep, leaving her there cold, wet, crying, and scared half to death. But this was their only chance. At least Katie was alive.

Her regrets faded into fear as she bent into a crouch and began running through the bushes, making as much noise as she could.

"Help!" she shouted as she ran. "Help! Murder! Somebody! Help!"

But how much noise was too much? She wanted to draw Mac off, but she sure as hell didn't want him to find her.

She could make out the Appleton house to her right. Some of the windows—and there weren't all that many of them to begin with—were lit, but mostly it looked dark and empty. She thought she saw movement around the side but couldn't be sure. Were all the women and kids hiding? Afraid of the storm or afraid of the shots?

Where was Levon now when she needed him? He looked like he could break Mac in half with one hand.

Her heart pounding, she kept thrashing through the bushes, moving away from Katie, and yelling as loud as she could. No way Mac could miss hearing her.

She paused between thunder claps and looked around, listening. She heard the rain, her own harsh breathing . . . and something else.

Scraping branches, breaking twigs . . . getting closer . . . coming this way.

Oh, Jesus, it had worked. She'd pulled Mac away from Katie, but now she had to find a way to keep herself alive until help came. Had to keep moving.

But which way? Where was he? What direction was the noise coming from? The sounds mixed with the falling rain and seemed to come from everywhere—like the rain.

Suddenly, the loud crack of a breaking branch to her right. *So close!*

Poppy bolted to her left, moving as fast as she could. The underbrush was thick here, and she had to move sideways to slip through. One advantage of being smaller than Mac—these thickets would slow him up even more.

She almost fell as the brush suddenly thinned and she stumbled into a small clearing. Now she could really move.

But she skidded to a halt when she saw the shadow a dozen feet ahead of her. She couldn't see his face but she recognized his voice from the single word he spoke.

"Bitch!"

As Poppy screamed and turned to run back the way she'd come, she saw a flash and heard a shot.

Missed!

She ducked into a crouch and veered left. She saw the house ahead.

Please let me make it there!

If she could put the house between Mac and her—and keep it there—she had a chance.

Another shot and suddenly she felt as if she'd been hit by a truck. A crushing, tearing, pain against her back, ripping into her chest, hurling her forward. She felt the ground slam against her front, felt the mud and pine needles slop against her face. And then she stopped feeling.

Her last thought before the darkness took her was terror . . . Katie . . . alone there . . . with no one to protect her. . . .

Katie . . . I'm so sorry!

20 Snake ran up to where Poppy lay and flipped her over onto her back. He dropped to his knees beside her and shoved the muzzle of the Cobra under her jaw. He wanted to pull the trigger now—God*damn* how he wanted to pull that trigger—but not yet. He gritted his teeth and held off.

"The tape!" he shouted. "Where's the tape? Tell me and I'll let the kid live!"

Not true. Not even *close* to true. But so what?

She didn't answer. His fury surged. But as he raised his left arm to give her a backhand slap across her face, lightning flashed and he saw her slack features, the blood on her shirt and the dark trickle from the corner of her mouth.

"Shit!"

Of all the goddamn luck. He'd never been more than a mediocre shot, and now, when winging Poppy was all he'd needed, he'd gone and killed her.

He jammed the pistol into his belt and began poking through her pockets. He'd already checked that rat-hole room he'd found her in.

Empty. Nothing on her. *Nothing!*

Snake jumped to his feet. The kid. She'd been running around without the kid. Which meant she'd left her somewhere.

And maybe the tape with her.

He looked around, trying to remember where he'd heard her first shout for help. . . .

Over there, wasn't it?

Snake started in that direction.

21 "Hear that?" Decker said as they stepped out of the car. "Sounded like a shot."

John strained his ears and wondered how Decker had heard anything above the rain, thunder, and slamming car doors. He squinted through the dimness at the red panel truck tucked behind the motley array of pickups. The Mulliner brothers had leapt from their pickup and were checking out the mud-splattered Jeep Cherokee that sat in the middle of the clearing.

"This don't belong here, Luke," the bearded one was saying. "This don't belong here ay-tall."

"We better get up the house," the bigger one said as he and his brother returned to the cab of their pickup and pulled shotguns from the rack across the rear window.

"Is that where Katie is?" John said.

Both stared at him from under the dripping peaks of their caps.

"You the little girl's daddy?" the bigger one said.

John nodded. "Is she all right?"

"She was this morning. Let's go."

John got directly behind the Mulliners as they miraculously found a path through the surrounding brush. He felt someone grab his arm.

"Better let us go first, Doc," said Canney's voice directly behind him.

John didn't look back. He shook off his hand and kept going. Katie . . . he was almost to her and dammit he was going to be *first* to her.

Uphill, and then into a larger clearing where lightning strobes revealed a rambling, ramshackle house that looked as if it had been designed by a schizophrenic. The bigger Mulliner—by now John had gathered that his name was Luke—picked up his pace and headed directly for a rectangle of light pouring from an open doorway.

Inside, Luke darted to his left and cried, "Lester!"

John ducked in behind him and froze in shock at the sight of an old man with a scoliotic spine lying on the floor, gasping, his shirt covered with blood.

"Katie?" John said, barely able to get the word out as he whirled in a circle, searching the shadows of this filthy little room, praying to see her face looking back at him. "Where's Katie?"

"Poppy took her," Lester said. "And he went out after her."

"Who?" Decker said.

"Guy with a patch over his eye."

"Snake!" Decker said.

Canney nodded. "Got to be."

"Shot me," Lester was saying. "Then he went after Poppy! Go find her!"

"You need doctorin', Lester," Luke said. "I'll get someone to stay—"

"Git!" Lester said. "This looks a lot worse'n it is. You gotta help Poppy. That guy went outta here with murder in his one good eye. Gonna kill her sure!"

John didn't wait to hear more. In a panic he dashed out into the storm and began shouting, "Katie! Katieeeee!"

He heard someone come up behind him and give him a rough shove in his back. He turned as saw Canney glaring at him.

"Knock that off!"

Rage flared. No one was going to tell him not to look for his daughter. John grabbed the front of Canney's shirt,

"She's out here!" he shouted. "We've got to find her!"

"But we're not the only ones looking for her," Canney said, pushing John's hands away. "If she answers you, Snake might be closer. Think about it."

John realized Canney was right. "But what—?"

Just then, one of the Mulliners came out of the house carrying a shotgun. He started yelling.

"Poppy! It's your Uncle Luke! Stay where you are. We're coming to find you. Let us know when one of us gets near you. We'll protect you." He turned to Canney and began pointing to different spots in the bushy undergrowth that rimmed the rear of the clearing. "Everybody fan out and move into the brush. Keep calling her name."

The two Mulliners moved off. John saw the three feds look at each other; then Decker shrugged.

"Unless someone can come up with a better idea," he said, "I suggest we follow their lead." He turned to John. "Maybe you'd better stay here and—"

"Like hell," John said. Without giving anyone a chance to stop him, he began moving off in one of the directions Luke had indicated.

The branches of the underbrush clawed at his clothes and his skin, raked at his eyes, but he kept pushing through, calling out, praying for a reply.

"Poppy, it's me! Katie's father! I'm here with your uncles." Over and over. "Poppy, it's me. . . ."

As he came to the base of a small rise, lightning flashed. He looked up and gasped. Someone was standing on its crest, someone huge, and he was holding something in his arms.

Something child sized . . . and limp.

Oh, God! he thought. Is this Snake? I should have a gun!

Then he heard a voice shouting to him: "Are you Katie's daddy?"

That wasn't Snake's voice.

"Yes . . . y-yes, I am."

The figure started crashing down the rise toward John. God, he was big.

"I think she's hurt."

"Oh, no!" John staggered forward, arms outstretched. Please, God, not now, not when she's so close to going home! "Give her to me!"

As the big man laid her gently in his arms, John crushed her to him.

Katie? And then he knew it was Katie oh yes it was Katie his Katie— *Oh, Katie, it's been so long!*—and she was soaked and she was cold but he could feel her heart beating and he wanted to drop to his knees and bury his face against the dripping rat tails of her sodden hair and sob out his uncounted joy and relief at having her back again, but he had to get her out of here, get her inside where it was dry and he could see her in the light and—

"I found her in a gully," the giant said. "I think she fell and hit her head."

Aw, no, not her head! Not again!

John turned and began carrying her toward the lights of the house.

"Where's Poppy?" the giant asked from behind him.

"She's hiding out here," John said, still moving away. "A man with one eye is trying to hurt her. Her uncles and some other men are here to help her."

"I'll help her too," the giant said. "I can find her. I'll save her from the one-eyed man."

John glanced back. As lightning flashed he saw the giant's face and a diagnosis popped immediately into his mind: *Fragile-X syndrome.*

"You do that," he told him. "And . . . thanks for finding Katie."

But the giant was already crashing away through the brush in the opposite direction.

"Hang on, Katie," John said as he edged closer and closer to the house. "Daddy's got you now and he's never letting you go."

Finally he was clear of the brush. He broke into a run and carried Katie toward the light of an open doorway.

"So you found her," Lester said as John ducked through the opening and dropped gasping to his knees.

John could only nod as he gently laid Katie on the dry floor and checked her head. He found a bloody, one-inch gash in her scalp—on the side opposite her old fracture, thank God—with a goose–egg hematoma swelling beneath it. Quickly he lifted her eyelids and watched her pupils constrict. Good! Her breathing was shallow but regular. She could have been asleep. Except for the blood . . .

Had she fallen and hit her head? Or had she suffered a seizure out there? Either way she'd suffered a significant concussion. He needed to get her to a hospital.

He glanced over at Lester. The old man was propped against an inside wall holding a dirty cloth against his bloody left flank. He looked pale but alert.

"Are you all right?"

"About as well as a man can be with a hole in his side, I guess. But I don't think the slug did much more'n puncture my love handle and one of my ass cheeks." Lester winced and took a swig from a big ceramic jug. "Hurts like hell, but this eases the pain. You want some? Take the chill off."

John shook his head. He knew he should check out the old man too, but he couldn't bring himself to leave Katie's side. Not yet.

At a noise behind him he turned toward the door, hoping to see either Decker or Canney, or even one of the Mulliners. But it was someone else.

John didn't get a good look at him—didn't give himself a chance. He saw the black eye patch and the next thing he knew he was charging across the room, arms outstretched, fingers curved into claws, an animal-like growl building in his throat. Six days of pent-up rage, fear, terror, frustration had finally found a target.

Snake!

He rammed his shoulder into the man's midsection and knocked him down. Then he was on him, pummeling him with his fists, battering at his face, wanting to rip the skin off him, pound him into the dirt, and keep pounding at him until Snake was flattened, until he was little more than a thin smear of bloody jelly.

But his attack lasted only seconds, and his red fantasy was shattered by the deafening explosion of a pistol only inches away and a tearing, concussive blow to his right shoulder that spun him completely around and left him lying on his back, writhing with the pain from his shattered shoulder, and Snake standing over him, his one eye blazing, his teeth bared, his dark hair plastered over the sutured lacerations that crisscrossed his shaven scalp, and his pistol pointed between John's eyes.

"You lied to me, VanDuyne," was all he said before he pulled the trigger.

But nothing happened. Through a haze of agony John saw Snake's index finger pulling the trigger over and over, heard the hammer falling, but no shots. He kicked at Snake's legs and knocked him off balance, but only for an instant. Snake leaped forward and smashed the useless pistol against John's head. As John fought to remain conscious, Snake straddled him and wrapped his fingers around John's throat.

"I've wanted to do this since I first saw you," Snake whispered as his thumbs pressed on John's trachea. "You and Poppy. Because of you two . . ."

John flailed at him with his left hand but the room was spinning and his vision was blurred and he had no strength and he needed air, oh God he needed air.

And just as his vision was fading he saw a shadow behind Snake, saw something moving, and then an amber liquid halo suddenly bloomed around Snake's head. The fingers around John's throat loosened as Snake stiffened and his one eye went wide, so wide, and his jaw dropped open and he sagged to his left and dropped from John's view.

Taking his place was a young woman with very short, very black hair, a chalk-white face, blood-caked cyanotic lips, and the remains of Lester's ceramic jug dangling from her fingers. The rest of the jug lay in pieces on Snake's inert form. She teetered left and right like a drunk, then dropped to her knees and stared at him. Her mouth moved but no words came.

Dimly, John heard Lester's voice in the background.

"You got 'im, Poppy! You got 'im good!"

22 Poppy wanted to ask about Katie but she didn't have any more air. She felt like she was drowning, like her chest was going to explode, and her legs wouldn't hold her up. Her vision had narrowed to a tunnel through a black fog, and to her left, at the end of the tunnel, she saw Katie. She tried to move toward her but fell flat on her belly. As she crawled her way, the black fog increased, pushing in, narrowing the tunnel. She reached out. She needed to touch her . . . one more time . . . just once more before the black fog took everything. . . .

23

After Poppy toppled forward, John struggled to sit up. He gasped in agony and his vision filled with bright spheres. He was pushing up with his left arm, but each increment of movement jostled the bone fragments in his right shoulder and it was like being shot again.

Finally, when he was upright, cradling his right arm with his left, he saw the woman Lester had called Poppy . . . crawling toward Katie, reaching for her.

"Aw, Poppy," he heard Lester say. "What he do to you? What he do to your *back?*"

And then John saw the bloodred bubbles clustered at the hole in her back, moving up and down with her increasingly shallow breaths.

Dear God . . . a sucking chest wound. Where had she been? How on earth had she managed to get here with *that?*

The room swam about him as John struggled toward her on his knees. Poppy . . . she'd saved his life just now, and saved Katie's many times, and now . . . what was she doing now?

John was close enough to see Poppy's glazed eyes, fixed straight ahead on Katie as she reached for her.

She knows she's dying, he thought.

And there was nothing he could do for her—not here, not in this place, even with two good arms. Nothing.

No—maybe there was.

He swiveled and ignored the screaming burst of agony as he let go of his right arm and reached for Katie's hand with his left. He got hold of her fingers and pulled them toward Poppy's outstretched hand, then curled Poppy's fingers around Katie's. He watched Poppy's face and thought he saw her smile as the light faded from her eyes . . . and the bubbles around the hole in her back broke . . . and no new ones took their place. . . .

Though John had never met her, had only spoken to her three times, he was almost overwhelmed by a terrible sense of loss, as if a rough gem had been swallowed by the earth.

And then he felt himself fading. The pain, the blood loss . . . he knew his blood pressure was heading for the cellar. He inched back and tried to put as much of himself as possible in contact with Katie, to keep her warm until help came.

The room began to fade . . . to blur . . . he wasn't sure but he thought he saw a huge man come in and drop to Poppy's side . . . thought he heard Lester speak to him . . . call him Levon and tell him to do something . . . thought he saw the big man grab Snake by his feet and drag him outside.

And then everything faded to gray.

24 He awakened to find the tiny room filled with people and babbling voices. He became vaguely aware of Gerry Canney asking him about Snake—what had happened here, where he'd gone. . . .

"Go?"

He started to say something about Snake not "going" anywhere, but caught Lester giving him a sharp look from across the room.

"Like I told you, Mr. Government Man," Lester said, "he came to and stumbled back outta here!"

John didn't get it but knew from Lester's glare that he should go along, so he mumbled something barely coherent about not knowing anything about Snake's whereabouts.

"I want him!" Luke Mulliner said, kneeling teary eyed over Poppy's sheet-draped body. "I want to find him first!"

"You'll find him," Lester said softly. "You may not be first, but don't you worry, Luke. You'll find him."

As Agent Geary fitted a makeshift sling around John's right shoulder, Bob Decker stepped up, cradling a blanket-wrapped bundle in his arms. He knelt and showed him Katie's face—her eyes were open but she looked dazed.

"Katie!" God, how he wanted to hold her, but his right arm was useless and he barely had the strength to lift his left. "Katie, you're safe now."

She only nodded vaguely. She was still shocky. Would she ever get over this?

And then he was being helped to his feet. Canney draped John's left arm over his shoulders and grabbed him around the waist.

"Agent Canney," John said. "And I thought you didn't like me."

Canney's grin was tight. "You're a royal pain in the ass, Doc, and I'm just moving you out of here—as fast as I can. I figure now that you've got Katie back, you won't be getting in my way anymore."

"You figure that right."

He hobbled outside on Canney's shoulder and looked at the sky. The storm had moved on. The rain had stopped and the sky was lighter now, hinting that the setting sun might peek through before it dipped below the horizon.

And then he looked around and saw them. The Appletons—the too short and the too tall, the straight and the crooked, the too pale and the mottled, the smooth and the lumpy—they stood about the clearing in front of their house, staring at the strangers who'd invaded their domain. A silent, eerie sendoff.

"Christ, this is a weird-looking bunch," Canney whispered. "Gives me the creeps."

"Recessive traits," John said.

"What?"

"Inbreeding. Brings all sorts of faulty genes out of the closet."

We make a pretty odd sight ourselves, John thought as he looked around at their little procession. Matt Mulliner led the way down the slope, followed by Luke carrying Poppy's sheet-wrapped body, then Geary, and Decker with Katie. Over his shoulder John saw Levon carrying Lester as easily as Decker was carrying Katie.

"As soon as we get you three to a hospital," Canney said, "we're coming back full force for Snake. We don't have to worry about keeping a low profile anymore."

"If you're talkin' 'bout that fella with the eyepatch," Lester said from behind, "I doubt that'll be necessary."

"We're sure as hell not going to forget about him."

"Don't mean you should. I'm just saying the pines has a way of takin' care of his sort."

John glanced back at Lester and caught the old man's wink. What was he up to?

He got his answer a few minutes later when they reached the clearing and found Snake facedown in a puddle.

Geary ran up to him, gun drawn, but it was obvious he was long dead.

"Must've tripped and fell," Lester said.

Geary and Matt Mulliner had a hard time lifting the body because Snake's face was sunk so deep in the muck at the bottom of the puddle. Finally it came free with a sucking *pop.*

"He must have 'tripped and fell' pretty damn hard," Canney said, giving Lester a hard look.

John wondered if Canney had noticed Levon's muddy hands, or the churned-up mud around Snake's hands and feet, as if he'd been kicking and clawing . . .

But Lester was unruffled. "Like I said, the pines has a way of takin' care of his sort."

And suddenly John realized that Snake's death closed the circle.

It's over, he thought, and with that he felt himself fading again. He had to lean on Canney a little more heavily until they got him into the back seat of the Roadmaster.

He was already riding the ragged edge of unconsciousness and the grinding pain of the transfer all but pushed him over, but he hung on because Decker was slipping Katie in next to him. John wrapped his good arm around her and snuggled her close.

At last, at last, at last, she was safe and back where she belonged. He kissed her cool forehead and felt as if he were going to explode with gratitude. Decker, Canney, the Mulliners, even the Appletons, but most of all . . .

He watched Luke seat himself on the passenger side of the pick-up, still clutching Poppy's sheet-wrapped body. He didn't seem to be able to let go of her.

Thank you, Poppy Mulliner, John said in his mind, from his heart, from his soul. *Wherever you are, thank you.*

As Decker, Geary, and Matt lifted Snake's body, John heard the bearded brother tell them to toss it into the back of the pickup—

"—with the rest of the trash."

"Katie, Katie, Katie," John whispered, squeezing her tighter, barely able to hold back the tears, "it's so good to have you back again."

She looked up at him. She seemed more alert now. She gave him a little smile, then closed her eyes again. She whispered a single word.

"Poppy."

John wished she'd said *Daddy*, but he'd take Poppy . . . he'd take anything. Just hearing her voice was enough.